M000268173

MIST-CHI-MAS:

A NOVEL OF CAPTIVITY

J. L. OAKLEY

Copyright © September 2017 by Janet Oakley

All rights Reserved. No part of this publication may be reproduced, distributed, or
transmitted in any form or by any means, including photocopying, recording, or other
electronic or mechanical methods, without the prior written permission of the
publisher, except in the case of brief quotations embodied in critical reviews and
certain other noncommercial uses permitted by copyright law.

ISBN 13: 978-0-9973237-2-6

Cover design: Libbie Hawker
Photo of Haida canoe: Guy Kimola

This is a work of fiction. Names, characters and places are fictitious, and any
resemblance to persons living or dead is coincidental.

Published in the United States of America

To love, to histories never told.

ACKNOWLEDGMENTS

Many thanks to Mike Vouri, retired Chief of Interpretation and Historian for the San Juan Island National Historical Park, who asked me to write a Pig War curriculum for them so many years ago. That undertaking led to my decades-long love of English Camp and American Camp, their histories, and beautiful San Juan Island.

I've always wanted to write about Hawaiians in the Pacific Northwest. This novel seemed to be one way to do it, but it's more than that. *Mist-chi-mas* is about the amazing story of the peaceful resolution of the dispute over the international water boundary between Washington Territory and British Columbia and the cultures and people of the Salish Sea. To all my dear friends at English Encampment, I say, "Hazzah!"

Many thanks to Andrew S. McBride for editing and to Mary Gilland of Independent Writers Studio for additional insights. To fellow HFAC authors, Mary Louisa Locke and Libbie Hawker for stepping up, thanks a ton. Helping hands are always appreciated.

BOOK I

SOLILOQUIES

When I was a lad, I played upon the grounds of Kawaiah'o, hiding kukui nuts in the red dirt for the ants to eat so I could make a necklace for my mother. After she died, I went to sea at seven years of age with my father. When he was killed in a storm, I was fostered by Captain Godfrey. We sailed north and south until we came along the Pacific Northwest coast. When I went ashore for water, I was captured by the great northern people, the Haida. For seven years, I was a *mistchimas*, a captive, the lowest of the low, until I saved my master's life and changed my status in his eyes. When I left, I was a man and better for it.

All life is a teaching. From those seven years, I learned that sometimes things happen beyond your control, yet somehow we survive. Events change us and broaden our spirit or they break us. Sometimes we are better for the teaching. Sometimes we are forever *mistchimas*.

Jonas Breed, unpublished manuscript

~

Dearest Jereminah,

Always remember that a woman's reputation is her only security in honest society. I was never one to run away from life, but when I was just shy of twenty, a scandal not of my making befell me. In danger of losing my good reputation, I had to flee across the ocean to claim a new life. Yet still, fearful of discovery, I felt forever bound to a lie that could unmask me at any instant and destroy my free and loving heart.

No matter your situation, you are always bound to something, dear daughter.

Jeannie Naughton Pierce, in a letter to her daughter, Jereminah.

THE MIST-CHI-MAS

Pacific Northwest, 1860

Abreeze stirred the ribbons on Jeannie Naughton's bonnet, causing them to tap her cheek. She tucked the ribbons away and took a breath of the clear, moist air. It was a beautiful, sharp April morning. As she stood at the rail, the HMS *Boxer* made the turn into Haro Strait and revealed a vista of forested islands and the high, white-headed mountains on the Olympic Peninsula to the south. Seagulls swooped and cried before the bow and from rocks jutting out along the islands' shores, seals poured into the water like hot molasses. As the gunboat steamed alongside the islands, the mountains rose up in a jagged blue-green wall, hiding their passages like lover's secrets.

She squeezed her five-year-old son's hand when he leaned his thin body into her skirt. When he looked up at her, she gave him a wide smile. Jeremy meant the world to her. She turned to the older man standing next to her. "Are we almost there, Uncle?"

"Soon enough." Archibald Campbell patted her arm, then gave it an extra squeeze. His smile disappeared. He cleared his throat. "And once again, you must adhere to all aspects of the story we have devised. It's for your reputation, lass."

"I know and I thank you for your kindness and protection."

She had only arrived at the trading fort in Victoria, British Columbia a month ago. Twenty-nine days of travel from Toronto by ship to the train on the Isthmus of Panama to the sea again on a steamer to San Francisco and then, Victoria. Now she was to meet the wife of the Royal Marine Camp's assistant surgeon and lay over for the next two days. It was good that Uncle Archie was a particular friend of Dr. Parker, but tomorrow Jeannie would have to face an unknown circle of women and without any advance intelligence, appraise them for their skill at inquiry on the domestic scale. She had to have her story straight.

I am the widow of John Percival Naughton departed this life two years ago, she said to herself. *He was in the Pacific trades. No, he never met his little son.*

"Come, Jeannie," Uncle Archie said. "Let's watch from there." He nodded to a spot on the rail close to amidships and motioned Jeremy to join him. "Then we should go inside. It's cold out here. We can return once we reach the camp."

His light brown hair fluttering under his wool cap, the little boy let go of Jeannie's hand and took Uncle Archie's. As she made her way over to the other side of her uncle it struck her how quickly the two had bonded since she and Jeremy had arrived in Victoria. As Uncle Archie helped Jeremy brace against the rail, Jeannie thought, *You are dear to me as my son.*

～

Forty minutes later, they arrived at their destination. Once the gunboat approached Garrison Bay and its small island, the wharf of the Royal Marine post came into sight as well as a commissary, a half-finished barracks, and a multitude of white-canvassed bell and wall tents. Set on a partially open field, half-freed from a forest of tall trees, Jeannie could see men clearing the trees from the encampment straight down to the water, although some magnificent old big leaf maples stood unscathed. To her right, she saw what she thought was a garden. Behind it all, thick wooded hills rose up and stretched back into the interior.

"What do you think, lass? It looks a wee raw, but it has promise, don't you think?" Her uncle's face, weathered by his thirty-odd years with Hudson's Bay Company in the Pacific Northwest, broke into a smile. "Not like the American encampment which is disheveled, undisciplined and stuck like a pig on a barren hill."

"I still don't understand, Uncle. The Americans are occupying the south end of the island and we are occupying the north. All because of a Hudson's Bay pig?"

"T'is true, the pig is dead, shot by an American squatter, and our Majesty's forces nearly coming to blows with that fool American, Pickett." Her uncle waved his hand at the scene. "But this isna over a pig. It's about the international boundary and the proper water line between our countries. The two countries have agreed to jointly occupy the island until it is settled by arbitration."

"Are the Americans truly so ill equipped?"

"I'm only jesting. I like the officers well enough though the Yanks threaten to overtake Victoria."

"Uncle." Jeannie hugged his arm. She loved Archibald Campbell. A native of Edinburgh, Scotland, he married her Aunt Liddy and took her back to York, Canada where she died along with their infant daughter during their first winter there. Grief-stricken, he transferred to the Pacific Northwest, first to Fort Vancouver on the Columbia River and then onto Forts Langley and Victoria. Over time, he became a major trader in the Hudson's Bay Company.

Uncle Archie smiled. "On the other hand, a Royal Marine is like any other man stuck out in the wilds. You will turn many a head today."

"Is this your game, uncle?"

He snorted, making his gray muttonchops bounce up and down. "God bless you, but you are headstrong and willful. No, kitten, you're much too precious to me. It will be of your own choosing." He

7

squeezed her hand and released it. His voice grew thick. "Yet you know I speak with love and affection when I think of you and Jeremy's future. I always will."

"And I will always be grateful, Uncle."

She turned her attention to the shoreline looming closer. She swallowed, feeling not so self-assured. Ever since she had left England, she had to be on her guard. If it had not been for this dear relative, she wasn't sure how she would have survived. When her marriage turned to scandal, she had been cut off from all family affections. Uncle Archie had literally saved her, with no questions attached. His initial rage at her family's lack of compassion turned to tender affection and support for her.

"You'll be like the daughter I would have entertained if she had lived. Forgive me for sayin' so, but your family's a pack o' fools. They never forgave me for takin' Liddy away and I wager they don't care one whit what happens to us." And that was that.

On the wharf, men shouted and moved rope and wooden planks as they prepared a berth for the gunboat. On deck, behind Jeannie and her uncle, activity had increased as well. Men furled sails and scrambled to put the HMS *Boxer* in order.

"We'll be landin' shortly. Remember, Jeremy and I join the lads while you take tea."

On land, a neat, strawberry blonde in her late twenties, introduced herself to Jeannie as the assistant surgeon's wife, Mrs. Gillian Parker. Jeannie was amazed to find such a congenial hostess in this wilderness. Though she dressed simply in a blue muslin day dress, she wore her hair in the latest style: parted in the middle with curls framing a pretty oval face. A fine straw spoon bonnet displayed white silk ribbons worthy of the most fashionable London establishment.

She's not at a loss with crinolines and tiny waists either, Jeannie thought.

Leading her arm in arm, Mrs. Parker negotiated their sweeping skirts through the barrels and bales crowding the rough fir boards of the wharf and took her on a tour of the encampment.

"The marines are clearing the area there for a blockhouse." Mrs. Parker pointed to an area directly on the water's edge.

"Because of the Americans?"

"I doubt that very much. It will most likely serve in the event of raids from northern Indians camped near Victoria. There was trouble a month ago."

When Jeannie stiffened at her remarks, Mrs. Parker pointed toward what was becoming a parade ground.

"You're perfectly safe here. See the wooden buildings being framed over there? The new non-commissioned officers' rooms and mess. The lumber came from mills on Vancouver's Island. Most of the marines quarter in the bell tents for now."

Jeannie stared. The tents looked like white witches' hats planted around the clearing. "Do the men find them comfortable?"

"They are marines, my dear. I slept in a tent myself when we first arrived and found it very accommodating." Mrs. Parker led her back toward the large maple trees Jeannie had seen from the gunboat. Outside one of the completed buildings next to them, an officer in his bright red jacket talked to another man in his shirtsleeves. He nodded at Jeannie and her hostess as they passed by. Mrs. Parker dipped her head. "My spouse, Dr. Thomas Parker. You'll meet him later. Do you see our garden?"

The tour went on for a few minutes more. To the west, all Jeannie could see was the wall of evergreen trees across the little bay. Behind her, the camp teemed with energy of an anthill as marines went back and forth carrying boards on their shoulders, felled trees and cleared. From up on the wooded hills behind the maple trees came the sounds of hammering. Building seemed to be in progress everywhere. As Uncle Archie had commented, it was a well-run and appointed camp. The smell of the bay and the fresh scent of cedar intoxicated her.

"Where do you live, ma'am?" Jeannie looked around for the officer's quarters.

"Up there. Just in time for tea."

Jeannie raised her eyes. A staircase made of hewn boards led the

9

way up a steep wooded hill. She swallowed. She hoped her sea legs were gone.

~

A few hours later, Jeannie joined her uncle and Dr. and Mrs. Parker for dinner down below in the nearly completed enlisted men's mess. The staff had set up a head table at the back of the room and decorated it with fern and salah branches. Beeswax candles glowed above the linen cloths seamlessly laid down the table's length. Mrs. Parker introduced her to the other guests over from Victoria for the weekend, including the sister of one of the officers. Jeannie recognized her from a tea given in her honor by a female friend of her uncle's. The young woman gave her a pleasant smile, then turned back to the unmarried officer she had cornered. Jeannie opened her fan to conceal her amusement.

Even here in this nook of the Pacific Northwest, unattached women sought to be attached.

Jeannie settled herself near Mrs. Parker and Uncle Archie. Jeremy was allowed to eat with them, but when she noticed that he was sleepy, Mr. Green, one of servants at the camp, escorted him away to the tent where he would be put to bed.

She kissed him on the cheek. "Sleep well, darling."

Jeremy rubbed his eyes. "Goodnight, Mama."

After dinner, there was a concert of guitar and fiddle, followed by dessert. Some of the guests went outside to get a breath of fresh air. Jeannie followed, setting her shawl high on her shoulders. She heard the summer nights here in the Pacific Northwest stayed light until after ten, but it was April and night was fast coming. Under the trees it was cool.

The party walked out towards the water. For a time she stood with them and watched the sky display streaks of corals and brazen oranges that deepened by the minute. Across the water, the little forested island next to the camp turned purple, then black. The buildings faded to gray. Inside, servants lighted candle lanterns. The fiddle slowed down to drowsy song. As if on cue, the group drifted back inside. Jeannie stayed behind to watch and listen to the night sounds.

Jeannie could sense the presence of the trees around her, the Douglas firs and cedars standing like gentle sentinels in the gloom. A subtle chill crept around their toe-like roots. Candlelight from the windows brightened their trunks like fairy lamps. She was so far from England, so far from the last place she had called home, but for the first time since she had left, she felt like she could finally put down roots just like those grand trees. She was going to stay in the Northwest.

"Miss?"

Thinking it was one of the officers come to escort her in, she thought of something witty to say and turned only to come face to face with someone wild and foreign. She put a hand to her throat.

He was a tall, lean man, half hidden by shadow, but she didn't miss his long dark hair hovering above broad shoulders nor his dress. The man was not in uniform or in any settler dress for that matter. Instead, he wore a hodgepodge of clothing including what appeared to be a linen shirt, a loose fitting coat made of a Hudson's Bay Company blanket, and dark wool pants. Around his neck was a thick necklace made of cedar rope. In his left ear, he wore an earring. So exotic was his appearance, she wondered if he weren't some native. His high cheekbones and beardless face certainly added to the picture. Then he moved and she saw he was a white man. Recovering her wits, the thought occurred to her that she might still be in danger.

"Mama!"

Coming out from behind the man, Jeremy sank into the folds of her dinner gown, causing the crinoline underneath the lavender muslin skirt to sway gently. When Jeannie put her hands on Jeremy's shoulders, he turned and smiled at the stranger.

"He seems to have found what he was looking for," the stranger said.

"Pardon?" Jeannie's voice cracked, a particularly unladylike breech of comportment.

"Found him wandering on the parade ground. Said he got lost going to the privy."

Jeannie's heart pounded. "Were you wandering around?"

"I got lost," Jeremy said in a sleepy voice. He pulled on her to pick him up.

Jeannie obliged, tucking his nightshirt around his bare legs. "I thought you were with Mr. Green."

"I was. I woke up. I heard bears." He leaned his head on her shoulder and put three fingers into his mouth. She hadn't seen him do that in some time.

Jeannie stroked his hair, the color of her own. "Then you shall come and sleep with me, but first I'll let uncle know."

"But the bears," Jeremy protested.

"There are no bears on the island." The man sounded amused. He moved into the light. She couldn't discern his nationality. He spoke in the flat tone of an American, but he might be a Hudson's Bay Company man. Rubbing Jeremy on his back, she rocked him.

"Thank you."

The man nodded. "Do you know where to go?"

"I think so."

He dissolved into the gloom. To her horror, two other men slipped in behind him. One of them was surely an Indian by his flat forehead and dress, but it was too dark to be certain. She had no idea they had been standing there. Her heart began to pound. Her head felt light.

"Are you done, *kahpo?*" a voice asked softly.

The stranger answered in a low voice. Accented by throaty clicks, the words were like babbling brook water and unfamiliar. Briefly, the three figures shared space with the shadows, then were gone.

For a hushed moment, Jeannie stood frozen, oblivious to the laughter and cheerful fiddle music inside the officer's mess. She wasn't exactly sure what had taken place. Her legs felt weak.

Dr. Parker appeared. "Mrs. Parker is asking for you. Why it's your little boy. A little overwhelmed by everything, I suppose." He started to say something else, then noticed Jeannie was quiet. "Is something wrong?"

"I don't know. The most curious thing just happened. Jeremy got lost on the parade ground. A man brought him here. I don't believe he was from the camp. There were Indians with him."

Parker laughed. "And Kanakas, most like. That sounds like Jonas Breed. He was here earlier to drop off a deer haunch. Favors us time to time."

Jeannie put Jeremy down. "You know him?"

"Everyone knows Jonas Breed or of him. He's an unusual man, captured as a boy by Indians just off the Queen Charlotte Islands. A *mistchimas*."

"Mist -she -moose?"

"Mist-chi-mas. Like in Christmas."

"What does that mean?"

"Captive, is one of its meanings, but in truth, it means slave."

"Truly? How awful. Did anyone free him?" She wrapped her shawl tighter.

"After a time, he freed himself. Now he's the best *shipman* in these waters *Boston* or Englishman."

"Shipman?"

"Chinook Jargon, my dear Mrs. Naughton. Means he makes his living on the waters."

"Then he's from Boston, back in the American states."

"No, *Boston* means American out here. The Jargon again."

Jeannie stared into the dark space. Though the man was gone, his presence lingered like a will o'-the-wisp. She pulled her shawl tight. *I'm more confused than ever. The language, the curious people. How will I ever manage?*

"She's away, *kahpo*. To her quarters."

Jonas Breed stood in the shack's doorway. "Did you find out who she is?"

"Mrs. John Naughton. An Englishwoman visiting the Parkers with her little son."

13

"Then she is married."

"*Was.* Someone say her husband is *melamose.*" Moki grinned. "*Kolohei.* Maybe you want to see her."

Breed looked past his friend into the clearing. The sun was long gone, leaving only a dark stand of alder and maple trees before him. The lantern light flickering on their trunks made them look like a line of pale, skinny heron legs. Somewhere off, he heard a dog bark. They were close to the Royal Marine encampment.

When Breed didn't answer, the Hawaiian added, "Maybe she was asking about you too. Heard from Freddie Po your name came up at the officer's table. Someone told her you were exotic. A curious man."

Breed shrugged. "I suppose. Can't pin me down. " He reached into his vest pocket for his bag of tobacco and filled his pipe. "It wouldn't be off to say I am curious. Wonder if my own mother would recognize me."

He really was changed. In his life span of twenty-six years, Breed had lived more than three lives, each hallmarked by people and place. The first life was in the Sandwich Islands where he lived a happy childhood before he went to sea. He spoke Hawaiian as well as English before he was two. The second life was his time among the Haida from adolescent to young man in the deep forests and waters of the Queen Charlotte Islands. It was an unexpected detainment, a life-altering school of survival that turned into admiration and trust. The third life was the present, as he grappled his way through a society that was once familiar and now half-estranged. His parents were long dead. He kept his own company with his own particular friends, bridging all three lives in one. He was on his own.

"*Kahpo.* You liked the lady."

"She had a pretty face, I'll grant you that. Wonder how she'll make here." He struck a lucifer and lit the pipe. "Time you were away too, Moki. Let Kaui know I'm around."

"Go with spirits." Moki turned, disappearing into the gloom.

14

THE TEA

The following morning, Jeannie returned to her hostess's home after spending the night on board the gunboat. As she passed by the trees where she had encountered the stranger, she wondered if it had happened at all. In the morning sun, the maples and cedars stood tall and welcoming. Beyond them were rows of tents on the cleared field. Outside some of the men sat on canvas stools, working on some project. One of the men smoked a pipe. An officer, his bright red coat buttoned up tight, came by the group and seemed to reprimand the men. A marine raised a boot and made a brushing motion. The officer knocked it away. Jeannie wondered who the unpleasant officer was and if he had attended the dinner party last night. But that was not her affair. She was returning to officer's row for a tea Mrs. Parker was giving in her honor.

At the top of the stairs, Jeannie stopped to catch her breath and once again admired the buildings in the clearing hacked out of a wooded plateau. The assistant surgeon's newly-built home was a simple affair with cedar siding, a shake roof and a small verandah under construction. The windows were trimmed in yellow. Below the half-finished railing newly planted bushes gave the small building a look of permanency. Behind the house and another half-finished building, a mix of Douglas fir, vine maple, and madrone rose up on a slight hill.

Lifting her hooped skirt, Jeannie stepped up on the porch. The door swung open and Gilly Parker came out.

"Good morning, Mrs. Naughton and welcome."

"Good morning, Mrs. Parker. Such a beautiful day." Jeannie followed Mrs. Parker into the front room that served as parlor and living room. It appeared to be as new as the verandah. The painted cloth on the walls above the wainscoting smelled so fresh that the scent of linseed oil disturbed the faint, sweet smell of some native plant set in a vase below it. There were muslin curtains in the window. Seated around the room were several ladies, dressed for the tea. They dipped their heads when they saw her.

Jeannie curtsied, keeping her back as straight as the cords that held her, but underneath her corset, a little beads of sweat went down between her breasts. She had already found out that even the little village of Victoria had its own rules and class structure as rigid as the one she had known back in England. She had to prove herself to this group or life would be miserable for the next few days. After Mrs. Parker took her cape and bonnet, she faced them.

"So this is Mrs. Naughton come lately to Victoria? My brother stationed there says there is no greater beauty than you, Madame."

A woman in her forties rose, as stout as the Hudson's Bay Company pig that caused such a commotion not long ago on the island. She introduced herself as the wife of a businessman in Victoria. The woman appraised Jeannie. "You are rather young."

"I am twenty-one. Not so young." Jeannie managed a smile. "I am not acquainted with your brother, but his words are very kind. I had no idea."

"We are a small community." Mrs. Parker pulled out a chair, arranging her skirt to sit down. "Twenty miles from Esquimalt to this encampment is a short sail. One must keep one's own society. Please, dear, do sit and become acquainted with us. And thank you, Priscilla, for your welcome."

Mrs. Stout sniffed into her handkerchief and sat down. Whatever else she was going to say was abandoned.

Jeannie sat down in the middle of the assembly, feeling enormous relief Mrs. Parker had spoken for her. The wife of the assistant surgeon would have strong social standing. Since their meeting on the dock, Jeannie sensed that Mrs. Parker would be an ally. Once a teacup was in her hands and the introductions over, the questions came. In a female society that sought station through family position, married, and children, Jeannie knew she had to field any questions well. It was a comfort to find the women friendly and eager to hear news from back east in Canada.

"Did you take the train across the Isthmus of Panama, ma'am?"

"Indeed, but no one took fever. Then to a steamer and San Francisco before coming here."

"You were married to a sea captain, I understand." Mrs. Parker commented with the assurance of someone who had researched her subject thoroughly.

Jeannie put her teacup onto its plate. "Yes. Captain Naughton was with a line in the Far East. He died of a brain fever in Madagascar." *Or so the story goes*, she thought.

Mrs. Parker sighed and all the women followed with sympathetic cooing. "Well we know the life of a mariner and naval man. Such dangers and disruptions to one's familial home. Our condolences, dear."

"But you have a child," another woman said to Jeannie. She was Miss Lean to Mrs. Stout, as thin as a rail with bony shoulders and a chin as thick as a warming brick. "He must be a joy, a reminder of the one you lost."

"Yes. Jeremy. He's just five. He is exploring the grounds with my uncle."

"Ah," the collective sigh went around the room again.

The conversation went on from there. Where was she from? How long did she plan to stay in the area? Jeannie satisfied their curiosity with an account of how she was born in a small town near Bristol and spent her childhood there before her father took a position near

London. She planned to stay at Fort Victoria for as long as her uncle was agreeable. Beyond that she did not share in her "marriage."

Jeannie took a sip of her tea. "You are so settled here. I never expected such polite company."

"A pearl in a bird's nest of trees," said Miss Lean. "Yet, the northern tribes give one pause. There were fearful attacks last year. Some poor miner enroute to the gold fields on the mainland was beheaded."

Jeannie dropped her cup into her saucer with an unladylike crash. "Oh, dear."

"With the presence of both British and American military forces," Mrs. Stout interjected, her mouth stuffed with a biscuit, "it is hoped they will be dissuaded from coming so near. It can be dangerous to be alone on the waters or out among the islands to the east of us. There are also the *Kanakas*." She finished stuffing, discreetly licking all her pudgy fingers.

Mrs. Parker leaned in. "Some call them Hawaiians."

"Kanakas here? From Owhyee?"

"Oh, indeed. They herd sheep at Belle Vue Farm, the Hudson's Bay Company concern on the southern end of this island. Have done so for seven years."

All this confused Jeannie. Kanakas in these islands? She had so much to learn. "But I thought the American troops were there." Jeannie took a little sip of her tea, careful not to spill. It was maddening keeping up such niceties while undertaking an understanding of the politics of military joint occupation. And maintaining her rich charade.

Mrs. Stout sniffed. "Indeed. The Americans moved their quarters from Fort Bellingham right onto the sheep runs and house their soldiers there. Since the initial troubles ended, however, we have had agreeable social commerce. Their officers are often here for socials."

One of the ladies asked for more tea and biscuits. The conversation shifted again. Jeannie took the opportunity to stand up and admired the porcelain knickknacks on a shelf. Next to them was a window. It was early afternoon now. The tops of the fine maple trees below the officer's quarters obscured the parade ground, but two marines in their bright red uniforms and monkey grinder hats hurried down the steps as bagpipes began to swell up like musical cats. They must be assembling for some afternoon drill, she thought. She wondered if Jeremy was at attention there with his great-uncle. *My little marine.* The thought made her chuckle.

"Are you staying the night, Mrs. Naughton?" one of the ladies asked.

Jeannie turned. "Yes, I am. Mrs. Parker has kindly invited me to stay here. She's been most gracious. My son and uncle are staying in the tents for the adventure."

"Then you'll join us for the dance the officers have arranged." All the women stirred, using their fans to murmur their excitement at that prospect.

Most likely wondering what kind of gown I'll wear. "Yes, of course."

"Wonderful!" said Miss Lean.

And with that, Jeannie felt that she had passed the first crucial test: that she was a woman of some support being the niece of a chief trader at Fort Victoria whose particular friend was Dr. Parker.

FORT VICTORIA

J eannie stayed with the Parkers for two more days, helping Mrs.
Parker unpack and arrange her household. The Parkers had only
arrived a few weeks before from Valparaiso, Chile. Often the
women took the air, walking along the shore and through the beautiful woods around the military grounds. Jeannie felt she had found a
true friend, a sympathetic older sister. This was confirmed as Jeannie
and her uncle prepared to return to the HBC fort in Victoria.

On the wharf Mrs. Parker took her hands. "You must come again,
Mrs. Naughton. What a pleasant sojourn we have had together." She
leaned down to Jeremy who was playing with two brightly painted
wooden figures carved by one of the enlisted men at the encampment.

"And you too, darling boy." She patted his head and sighed. "Come
again soon."

I will, thought Jeannie. The beauty of the countryside and the
masculine order of the place had made an impression on her.

Back at Fort Victoria, Jeannie settled in the daily routine of the
Hudson's Bay Company. As she was a member of a trader's family, she
had a place of welcome at the company table. Wanting to be useful,
she put herself to work helping her uncle with his inventory. She
knew how to keep accounts, something she had learned from her

father's business, Hackmore & Son. She was not allowed to work in the main store as she was a proper woman, but under the pretense of keeping house for him, she attended to business in his back office.

Word soon got out that trader Campbell had a niece. A stream of young men began to appear, wishing to settle their accounts or to discuss company business. From her perch at Uncle Archie's desk she often heard some of the comments.

"Mr. Campbell, may I inquire on the health of your niece? Or "How is that lad of hers? Keeping his mother occupied?"

If she was not, a *card de visite* appeared next to her tea table. If she was summoned out, she curtsied and made the acquaintance of well-scrubbed and well-mannered gentlemen. One of them, Harry Ferguson, a fast-rising clerk in HBC, began to show up at the company store and go over his account books regularly. Jeannie eventually consented to go on a walk with him, but she soon found that though he was well read, he seemed to think female company meant poetry and castles in the air.

Give me action, Jeannie thought. Still, he was pleasant. As she got to know him better from exchanges at the store, she saw his virtues.

"He's hardworking," Uncle Archie said one afternoon at tea. "And an honest man in his dealings. He has a fair way with the Songhees people."

Jeannie thought he was fair looking in appearances too. His curly brown hair always seemed to be at odds with male fashion which meant plastered down and parted to the side. And he had an endearing laugh.

When she had free time, she would take tea with Miss McMurray who gave lessons in comportment and elocution to the daughters of HBC workers. Or, leaving Jeremy with her uncle, she would step out of the company grounds. There were many sights to see outside of the fort. Victoria had shops with excellent assortments of food, clothing, millinery, furniture and toys from London or the colonies in the Orient. Across the way there was the large longhouse of the Saanich people. Beyond that, the tall masts of the British naval ships could be seen playing hide and seek with the tall stands of fir behind them as they moved out to the Strait of Juan de Fuca.

Most of all, she relished the time she spent with Jeremy. When he was not running around with the other children at the fort, together they would paint with water colors, count ships coming into the harbor "Why is that ship called a bark, Mama? A bark is what a dog does." They guessed each ship's origin in the world or on rainy days practiced writing their names on slates and puzzling over the riddles in old copies of *Merry's Museum:*

I am a word of 6 letters.
My 1, 2, 6, 5, is what Oliver Twist asked for.
My 3, 2, 1, is a nickname for a boy.
My 4, 2, 1, 5, everyone loves.
My 1, 2, 3, 4, every good house-keeper dreads.
My whole is my dearest friend.

"Oliver asked for more, didn't he?" Jeremy leaned against Jeannie and looked up, his brown eyes full of mischief.

Jeannie tweaked his nose. "Yes, he did, darling." *You're such a precocious boy*, she thought. *Reading from newspapers since you were four.*

Once Uncle Archie had asked him, "What do you want to be when you grow up, Jeremy?"

"I want to be me. Just a bigger me."

Jeannie hoped that he wouldn't grow up too soon.

On the fifth of May, after they had taken a stroll down to the beach below the fort, Jeannie and Jeremy encountered Jonas Breed standing by the west gate where the wood palisades made of cedar logs rose eighteen feet high. In the bright afternoon sunlight, Jeannie could see him more clearly and he didn't seem so wild looking. Dressed in a black frock coat associated more with a preacher than a *shipman*, his brown silk tie was carefully placed and arranged. He had hair as dark as charcoal and eyes the color of deep blue sapphires. A fine, straight nose and a thin, thoughtful mouth complemented his high cheeks weathered by the wind and sun. Like a Welshman, she thought. They were dark like that. She flushed when she realized she was paying too much attention to him.

Breed removed his slouch hat. "Are you are settled in comfortably, Mrs. Naughton?"

Jeannie wasn't sure how to respond. They had never been formally introduced. Surely, such propriety mattered even out here.

"We are indeed, Mr. Breed." Jeannie had to hold onto her straw bonnet to look up at him. A sweet breeze blew off Victoria Harbor where both the Hudson's Bay fort and the colonial settlement shared space above the muddy beach. Further out, local craft and Hudson's Bay Company ships sat in the water tied to mooring rings as there was no wharf.

Breed looked down at Jeremy embedded in the folds of Jeannie's ample plaid skirt. "And I suppose you helped too."

Unfolding the cloth around his head, the boy grinned up at the man. "Uncle Archie has a telescope," Jeremy announced.

"He does, does he? Very handy." Breed straightened up. "Did you know the boundary surveyors are using such a thing to find the border? They use the moons of Saturn. Triangulate right off them."

"Ah." Though she had been in Victoria for only a couple of months, one would have to be dead not to know about the international boundary survey being conducted by a joint British-American commission. Three years after it started, the survey of the land border between the United States and British colony of British Columbia was nearly half done.

"Is this something that interests you, Mr. Breed?"

"Ah-ha. I worked with the American survey party at Semiahmoo."

"I saw the moon last night. It was big," Jeremy said, coming out of his hiding place.

"Did you now?" Breed chuckled. "It was bright. Did you take it out of the sky and put it in your pocket? You can if you put your fingers around it."

"I did, but another moon was there."

"Oh, that's the moon's twin. Stays there so it won't get dark at night. While you're sleeping, it climbs right back up into the sky."

"Oh."

Oh, indeed. Breed flummoxed her. Jeannie had never heard anyone other than her uncle spin such an elaborate tale for her young son. Yet, no other man had taken such an interest in Jeremy. She found it touching. She wondered if Mr. Breed was married and had children.

They passed together through the huge red doors of the gate and into the fort. An ox cart loaded with freight came lumbering by on its way to the general warehouse. The curved horns on the big oxen lolled side to side as they tugged against the weight, sinking into the mud at every step. Jeannie pulled Jeremy out of the way, avoiding a large pile of horse manure as she did so. As the cart passed, it spit a clod of mud against Jeannie's skirt. Jeremy reached down and brushed it off.

Breed laughed. "A true gentleman. Are you going to your uncle's?" He waved his hand at the bustling thoroughfare running through the middle of the fort under a wood tower. The block-shape residences of the Chief Factor and his second, shops, Men's Quarters, and Bachelor's House lined the palisade walls.

"Yes, I keep house for him." She watched the oxcart rock its way along the muddy way. She was about to say something else, but was interrupted by someone yelling at Breed.

"*Hey, chee chako. Maika klootsman yaka?*" Over by the sale shop, three men—more ruffian than settler—hooted back from their island of log poles used as a sidewalk. One of them offered his pipe.

"What is he saying?" Jeannie asked.

"Now, Mrs. Naughton, do you really want to know?"

"Yes, Mr. Breed."

He nodded her request. "They wonder if you're my sweetheart." Breed grinned. "At this point, I'll excuse myself. Good day to you both." He dipped his hat to them, then joined the men at the square whitewashed building.

Jeannie felt her cheeks redden.

24

Back at her uncle's office, she asked him what he knew about Breed. "Those stories about him, are they true?"

"Which stories?"

Jeannie blotted a newly penned entry and let it dry. "That he was captured as a boy by Indians just off the Queen Charlottes Islands. Gone to shore for water and taken. Is it true he was kept to work like a slave?"

"Now, where did you hear that one?"

"At the Royal Marine encampment. Is it true?"

Uncle Archive seemed to consider his words. "Aye, a *mistchimas*. A slave."

"I thought that meant captive."

"He was kept as a slave."

"How dreadful. I thought slavery was illegal in British territory."

"It 'tis, for over forty-three years, but you canna tell the natives here. It's not like the evil trade in the States that still continues today, mind you. That is a pernicious thing. Here they take captives for wealth and status. Only we won't let them bring the poor souls inside a British fort, not even to haul their trade."

"We just look the other way?"

Archie closed his account book thoughtfully. "Now, dearie, you canna change them. What we do try is to prevent the northern tribes like the Haida, Tlingit, raiding for slaves from the local tribes."

Jeannie gripped her pen. "Didn't someone look for him?"

Uncle Archie cleared his throat. "No, they dinna know there were survivors on shore. Dinna know he was taken alive and hidden." He stacked his papers on his desk and put away his pens into their holder, an indication that the conversation was over. It bordered on things a well-bred woman shouldn't have to worry her head about.

"Where's the wee laddie?" he asked.

"Why, looking through your telescope. He said he wanted to find Saturn's moon."

"That he will. We'll look tonight."

OF THE VARIOLA MAJOR

Life at the HBC Company and the settlement of Victoria continued to both intrigue and amuse Jeannie as she further explored her newfound home. Jeremy discovered friends to play with both in and outside the fort. As spring unfolded with tentative sun, their days settled into pleasant routine. Then rumors stirred that a contagion had broken out in the Saanich village.

At first, it was said to be some sort of grippe, but then hard intelligence came that it was the variola.

"Is it true, Uncle? Smallpox is in the village?" Jeanne asked as they stood at gate to the fort. The harbor lay out before them.

"Aye. Ye can hear keening in the village."

Jeannie looked across the inlet, beyond the town, where Saanich and its long, rambling buildings of split cedar boards stood. As sure as the smoke rising out of the spaces between the planks in the roofs, she heard wailing.

She put a hand on her arm. When she was a little girl, smallpox vaccinations became mandatory. She remembered when Papa took her and her sisters down to the apothecary in Plymouth where Dr. Allen had scratched her arm. It had gone well. No one became sick.

But Jeremy was not vaccinated. "I best bring Jeremy in close," she said, wishing she could just take him away.

"Aye, that would be a sensible thing to do. There are no vaccination vials at hand."

Jeannie's world changed. The trading fort and the little village outside shuddered and shrank. The big gates were shut. She confined herself to her uncle's quarters, keeping Jeremy close by. They spent their time playing Nine Men Morris and quoits or making tents from handkerchiefs for the royal marine figures from the encampment. She did leave to speak to the doctor at the infirmary and offered to help with any baskets being assembled to help the stricken. Her reasoning was simple: she was not only vaccinated, but she twice nursed those with the disease. She knew what supplies to assemble. She was startled to learn that the doctor had gone to Port Townsend, leaving only a clerk who commiserated with her over vaccinations.

"My wife is vaccinated, our son is vaccinated," the clerk said, "but all her kin are not, as well as the northern Indians encamped nearby. It's been nearly ten years since an outbreak here. No one has felt the need."

Jennie shuddered. When she returned to her uncle's quarters, she decided they would not even go outdoors. Yet Jeremy became sick.

At first he had a headache and loss of appetite, something she soothed with bark tea and readings while he sat on her lap. But when a terrible backache came on followed by a high fever, she feared for him. His arching back signaled the worse was to come. Like winter frost deepening on a glass pane, she felt ice form in the pit of her being. The next day, the dreaded small red spots of the disease began to appear, quickly spreading from his face to the rest of his body in one day. And then his mouth and nose and every part of his body except for his left ear.

"He has the variola major, the confluent type" the post doctor said upon his return. "I'm so sorry. I believe that it has gone to his spleen. There is nothing I can do."

Confluent. The worst and deadliest form. Jeannie tried not to show fear around her little boy, but when she left his sick room with the doctor, she sank to the floor and prayed.

So they waited. Each hour Jeremy became weaker. His slight body was wracked with pain. Blood oozed from his nose. The pox grew close together, doubling up like bee stings on top of one another. She tried everything she knew and did her best to comfort him all the while praying for a miracle.

∼

"Momma, I'm so hot. Get 'em off. Get 'em off." The little voice rose from a moan to a scream. Jeannie stirred in her sleep, then sat up straight in her chair.

"Jeremy?" The room was dark, but she could see the ghostly shape of her little boy writhing on the cot next to her. "Jeremy?" She tossed away her quilt and knelt down barefoot beside him. She wanted to scream out too, but she must stay calm for him even to the end. *Please, dear Lord, I don't want to lose him. He's all I have.*

She quickly lit a candle on the nightstand. Its light bloomed, then flickered on the fir headboard. "Shh, darling. Momma's here." She touched his ear, the only part of his thin body still not puckered with pox. "Shh." Her throat felt unbearably dry, but not like his skin all racked with fever. Its heat had come back with a vengeance.

"Darling." Jeannie shifted her position and gently lifted back a strand of damp hair half stuck to a sore. His forehead felt rubbery and cool. It was then she realized that it wasn't Jeremy who had screamed. It had been her. His eyelids crusted with pox were shut tight.

"Jeremy, please say something. Jeremy." When he didn't respond she got up on the bed and lifted him into her arms. His arms fell away limp. She put her ear to his mouth and heard nothing.

"Jeremy." She shook him gently but he flopped like a rag poppet on a string.

Something deep and primeval rose in her chest, a great giving away of emotion she thought impossible. Her scream brought her uncle into the room, his lamp raised high. He hung it up above her and put a hand on her shoulder. She could barely feel it.

"He's gone." She moaned, rocking back and forth with Jeremy at her breast. "Gone."

Uncle Archie gently turned Jeremy's face and placed a hand on his throat. He felt for a pulse. "Aye. Poor sweet, little laddie."

"I should have kept him near me." Jeannie's voice cracked. She began to rock him again, his hair wet from the tears dropping onto it.

"It wasna your fault," Uncle Archie leaned over and gave her a kiss on her head. His lips trembled. "He probably was exposed when he went out to the muddy beach to play with some of the *bairns* from the Saanich village. It was before anyone knew." He coughed, his voice thick.

The memorial service was attended by members of the Hudson's Bay Company as well as officers and their families from the British naval station nearby. No one followed her out to the cemetery for fear of catching the disease except for Uncle Archie. When they arrived at the cemetery, they got down from their buggy and followed the wagon holding the little fir coffin. Jeannie walked behind it, her black veil and dress floating like streamers in the breeze. She moved like a wraith, a spirit so close to self-consumption that she was in danger of drifting away. Once she tripped as she followed her uncle out to a forlorn place set next to a stand of ancient cedars. She would have fallen had he not caught her, but she did not care. After simple words were said, she was left alone.

For a long time she stood at Jeremy's gravesite, her veiled head down and her hands folded in front. Oblivious to everything around except for the clump of ferns and flowers strewn on the muddy mound, the afternoon deepened. She ignored her uncle's pleas to come home, ignored the breeze coming up and hinting at rain, and ignored the aimless rustling of the cedar boughs around her. The one thing that had defined her for the past five and half years and changed the course of her young life forever was gone. She was rudderless, without meaning and above all, without the splendid joy she experienced each day after Jeremy came into her life.

Uncle Archie stepped up to Jeannie and gave her a hug. "Won't ye come now?"

"Please, Uncle. A little longer, if you please. I'll find you."

"Aye, then. I'll go sit in the buggy." He shook his head, tears caught in his whiskers. "Dinna tarry too long." He backed off and left her alone.

Jeannie closed her eyes. The only sound around her was the light lift of the wind in the trees. She was glad for the silence.

Jeremy. Her chest tightened, threatening to take her breath away. She wanted to scream and throw herself down, but she knew it would only make her sick. She could not bring Jeremy back. She stood dumbstruck. Tears rolled down her cheeks and pooled on her round black collar. She had never known grief so paralyzing. Finally, she gave into it and sobbed until there weren't any tears left.

Sniffling, Jeannie sought the crumpled handkerchief in a pocket and wiped her face. She struggled for control of her emotions. She closed her eyes and, then abruptly opened them when rain began to splatter on her hat and veil. At her feet, little pools of water bloomed on the grave.

"Oh, no. Jeremy. You'll wash away." In desperation, she dropped to her knees, clawing at the dirt to scoop the water out. The muck soaked her skirt and clotted her gloved hands but she continued to mound and pound the cold earth. "Jeremy. Why?" She caught her breath when she felt a hand on her shoulder.

"It's me, Mrs. Naughton. Jonas Breed."

Under her black veil, Jeannie wiped a tear off her cheek.

"I'm so sorry, Mrs. Naughton." Breed's voice cut through the patter of the rain. "He was a grand little boy. *Hyas skookum.*"

"Thank you." Jeannie looked down at her knees. She was an island surrounded by water. A portion of her hair had come undone. She began to tremble.

Breed held out his leather-gloved hand. "Let me help you, Mrs. Naughton. The weather's not likely to improve."

At first she hesitated. He was a stranger, after all, but she eventually gave him hers. He gently pulled her up. When she was steady she let go.

Breed was dressed rustic again in his Hudson's Bay coat. He had a canvas haversack over his left shoulder and a rifle in his right hand. A felt hat channeled the rain from his head.

Jeannie sighed. "Forgive me. I'm not myself. I thought..."

"The grave will withstand the rain. When you're up to it, you can plant fern or salah. Maybe even a native rose. They'll help hold it together."

"You think so?"

"I know so. You want one more minute alone? I was just cuttin' through."

Sniffing back a tear, Jeannie nodded.

"If you like, I'll walk you to your uncle's buggy then I'll have to skedaddle. Gotta stay dry. It's going to blow real hard tonight." He smiled. "I'll just meet you over there."

KAUI KALAMA

B y the eighteenth of May, no new cases of the variola were reported on Vancouver's Island. However, the deadly cycle continued on to the islands in the north and east as Indians returned to their villages and brought the disease with them. During this time, Jeannie stayed in her room with the shutters closed, begging off her uncle's entreaties and those of the Head Factor's wife who came to console. She left her room only for the privy. Sometimes she dressed. Sometimes she lay abed, taking her meals on a tray.

After days of this, Uncle Archie pleaded with her. "Jeannie, lass, have ye no concern for your wellbeing?" Will ye not go outdoors and take the air? There's no danger now of the variola. Besides, ye've had the vaccination."

Jeannie only leaned into the wall.

One morning, she woke and found Jeremy in her room. He was wearing a linen night shift, its hem just below his knobby knees. Without a word, he took her hand, pulling her from her bed, drew her into the narrowing room that began to sway and clack. They were on a train, going across the Isthmus to the Pacific. The heat and humidity exhausted her, but Jeremy embraced their adventure with enthusiasm and delight. He led her back through the cars, pointing out the birds and monkeys in the trees as the train swaggered through the jungle. At the last car, he paused and opened the door to the caboose, inviting her in. She lifted her black mourning skirt and stepped into a field of lavender, like the one in her grandmother's garden in King's Lynn. The pale sky was high and light with clouds. A gentle breeze scattered the scent as the fragrant blue wands bent.

Jeremy let go of her hand. "I'm going, Mama. Just over there. Remember me." He kissed her, sending a wave of love that passed through her like a warm summer breeze. He turned and faded away.

A knock came at the door behind her, making Jeannie startle awake. When she opened her eyes, she was lying in her bed, her quilt twisted around her. Her heart felt like it would pound out of her chest.

"Jeremy!" Jeannie sat up like a shot, hugging her quilt blanket against her breast. "Jeremy." She put a hand to her cheek. The kiss felt as real as the second knock on the door. Thinking it her uncle, she begged off for the moment, but he apparently did not hear her and opened the door.

"Well, dear," Mrs. Parker said in a matter of fact voice, "we mustn't be *deshabille* all day long." Sweeping across the floor boards, she went directly to the windows and pushed out the shutters before Jeannie could make one note of protest. Sunlight streamed into the room. Jeannie turned her face away. Somewhere off the door closed.

Mrs. Parker sat down on a chair next to her. "Now what is this all about? Hiding in your room. It's time to come out and address the world as well as you can handle."

Jeannie looked down at her hands. "I can't. I just can't."

Mrs. Parker took her hands. "I know, dear." She sighed, the lace on her cap trembling. She rubbed Jeannie's fingers with her thumb, like she was wiping away something delicate. "Poor dear. What a sweet little boy. I felt he was like my own."

Jeannie sniffed, trying hard not to fall into tears again, which was so easily done. "Thank you. You are so kind, Mrs. Parker."

"Pff. Gilly to you, my dear Mrs. Naughton. Jeannie. May I call you so?"

Jeannie nodded weakly. She looked up. "Why are you here?"

"To see you, of course, and to bring you courage." There were tears in Gilly's eyes. She lowered her voice. "I lost a little girl to a fever a long time ago. My only chance at motherhood." She squeezed Jeannie's hands. "You must keep busy and you must not give up on life."

"You lost a child?" Jeannie's voice croaked.

"Priscilla. She was three years old." Gilly brushed a strand of Jeannie's hair off her forehead. Jeannie found that she didn't mind at all. For once, she felt interest in another's troubles.

"What happened?"

"We were in India, you see. Terrible heat. 'Cilla got some fever and was gone just like that. I had to leave her behind when we left."

"Oh."

Gilly cleared her throat. "I have been thinking. They tell me the islands are rather beautiful this time of year. Do come and enjoy the fresh air and company of those who wish to help you through your period of mourning. It will do you good. You can stay as long as you wish. There is little female company for me and I would be delighted. Your uncle already has agreed if you wish." When Jeannie hesitated, Gilly smiled wistfully. "You don't have to do a thing. Not unless you want, but I will tell you, doing is better than lying about."

Jeannie and Gilly arrived at the Royal Marine encampment the next Sunday. Once they were on the dock, Gilly locked arms with Jeannie. "See? I told you the building phase is continuing with great speed. Accommodations are most pleasant."

Jeannie gripped her valise. Since her stay over a month ago, the change was quite amazing. The marines still lived in Silbey tents, but another long barracks was under construction as well as other important support buildings. The sound of hammers echoed through the trees.

Gilly pointed out the additional officer's homes being built. "There's an officers' mess as well. Come, let's refresh ourselves. Then become reacquainted to our little community. A marine can bring up your trunk." With that, she took Jeannie's valise and led her to the stairs where the Parker's modest home sat on a natural terrace half-way up the hill.

It's been painted, Jeannie thought. White on the body. Yellow on frames and eaves. She welcomed Gilly's invitation to settle into a room which must have been her friend's own study. In addition to a small writing desk, there was a comfortable chair for reading or sewing projects. A cot had been set up for her. "When you are presentable, do join us for tea." Gilly closed the door leaving Jeannie alone. She sat down on a chair by the desk and immediately began to weep.

"I must stop doing this," she whispered, but the tears continued. Eventually, she blotted her eyes with a black-edged mourning hand-kerchief. Taking a deep breath, she put away her things. The Parkers, in anticipating her, had laid out linens, a pitcher and bowl. Nootka roses were in a vase. Jeannie added a small tintype of Jeremy taken in Toronto when he was four. At the window, the lace curtain lay calm against the multi-pane glass. She pulled it aside at the grating call of a Steller's jay complaining about some offense. Despite the bird's distraction, the woods were still, lazing in the afternoon heat. *Jeremy would love this place*, she thought. *But now I must put these things aside.* With that, she checked her hair in the mirror and went out to join the Parkers.

～

"There is always the first step," Gilly said that afternoon. "No one can take it for you, but I promise, I shall be here for you."

She was true to her word. Never pressing, but always leading, Gilly drew Jeannie out of her grief and back into life. Sometimes it was in the company of Dr. Parker who very gently assured Jeannie that she had done everything she could for Jeremy. If he was away visiting his American counterpart at Camp Pickett or at the main naval hospital back on Vancouver Island, Gilly and Jeannie had the place to themselves. For that, Gilly provided projects and jobs. There were medicines to record and bottle in the infirmary and salmonberries to gather in the woods. Receipts to collect from the weekly newspapers piled up from the last monthly mail boat. Linen and underpinnings to mend. For Jeanie, this activity was the very best anecdote to tragedy. When Gilly and Jeannie weren't engaged, they read on the porch.

As the days went by, Jeannie adjusted to the regimented life at the camp. Though they were on an island in the wilderness, Royal Marine discipline was maintained. Reveille sounded each morning. There were drills and inspections and various soundings of bugle and drums. Occasionally, the droning of bag pipes filled the air. Order led to a scheduling of her own day. By the end of the first week, she felt more outwardly focused and could even laugh at her companions' observations and jokes. It helped that Gilly Parker had also lost a child. Because she had chosen to go on with life and embrace it fully, Jeannie gathered courage, too.

She also gained a new purpose. Jeannie had come to Victoria because of Jeremy. With him gone, she had to decide whether to stay or go. Events soon helped shape her desire to stay.

One hazy morning when Jeannie walked near the vegetable garden above the stony shore, she saw the high black bow of a *salt chuck* canoe coming up toward the camp. She shielded her eyes with a hand and watched the canoe negotiate the waters at low tide. Six men were in the canoe, all Indian except for one—Jonas Breed. Bringing the canoe alongside, Breed, who was sitting in the front, ceased pulling and put the paddle on his knees.

"Good morning, Mrs. Naughton," he said. His sudden greeting surprised her. "A fine day for a stroll. Mind the stinging nettles"

Jeannie turned. In watching the canoe, she had wandered into a good-sized patch of the soft, jagged green leaves at waist level. Even though her heavily petticoated skirt and gloved hands would protect her from their stinging hairs, her arms were bare. "So I am."

"You could back out or we could beat them down with our paddles and give you a lift."

Jeannie laughed. "Have you come for a visit?"

"*Ah-ha*. Dr. Parker is in, isn't he?" Breed stiffened when she answered he was not.

"*Iktah mamook, kahpo?*" the Indian behind him asked.

"The *docktin* is gone." Breed frowned. He seemed shaken by the news.

"Is something wrong?" Jeannie asked.

"I'd hoped he'd be here. We've come all this way."

"Have you asked at the American Camp for the surgeon there?"

Breed scowled. "He's only a civilian and he's gone over to Port Townsend. They've got a bloody steward in the infirmary and he's drunk."

Jeannie ignored his profanity. "The subaltern's gone to see a man who injured himself logging. Mrs. Parker is at home, though."

"I'd doubt she'd come. It's the variola."

"Smallpox is here on the island?" An image of Jeremy in his last struggles flashed before her. She put a hand to her throat.

"At Kanaka Town, over by Belle Vue Farm." Breed muttered under his breath, then said something to his companions. He jabbed his oar into the water and together the men began to turn the canoe around. "Thank you, Mrs. Naughton. I won't trouble you again."

She watched them turn. The presence of variola was alarming, but she had to know more. "Mr. Breed, who is sick?"

Breed stopped the canoe and looked back at her. "A friend. *Hyas tillicum. Naika kloshe ow.*" She didn't understand him, but the emotion in his voice told her the person was special.

"How sick is he?"

"He has the spots, already forming and full of pus. A high fever, with chills, but it is abating somewhat." Breed held the canoe in place with his paddle. "My apologies, Mrs. Naughton. I did not mean to remind you of your loss."

Variola. She felt foolish standing in a patch of nettles, but she could not help herself. She wrung her hands as she worked through her emotions. She never wanted to go through tending a variola patient again. She couldn't bear it. But a strange calm came over her, a whispering in her ear. She knew what Jeremy would think.

Mr. Breed looked cast down. She saw hope recede in his face. Yet he had given *her* hope. Several days after Jeremy's burial, she had gone out to his grave and found it tended. The mound had settled from the rain, but had been reworked so it would not lose any more volume. Near the wooden grave marker, salah had been planted. Underneath the bush was a clump of miner's lettuce —a tiny plant with green heart-shaped leaves and delicate pinkish-white flowers. It had been done tenderly, but when she asked her uncle if he had done it, he said no. Nor could any one answer. Now she believed it had been Jonas Breed.

"I could go," she blurted out, then froze at her audacity. She had no idea what this place was like, let alone the enormity of her task. Yet, that little voice gave her courage to act, pushing her forward.

"You?"

"Yes. I've been vaccinated and exposed. Further, I have also nursed smallpox and measles in Toronto." She lowered her voice. "Long before Jeremy got ill. I could nurse your friend."

Breed turned his oar over in his hands. Jeannie stared at its sharp end. It looked like a dagger, aimed at the pain she was feeling in her heart. "He's a Kanaka, Mrs. Naughton. Some might not approve. That's a fact."

"Christian kindness needs no approval, Mr. Breed."

He smiled faintly at that. "You're very kind and you don't know what you are getting into. He's not the only one ill. So, *mahsie*. I thank you, but I should go now."

Don't give up. The little voice grew stronger, bringing with it the deep scent of lavender from the Royal Marine garden. *Like the dream she had of Jeremy*. Jeannie stepped closer.

"Do listen, Mr. Breed. I'm not acting rash. I can come for a fortnight if needed and give what I aide I can. If you wish, I shall ask Mrs. Parker's opinion."

Breed frowned, but Jeannie thought there was a spark of hope in his eyes.

∾

Jeannie felt Gilly Parker's discomfort about going to nurse Breed's friends as soon as she announced it. The older woman's lace tabs on her cap twitched as she rose from her settee. Her cheeks matched the color of her strawberry blonde hair.

"Mrs. Naughton is my particular friend, Mr. Breed. There is danger there."

Breed put up his hands. "It's not my suggestion, ma'am. I will find another way to help my friends. I must be on my way."

Jeannie did not give up. "Do hear me out, Gilly. I've been in little pieces since Jeremy died. If I could do just something. I'm not afraid." *Well, not too afraid*, she thought. "So far my vaccination has proved true." She looked at Breed. She didn't know him from Adam either.

"It's not just the matter of not being afraid, dear. It's the impropriety; it could cause a scandal, though I do say that I know Kaui Kalama. He is a decent fellow and 'tis right to help him and the others. I would go with you, but I cannot." Gilly wrung her lace-gloved hands and looked as though she was approaching final pronouncement, when Breed cleared his throat.

"The number of sick is small. They are quarantined. Their priest vaccinated the rest and I do not fear it spreading. " He nodded at Jeannie. "Mrs. Naughton would be treated with respect. I'll ask Mrs. Kapuna to be her chaperone."

Gilly sat down and smoothed her skirt. "Dear Mr. Breed, you confound me. You are no help." She sighed. "But I do seem to be losing the argument. You want to do this, dear?"

Did she? Jeannie's heart pounded. She could not go back on her word now. She was committed. But how could she say that she would do it for Jeremy? "Yes."

"Well, it's most unconventional, though I know, dear, that you have occupied yourself at the infirmary for the past few weeks. And it is the Christian thing to do." Gilly sighed again. "Lord, what will Dr. Parker think that you should go in his place? It's unconscionable that both governments do not feel fit to vaccinate them all. Kanaka and Indian alike. This should never have happened." She folded her hands in front of her and bit her lip. "All right, I shall help you pack. Mr. Breed, you better take care. I will expect a full accounting."

~

While Jeannie gathered and Gilly packed medical supplies, Breed went to see a friend in the commissary just down the beach. The large double doors were open. The commissary was full of activity as a sergeant directed the stacking of arms and munitions inside and Royal Marines in their shirtsleeves rolled barrels up the dock outside. His friend was not there. He got the attention of one of the privates grunting his way up the ramp.

"Is Sergeant Prettyjohn about?"

The private stopped. "He's up in the woods with Lieutenant Sparshott, on the wood pile." He gave Breed a quizzical look, then straightened. "I say, you're that American chap from the northern Indians. Jonas Breed."

"That's right. Give him my compliments." He turned to go, only mildly disappointed that Prettyjohn was gone. His Devonshire friend would inquire after him later. He had walked down to clear his head because in agreeing to take Mrs. Naughton to Kanaka Town, he not only opened her to scrutiny, but himself as well.

It had only been seven years since he had returned to white society. What was proper and what was not proper was sometimes a complete muddle. A motherless boy gone to sea at seven, he had only his memories of his father's captain's table and the rough ways of the seaman. He was sailing into uncharted waters here and it gave him a headache. Mrs. Naughton was a proper young woman. He did not desire to compromise her in any way due to his lack of knowledge about such protocol. He guessed like the Haida, a highborn woman should be accompanied by a chaperone. But was Mrs. Naughton highborn? What exactly was her station? He only knew that she was the niece of a Hudson's Bay Company trader he respected and liked.

"You, sir. What right do you have being here? You're not one of those bloody Yanks misappropriating the Queen's property?"

A tall sandy-haired man with muttonchops strutted out from the commissary. He was in full uniform, the red cloth neatly brushed and leather boots polished. Breed couldn't imagine him on any wood detail. Ignoring him, he continued back toward the wharf.

"I say! What are you doing here?" Boot steps pounded behind him.

Breed turned. "I'm only passing through. At Mrs. Parker's behest."

"Mrs. Parker?" The English officer strode up to him. On the ramp, the marines stopped working. "On whose permission?"

"The lady. And who are you, sir?" Breed tried to keep the disdain from his voice. The man broadcast his ilk like squid ink. "Haven't seen you at Captain Bazalgette's table."

The marine sputtered at that, his eyes narrowing. Breed let the marine think he was someone of importance, being familiar with the camp's commander. Bazalgette was, in fact, Breed's friend, someone who had known his foster father, Captain Geoffrey.

"Lieutenant Thaddeus Cooperwaite." He muttered his company's name.

A visitor, Breed thought. Not from here. He turned and left him sputtering.

KANAKA TOWN

"Sit in the middle, Mrs. Naughton."

As Breed held the canoe steady, Jeannie stared at her mode of transport. It was one thing to state that she was willing to travel to Kanaka Town where her patients awaited, but it was another matter to actually go in the same fashion in which Breed had just arrived.

She had seen a Haida canoe at Fort Victoria. Over sixty men were in it. Made of a single cedar log of fifty feet in length with a carved sea wolf attached at the high bow, it had moved with astonishing speed.

Breed's canoe, however, was much smaller, with a simple, more abstract extension in the front. The outside looked like it had been rubbed black with charcoal until it shined while the inside was stained with ochre. It seemed completely unsteady and unseaworthy. How would it carry her, Mr. Breed and the six Indians who accompanied him, not to mention firkins and the boxes with medicine covered with canvas that filled every manageable space? She sat down on its gunwale and worked her way onto the seat, clutching her valise.

"And who are your paddlers?" she asked Breed above the sound of the waves washing on the shore.

"Not paddlers, Mrs. Naughton. They're pullers. We pull the sea with our paddles." He handed her two wool blankets and instructed her to tuck them around her, then gave her an India rubber cape. "They are friends of mine and very skilled. We'll get there soon enough."

Not soon enough for her. Jeannie's unease continued once they got out of Garrison Bay and into Haro Channel. *What have I gotten myself into?* This was madness. Worse, she hadn't even thought about what sort of community she was going to nurse the sick in. Did they even speak a form of English?

Yet, as they sped southward along the water of the Haro Channel, she marveled at the strength and skill of the men. *Their discipline!* They moved as one. Most of all, she marveled at Jonas Breed as he dipped and bent with fluid strength in front of her.

They stayed away from the heavily forested shore to avoid the drag of the current there and took advantage of the tide going out in the channel. Sometimes they passed high cliffs of crumbling rock where madrone and Garry oak crowded at the top like the points on a crown. They saw coves clogged with great ropes of bull kelp.

Breed turned around. "Are you all right, Mrs. Naughton?" he bellowed over the wind.

Jeannie grabbed onto her bonnet and managed a frozen nod, but when the canoe lolled to the right she let out a shriek and grabbed hold of the gunwale again. Breed shouted something to her, then sank his paddle into the waves as the stern of the canoe fishtailed and rose up behind her. The water sprayed against her India rubber cape. She gasped and closed her eyes only to open them to the sound of a voice singing over the rush of their journey. It was Jonas Breed's.

"King Louis was... king... of France... 'fore... Rev...lution" were the only fragments she heard and then "way haul away, we'll haul away Joe," picked up by the men around her. It seemed that the canoe steadied and straightened its course because of their strong determination. The man behind her began to play a steady beat on his drum. One-two-three-thump. One-two-three-thump. "Ah-ho. Ah-ho." The two songs blended, weaving in, out and over the ebbing tide. Off to the west, a lone seagull rose to the sky and balanced its flight with outstretched wings. With Vancouver's Island behind it, Jeannie watched for a long time. The pullers stayed strong and she eventually lost her worry that they should be thrown into the sea.

Four hours later, in the late afternoon, they arrived at a treeless bay on the southwestern side of the island. Along the exposed shore, she could see a spattering of simple huts made of split cedar boards. They were as weatherworn as the gray heaps of driftwood and logs lining the sandy beach. On the roof of one hut, crows gathered like solemn judges. The whole place looked forlorn and uninviting. *Or is it because I am chilled to the bone?*

The birds rose up and flapped away when a man came out of a hut and ran down to the canoe. At his alarm, a few more men appeared. They waited for the canoe to come in on the crashing waves. When the bow hit shallow water, the men lifted and dragged the canoe up onto the gray, stony beach.

"Where is Doctin Parker?" the first man asked. He was a short burly man with bowed legs and potbelly. He wore a hat woven of cedar root, but his jacket was an old sea captain's. His skin was the color of a walnut.

"He's away, Charlie," Breed said as he half-carried, half-pulled the canoe. "I've brought Mrs. Naughton, late of Fort Victoria. She has volunteered to help. How many are ill now?"

"Five. Kaui is very sick. So is Kanaka George."

Breed nodded grimly. "Keep an eye on them all. Don't let any of them run into the water. They'll be *memaloose* for sure." He turned to Jeannie who was frozen in her place in the center of the canoe. Literally. "Let me help you out, Mrs. Naughton."

He motioned for her to leave the rubber cape in the canoe. He helped her stand, then clamber (*most unladylike*, she thought) out of the canoe. Her teeth began to chatter. Breed took off his coat and put it on top of the blankets covering her shoulders.

"I'll take you to the hut where my friend is, but first is there anything else I can do for you?"

Jeannie nodded numbly, wrapping the bundle of coat and blankets tight around her body. Her teeth continued to chatter. "If you please, Mr. Breed, where is the privy?" No chance of comportment here.

Breed pointed to a ramshackle structure made of long cedar boards near the base of the rise. Pulling the coat tight against her, Jeannie slipped across the stony beach to it. Behind her, Breed gave out instructions for moving the gear left in the canoe. When she returned, he offered his arm and led her to the place where her patients waited.

It was smoky inside the one-room hut, but warm. A lean-to provided additional space for sleeping. Lamps were hung from the rafters as well as smoked salmon and laundry. Several pages torn out of *The Colonial*, a newspaper at Victoria, graced the walls. A small cast-iron stove crackled and popped radiating heat out into the space. She went to it immediately and rubbed her cold hands together, then looked toward the bed in the lean-to where a young man was lying. She was surprised to see another man sleeping on the floor next to him. Two men and a woman sat beside them. She assumed all of them were Indian, but some had features she hadn't seen around Fort Victoria. They wore European clothes, although some were bare-footed. By lantern light, everything seemed distorted and in shadows.

Breed came in behind her with a tin coffeepot and put it directly on the stove. "We'll get you warmed up as soon as possible, Mrs. Naughton."

Jeannie hugged her blankets. "They should be outside, Mr. Breed."

"It's too late. They've already been exposed." He greeted the men and women by name and introduced Jeannie. "This is Alani Kapuna. Over there is Jimmy Two Band." The names came at her at a rush, musical and foreign.

Jeannie tentatively smiled back. "Who is vaccinated?"

"Charlie, Billy Po, and Alani and Moki Kapuna are vaccinated. In fact, all but a handful. Hasn't been an outbreak in this area for four-teen years. Indians and Kanakas seldom get vaccinated. Tens of thou-sands of Salish people died in the last fifty years."

45

Jeannie swallowed. "Jeremy wasn't vaccinated. The doctor said he was too young, that there was no need. That I should wait." She rubbed her arm. "I had mine long before he was born." She heard her voice break as grief rose up and thickened her throat.

"It wasn't your fault," Breed said.

"Thank you, Mr. Breed. That is kind of you to say, though I often do not believe it." She removed the blankets on her shoulders and put them on a ladder-back chair.

"This is my friend, Kaui Kalama." Breed pointed to the figure rolled up in a blanket. "I tried to get liquids into him earlier. Made a tea for the fever. The sores are troubling."

Jeannie stepped around the man on the floor and looked at Kaui. Even in sickness, he was handsome. He had short, wavy brown hair. Brown-skinned with high cheeks and a straight nose, Jeannie couldn't help but notice the thick dark lashes on his closed eyes. Bracing herself, she touched his forehead, avoiding the crop of sores near his temples. It was very warm. She felt his pulse, trying to remember all the things Dr. Parker told her at the English Camp dispensary, but more importantly what she had learned from the surgeon at the Esquimalt Naval Station about variola since Jeremy took ill.

Breed pulled back the covers. The patient's arms and shoulders were covered with pustules that looked like tiny buttons ringed with red. The pustules grouped together in threes and fives. Some were pus-filled. He smelled of fish oil.

"They worse, Alani?" Breed asked the stout woman sitting on a stool next to the bed.

"I think they will break soon," she answered. "He wants to scratch them all the time."

He must be in his fourth day, Jeannie thought. The blisters showed up usually by the fourth day, then the pus broke out. By the ninth day, they would begin to dry up and form scabs. Jeremy didn't live that long.

"How are you?" Breed asked Alani.

"My head hurts, but I be okay Jo-nuss. I am sick before."

46

"Mrs. Kapuna got sick a while back," Breed told Jeannie. "She survived. Her family did not."

Jeannie took this bit of news personally, but she noted the respect Breed showed the woman by addressing her as "Mrs." She nodded shyly at the woman.

Breed looked around the room. "Where is Kapihi and Noelani?"

"They ran away. Billy Po and Moki looking for them."

"The little rascals. When they get back, put them in Hetta's hut."

"I don't think so. I think Hetta is sick."

Breed sighed. "What will his *klootsman* think?" he asked, waving his hand at Kaui. "She'll give me stink talk for sure for not watching them." He said something in a language that had a musical flow to Jeannie's ear. The woman laughed, her fine straight teeth showing.

"You are very bad, Jo-nuss."

Breed grinned back, but the smile fell when the man on the floor groaned. "*Auwē*," he said. "Would you look at him too, Mrs. Naughton? He's one of the shepherds at Belle Vue Farm come for a week's visit. Couldn't let him leave once he showed signs." He picked up a stool and put it next to the man's pallet. "His name is Kanaka George."

Jeannie sat down on the stool. The man looked old with his white hair but any creased lines around his eyes and forehead were blotted out by the telltale spots. His face was ashen. He opened his eyes and stared back at her, then looked beyond her.

"Jo-nuss?"

"I'm here, *kahpo*. Brought someone to help you."

"*Mahsie*." Kanaka George licked his lips. "My throat is so sore."

Jeannie said nothing, but she knew that was a dangerous sign of the disease.

"Could you heat a bucket of water?" Jeannie asked. "Not too hot, but as hot as can be comfortable. And if I could have that saleratus that Mrs. Parker gave me, I can bathe them both. None of them can be chilled."

For the next several hours, Jeannie tended Kaui Kalama, Kanaka George and two others in the hut. She made a soup of desiccated meat and vegetables and handed it out in bowls. Jeannie was surprised to see they were made of Spode china. Then Jeannie prepared a soothing bath of saleratus. When the soda powder was dissolved, with Alani's help she sponged it on their postules.

Jeannie made sure that her patients did not become cold. "But you must keep their clothing and covers loose," she told Alani. "Over warming is dangerous. It will only aggravate the boils." When Kaui started a round of chills, she had a blanket warmed by the stove put directly on him. Extra blankets were some of the items in the boxes in the canoe and were put to use, applying them in rotation. Soon she was looking after everyone and quickly lost sense of time.

At one point, Breed took her outside for a breath of fresh air. At nine-thirty at night, the last of the summer sun was going down in the west. In front of them was Haro Strait, its waters flat and cold. Across its expanse, was the blue-gray shape of Vancouver's Island. Brilliant corals and pinks slashed against an increasing lavender hue until they all deepened. Breed and Jeannie stood on the beach in silence and watched the night come on. It became cooler. Waves scurried in on little crab feet across the sand and stones. Jeannie wrapped her shawl tighter around her.

"Don't get chilled, Mrs. Naughton."

"Thank you, I won't." She was tired and there was a whole night ahead of her, but she suddenly felt good and content like something was lifted from her shoulders.

"Those children who ran off," she wondered. "They'll be all right?"

"They're fine. Didn't really go anywhere. Moki Kapuna found them hiding on the beach. Got them stowed in that tent down there. Just as a precaution, even though I had them vaccinated when a British surgeon came visiting Belle Vue Farm a time back. They should be all right. It's their father I'm afeared for."

"And you are vaccinated?"

"*Ah-ha*. A long time ago." He paused. "I appreciate what you are doing, Mrs. Naughton. For all of them." He stood off to the side, keeping the chill of the approaching night away in his multi-striped Hudson's Bay blanket-coat. He didn't look at her. Just out onto the shore where the waves were coming in lazily, line by line.

"Mr. Kalama must mean a lot to you to come so far," Jeannie said.

"He's my *kloshe kahpo.*"

"Caw-poh. What does that mean?"

"In Chinook Jargon, it means 'good' or 'close brother.' Like a blood brother."

"I thought that he is Kanaka, not Indian."

"He is. We have known each other since boyhood." He paused, like he was weighing his thoughts. Finally, he said, "We were captured and shared the same place under the great house in the north. We were *mistchimas* together."

"He was with you with the northern tribes?"

Breed looked at her in the fading light. "*Ah-ha.* I was fifteen when we met."

For a moment, the air around her seemed to chill. A strand of her hair brushed against her cheek. She had seen the long houses at Saanich so she imagined a confusing scene of Breed and Kalama being bound to something underneath a hundred-foot long native house of massive cedar posts and boards, putrid mud and muck soaked into their tattered clothes and bare feet.

"How did that happen?"

"Meeting Kaui?"

"Forgive me. I was thinking of your capture. I beg your pardon. I shouldn't have asked."

Breed shrugged. "I suppose since I brought you here, you have a right to know something about me. I'm not ashamed." He gave her his full attention. "I was just a lad on a British shipping vessel out of the Sandwich Islands. We had just finished making a run of goods up to Fort Simpson and were on our way back down to Vancouver's Island, when we anchored in a cove for fresh water. Part of the crew was on shore when we were attacked. Swarmed us like a bees. "

Jeannie gasped. "What did you do?"

"I dove for the bushes and watched them kill my mates one by one. The ship got away and left me behind."

Jeannie shivered. "How awful. How did you survive?"

"I hid out for about a week living on berries, but got so hungry and

49

bit by mosquitoes, I finally gave up and just marched down into the Haida encampment. Scared the daylights out of them as I come at night and looked like a *memaloose* spirit. A dead spirit. If I was going to die, I figured I was going to go singing my lungs out. 'Rock of Ages,' I think it was." Breed rubbed his cheek where his whiskers were showing.

"But they did not harm you."

"No. It wasn't easy, but they didn't kill me."

Jeannie decided not to pursue this subject any further. He would tell her if he wanted. She pulled her shawl tighter around her shoulders and struggled to find something else to talk about when there was a cry from the hut.

"Jo-nuss." Alani appeared on the porch, wringing her apron with her hands. "*Hele* on. Hurry. It's Kanaka George."

Breed sprang from Jeannie's side, his boots making the pebbles clattered as he ran. Gathering her skirts, Jeannie hurried behind him.

Inside the lamp-lit room, Jeannie found Kanaka George her patient struggling to sit up. He arched his back and rubbed it like he was working some evil out of it. Breed put his hands on Kanaka George's shoulders to steady him. Alani comforted him in a low voice.

It's the pain, Jeannie thought. Jeremy had gone out of his mind with it.

She crouched to look at him and realized that his eyes were only half-open. He was lost in a restless nightmare. "Would you be so kind, Mrs. Kapuna. There is a little green bottle in the wood box. It contains opium. Two drops on the spoon should help."

After administering the sedative, Jeannie helped Breed lower the man down onto his pallet. "Remember to keep his clothing and covers loose. I'm making gruel of maize because we must make sure they all eat. It is supposed to be very nutritious."

With that, she turned to the other patients under care in the little lean to. Kaui Kalama lay crumpled on his bed, his bedding soaked. Alani and Breed helped him into a sitting position while the linens were changed out. Only when he was flat again, did he open his eyes.

"*Kahpo*," he whispered.

Breed put a hand on his shoulder. "Don't talk, *ow*. I'll be here for the by and by. Think of Sally and your *keiki*."

Close to midnight, Breed made Jeannie stop. Doubling up some cattail mats on the floor, he ordered her to rest. "Stay with her, Alani." He gave Jeannie a warm wool blanket. The last thing she remembered was Breed opening the door to the stove. The glow from the fire inside illuminated his face with strong, golden tongues of light. She fell asleep and dreamed of that face long after he left the hut.

The next morning she woke to loud voices outside. One of them was Breed's.

"You can't come near, Krill. There's sickness here."

"Small pox?"

"*Ah-ha*."

"Then it's true. The more the better. There's whiskey for them."

"Get your stinking whiskey out of here, Krill. It'll only make them worse."

"They're going to die anyway. Where's that sweet Alani?"

Jeannie heard Breed swear then the stones under his boots crunch as he quickly advanced towards someone. Throwing aside her blanket, she sprang up and cautiously opened the door. Down to her right she could see Breed walking towards someone down by a beached *salt chuck* canoe. There were several other men with the stranger. Breed was carrying his rifle. Wrapping her shawl around her head, Jeannie stepped out onto the narrow porch. The stranger was a big burly man about six feet tall and with arms like anvils. His windswept hair and bearded face were chestnut brown; his dress a combination of military coat, jersey pants and an India rubber poncho to keep the morning chill off. When Breed came up to him, he held his ground. His men ranged behind him.

"This is a free country, Breed. Folks can do as they like"

"*Ah-ha*, it's free, but do they want it?" Breed swept his hand towards Krill's men. "Have they had the *variola*?"

A couple of the men looked uncomfortable, but didn't dare move with Krill there.

"How widespread is it?" Krill asked.

"It could be in all the huts by now. Best to stay away."

"Does the surgeon at American Camp know?"

"Probably not. He's away."

"Too bad." Krill started to say something when he noticed Jeannie up on the porch. "Who's that? Your *klootsman*?"

"Watch your mouth, Krill. That's Mrs. Naughton from British Camp. She's a particular friend of the Parkers."

"Why she here?"

"So trash like you don't get it."

Krill laughed. "I'd like to get it." He cupped his hands in front of his chest and said "*Hyas tatoosh.*"

"Go to hell."

The men behind Krill howled with laughter, but the sudden arrival of a party of Indians and Hawaiians coming down the trail from the ridge silenced everyone. By the time the new men joined Breed, Krill had signaled his men to put the canoe in.

"I'll be back when conditions are more encouraging," Krill shouted above the waves on the shore. Krill bellowed at his men to pull harder. Once it was on the water, he joined them in the canoe. There was some fumbling to get the paddles going, but eventually it was under way.

Jeannie watched them go from the porch. She hadn't understood the meaning of the exchange, but knew it was directed at her. It was also apparent Jonas Breed did not like this man. The new group of men stood with him while the canoe went off then dispersed to another hut. Breed eventually turned around and came back.

"You shouldn't be up. You hardly slept."

"I heard yelling outside." She dropped the shawl to her shoulder, keeping it close to her neck. "Who was that man, Mr. Breed?"

"That was Emmett Krill, a leading citizen of San Juan Town and his board of directors."

"What does he do there?"

"What doesn't he do there? I don't think Camp Pickett was set up two hours when he and his cronies showed up on Griffin Bay. The British and Americans were going to fight over a pig, but when opportunity knocks, who cares? Now mind you, some of the people there are legitimate, but Krill deals with a more unsavory crowd."

"Does the army allow their men to go down there?"

'Oh, they're not allowed, but I could show you a list of the number of men in detention or court-marshaled for a dalliance at San Juan Town or downright drunkenness from going there." Breed's face grew dark and his mouth hard.

"Can't the American Army or Royal Marines do anything about it?"

"The American commanders have tried, but while this island is jointly occupied and the international water boundary dispute undecided, there will be a hue and cry about the military getting involved in 'civil' matters." Breed came up by the porch. "I hope you slept well, under the circumstances. I'm arranging for one of the huts to be swept out. It has a cot. You'll sleep there from now on. Mrs. Kapuna will accompany you."

"That's very kind, Mr. Breed." She stepped out to the porch rail. The morning smelled of seaweed and roasted coffee beans. So refreshing after the smell of illness in the hut.

"I made coffee. Want some? Or would you prefer tea?"

Jeannie said the coffee would be fine. He went down to a fire pit where a coffeepot hung on a rod. He poured her a cup. Its aroma drifted back to her over the salty damp beach.

"Smells rather good. How did you roast the beans?"

Breed pointed to a frying pan. "Army receipt. Will you join me, Mrs. Naughton?"

Jeannie lifted her skirts to come down the algae-stained steps, worried he might see her only indulgence—her green and black striped stockings. She made her way to his outstretched hand, surprised to feel awake at this hour, whatever time it was.

He handed her a mug. He lifted his mug then took a sip. "Cheers."

She raised her tin cup back. "It's delicious."

"*Mahsie*. Pot has a green alder chip in it."

"I never heard of such a thing, but it's delicious." Jeannie looked west out to the lavender shape of Vancouver's Island across the wide strait. A thin trail of smoke reached up to the sky. Someone's homestead, she thought. She cleared her throat. "I thought I heard a sheep bleat last night. Are they around here?"

"Belle Vue Farm isn't far away. Sometimes you can see the tip of their big barn's roof from here."

"My uncle says the American soldiers occupy it."

"Just the sheep runs above. The farm is down below." He sipped his coffee. "I suppose they wish to overlord it, but that won't happen until someone decides which nation the island belongs to."

"Do you think it will be decided?"

"In time."

Jeannie took another sip of coffee. There were so many things she wanted to know about the island and about him. "I thank you for telling me your story of your unpleasant capture last night. Shall I ask where were you born, Mr. Breed?"

He looked surprised.

"Oh, you've had such a wandering life. I just wondered."

He shifted his feet and took on a far-off look. He paused for some time. "I was born at sea. My father was an American trader in the South Pacific. Wintered in the Sandwich Islands. He met my mother there. She was Welsh. She was in a mission party going to Australia, but Honolulu was as far as she got."

He is Welsh, Jeannie thought. And the Sandwich Islands. How exotic. So he is comfortable with its people. Mr. Breed continued to surprise her.

"Did you grow up there?"

"I lived there the first years of my life, not far from the American mission. I played with the royal children on the grounds. Then my mother died. I believe I was five."

"I'm so sorry. To be so young and lose your mother." She felt a twinge of irony that he had lost a mother at a young age and she had lost a young son.

Breed shrugged. He put his mug on a log and took out his pipe. "I remember her being a pretty thing, with a great singing voice. The first great love of my life." He tamped tobacco into his pipe with his thumb.

"What happened after that?"

"I was schooled in Honolulu for a year or so, then at seven joined my father on his ship. I loved it from the moment I was on deck. He was a good ship's master. I wanted to be like him. We were going to go around the world together."

"Something happened? Your capture?"

"*Wake.* No. My father died in a storm. Rigging from the mainsail fell on him. The ship was lost along with part of the crew. We were down near New Zealand. A captain who rescued us knew my father. He took me as his own and fostered me. I was ten. I guess I was British after that."

"Orphaned at such a tender age," Jeannie murmured.

Breed put his mug down on a log. "*Ah-ha.* A number of HBC ships —Hudson's Bay Company—come to the Sandwich Islands to winter and replenish their masts and riggings. They have a trading fort right down by the water. Fly their flag just like at Fort Victoria."

Breed lit his pipe with a lucifer and shook the flame out. "Captain Godfrey began to haul salt salmon from the Fraser River runs up at Fort Langley north of here to Honolulu. Sometimes he went north up the coast to the Queen Charlotte Islands. He was a good man. He died from his injuries from the attack on our ship."

They talked for a while longer. Eventually, Breed pointed his pipe back at the hut. "We should go back in. Kaui's limbs are warm. His fever's down, but I'm worried about George. He hasn't improved." He picked up his mug.

They turned to go when Alani came out. "Jo-nuss."

"What's wrong?"

Alani wrung her hands on her apron. "I found some blood on Kanaka George's shirt."

Jeannie started to go forward, but he stayed her. "We'll hope for the best. That's all we can do. I think the crisis is coming."

The crisis came in the afternoon with an ugly familiarity. Kanaka

George's fever returned with a vengeance. He became insensible and breathless; his skin hot and hard. Jeanie tried to help him with baths of saleratus and keeping his skin clean with castile soap, but the pain in his back increased. The laudanum did not seem to help and he often cried out.

During this time, Breed worked with her, following her instructions. *How odd. What do I know, beyond the pain and helplessness of losing a dear one? What right do I have to lead?* Yet, Jeremy's voice spoke inside her, urging her to try. She struggled to recall what she had read at the Royal Marine infirmary and the questions she had asked Dr. Parker.

Toward evening, the old man's struggles lessened, as though he was resigned to the approaching maw. A dull veil crossed his eyes. Then Jeannie saw a reddish liquid appear between the pustules.

"Mr. Breed," she said, her voice shaking.

"I know." He sat down on a stool next to her. "It will be soon." He smiled wanly at Alani who stood by the woodstove with tears rolling down her face. "Do you want to gather the others?"

Kanaka George died an hour later. No sooner had Breed pulled a blanket over his face, to Jeannie's astonishment, a great keening rose from inside and outside the hut. Not one for superstition, she felt as though a cold hand had brushed against her neck when someone began to chant with a mournful voice. In the shadows flung against the wall by a lantern, she thought she saw dancers.

Breed sighed. "Moki, when the time comes, will you see that he's taken to the outlying hut? We'll have to keep him there until we can safely take him up to Belle Vue. Until then, no runners. We must wait until all this has passed."

A Hawaiian in his thirties nodded solemnly. "I'll see to it, Jo-nuss." He pulled down his felt hat and stepped outside. Jeannie was surprised to see that it was still light out. For the past twelve hours, they had kept the windows covered as light hurt their patients' eyes. She began to shake. For all her efforts, the old man had died. A tear cut loose down her cheek.

"Mrs. Naughton." Breed helped her up. "You need to rest."

"What about Mr. Kalama?" With all her actions concentrated on

Kanaka George, she did not see that Kaui could be coming into a cata-
clysm of his own.

"I'll sit with him. Now Mrs. Kapuna will help you to her hut."

～

For the second time in two days, Jeannie woke to the sound of voices.
For a moment she was disoriented, lying under a rough patch quilt on
a cot. Over her head, the arms of cedar posts and rafters lay out like
panes in a quilt of their own. The cedar shakes were the filler. She was
in the hut Breed had set aside for her. It smelled of smoke and the salt
tang of Haro Strait.

She closed her eyes, a heavy weariness steeped in her back and
arms. Her throat was dry. For a moment she wondered if she was
getting sick. The thought made her draw the quilt closer, as an image
of Jeremy's first signs flashed before her, but common sense took
hold. She was only feeling the effects from her exertions of the past
two days. They would pass.

I'll not be sick, Jeremy. Who would tell your story?

The voices outside moved up to the roof top, squabbling and
cawing. Ravens! Or crows. She still couldn't tell the difference, but
their sharp, indignant tones made her smile. Mr. Breed had said they
had import to the Salish people around here.

"Missus Naughton?" Alani's low voice came through the hand-
hewn door, then a knock. "Are you awake, Missus?"

Jeannie sat up, patting her chest. She had been sent to bed half-
dressed in her chemise and drawers with her stays loosened. She
swung her shawl around her shoulders. "Yes, I am. What time is it?"

"Ten o'clock."

"Ten o'clock!" Jeannie threw off her covers and ran to the door and
into Alani as she came through carrying a cloth-covered tray. The
woman swung it around to her hip and caught Jeannie.

Jeannie tried to go around her. "Kaui. I must see him." She felt cold,
the dread of another death seizing her in panic.

Alani held her firm. "Shh-shh, Missus. Jo-nuss say not to fret yourself. Kaui, he passed the crisis. He awake and talkin'." When Jeannie stayed still, Alani put the tray down on a small table and took off the linen covering it. The aroma of coffee filled the room. "I brought coffee, missus. And a biscuit." She gently guided Jeannie back to the bed, then gave her a cup. "I think his scabs will form just fine."

"Thank God." Jeannie's hands shook.

"You rest. I sit." She gestured to a stool by the bed with legs made from cedar branches. When Jeannie was seated, Alani covered her with a shawl. "You one very dear woman, Missus Naughton. Thanks to your *kokua*, we are betta."

Jeannie felt tears coming on. "Not everyone... Poor Mr. George." *And Jeremy.* She sniffed, embarrassed to be emotional in front of her. But the tears rolled down.

Alani gave her a handkerchief from her apron pocket.

"Thank you."

The woman's dark eyes glistened. Ever since meeting her, Jeannie thought she had a powerful face, but now she reflected that she was quite beautiful. Her brown skin was smooth and ageless. The lashes of her eyes black. She was also warm and kind.

Niceties do not matter here. I'm not in England where my whole life was ensconced in niceties. What good had that done there when I needed help the most?

"Was Mr. George a good friend?"

"Oh, yes, I knew him well. He was one good man. He work for HBC many years."

"I'm so sorry. So cruel. Mr. Breed said that you lost family to the *variola*."

Alani looked down at her lap. "My husband... my *keikis*. All gone." She shrugged it off. "I have a new husband now. Moki." She smiled faintly. "But I think maybe you understand."

Jeannie put her cup down and reached out to Alani. She was glad when Alani took her hand. "Yes, I do. And I thank you for your kindness."

Jeannie meant it. Somehow, things were changing for her. She had been so confused after Jeremy died. Although her grief could still consume her, she felt a new energy opening up paths for her. In some ways, it was an incaution, but somehow she really didn't care what people thought. If friendship was here, she'd accept it.

Alani stood up. "Would you like to dress? Then you see how everyone is doing."

Jeannie said, "Yes."

AMERICAN CAMP

Jeannie's stay fell into routine as her patients improved. Each day she rose early for a light breakfast prepared by Alani. Afterwards, then she would attend to the ill in the hut as their pustules dried up and scabs fell off. Later, she tended to housekeeping. In the afternoon she might walk the beach or read. Evenings she spent in the hut, where they told stories or she would read from one of the novel she had brought with her.

As she became more acquainted with the citizens of Kanaka Town, she recognized a hodgepodge of nationalities. Though most were Hawaiians, there were Indians, too, from various Coast Salish tribes in the region, and a lone Irishman. All were bound together by wives and husbands. Kaui Kalama's wife, Sally, was Nooksack with ties to tribal communities further north. Of particular interest to Jeannie were their children, Noelani and Kapihi.

At first, her only glimpse of the children was when she went out to walk along the beach. They stayed in their stand-alone tent Breed had quarantined them in, sometimes peeking out as she went by, but never showing themselves fully. Then one day, on her way back from the privy, a willowy girl with waist-length hair came out from behind the flap. Her dark brown eyes looked at her with fierce curiosity.

"Good morning," Jeannie greeted her. "Are you Kaui Kalama's girl?"

The girl froze, the eyebrows on her brown moon face rising in surprise. She leaned into the tent pole for a moment, then nodded.

What a darling girl, Jeannie thought. Her dress was nothing more than a knee-length chemise of faded blue. Her feet were bare. Breed said that Noelani was twelve.

"Are you the *wahine* who gives *kokua* for my papa?"

"Papa? Where's Papa?" From behind Noelani, a chubby boy with short-cropped hair rushed onto the deck in front of the tent. "Where's Papa?"

Noelani drew the boy against her. "Shh."

Jeannie put a hand to her mouth. Something about the boy reminded her of Jeremy, but it was not a sad recollection. The boy made her laugh, that unaccustomed feeling warming her. "And you must be Kapihi. I've heard Mr. Breed say your name many times."

The boy's eyes grew wide. "Really? You know my *kahpo*?"

Jeannie grew serious. "Cow-po? He's doing much better if you want to know."

The girl stepped forward. "He means Jo-nuss. He is our father's *kahpo*, big brother."

"Oh." Jeannie put a finger thoughtfully to her lip.

Kapihi squeezed his arms around his sister. "Can we see Papa?"

Jeannie's voice soften. "Pretty soon. We need to wait a little longer."

It was not much longer. Later that afternoon, the children were allowed to see him for the first time, standing at the door to the hut. Kaui sat against the wall with a blanket over his shoulders. When he saw them, tears rolled down his face. "*Klahowyah, keiki.* Don't come in. Papa's still sick, but I so happy to see you."

"I am happy too, Papa," Noelani said. "I miss you. I will make a *lei*."

Kapihi stepped forward. "Me, too. I will make it this big."

"That's a very nice thought, Kapihi," Jeannie said. Wrapping her arm around his shoulders she ushered him back to the invisible line at

61

the threshold. "Why don't you do that right now? We mustn't overtire your father."

From that moment, she became the children's particular friend. They sought her out at every opportunity. When she was able, she would sit in front of her hut with a slate and help them practice their letters and sums. Sometimes, she would read from a ragged *Merry Museum Magazine* come from who knew where, just as she did with Jeremy. She marveled that the children were so open and confident in their friendship. When they leaned against her and helped to turn the pages, she felt a rich comfort. Sometimes they read the puzzles aloud or figured them out on the slate. When she was low in spirits thinking about Jeremy, they lifted her up. They often had her laughing.

One day, while she was at Kaui's bedside spooning out soup to him, she heard a commotion was heard outside. Breed went out to investigate.

"Corporal?" Jeannie heard Breed say.

A man with an Irish lilt answered. "Beggin' your pardon, sir, but is a Mrs. Naughton here?"

"She's inside."

Jeannie put down her spoon.

"I'm from Camp Pickett," the man continued. "We heard the infection was gone, with only one loss."

"*Ah-ha.* The crisis is over."

"Splendid. I have a message from Captain Pickett. He asks if she would honor the officers with her company this evening."

"Why don't you ask her?" Breed came to the door. "The Americans have called, Mrs. Naughton."

Jeannie gave Kaui the tin cup of broth and the spoon and went out onto the porch.

The soldier had his back to her and was knocking sand out of one of his boots. She smiled. She had never seen an American soldier before. He wore a dark blue cap and jacket and light blue pants without cuffs. He tapped his hands as he looked around the settlement. When he turned, she noticed a brass Company "D" and bugle emblem on the front of the cap.

He straightened up. "Ma'am. Captain Pickett requests the honor of your presence at his table this evening." It sounded like a rehearsed speech, but it was well delivered. He laid an envelope on the porch railing and stepped back. "Are you able to travel?"

"I'm sure that I can, if my work is done here. I am, however, hardly presentable for company." Jeannie turned to Breed. He leaned against the doorway with a slightly bemused look on his face. She wished she could read it. After a fortnight, he was still an enigma to her.

"I believe your work is done here, Mrs. Naughton. You've earned your rest." Breed turned to the soldier. "Will you be returning shortly?" he asked the soldier.

"At her pleasure." The corporal straightened up, nodding towards the envelope. "I have been asked to return with an answer." He walked down toward the fire pit.

Jeannie took it and slipped out the note. It read:

Madame, it has troubled me that you have been in Kanaka Town for this length of time, performing this gruesome duty unspeakable for a lady of your character. I must seek to give you relief. If you would give me the honor of presenting yourself to me this evening, I would be most flattered. Our post's surgeon will be at your disposal for any necessary rehabilitation. I'm sure you will find the quarters here most agreeable despite their rude state and the company of ladies here a better class. I can send an escort with you back to English Camp at your leisure.

Faithfuly yours,

Captain George E. Pickett, U.S, Army

Jeannie folded the note and put it back into the envelope. "Captain Pickett is quite the gentleman," she said to Breed.

"He's a Virginian."

"What does that mean?" She knew nothing about the America states of let alone the territories.

"Some of your countrymen find him completely compatible."

"He does not approve of my being here, due to the infection. Still,

63

he wishes me to come this afternoon as his intelligence says we are clear. He will arrange for my return to the Royal Marine encampment."

"Do you want to go?

"Oh, yes...yes, please. I believe it's safe to go."

Breed called the soldier back. "Tell the captain Mrs. Naughton will be ready to travel within the next few hours."

"Should he be sending an escort?"

"No, I'll bring her myself." Breed stood at the small railing. "Is the sutler around? I wonder if he's seen Andrew Pierce."

"A schooner came in this mornin.' I believe Mr. Pierce was aboard."

"Excellent. I'll see him then."

After the soldier left, Breed ordered preparations for Jeannie to bathe. Next to the base of the wooded ridge and several yards away from the huts, men placed a wood tub behind a curtain of blankets with an additional area roped off for dressing.

"My friends will heat water and put it into the tub. When it is ready, you can hand your clothes over to Alani. She will put them into the large fire being built on the beach."

Jeannie nodded that she understood. She would wear clothing she had previously set aside for the journey back to English Camp. It was the best way, so not to carry out the disease back with her.

"And you, Mr. Breed?" She did not think that he had any wardrobe beyond what he always wore, but he answered that he would do the same.

"When everyone is well again, we'll take everything out and burn it or scrub it down with carbolic acid." he continued. "Once the contents are out and dealt with, I'll smoke the buildings out with sulfur."

So Jeannie bathed and Alani guarded. When she emerged from behind her blanketed wall into the dressing space, she was as fresh as she ever would be.

"You'll be going home after your visit to the Boston camp, missus?" Alani asked as she helped to lace up Jeannie's corset over her chemise and adjust her petticoats.

"Yes, I'm afraid so." Jeannie swallowed. She felt sad to be going. She was very fond of Alani. "Mr. Breed says my work is done here now. All should recover with no ill effects other than the marks, I'm glad to say."

"*Auwē*. We will miss you," Alani said. "May I sing you a *mele*? To say '*Mahalo nui loa* for your *kokua*."

Jeannie smiled. "I would be honored. That would be very nice." *Though I don't know what a maylay is.* She slipped her skirt over her head. She hooked her skirt in place then buttoned up her blouse front. "There. I'm ready. Let's go next door."

Outside, Jeannie put on her bonnet and walked over to see Kaui.

Jeannie looked into the hut. Her patient was sitting up against the wall, bundled in blankets. He still looked pale, but the pox had not ravaged him as she had seen in others. The scabs on his face and arms were finally gone, except for a couple on his face. There would be some deep scars on his cheeks, but nothing other than that. Under his liquid dark eyes, the brown skin was purple. It made him look sorrowful, but in the short time she knew him, he had never complained.

"You will come again?" he asked.

"Yes, I'll come again if I can." She smiled at the children sitting next to him and felt a pang of longing for her lost boy. She adored them both but her heart had a special place for Kapihi. It was so comical the way he hung on every word Breed said and copied his actions when he wasn't in the room. She held out her arms to Kapihi and Noelani and they ran to her. Jeannie embraced them each and kissed them on their heads.

"Horses are ready," Breed said as he came up to the porch. "But first... my friends would like to say farewell." He set up a canvas camp stool on the porch. "Will you sit, Mrs. Naughton?"

"All right." The children following her outside, Jeannie smoothed out her skirt and sat down on the stool. She was surprised to see a little group form near the steps below her. A large woven cedar mat was placed on the ground. Moki Kapuna sat down with a large tan gourd. Another man knelt beside him with two sturdy sticks in his hands. From around the corner of the hut Alani appeared with a crown of ferns in her black hair and a long necklace made of thick twisted cedar rope draped over her red blouse. She had removed her apron and shoes. Her skirt swayed as she walked.

"*Aloha*, Mrs. Naughton."

"A-low-ha." Jeannie had heard that word so often the past days, she now embraced it as her common greeting with everyone.

Alani smiled and turned to the men.

Moki Kapuna began to pound and rap the gourd twice on its side until a boom-da-da, boom-da-da beat was established. The other musician tapped the sticks together. Then Alani began to dance, her full body swaying as gracious as the eelgrass near the shore.

At first Jeannie was shocked. She had once heard a pastor in Plymouth, England remark on the pagan dances of the Sandwich Islanders. He had seen them while on the island of Maui and said the missionaries had every right to squash licentious behavior. But as Alani danced, Jeannie thought, how beautiful. Then the woman began to sing in a deep alto voice full of grace and sorrow.

Auhea wale `oe e ku`u aloha `eâ

Ne`ene`e mai `oe, ne`ene`e mai `oe ...

A pili pono

Jeannie felt a chill go down her spine and pulled her shawl tight around her shoulders. "Do you know what it means, Mr. Breed?"

Breed cleared his throat. "Yes. I do. Essentially says Listen, you bird, my companion who weathers gossip of the cold night, this cold is nothing to me. The heart's desire is ever urgent." He smiled. "It was composed for Alexander Liholiho, Kamehameha IV. I think he came to the Hawaiian throne in '55." He shifted his feet. "Well it says to come close. It was written for his wife, you see."

"Oh." Jeannie blushed.

Alani moved back and forth in front of the mat, her body as graceful as the most winsome maiden. Her brown hands caressed the air in front of her face, sometimes reaching out as though her fingers were rain falling gently from an unseen sky. Jeannie wondered what the song really meant. She heard the words *ke aloha* and knew that *aloha* also meant love.

The *mele* and the dance was over too soon. Alani bowed down in front of her. The men rose up from the mat. *"Mahalo nui loa,"* they said in chorus. Thank you very much.

Jeannie stood up. She smiled self-consciously at the small group, including Kaui standing in the door of the shack and the group below. "Thank you. All of you be well." She put her arms around Kapihi and Noelani.

"Mahsie," Kaui said he leaned on the door frame. "Go with the spirits."

"Mahsie. Mahalo." The flood of thanks from all sides overwhelmed her. She had made friends at Victoria. Here the word "friend" felt genuine. She stepped down off the porch. The day was bright and warm. Overhead, the sky was blue with white clouds stacked up high like teased wool. Even the cold water of Haro Strait looked inviting, the waves slapping lazily on the gray stony shore. There was a pungent, salty sea scent to the air, as refreshing as the first day of the world.

"So where are we going?" Jeannie asked as she stood by her horse.

"The U.S. Army calls it Camp Pickett, but most of us say American Camp. Part of the joint occupation agreement. No more than one hundred military at either place." Breed helped her get up on the sidesaddle. "I hope the saddle's comfortable. Local cobbler made it."

"I can manage." Jeannie hooked her right leg over the top pommel and put her left leg in the stirrup, then arranged her skirt and petticoats over her legs. After tying her gear behind her, Breed mounted his horse. He pointed up to the forested sandstone ridge. "It's a straight shot up. I can lead your mare if you wish."

"Thank you, Mr. Breed. You're most kind."

"Moki," he called out to the group gathering around them.

"Kahpo?"

"I won't be back for a while. I've a business contract with Peters. You want something from Whatcom?"

"Sure, bring me a new stone for my knife. Feller took mine."

"O.K. You see Doctin, tell him I'll be back by Sunday."

Breed raised his hand to his friend. Taking the reins of Jeannie's horse, he led her over to the trail going up. He turned in his saddle and gave her a reassuring smile. To the others he said, "*Aloha.*"

"*Aloha!*" the greeting came back.

"Bye, Jo-nuss!"

"Bye, Kapihi!" he called back to the boy who had just joined the group. "Be good."

Jeannie smiled when the answer was a boisterous giggle.

The ride started out pleasantly. Both of her legs on the left of the horse, Jeannie squeezed them tight against the pommels to keep her balance as Breed led her horse up the trail. The path was dry but pocked with holes and rocks and lined with patches of rough grass she couldn't name. For a while, she held her seat until the mare tripped throwing her against its neck. For an awkward moment she clung to its mane, the stiff hairs scratching her cheek. The animal staggered then righted herself.

"You all right, Mrs. Naughton?"

Jeannie looked out and saw that Breed kept the animal's head up by the rein until it regained its composure. Jeannie wasn't sure if she found hers. Her heart was pounding when she sat up straight again.

At the crest of the hill, Breed handed her the reins and to her surprise, got down. "If you take your left foot out of your stirrup, I can check your cinch. Just in case it was loosened."

Jeannie curled her legs up. He pulled on a strap, then put the stirrup down. Breed standing so close to her made her face warm.

"That should do." He went back to his horse and mounted.

They could see in many directions. As he promised, she could see the roof of a large barn and those of shacks organized like a neat little village. Hudson's Bay Company Belle Vue Farm. Extensive fencing suggested a well-managed station. The large island of Vancouver was across the Haro Strait, tiny islands protecting the entrance into Victoria's main harbors on its southern tip. In the distance a steamboat made the turn at the Strait of Juan de Fuca and entered the channel. This is what the fuss is all about, Jeannie thought, and why San Juan Island was presently occupied by both countries. The United States wanted the international boundary here. The British wanted the international boundary to be Rosario Strait on the other side of the islands to the east. Then they would have all the islands.

There was little activity on the water today except for the steamboat and the arrival of a pod of killer whales that immediately began to feed on the summer run of salmon. Standing up in his stirrups, Breed pointed out the plunging black dorsal fins out in the channel.

"The Haida say a young man ran with them. He fell into a stormy sea and was rescued by people wearing black and white animal skins. He stayed with them for a time, but when he wanted to go back to his village, they told him who they were. They were the killer whale people and they wanted him to stay."

Jeannie craned to see them. "Do you believe that, Mr. Breed due to your time among the Indians?"

"Yes and no. It's a story, but maybe it's true. We are all on earth together."

"My uncle told me that local Indians believe the first man came out of a clam shell."

"They're sea people. It's no different than first man made from dust." Breed sat back down, deep in thought. For a moment his mouth set and his eyes grew distant, but the mood snapped and he was himself again. He cleared his throat. "Ever see a totem pole?"

"I've seen a drawing of a Haida pole. It had animals stacked on top of each other. A bear was eating a frog. Is it a fairy tale?"

"*Wake*. Not a fairy tale, though such poles do tell stories. Sometimes it's about how the world came to be. Other times it's stories about the families who own the poles. Before there were human beings, there were only animals. Bear eating Frog is an old story. See the eagle over there?" Breed pointed to a snag high up the hill. On one of its gnarled, bare branches sat a white-headed eagle.

"I see it."

"Among the Haida there are the Raven and Eagle Clans and their houses. Each clan claims stories and objects that belong only to it. Their masks and family crests poles tell their stories. The crests are like those knights in *Ivanhoe*."

"*Ivanhoe*? You've read it?"

69

"Of course. Many ship's captain has the book their library. I read it as a boy." Breed went on. "Eagles are powerful. They can take messages to the spirits."

Jeannie shifted in her saddle when her mare dropped her head to pull at the tall grass. "You said you didn't believe, Mr. Breed."

He smiled faintly. "No, I don't. I don't see *tamahnous* everywhere."

"Tama-noose?"

"Spirits." He smiled again and nodded his head at the eagle who had turned its haughty head in their direction. "But I believe in that fellow." He sighed. "I was just a boy then, lost in a different world." Breed grew serious. "When I was a captive, my master sent me into a deserted Haida village up high in the Queen Charlotte Islands. The village had been empty for years because a villager had gone to trade and brought the variola back along with the goods. Wiped them all out."

"How awful." Jeannie put a hand on her stomach.

Breed didn't appear to notice. "Not a soul was left, except their totem poles—great columns with all their family crests on them. They were leaning every which way like tombstones, their long houses with doors open like hungry black mouths." Breed looked back at the eagle. "Stretched out in trees behind the village were a hundred eagles. I thought of my mother and father, and my companions lost in the attack on us. The eagles answered."

"Truly?" Jeannie put a hand on her chest.

"Truly." Breed sat back down in his stirrups, pulling his horse back from the ridge. A breeze was blowing gently and it caught both horse and rider. The dark hair on Breed's forehead lifted slightly. A long, thin scar ran high up against the scalp line. She wondered how he had got it.

"I have only seen the Indians at Fort Victoria," Jeannie said quietly.

"Then you have seen only the surface and the pull the traders have had upon them."

"You must know them very well, the Haida in particular."

Breed turned to her. "I only know what I've experienced and what they have invited me to learn. Even what I've seen does not come close to who they really are. White people have taken my captivity and enslavement as cause to misjudge them, to dismiss them as savages, *siwash*. All I can do is show them my respect. They are deeper and more varied than anyone knows. They love their families, have a great sense of humor, and delight in the natural world."

He sat back on his saddle and change the subject. He pointed to the coastline below them. "Coast's mostly like this," he said. There was a bay to the north and coves guarded by treacherous foaming-white surf and hidden rocks. To the south, the shore became more open and prairie-like but still wild and unruly. *Like you are,* Jeannie thought.

She marveled that only fourteen days ago she had been out there on the water looking in as they paddled. Equally, she marveled at Breed's ability to keep the subject of his captivity tightly guarded. In their days together, this was the second time he had said something that even hinted at it.

"Some say volcanoes formed the rocks, then a giant glacier came through," he stated.

"Do you believe that, Mr. Breed?"

Breed laughed. "You're philosophical today, Mrs. Naughton. I—"

"There you are! Figures you'd be with some pretty lass. Good morning to y'all."

Both Breed and Jeannie turned around and stared. Coming out of the grove of madrone and cedar trees was a tall blonde man dressed in a naval captain's coat. Jeannie thought him about Breed's age, but more weathered, a seaman to the core. His face was tanned, his high cheekbones and straight nose sunburned. His bushy eyebrows were bleached to the color of winter butter. She wondered about his connection to Breed.

He bowed to Jeannie with a sweep of his cap, causing his knapsack to fall against his head. Tied down to the bundle was a long sword sheathed in an elegant leather cover. It swung precariously over him and startled Jeannie's horse. As she calmed it down with a pat, Jeannie couldn't help giggling. The stranger was quite a study in the vagabond life.

"Collie Henderson," Breed said. "You sure dawdled getting here."

"I was detained by Mother Nature, *kahpo*. Quite an adventure which I will tell you in private company later. Glad to see you looking well. Heard there was the variola in Victoria and here. Any lost?"

"Kanaka George, the old shepherd from HBC, I'm sad to tell. Kaui Kalama was pretty ill, but he survived. The rest are recovering fine." Breed turned to Jeannie. "May I present Mrs. Naughton, late of English Camp?"

Collie Henderson bowed again, but held back his gear with his hands. "Ma'am. Mr. Naughton is most fortunate."

Breed said, "She was kind enough to come here to help the sick. Kaui in particular. We're off now to see the Virginian. Want to come? Mrs. Naughton will be staying over until she is escorted back to Garrison Bay. I have a delivery for Peters."

"Sure. You might need an escort. Saw some soldiers out squirrel hunting. Drunk as skunks, begging your pardon, ma'am. Krill must've got in a new shipment. Among other things." Collie made a sign to Breed. Breed frowned.

"Captain Pickett has his hands full, that's for sure." Breed shifted in his saddle, making his horse turn its ears back at him. "Half his company is either in detention or doing hard labor at the wood pile."

"Is Krill the man we saw the other day?" Jeannie asked Breed.

"That's right."

"Krill was here?" Collie took off his cap and wiped his brow with his sleeve.

Breed glowered. "Came right into Kanaka Town. Left when he learned there was smallpox."

"Pox on him, if you'll excuse me, ma'am." Collie muttered something under his breath and slammed his cap back on. "Krill'll get his own one of these days. It won't be the liquor either."

Breed coughed and Jeannie wondered if it was a signal to Henderson that he should stop talking and start walking. Jeannie was relieved to be going. She was anxious to get settled into her new quarters.

With Collie walking alongside Breed's horse, they made it to the top of the hill and onto a rough-cut road that seem to run north and south through half-cleared woods. Breed turned his horse to the south.

Jeannie heard American Camp before she saw it. Like the Royal Marine encampment, the sounds of hammering told her that it was under construction too. Dr. Parker had informed her that during the crisis over the murdered pig the summer before, Captain Pickett had taken down many of the buildings at Fort Bellingham on the mainland and sent them over plank by plank. They had been put up on the open prairie seventy feet above sea level and remained.

How exposed they are, Jeannie thought as she and the men came out of the trees and onto the edge of the military ground, essentially an open prairie enclosed by a white picket fence. Inside, several Silbey tents and a long building under construction stood to the left of the parade ground. To the right was line of housing she suspected was for the officers. At the back was a lone blockhouse. On either side, the land sloped down through rolling grass and woods, but up here, she thought, the wind must howl through the outskirts of the picket fence surrounding the camp.

"Where is the Hudson's Bay Company farm from here?"

"It's down the hill to the right." Breed brought his horse to a halt outside the tall whitewashed sentry box to the camp. There was some activity out on the parade ground, which the sentry at the gate was watching with unsteady concentration. Jeannie wondered if the man was recovering from a self-inflicted malady. He looked drunk, but she didn't dare say.

"That you, O'Malley? Breed patted his horse's neck. "Looks like you lost more than a stripe."

"Aye, I did, Mr. Breed. Shameful business." The sentry beamed. "I've been recuperating from me loss ever since."

Breed straightened up. "I've brought Mrs. Naughton. She has been invited to Captain Pickett's table this evening."

"Beggin' your pardon, ma'am, but his lordship is detained in San Juan Town. There was an incident last night lately discovered. See that building over there? You'll find the officer of the day, Sergeant-Major Grimes, there. He'll make you comfortable."

Breed turned to Jeannie. "I'll see that you're settled, Mrs. Naughton. I'm sure everything is under control."

"Thank you, Mr. Breed." Jeannie wasn't so sure about her new situation. There was such a different feel to this camp, a little undernourished in contrast to the Royal Marine encampment. Sergeant Major Grimes, a man with a neatly trimmed beard and mustache immediately put her at ease. She dismounted and was ushered to her evening abode.

She said her good-bye to Breed outside the small, newly built officers' quarters where she would share quarters with a Mrs. Jenkins and her daughter.

"Is all well?" Breed asked as he untied his horse from the hitching post.

"Indeed it is. My quarters are very satisfactory."

He dipped his head. "Then I'll say good-bye. There is a military road of sorts from here to English Camp. A pleasant ride through valleys and woods. Perfectly safe. I'm sure an escort can take you or even some of the officers themselves as they enjoy good relations with the officers at Garrison Bay." Breed held the horse close to him and stroked its nose. "Mrs. Naughton."

"Yes, Mr. Breed."

"*Mahsie* for your kindness. I wasn't sure if it was such a good idea, especially with Mrs. Parker to answer to, but thanks for what you did for my friend, Kaui, and the others. You were courageous. I hope it hasn't hurt your reputation."

Jeannie felt a sting in her eyes. Her little son's spirit was so close, a soft breath at her neck. It made her think of eagles. "It was not anything, I assure you. I am the one who is grateful that you accepted, Mr. Breed. You have restored my confidence. I thought that I could save my son and I could not, but there I did do some good." She began to choke up and avoided his eyes. Behind him Collie Henderson waited. Giving Breed her gloved hand, she said farewell. "I hope we meet again."

Breed bowed and left.

~

"So where did you take Kanaka George's body?" Collie asked Breed as they walked their horses past the laundress shack. A young woman stirred a boiler full of soldiers' shirts and flannels with a heavy stick, the steam making her Irish face even more red. Close by, someone chopped wood for the fire.

"He's laid to rest at Belle Vue Farm. Mr. Griffin made the arrangements from there."

"Bloody business. Truly sorry, Jonas."

"I only knew him for two years, but he was a solid HBC man. Never complained nor shirked his duty. I enjoyed his company."

They were beyond the white picket fence surrounding the camp and coming clear of the last outbuilding that made up the American military ground. They passed into the sweeping, grassy expanse that comprised the southern tip of San Juan Island. Directly below, the Hudson's Bay Company farm spread out in front of them, the neat log houses lining the lane in rows pointed west to Haro Strait. The huge English barn with its double bays and corrals spoke of organization and attention to detail. When a sheep bleated from one of the pens made of logs, Breed thought it sounded like a farewell cry. The farm was probably not going to last too many years longer.

"You're looking thoughtful." Collie's comment broke Breed's mood.

Breed laughed. "Mind your business."

"Thinking of Mrs. Naughton?"

"You're a fool, Collie."

"Am I? Gone three months and I find you with a pretty face. Who is she anyway?"

"She's the niece of Archie Campbell, a trader at Fort Victoria. She lost her little boy a few weeks back. She's rehabilitating with the Parkers at English Camp."

"How did she end up at Kanaka Town?" The men had descended down onto the wide main lane of the farm. Breed stopped to allow Collie to hitch up his gear.

"She offered to help nurse Kaui and the others. Whole town's fond of her."

"She's married."

Breed snorted. "Widowed." He wasn't sure why Collie's comment irritated him. He certainly found the woman charming and could admit her friendship was very satisfying. She just wasn't someone he could hope for. He let his horse tug at the grass by a fence post. "Her husband died a few year back plying the East."

"You have another opinion?"

"Meaning what?" Breed's irritation prickled.

"Oh, a woman alone with a child. Think she's a grass widow?"

Breed put his hand out. "Enough, Collie. That's enough."

"Then she's a special lady, indeed."

Breed let out a guffaw. Collie would say something like that, though he didn't understand his friend's continued good opinion of him, despite their long-standing acquaintance.

They had met under unusual circumstances. Twice.

Collie Henderson was the son of a Scots whaling captain employed with an American firm. His bark often wintered over in Honolulu. Breed was seven years old when they first met. He had been down on his knees, digging near a coconut palm tree inside the coral rock wall of Kawaiahao Church, when Collie, a big boy for his age, came up to him.

"What are you doing?" Collie asked, his voice a bit too loud.

"Burying kukui nuts to make necklaces for my aunties at the mission."

"Why would you do that?"

"So the ants will eat the meat and clean it out."

"I thought you were easy pickings," Collie told him later. "You were a scrawny runt. I wanted that coral piece around your neck. Didn't count on your aim."

Collie was going to give him a licking and he could have, but Breed was fast and in three quick shots, knocked the bigger boy to the ground with well-aimed kukui nuts. Out cold.

Breed didn't see him again until fifteen years later in the Puget Sound stranded on a rock at high tide.

A ewe bleated again, bringing Breed back to the lane they were standing in.

"Why we coming here, by the way?" Collie patted his stomach. "I'm starved."

"I heard Sikhs was somewhere around here. Stayed away because of the sickness." Breed looked over the pens to see if he could see his Coast Salish Indian friend.

The bleating of one of the ewes multiplied to a chorus as a shepherd came into the pen and with his croft and dog, gathered the flock together. Another Hawaiian swung the gate open and the sheep poured out. *Sheared and freshly dipped*, Breed thought. The smell of tobacco juice was strong. The sheep quickly moved down the hill to the prairie grass, the dog gathering them the way the shepherd whistled.

At the manager's house, Mr. Griffin himself came out and greeted them on the stoop, his slouch hat in hand. He wore a jacket and tie but he could not hide his hands stained from work. He was a youngish man with a beard and trimmed muttonchops that reflected current fashion. Hailing from Hudson's Bay headquarters in Montreal seven years before, Charles John Griffin's reputation as an agreeable man with anyone he met earned him respect from Americans and English alike.

"Joy of the morning to yer, Mr. Breed. T'is good to see yer in good health. How's everyone now in Kanaka Town? All's well, now?"

"*Mahsie*. All's well."

"And Mrs. Naughton?"

"On her way home tomorrow. She's having dinner with Captain Pickett tonight."

The farm manager put on his hat and stepped into the lane. "Excellent. A bloody business, this variola. Mrs. Naughton's a fine, compassionate lady to help contain the infection after losing her little son. And you, sir, as well. We all thank ye."

Breed dipped his head.

Griffin looked beyond Breed to Collie who had taken over the reins of Breed's horse while he talked.

"What brings you to Belle Vue Farm, Mr. Henderson? I haven't seen you since the winter storms. Where have you been?"

"Out chasing pirates." With that he drew out a large sword of samurai design from the scabbard on his back. "Or rather, they had designs on us."

Breed pinched his nose. Collie either was on the border of a tall tale or his excursion for locating trading partners had taken a turn for the worse.

DINNER PLANS AND FANS

After Jeannie refreshed in her room, she joined her hostess, Mrs. Jenkins, the sister of one of the officers and her sixteen-year-old daughter, Lucy, on the long porch.

The housing for the American officers lay in a row on the west side of the parade ground. Three in number, the commanding officer's house, a two story affair, rose tall over the two quarters for the bachelor officers. All were white-washed houses with green Venetian blinds. To Jeannie's eye, they seemed typical military construction, though she couldn't help compare the general area to the beauty of the Royal Marine encampment with its two stately big leaf maple and woods on the hills hugging the parade grounds, the water in front. This place was wide open. The wind tugged at her hair and sleeves. It hadn't stopped blowing since she arrived.

How tired I am. She felt the weight of the past two weeks rest heavy on her shoulders. Only one more night and then she would be back at the Royal Marine camp, the place she was starting to call home. She scrunched her shoulders slightly so as not to suggest any lack of equipoise to Mrs. Jenkins, then set her shawl off her shoulders.

Jeannie moved to the rail. Mrs. Jenkins followed, then jumped when her hooped skirts bumped into Jeannie.

She's afraid to stand next to me. Is it the variola? *That I'm English? Or the people I nursed Kanakas?*

Mrs. Jenkins recovered with a flourish of her fan, murmuring some apology.

Jeannie put the back of her gloved hand to her lips and cleared her throat. Conversation wasn't going anywhere. "Have you been here long, Mrs. Jenkins?"

"Entirely too long. It took nearly three weeks just to get from Philadelphia to San Francisco then another four days to Port Townsend. The train on the Isthmus was dreadful." She fanned herself like she was still in jungle heat. "And now the prospects my brother was so enthused about are not forthcoming. What will Albert think?"

"Albert? Your brother?"

"No. My husband." She sniffed. "He hoped for some contract with the military here, but it seems that the locals have that sewn up." The fan snapped again. "I cannot tell him about the dangers here. Savages that take heads and those filthy Kanakas. He would be appalled."

Having just spent a fortnight with both categories of people, Jeannie thought she should say something, then decided she had better not.

Mrs. Jenkins turned her attention to a bald eagle gliding above the camp. Jeannie's eyes followed. Turning in an aimless, descending circle, its white head looked gold in the summer sun. She remembered what Mr. Breed had said about eagles. It could communicate with the spirits. *Jeremy, I love you. Eagle, tell him that.* It finally flew down the hill and out of sight.

Lucy Jenkins soon became bored and sat down on a chair to examine the contents of her reticule. The silence became oppressive. Jeannie fought to find something else to talk about, but Mrs. Jenkins spoke first.

"Was it difficult, my dear, to tend to such wickedness as the variola? I should have died to have to go to such a place."

"I did not have to go. I wanted to do some good. Smallpox is not particular. It found its way into my uncle's house." Jeannie's stomach tightened. Blinking, she turned away as her eyes filled up. She used her black trimmed handkerchief for any stray tear.

"Oh." Mrs. Jenkins's voice sounded like a squeaky mouse. "Well, I should say. There it is." She sniffed, fiddling with a pendant at her considerable bosom. She wore a bright green and yellow silk plaid dress Jeannie supposed was in season somewhere.

"I heard that wild American was there, a Mr. Bread. Lived with the northern Indians."

"Mr. Breed. He was a perfect gentleman." Jeannie stepped away from her.

"A virtual slave, I hear tell. Made to do the most menial things for a white man."

"That I do not know, madam. I fear it is someone's flight of fancy." *Who did Mrs. Jenkins think she was?*

"Ah."

"Mother, when are we going to dinner? I'm quite famished. And didn't you promise me there will be introductions?" Behind Jeannie, a fan snapped open violently.

Mrs. Jenkins's mouth made a perfect "O." She scolded her daughter not to speak in such fashion. "There will be gentlemen present, I dare say." She smiled weakly at Jeannie and sat next to Lucy. Jeannie heard the chair creak behind her. She was left on her own, wondering how the evening would fare. Hadn't Gilly Parker warned her that there might be some scandal?

At six o'clock a sergeant came over to escort the women to Captain George Pickett's quarters next door where Pickett personally greeted Jeannie and the Jenkins women at the door. For the second time that day she mused that she was the same height as the captain. With dark shoulder length hair, mustache and a long unruly goatee, Pickett was only a little over five and half feet tall. What he lacked in height, however, she had already learned he made up in audacity, charm and a strong scent of Jamaican rum cologne. He offered her his arm and led her into the candlelit dining room.

Gathered around the table was a collection of men and women from the area. Pickett gave immediate introductions. "May I present

81

Mr. and Mrs. Lyle Marshall of Port Townsend, my second lieutenant, James W. Forsyth, two British naval officers from the HMS *Satellite*, Lieutenant Fuller—Mrs. Jenkins' brother visiting from Fort Steilacoom, and Andrew Pierce from the settlement of Seattle."

The men rose as the women were escorted to their seats at the table. The Jenkins women were treated with courtesy, but from Lucy's pout not enough. When Pickett pulled out her chair, Jeannie thanked him for his hospitality and sat down.

"Now, Mrs. Naughton," Captain Pickett said as he sat down. "Do tell us all about your time in Kanaka Town. It has concerned us all, considerin' someone has left his earthly bounds." He put his napkin in his lap and sipped water from the crystal glass at his place.

Jeannie glanced around. The table was set just as fine as the officer's table at the Royal Marine Camp with a linen cloth, several candlesticks spread out down the middle, and a large hurricane lamp set in the center. The candles cast soft yellow light on all the diners.

Captain Pickett winked at her, but she pretended she did not notice. "An act of bravery, I might add," Pickett went on. "Do tell."

Jeannie wasn't sure what account to give or whether it was a proper subject for the dinner table, but they seemed anxious to know about her time with the people of Kanaka Town, so she told them of her days there. When she was done, Pickett directed the dinner guests to a discussion of health in general. He sat at his place at the head of the table, his long hair curling at his jacket's collar, like a country gentleman hosting guests at his estate. Jeannie could understand why Mr. Breed said he was popular with both military camps and civilians.

It soon became apparent that the women were not taken with her account. Mrs. Jenkins' lips seemed to get acutely puckered as Jeannie went on. Mrs. Marshall, the merchant's wife, burst out that the whole affair was unseemly.

"Don't you think, Mrs. Jenkins, a woman should be more particular in what she chooses to undertake?" Mrs. Marshall's rag curls banged against her neck.

"I do indeed. Don't you, Mr. Pierce?"

Andrew Pierce was mid-bite on an appetizer of oysters. He looked startled, then blushed at Jeannie sitting next to him. "You caught me off-guard, ma'am. I'll have to think on it."

"I don't believe that there is anything to think on," said the captain of the HMS *Satellite*. "Women served valiantly in our hospitals in the late Crimean War. Miss Nightingale for one. An extraordinary woman. Saved many a soldier's life."

Mrs. Jenkins and the other ladies shrank back when the military men agreed. The matter of Jeannie's incautious adventure was settled and to her relief, in her favor. The men agreed that containing the smallpox was imperative. It touched her deeply when they gave tender acknowledgment to her loss and the irony she could not help her son.

Dinner was served in the French style with all the dishes on the table and the serving plates assisted around. Pickett continued playing host, leading the conversation and letting topics flow from local politics to news of the social season. Occasionally, he'd interject, "Sir, ah believe that is the most interesting thing ah heard" or something to that effect. Jeannie found his accent hard to understand.

During the second hour, the conversation turned to more national subjects, though Jeannie noticed that by some unspoken agreement, they did not speak of the growing discord and talk of secession back in the States she had heard during conversations in Victoria. Instead, the conversation settled on Pickett's exploits in the Mexican war. The British officers were interested in the tactics of General Winfield Scott. Pickett obliged them with an arrangement of saltcellars and candlesticks on the table.

As he laid out the battlefield, Jeannie was amused to see that he had brought Mrs. Jenkins and the other women to a complete stop. Their fans covered faces and asides were muffled. The officers leaned over and the battle began. When Pickett was done, salt had been spilled and a candlestick dripped its beeswax onto the linen cloth. To that, everyone clapped. The officers raised their glasses as Pickett returned to his seat in good cheer.

Servants reappeared and removed the dinner plates from the table.

Berry pies and clotted cream took their place. Over oohs and ahhs, the company settled down.

"Did you read in the *Pioneer and Democrat*," Mrs. Jenkins said regaining control of the conversation, "that people in New York are actually contemplating the burning of the dead as a means to make more space in their cemeteries? Apparently the practice is known in Europe. It's scandalous." The woman's eyes rolled back in her head, her jet earrings swinging. "They call it cremation. Imagine."

Dead silence fell on the diners. Jeannie felt cold. She looked down at her dessert bowl and wished the woman would hush. Mrs. Jenkins seemed to go out of her way to make Jeannie uncomfortable. She was relieved when her dinner partner, Andrew Pierce, jumped in.

"Ladies and gentlemen, having just gone through the most horrendous battle of our time on the fields of Montezuma on this table top, perhaps, it would be best to change the subject, in deference to Mrs. Naughton's loss. I propose a more entertaining subject: hydropathic marriages. Mrs. Jenkins, I understand you subscribe to the ideals in the *Water Cure Journal*."

Mrs. Jenkins seemed startled the subject had been changed so rapidly, but with her fork poised over her pie, she jumped at the chance to talk about the topic at hand.

"I do, indeed, Mr. Pierce. How kind to mention it. There is great advantage to cold baths and eating vegetables, and finding a proper mate. Being the mother of a daughter, I naturally lean towards this persuasion." She dipped her fork into the berry concoction and chewed delicately.

"Then you are a Bloomer?" Pierce took a sip of his wine and said nothing more.

Jeannie felt a ripple go around the table, the strongest from Lieutenant Fuller, Mrs. Jenkins's brother. As the woman launched into her philosophy and opinions, Jeannie couldn't help note Fuller was making himself as small as possible. Andrew Pierce, on the other hand, had just handed them the final entertainment of the evening. A faint smile appeared beneath his neatly trimmed moustache. She wondered if all Americans were like this.

After the close of dinner, the women went into another room for sherry while the men went outside to smoke. During that time, some fences were mended when Mrs. Marshall shared with Jeannie that one of her best friends was from Hampshire, England, currently homesteading a few miles north of her in Port Townsend. At ten o'clock, they all came back together for a final goodbye. Immediately, Pierce worked his way to her side and gave her his full attention.

"Shall I escort you back?" he asked.

At first, Jeannie thought to refuse him. It had been an entertaining, but exhausting end to a long day and she was in no mood for further chitchat. But Andrew Pierce had defended her and she at least owed him a turn on her arm.

"Thank you. Mr. Pierce. That is very kind of you." Jeannie turned to her host. "Good night, Captain Pickett. You have been most welcoming." She gave him her hand. The military men and Mr. Marshall stood at attention.

Pickett bowed. "I greatly admire you, Mrs. Naughton. I hope you will return to my company as soon as you are able. I am faithfully and forever yours. Please give my regards to my counterpart at English Camp."

Outside the summer light still hovered to the west. Jeannie thanked Pierce for interceding on her behalf. "It pains me to hear anything about death in light of my child's passing and Mr. George in Kanaka Town. Mrs. Jenkins's remarks on this new practice of cremation were especially upsetting."

"I am happy to oblige." Pierce offered his arm and escorted her to the steps of the bungalow. The door was already open, spilling lamp light out onto the porch.

"I hope you find your quarters comfortable, Mrs. Naughton."

"They are, thank you."

"Oh, I'm sure anything would look like a castle after what you have endured. You were very brave, but you were in good hands with Jonas Breed."

"Do you know Mr. Breed?"

"We've done some commerce together. He's done mail runs for us at the risk to body and limb. Just a year ago, as he cut across from San Juan Island to Shaw Island, the northern tribes pursued him.

"They pursued Mr. Breed? He has lived among them."

Andrew snorted. "All the more to want him, if they recognize him. He is thought to be *hyas skookum*. That is to say, a spirit worth taking."

"But he got away."

"Yes. With his men, he out-paddled them and hid in a cove until they grew weary of waiting him out and found another victim."

"Victim?'

"Some poor miner making his way over to the minefields on the Fraser River. It's too grotesque to tell you, my dear Mrs. Naughton."

"Oh." Jeannie fiddled with her shawl. The evening had cooled off though still light.

"Not to worry. He can quite take care of himself."

Jeannie chanted the subject. "What do you do, Mr. Pierce?"

"I own a mercantile business in Seattle. I do business with the sutler here. I supply all manner of provisions for the soldiers as well as for the settlers when needed."

"Do you come often?"

"Perhaps I will now that you are settled on the island." He grinned widely, then laughed. "Begging your pardon, ma'am."

Further down the hill to the south of Camp Pickett and Belle Vue Farm, Breed, Collie and Sikhs, his Songhees friend, were laughing as they sat around a campfire. The night was fast approaching, but the Olympic Mountains and Vancouver's Island still glowed in the honey color of sunset. A cooling breeze wafted off the water hinting at fog in the morning, but Breed didn't care. To be with friends and free of the worries of the past two weeks was release. Kaui Kalama was safe and so were the others at Kanaka Town. Things would soon be restored to order. He had much to be grateful for.

The men decided to camp above the lip of South Beach, sleeping on blankets and their coats. In the morning they would fish for salmon, a Salish canoe pulled up beside them with the gear ready. As they talked, they passed around a bottle of whiskey. The only ones not drinking were Breed and Sikhs. As they sat on driftwood logs, Breed took account of the past day in which he had been reunited with not only Collie Henderson and Sikhs, but with two others, Neville Hector and Andy Po, a Chinese friend from Victoria.

It's good to see you, Doc-tin," Breed said to Neville. "You were missed during the contagion."

"My apologies, but due to the violence between the Haida and Sikh's people last month in Victoria, I thought I should not take my chances coming up from Port Townsend." Doc-tin adjusted his slightly bent wire-rimmed spectacles before pouring whiskey into his tin cup. He was wiry man with thick black hair growing on the top of his head like a spiky sea urchin on a rock. A horse veterinarian by trade, he was often called on for his doctoring and surgical skills, thus the name Doctin. In Chinook Jargon *doctin* meant "doctor." "Where is Kaui now?"

"Kaui's with his wife Sally and their *keiki*. She's come back now the danger is over. They need some time, then he hopes to return to work."

"Wonder how long that will last?" Collie put his cup down to light a cigar. "If the islands go in the Americans' favor, Hudson's Bay Company will have to go. Then where will the Kanakas all go? Back to Honolulu?"

"Kaui's here to stay. He has family now," Breed said.

Doc-tin leaned over his cup. "And if the islands go to the English? What will happen to your grand plans for limestone at Farseeing, Jonas?"

Breed laughed. "Ah, that. For the towns and cities to come. I'll just keep working on the site and put my claim in either way. Farseeing has promise. I'll take it."

For the past few months Breed had been working a prospect of limestone on the northern end of the island, using his circle of friends to get limestone out and processed in his small kiln. Neville Hector was a member in that circle.

Like Collie, Doctin had become part of Jonas' retinue simply by being in the wrong place at the right time. Breed didn't know him from Adam that fatal August night when Breed pounded on his cabin door on Lopez Island six years ago to warn of a Tsimshian war canoe with some forty warriors landing on the beach below.

"I thought you were some blasted savage," Doctin told him a couple of years later. "And my partner thought you were a HBC man wanting to get us off our claim. I almost didn't go with you, except for one thing."

"What was that?"

"I guessed you were the *Boston* who lived with the Haida. The *mistchimas* who showed up at Fort Victoria a while before. Therefore, friendly."

"*Ah-ha*. And you were the *doctin*."

After that first encounter, Breed and Doctin became steady friends, often traveling together, but Doctin was never at ease on the open waters of the Straits of Haro and Juan de Fuca and Puget Sound. He was always fearful of the northern tribes.

Breed put another piece of driftwood into the fire. "When did you get here?"

"About an hour ago. Schooner dropped me off down by Cattle Point. Met Andy Po on the way up." Doctin swirled the whiskey in his cup, then drank it.

"Then you had a safe passage."

"*Mahsie*, Jonas. I did."

Breed and his friends talked around the fire for another hour, then all but Breed and Sikhs went to their blankets. Breed resumed musing over the past two weeks in Kanaka Town and their future there. This was the kind of night Breed liked the best. The only light came from the low fire and the million stars above them. For once, the sky was clear, revealing the deep and vast Milky Way. He wrapped his Hudson Bay blanket around him.

"Jo-nuss?"

Breed looked up from the fire. He was night blinded for the moment. He could barely see Sikhs. "Hmm?"

"When you are going to Timons?"

Breed grinned at Sikhs who was about ready to burst out laughing at this novice but deadly mistake of looking into a fire.

"As soon as we catch something to smoke. Then I'll go to my claim." He turned to the dark, trying to blink away the red circles of light floating in his eyes.

"*Hee, hee*. You take all night, *chee chako*. We catch salmon when you can see. Then go."

WICKERY

J eannie returned to the Royal Marine encampment the following
morning escorted by a small contingent of soldiers from American Camp.

"Are you quite worn, dear?" Gilly pulled at Jeannie's hem as Jeannie
sat sidesaddle on her mule.

Am I worn? Jeannie certainly felt it. Why the Americans preferred
mules over a horse, she couldn't say, but her back hurt from riding
side saddle. And Blue the mule was unyielding and opinionated.
Worse, after three hours of following the soldiers home on the military road, her posterior had suffered a most unladylike death. She was
glad for the coolness of the woods that guarded the path to the Parkers' home and glad for the far-off scooping drone of a bagpipe as
someone put air into it. When Dr. Parker lifted her down to the
ground, Jeannie nearly collapsed into him. Her legs felt as steady as
India rubber.

"There now." Dr. Parker handed Jeannie off to Gilly.

"Mrs. Parker," the doctor said as he accepted Jeannie's valise from
the soldier who had it tied to his mule, "I think Mrs. Naughton needs
a cup of tea. The ride is generally a pleasant one, but it appears to have

been taxing." He smiled at Jeannie. "Welcome back. You look quite handsome, Mrs. Naughton, despite your recent exertions."

Jeannie found her footing by slipping her hand through Gilly's arm. "Thank you, sir. I'm happy to be back."

He started to say something else, but asked instead if the Yanks had given her trouble.

"Not at all. They were very accommodating."

"Delighted to hear. We'll be returning there on the fourth." He nodded at the soldiers. "Go down to the commissary. They will give you some refreshments before you return to your camp. Thank you for your service to Mrs. Naughton." As soon as the soldiers were off, Dr. Parker announced they should head back to the house. "I wouldn't mind a cup of tea myself."

In the guest room, Jeannie found flowers by her writing box and a letter from her uncle.

"My sweet lass,

I hope this finds you well. I was a bit alarmed to learn that you ventured down to a place of infection. It is a relief to hear that you are well and had a helping hand in preventing further contagion, but I hope that you have come to your senses and will remain with the Parkers. If I had been informed early on, I would have protested most vigorously. What possessed you, I cannot say, though I can accept that your grieving heart wanted to do something?

I was pleased to hear that Jonas Breed was in attendance for he is someone I trust. One cannot be too careful these days. The American encampment draws the most unsavory people down at San Juan Town. I'll say no more as it is too indelicate for your sensibility. So do behave and accept this reprimand with the gentlest of admonitions. I hope to see you soon.

Lovingly, Uncle Archie

She turned the letter on its side. There was a scribble in the margin: "Harry Ferguson has inquired about you. It appears that news of your adventure has made its way back here. He asks about your return. I suggest that you make known your feelings on his intentions. Your mourning will be over by Christmastide."

91

Well, Jeannie thought. *He has done his duty.* And I shall behave. There is so much to explore around here I shan't fall into wickery.

Wickery, however, presented itself in another way.

Some days after she returned to the Royal Marine encampment, Gilly had a visitor. Jeannie had been quietly reading on the front porch, when a tall man wearing a gray top hat bounded up the steps. He went immediately to the door and knocked.

Jeannie put her book down. *Now who was this come to the Parkers?* When the stranger removed his hat, she saw that he had the same strawberry blonde hair as Gilly's.

A servant opened the door, took his card and disappeared. There was an unnatural pause and suddenly he was looking at Jeannie.

"Beg pardon, madame. I didn't see you there. I'm calling on my—"

The door flew open and Gilly came through straight into the man's arms. "Why, John, what happy thing brings you here? Is Valparaiso is no longer amicable?"

"The place is dull," he said. "Dull people, dull sales, dull winter. I'll leave it to the Chileans to carry on. I've closed out my account and brought my fortunes up here." He kissed Gilly on her forehead, then turned his gaze to Jeannie who didn't know whether to be taken aback by such familiarity or return his infectious grin.

Gilly laughed. "This is my twin brother, Mr. John Forrester. John, this is my particular friend, Mrs. Naughton, lately of Toronto. Her uncle is a trader at HBC in Victoria. She is here mourning the loss of her young son."

Forrester bowed deeply from the waist. "My deepest sympathies."

Jeannie rose and curtsied. She felt conspicuous in her black mourning clothes, but Gilly, ever vigilant, did not allow the happy reunion to descend into clouds.

"Now, when on earth did you arrive? You gave me no such intelligence, you naughty boy." Gilly settled her skirts and petticoats down on a bench and patted a place for her brother.

Forrester put his hat on the wicker side table. Obliging her, he told tell them of his trip from Valparaiso to San Francisco, where he attended a play and had his picture taken at Ford's Daguerrean

Gallery. "I left there ten days ago. I should have taken a steamer. The trip up to Victoria was rather rough. We encountered high rolling seas around the Columbia bar. An overnight stay at Victoria, then I found a schooner coming this way. I say, I saw a rather large black and white fish coming over. I think that nothing is dull around here."

"Indeed, brother," Gilly said.

Jeannie smiled. Black and white fish. It had to be a killer whale like the ones Breed showed her. Though charmed by her friend's joy at being with her brother, Jeannie mourned the truth that her sisters didn't know where she was and most likely didn't care.

A light dinner was quickly arranged in the Parker's small dining room with Dr. Parker at hand from the infirmary. Forrester proved to be a delightful addition to the Parker family circle. Well-traveled, he had a great sense of adventure. Jeannie found him a charming counterpoint to Gilly's sense of propriety and economy in any undertaking.

As the last of the dishes were put away, the talk turned to the area surrounding the camp.

"I heard that there is limestone in good quality and quantity here," Forrester said. "A good enterprise for the undertaking."

"There are diggings not far from here," Dr. Parker said. "And the land is very fair for cultivation, but one is wont to be careful to make any advances as the islands are in dispute and neither Yank nor Englishman may make designs until it is decided."

"Then we shall have an adventure and plot our fortunes. It should go in our favor. Do fancy riding horses, Mrs. Naughton?" Forrester asked.

"I do."

"Why not go on an excursion once our meal has settled? I promise that with Gilly as guide, we shall see the sights like we would on a Grand Tour of the Continent. How about you, Thomas? Can you steal away from your instruments and bottles?"

Dr. Parker dipped his head. "I will have to play catch-up. I have an appointment."

Jeannie laughed. "I should very much like to go." Having recovered from the ride down from the American camp, she was eager to go out again. There were many forested steep inclines and flats behind the encampment she had been able to explore on foot with Gilly, but anything further out required a horse.

"Then, it's done. The expedition will begin at two o'clock sharp. Unless, dear sister, for the want of horses."

A few hours later, after Forrester helped Jeannie and Gilly onto their sidesaddles, they rode out the same military road she had come home on, a widened trail cut through the mixed woods of big leaf maple and fir. The afternoon was warm and clear promising bright sky well into the summer evening. On top of a natural bench, they turned north onto a pleasant track, recently cleared by the marines. The woods were full of birds that called with squawks or soaring song. A squirrel made his complaint. Jeannie breathed in the fresh scent of the green woods which filled her heart with solace.

Jeremy. You brought us here and here I shall stay, my darling.

"Attention! Marines halt."

Jeannie jolted awake from her reverie. Ahead of them was a small group of marines leading a horse burdened with the carcass of a young buck. Its horns stuck out from the horse's flanks. In their sleeves and braces, one man with fair hair and muttonchops immediately put on his red jacket to indicate that he was an officer. As they came closer to the men, their eyes drifted to her. Jeannie sat higher on her seat, feeling the mare beneath her pause for some command. Jeannie stroked its neck.

"Good day to you," the officer said. He had the accent of someone from Devonshire, England and a sculptured face. Though he smiled at them all, he suddenly focused on her, his eyes growing wide in astonishment, then shutting down before he turned back to Gilly and Forrester. "I am Lieutenant Thaddeus Cooperwaite."

Gilly wasted no time in establishing who she was. "I don't know you, sir. I have not seen you at the officers' table."

"I've been at the naval station at Esquimalt, but now I have returned here at my division's pleasure. You are Mrs. Parker, I believe."

"Yes, and this gentleman is my brother, Mr. Forrester. This is Mrs. Naughton."

"Ladies. Gentleman." Cooperwaite was courtly, but he gave Jeannie the chills. There was something about his smile under the mustache that seemed forced to her. His eyes were a strange light green with dark rings around the pupils. The eyelid on his left eye drooped.

He recognizes me. He knows something about me. She gripped her reins tight.

"Well, carry on lads." Forrester took charge of the expedition and kicked his horse ahead. Gilly and Jeannie followed with a lurch. Jeannie had to right herself hoping her right leg over the pommel would help her hold on. She was glad to be away from Cooperwaite. Eventually the trio slowed to a walk, resuming their leisurely ride through the woods. Jeannie did not look back and focused instead on the green arches passing high above her. Her heartbeat slowed down.

"That was a splendid young buck the marines had," Forrester said as he rode beside her, "but there's many a time I had one of my own." He went on to tell amusing accounts of hunting in England as a boy and in Chile where there was a large English community.

Jeannie continued to feel less threatened and joined in the exchange. They eventually came down out of the thick woods and into a large open area of grass dotted with Garry oak trees and maples. There were signs that a forest fire had cleared it years ago. They pulled up while Gilly decided which way to go. A twinkle came into her eyes.

"Oh, brother, how we used to race across our father's fields. I feel so young at heart today with you here."

Forrester looked at Jeannie. "Mrs. Naughton?"

At first, Jeannie was hesitant. She knew they were asking if for one brief moment, they could be the companions of their nursery once again. That meant she would be alone, but Cooperwaite was no longer around and she was perfectly safe here. For a moment, she felt uneasy, but eventually, she put it off. "I shall try to keep up, but I'd rather take my time and spare my dignity."

"I know," Gilly said, "There is an old giant maple hence—see that path to the left? It bends a ways in. Stay on the path and meet us at the tree."

Jeannie looked in the direction Gilly pointed. The lane was bordered by tall grass browned by the sun and young saplings, but it was clearly marked with wagon ruts and wide enough for two. Further out it entered into clumps of trees and bushes and back into a wall of towering fir and cedar. As soon as Jeannie agreed, the two siblings cantered off.

"Don't tell Dr. Parker..." Gilly's voice trailed off

The horses cantered away, leaving Jeannie pulling on her mare's reins to stay back. Heart pounding, for a moment she thought she might lose the argument, but eventually the little bay calmed down and they moved ahead at a walk.

In the clearing, the June day sun cast a hazy warmth Jeannie knew was unique to the Northwest. It might be cloudy, but she could still get a burn. She checked to see that her *mousquetaire* hat would do its duty, letting the horse pull at the head of tall grass as they passed by.

She patted the horse's neck. "Enough, Rosie." Rosie pricked her ears back, then quickened her pace when Jeannie urged her forward.

The trail was tighter than she realized as she got to the bend. Bushes sporting reddish berries seemed to reach out their soft leaves out to her. Unseen creatures stirred in the hushed trees behind them. For the first time since she had arrived here, the woods didn't feel quite right. Hair at the nape of her neck tingled. She looked behind her to see if Cooperwaite had come back, then for Gilly and her brother, but she was alone in the green. The only sign of her friends' passing was torn leaves from the berry bushes. As she rode on, she was relieved that the trail widened again to path big enough for two wagons.

"Walk on," Jeannie said. Rosie stepped up her pace bobbing her head side to side. Jeannie relaxed as she got further away from the narrowed trail only to grab at her mane and pommel when Rosie danced sharply to the left.

There was a loud splintering sound as the brush gave way to two black horses plunging onto the trail. The whites of the horses' eyes gleamed. Their ears lay flat back against their heads. Astride them were men with long matted hair under slouch hats. Jeannie let out a little cry.

One of the men circled her. "Well, fiddle-ee-dee. Ain't it the young miss of Kanaka Town? Fancy you should be out alone." The rider came so close the sour smell of liquor on his breath nearly gagged her. His teeth under his ragged moustache were yellow.

"I'm not alone. Mrs. Parker and her brother are ahead of me."

"Indeed, indeed. Very thoughtful of them. Will you be needing an escort to your rightful place?" The man took off his hat. "Allow me, I'm Emmett Krill, Esquire.

Jeannie felt the color drain from her face. The man at Kanaka Town, the one Mr. Breed said was no gentleman. Her arms became cold. "I'd rather not." With that she urged Rosie forward, but the other rider blocked her.

"Now Perkins, that ain't a sociable way to treat a lady such as this. Mus'n forget our manners." Krill reached over and touched the little flourish on her hat. "Such a lady."

Jeannie slapped his hand and tried to turn her horse but she was up against the bushes. "Let me pass." She struggled to keep her voice calm.

"Perkins, why don't you get her some of those nice thimbleberries yonder? Do you fancy them?"

Jeannie pulled Rosie back, but Krill pushed his horse right into her legs. "I don't mean no harm. I'm just putrified by the lack of your hosts' consideration, leaving you here and all."

Jeannie snapped. Clutching the reins in her hand, she swung them into his face. Krill yowled and raised his fist to her.

"Why don't *you* keep your damned hands to yourself, Krill," a voice behind her boomed. "Get away from her."

Krill and Jeannie turned at the same time.

Sitting astride a gray on the narrowing trail, Jonas Breed looked in full fury, a rifle laying across his lap. Jeannie wrenched herself out of Krill's way and tried to back her horse.

"Well, well, his honor Mr. Breed. What brings a *siwash* lover out here?" Krill pulled slightly away from Jeannie, freeing her legs.

"Stop your mouth and let her go."

"You're a bit outclassed," Perkins said.

With no warning, Breed threw something at Perkins's face causing him to yelp and slap a hand on his cheek. He swayed in his saddle.

"He cut me." Perkins wiped blood from his cheek and stared at his fingers.

"What'd you do to him?" Krill roared.

Breed grinned and tossed a stone in his hand. "Get away from her."

"The hell, you say. Perkins?"

Suddenly two hands reached up and pulled Perkins off his horse with a thud. Jeannie craned her neck in time to see someone pull him to the bushes by his coat collar giving her a start almost as frightening as Krill's first assault. The attacker was an Indian. He wore a European shirt with the sleeves ripped off and pants, but he bore the practice of head flattening which made his forehead rise back from his brow like a steep hill. His long hair gave him a menacing appearance. He smacked Perkins' horse away, giving Jeannie room to break free. She looked at Breed for an answer.

"Go!" Breed yelled.

Jeannie kicked the mare to action but Krill blocked her with his horse. Behind her, she heard Breed shout and charge. Krill yanked on his horse's reins and to her great relief, bolted into the thicket on the other side of the trail.

"I'll kill you, Breed" Krill roared as he was swallowed up in the brush and trees.

"*Ah-ha*. You say so." The Indian gave Perkins a kick in the rump as he scrambled to follow Krill. Once Perkins had his horse's reins, he couldn't go fast enough.

"Leave him be, Sikhs. He's not worth it." Breed pulled up beside Jeannie who had begun to shake. "Are you all right, Mrs. Naughton?'

Jeannie bit her lips and nodded she was fine.

Breed gave her a faint smile. "Yes, I can see you are fine."

"I am, truly. Will he come back? He threatened to kill you."

"Krill's full of steam. A lot of *hyas wawa*. He'll go off and smolder for a while. Might even apologize, but don't trust him."

"I won't, but don't tell Mrs. Parker. She'll only fret." Jeannie swallowed.

"As you wish." Breed looked around and sighed.

Jeannie loosened her grip on the reins when the Indian came alongside Breed. Up close, she realized that he was an older man, perhaps of middle age, with crow's-feet around his dark brown eyes suggesting warmth and kindness. His face was sunburned to a light copper color. His bare arms were muscular.

"This is my friend and teacher, Sikhs of the Songhees."

"How are you, Mrs. King George?" Sikhs said. "You got one good scare. Maybe he got one better." Sikhs nodded in the direction of the bushes. "What do you think, Jo-nuss?"

"I think it's time to get Mrs. Naughton back to her company. Then we'll skedaddle." Breed settled into his saddle and pulled back.

As if on cue, the thunder of hooves came down the trail as Gilly galloped toward them with her brother behind. Breed dipped his head at Jeannie. "On the other hand, good day. You're in good hands now." Nodding to Sikhs, the men melted into the bushes behind Jeannie.

"Oh, dear Lord," Gilly said as she cantered up. "What has happened here? Where are the Marines?" She looked around.

Jeannie straightened. "Not to worry. I was having difficulty with my horse. Do forgive me for your trouble."

"I heard a commotion, that's all. Thought I saw someone here just now. " Gilly studied both sides of the trail before smoothing Jeannie's cheek. "Are you sure everything is all right, dear?"

"Yes. I'm quite alone and I'm fine." Jeannie raised her yes to Forrester who didn't seemed convinced. He kept looking at the torn bushes next to her.

Jeannie brushed out her skirt, her hand trembling just a bit. "I'm ready to go on, now." In fact, she hoped they would leave immediately for fear Krill was watching them. She listened for motion in the bushes and woods and to her relief heard nothing.

Gilly sighed. "Well then. Shall we resume our adventure or are we out of steam?"

With Breed gone, Jeannie thought, *we are surely out of steam,* but instead, she said, "Most gladly."

~

A half mile away, Sikhs joined Breed in a small clearing.

"See anything?" Breed patted his horse's neck.

"Krill and that trickster are gone. Heading south toward American Camp."

"Found the same thing. Must be making tracks to San Juan Town. Wonder what he was doing up here? Doesn't have contacts at English Camp as far as I know."

"Thought King George soldiers told him to stay away? Not bring his stuff around?"

"Maybe because they get rum rations and don't need it." Breed grinned. A Royal Navy tradition.

They spoke in Straits Salish. It gave deeper context and meaning than Chinook Jargon, which they often spoke in out of laziness. Though Sikhs' English was good, Breed wished peoples could understand Sikhs in his own language. He was a great speaker and story-teller. Since living among the original people of the Pacific Northwest, Breed had learned to be patient and listen, something American settlers seemed to lack in skill. Americans wanted things now and in writing. When a great speaker like Sikhs spoke, you listened, no matter how long they took. Sikhs could talk and talk when he got going.

Sikhs patted his knife sheath. "I think Krill's gone. Perkins too."

"Good riddance. They're nothing but trouble. San Juan Town's growing. So are sales of liquor and the women. Pickett has his hands full."

Breed looked back through the thick woods from where they had come and thought of the young Englishwoman, Mrs. Naughton. He had seen everything from the beginning. She had taken the scare pretty well. Krill wasn't known to pester women like that, especially someone protected by an officer in the Royal Marines such as Dr. Parker. That would be risky, bringing the ire of two militaries down on him. What had made Krill so bold?

And what of her? Mrs. Naughton unsettled him every time he saw her. Those days at Kanaka Town had become precious to him. He liked the way she talked and what she talked about. He liked the way her light brown hair got loose from its pins and curled around her face. He liked the way she opened up to his friends, showed real kindness to Kaui Kalama and his *keiki*. He admired her courage too. To marry so young and have a child, then lose it. A wisdom the pampered prisses Breed had encountered since coming back into white society would not understand.

Krill had touched her hat. *I'd like to touch her cheek and kiss those honey lips.*

"Jo-nuss? You sleeping?"

"Hmh?"

"You like you were in a dream. I was saying that Krill hurts everyone, especially my people." He swatted a fly troubling Breed's horse. "Why do Bostons want to get everyone stupid with drink? The King George people keep it out of the trading forts."

"Something to do with free enterprise. Most call it smuggling."

"Someday he will lose his head," Sikhs said.

"Someday, we hope, Sikhs, he ends up in jail, then the noose for the murders I'm sure he has done. Gotta catch him red-handed first."

To that, Sikhs spat.

Breed slipped his feet out of his stirrups and rolled up his sleeves. On his left arm near the wrist, he exposed a tattoo done in brown and black. Its design was an orca eating a seal. He had carried it since he fallen under the Haida as a boy, a symbol of his servitude. Forced to submit, its application had been painful, but over time it had become a part of him. He made a fist, causing the design to shift.

Mistshimus. Slave. It was a shameful thing in the native communities, but Breed had learned to rise above it, earning their respect the hard way. Including Sikhs.

Sikhs was his first real friend after he had come back from the north in 1854. Just twenty years of age, after seven years of captivity, Breed had been high-strung then, not completely sure of his safety with Haida in the area. When he came ashore at Fort Victoria, he was taken immediately to Hudson's Bay Company headquarters where company men offered him food and white man's clothing. His hair was shorn so they put a captain's cap on his head. They also asked him questions in English, but he had trouble speaking in a tongue he hadn't heard in years. Sikhs had been in the fort when Breed first arrived and had gone out to see what the commotion was all about.

"I was surprised to see a Boston *mistchimas*," he later told Breed. "I knew right away by the tattoos on your hand and ankles and your short hair. But I was more surprised when you called me "Uncle," and showed me good manners."

Breed remembered that they spoke first in Chinook Jargon and then tested some of the dialects from around Vancouver's Island. In Chinook Jargon, *sikhs* meant "friend" and Sikhs had truly been that, but to this day Breed was one of the very few who knew Sikhs' real name.

The first week was difficult for Breed. He felt displaced and awkward in social situations and uncomfortable being indoors in small, closed up houses. English words began to come back to him in a flood, but at night he dreamed in Haida. There was no place to be alone. He was watched intensely both from curiosity and from distrust, but eventually, he was given free range of the fort. Sikhs often came to see him. When fall came, Breed left with Sikhs for a village on the American side of the Strait of Juan de Fuca where Sikhs had a daughter who had married into the S'Klallam people.

Sikhs coughed. "What do you want to do now, Jo-nuss? Go find Krill?"

Breed shrugged. "We can pry around. I heard that there is some sort of celebration taking place down at American Camp in a couple of days. The British officers and their particulars are going down. I've been invited."

Sikhs raised an eyebrow. "What are you? Some *muck muck?*"

Breed grinned. "I'm not exactly aspiring to that. They probably want sort of intelligence they are not getting from the locals."

"I hope there is food."

RACES AND DANCE CARDS

Two days after the confrontation with Krill and Perkins, a delicately printed card arrived inviting the Parkers and their guests to a program of horse races and a grand ball. All the officers had been invited.

"What shall I do?" Jeannie asked Gilly on learning that she had been invited too. "I am in mourning."

Gilly patted her hand. "But you are not relegated to the corner. You may come and enjoy the festivities. Your mourning period is proscribed, but a grieving mother is allowed more leeway than a widow in mourning. I'm rather afraid that you should not dance. It would be unseemly. But out here, I'm told, three months of full mourning for your boy will be appropriate enough." Gilly sniffed. "Of course that is the official word. In your heart—well—that cannot be measured."

Jeannie looked away. *In my heart. When will it be full again?*

On July 4th, at the crack of dawn, Jeannie and the Parkers left to go American Camp. This time Jeannie went with Gilly in a buggy driven by Dr. Parker. Forrester rode alongside them with some of the officers. *At least I shall ride in comfort for three hours.* Then she remembered the ruts on the military road cutting across the valley.

They eventually arrived at American Camp. In an opening to the north of the picket fence lining it, soldiers and civilians were playing a game. To her surprise Breed was at the center, throwing a ball underhand to a soldier in shirtsleeves. The soldier held a long wooden bat in his hand.

"What game do they amuse themselves with?" she asked.

Dr. Parker turned around. "I believe they call it base ball. I'm told back in the States a number of towns have their own teams of players."

"Is it like our cricket?" As they passed by, Jeannie watched the soldier swing and miss. "Is the soldier a batsman?"

"Aye, and Mr. Breed would be the hurler. He has a good arm." He went on to explain what he knew about the intricacies of the game and how it was not like cricket, but Jeannie wasn't listening. She recalled how Breed had thrown a stone to unseat the ruffian abusing her. She admired him even more as he threw the ball and the soldier swung and missed again. It also made her smile to make this new discovery about him.

They continued on around the camp's outbuildings and down to the racetrack set on the prairie below American Camp, a wild and wide open expanse of hills and wind-tossed beaches facing west toward Haro Strait and Vancouver's Island. Awnings and a Silbey tent had been set up to accommodate guests which Gilly said were coming from as far away as Victoria and Bellingham Bay. One of the awnings bucked like a kite as a breeze off Haro Strait tried to get it airborne. An extra rope and peg settled it down much to the amusement of the ladies under it. Interspersed among the hooped skirts like kingpins between egg cups were the soldiers and officers of the two military camps dressed on the hot summer day in their red or blue wool uniforms. Separating from the group of officers, Captain Pickett greeted Jeannie and Gilly like they were the goddesses of grace and beauty.

"Good day to you ladies and welcome." Pickett gave his hand to Jeannie and helped her down. Always the gentleman, Jeannie thought as a young subaltern with very large drooping mustaches steadied the team of horses.

Once Jeannie and Gilly were on the ground, they were escorted to an awning where a group of ladies sat on canvas folding chairs. The day was hazy but before them the expansive water that flowed miles across the straits to Vancouver's Island and the Olympic Mountains to the south sparkled like cut crystals. The sun was not far behind.

Gilly immediately found someone to talk with and preparing her hooped skirt before she sat down, joined in the ongoing conversation. Gilly introduced Jeannie to two women she knew. Jeannie was relieved that none of the British ladies were from her part of England. Lately, she was aware of Devonshire men in the marine ranks and she feared that someone might recognize her. *Would they know her family? Worse her late husband who was from that region of England?*

"Ladies and gentlemen, the race is about to begin. Please bring your horses to the starting line."

"Is the brown bay your favorite, Mrs. Naughton?" United States Captain James Forsyth suddenly appeared at her shoulder with Andrew Pierce, both of whom Jeannie had met at Pickett's dinner. Forsyth nodded at the Hudson's Bay Company horse. "Or are you interested in international harmony and support all favorites?"

Jeannie laughed to see the horses gathered at the start. "I suppose in the interest of the joint occupation I should cheer for all, although in reality I should cheer any poor brute to make its way safely to the other end of the prairie."

"Then you should cheer for Captain Pickett's horse. It's the black one next to HBC horse."

"So I shall." She studied the horses stamping and tossing their heads in anticipation. Their riders sat astride and worked the reins in their leather-gloved hands. Soldiers and marines struck wagers. Beyond them a new group arrived. It was Jonas Breed and Collie Henderson followed by Breed's Indian friend, Sikhs. They stood off in the middle behind the starting line as though they didn't want to commit to either nationality.

You are not wild, today, she thought, though the cedar rope necklace he wore on the day he confronted Krill was still visible under his linen shirt. He was coatless, but wore a tan canvas vest over his shirt and braces. He makes no apologies for his casual dress, she thought, but with the heat of the day increasing, there were others, for sure, who were itching to join him. When he spoke to Henderson, she felt a little prick in her throat.

Jonas Breed. Why does he bother me so?

For the past two years, she had always been on guard of her true situation. The attentions of Harry Ferguson and the other gentlemen at Victoria were flattering, but she felt wary around any man except her uncle and lately Dr. Parker. She would not be led by false flattery or excessive attention. She knew when she was being treated like a simpering female unable to think for herself, with no head on her shoulders to make any decision for herself.

She knew about danger to her reputation. Her experience had taught her that. But experience could not help her with Jonas Breed. She could not read him. She only had instinct and after her time at Kanaka Town, it said to trust. Completely.

"Pay attention, Jeannie," Gilly whispered as she opened her fan. "I believe that Dr. Parker has put a bet on the HBC's bay and the race is about to begin." She raised her voice slightly. "Brother dear, are you are participating?"

"My pockets are lean," Forester said behind them. "Do go on and enjoy yourself, sister." He tipped his top hat to Jeannie. "Mrs. Naughton."

A signal flag was raised at the line, Voices stilled, leaving only the sound of a hawk lazily calling its territory. The flag rustled in the mid-morning air for a brief time, then dropped like a stone. The crowd roared. The horses charged, throwing dirt and grass on the closest observers. Jeannie stood up as the riders got further away. Soon all the ladies were standing except for Jeannie's sour nemesis, Mrs. Jenkins, still a guest of the Americans.

"It's a jolly good race," Gilly said above the cheering, "See how the brutes fly."

They're flying all right. Heads down, riders low on their necks. Jean-

107

nie's heart skipped, as she remembered the first county fair races she had seen as a girl. Her father had bought ribbons for her hair. A happy time then.

"Huzzah," a Royal Marine shouted.

Jeanie looked up, clutching imaginary ribbons in her gloved hand. The horses were fast approaching the flags at the end of the makeshift track. The grass behind them lay flat and mangled. Two came so close together, they seemed to move as one then suddenly separated like oil on water.

"What on earth is that black horse doing?" Gilly said, standing on tiptoe. "It's gone astray."

"In truth it has." Jeannie laughed. "And from the look on Captain Pickett's face, he is not happy." Instead of going straight to the finish line, his horse had veered off to the right, its rider in a heated dispute with the animal over the direction they were going. Jeannie wondered how much the captain wagered.

"So much for the legendary horse breeding of Virginia," muttered an American officer off to the side. "I need a drink."

Gilly flashed her fan and leaned in. "Indeed. The gentleman's not happy. But with the Hudson Bay's horse declared the winner, we must bring our two countries together. I believe that is cider being served on the barrel. Time for refreshments, Jeannie." She nodded to the other English ladies and they followed, their skirts in swaying obedience. The ribbons on their hats rippled in the warming air.

Representatives of two nations gathered at the cider barrel and took turn drinking from japanned mugs. Jeannie looked for Breed among the small crowd, but instead saw the Royal Marine she had encountered on the day of her ride with Gilly and her brother. *Thaddeus Coopersmith? Cooperwaite?* He advanced toward her. Remembering how he studied her that day gave Jeannie the chills. She searched for Gilly but Gilly was occupied with her husband and brother and further up the hill. Jeannie stepped away from the barrel to the edge of the crowd. She spied Breed and his men gathered down below, but the marine was upon her before she could move.

"A joy to make your acquaintance again," the marine said. "Did you enjoy the race?"

Jeannie was too shocked to answer.

"Forgive me. I'm Lieutenant Thaddeus Cooperwaite of Her Majesty's Royal Marines. We met on the road just outside of our Royal Marine encampment." He bowed. Jeannie acknowledged him with a nod, but wanted nothing more than to run down to where Breed's mariner friend Collie Henderson had unsheathed his sword and was showing it to some American officers.

"May I inquire if you enjoyed your outing?" Cooperwaite was not going away.

Jeannie thought, *No I did not. I was frightened as a matter of fact.* "Yes, I did. I have excellent hosts."

"Indeed." Cooperwaite smoothed out his mustache. Up close, Jeannie saw why his left eyelid drooped. There was a scar on the side of the eye. "I'm afraid I didn't get your name," he said.

"Mrs. Percival Naughton. Excuse me." Jeannie turned away. She watched Collie Henderson swish the sword around in the air, then blade up, let a silk handkerchief fall lightly on it. It split in two with no effort on his part. He acknowledged their admiration with a grin, then sheathed his sword in one clear stroke. Jeannie watched Breed clap Collie Henderson on his back. "I must go," Jeannie said.

Cooperwaite drew himself up. "Before you take your leave, may I be so bold as to ask where you are from in England? You remind me of my home near Christchurch."

Jeannie swallowed. It took all her courage to turn and face him. "I'm afraid I've never been there. I'm from Bristol. Pardon me again." With that, Jeannie set off to see Breed, hoping Cooperwaite wouldn't follow.

Jeannie was nearly upon them when her skirt caught on a thistle. She stopped to pull it off. Suddenly, the men's conversation cleared, their voices loud in the morning air.

"...the beheading part or the canoeing part?"

Jeannie dropped her skirt and stared. A chill ran up her arms. Were they talking to Breed?

"Now see here, Tuttle," one of the American officers said. "We all know where Jonas stands on that. He's warned folks a few times when there was trouble brewing with the northern Indians. Remember, two years ago, no one lived on this island excepting for Griffith and his men at the Hudson's Bay farm. Only American was the customs officer who had enough sense to camp next to the sheep. Jonas warned him fair and square."

A bewhiskered man with a slouch hat and paisley braces spit out some brown, juicy tobacco toward Breed and said in a sing-song drawl, "It ain't no lie what he is to them. Y'know'd that poor schooner was overtook by them savages on its way from Whidbey Island to Port Townsend. Boarded it and slaughtered them all. Took their heads, those sons-of-bitches. Boiled their faces off and hung them in their lodges along with their salmon catch."

"That's enough of this truck," the American officer said. "Not on this day of celebration." Tuttle grumbled "Damn sigh-wash," under his breath, but he said no more. Jeannie watched him give Breed a nervous glance. Then Andrew Pierce noticed her.

"Look who's come to join us. Mrs. Naughton!" He took off his hat and bowed.

"Mr. Pierce," Jeannie said graciously. For her part, she did not acknowledge that she had heard a good portion of their conversation nor that the tension around the group still hung around them like wet laundry.

"How did you like the first race, Mrs. Naughton?" Pierce asked.

Jeannie laughed lightly nodding to the men as they opened a space for her. She was conscious of their admiration of her person. Female company at this level, Gilly once told her, was enjoyed on an international scale, but one must not encourage it. "Very exciting," Jeannie said as she held onto her black Indian-silk parasol. "A joyous romp."

"I hope your ride over wasn't a romp. Was it pleasant, Mrs. Naughton?"

"It was indeed. Thank you, Mr. Pierce." She smiled at all of them, but when she caught Breed's gaze, she knew he had seen something. His eyes questioned her.

The man named Tuttle cleared his throat and backed away, making a wide sweep past Breed and Sikhs. The American officer who had defended Breed earlier took his place. Jeannie tried not to stare at the Indian. She could not quite get used to his flat head. Though he was dressed in European pants and shirt, she wondered if he was a "northern Indian." The thought intrigued her. For someone who had been enslaved by one such group, Jonas Breed seemed calmly forgiving. Then she remembered that Breed had said Songhees, a local tribe.

Up on the hill, a bugle sounded. "Ah. Looks like the second race is to begin." The American officer, nodded in the direction of the starting line. "Shall we return, gentlemen?"

The men concurred, except for Breed and Collie Henderson.

"I shall certainly like that." Pierce turned to her. "Mrs. Naughton?"

For once, Jeannie asserted herself. Andrew Pierce was a decent fellow, but he wouldn't offer her the kind of protection she was seeking. "I'd like to stay and speak to Mr. Breed. I believe that he has something to communicate to me."

"Very well, Mr. Breed, you'll escort her back?"

"*Ah-ha*. The few paces it takes." Breed kept his face still, but there was mischief in his eyes.

With that, the men left, leaving her alone with Breed and his friends.

"Are you well, Mrs. King George? You seemed troubled when you came down."

Jeannie flushed. Behind him, Collie and Sikhs waited.

"Skedaddle, for a moment, would you?" Breed said to them. "I'll join you shortly,"

"Sure, *kahpo*," Sikhs said. "*Maika kloshe tum tum toketie.*"

Breed frowned. Whatever they had said, she was beginning to feel foolish for running away from Gilly. What would she think of my being unescorted? Jeannie seemed always at odds with some societal norm.

111

"So." Breed's voice startled her. "What did that marine want?"

"You saw him?" Jeannie was as surprised as she was embarrassed.

"I've met him before," Breed went on. "Cooperwaite. He's an arrogant sod. I saw you spurn him. Why?"

"He unsettles me. That day we ran into Krill, he was with a party of hunters from the Royal Marine Camp. He was very familiar with me."

Breed cocked his head. "Did he say anything to you?"

"No," she lied. "But he won't take leave of me." Jeannie gave her parasol a half turn. *Why on earth did she come down?* She sounded like a pouty schoolgirl. Next she would be stamping her foot.

"Mrs. Naughton? Jeannie. May I call you that?"

Jeannie's heart thumped. "Yes."

"Good. Such a mouthful, Mrs. Naughton. You're my friend as your days playing Nurse Nightingale at Kanaka Town made you so." He looked up the hill as a second bugle called. "As such, we can say anything in confidence. This Cooperwaite unsettles you for what reason you cannot say, but that is enough for me. What would like me to do?"

Jeannie pressed her parasol against her shoulder.

"Shall I behead him?"

"Mr. Breed—Jonas."

He chuckled. "I know you heard the conversation with the American Tuttle."

"I did not."

He put up a finger. "The truth. With friends there is always truth."

Jeannie blushed. "That man said perfectly awful things about you."

"It's not the first time something has been said."

"Is it true about the schooner?"

"*Ah-ah.* A terrible thing."

Jeannie put a hand to her throat. She felt cold. Could that have happened to them when they were on the water racing to Kanaka Town? A few yards behind Breed, the Indian waited with Collie.

"Do you want to go back?" he asked.

"Please."

He gave her his arm, signaling to his friends. "If you wish, I'll poke around about him. I have friends at English Camp."

"You are too kind, but you needn't."

"But maybe I will. I think only of myself. I'd like to throw him a punch."

"Jonas," she whispered.

Breed laughed and led her back up to Gilly where he handed her over. A quick dip of his head and he was gone. Thankfully, so was Cooperwaite.

The rest of the day continued to be fair. The sun moved further to the west, dragging the summer afternoon with it and an increasing array of clouds. The races over, the party adjourned and made their way up to the American parade ground.

At six, there was a sit-down supper for the officers and special guests. The soldiers set up a large tent on the parade ground and hung bouquets of ferns and wild flowers from the corner posts. They placed boards upon wood horses for tables. Laid out in banquet style with white linen cloths and silverware, the diners could have been supping at the finest establishment. Only the patches of summer sun and shadows on the grass around them and the teasing gentle breeze reminded them that they were outdoors.

Jeannie sat with the Parkers at Pickett's end of the table. Pickett was entertaining Captain Prevost from the HMS *Satellite*, as well as members of the American survey party still surveying the international land boundary at the forty-ninth parallel. Jeannie looked for Breed and was disappointed when she didn't see him. Later, he arrived with a group of men she did not know and sat at a table set for bachelors. Unfortunately, Breed was so far from her end of the tent, she could not glimpse him without craning her neck and that would not do. By the time dinner was over and cake and coffee served by one of the Chinese servants at the camp, he was gone. Still, it lifted her heart that he had come, even if he was unattainable.

While the women tended to their hair and dress in an American officer's bungalow the men walked to the blockhouse and smoked cigars by the post fence. Out in the center of the parade ground, soldiers finished raising a wood platform, stringing lanterns between the corner posts. Soon after, an orchestra from the Royal Marine Camp set up chairs on a corner of the stage and began to squeak and haw as they tuned their instruments.

"A pity you cannot put on your dancing shoes," Gilly said as she peeked out on the scene from the cramped room where the bed took up half the room. "I have never seen so many men anxious to make your acquaintance as I have today. But you may have your name on the dance card and visit." She moved a hatbox on the floor and avoided stepping on the woman next to her pulling her stockings on.

Jeannie said nothing. Adjusting her crinolines, she slipped on the new dress Uncle Archie recently purchased for her. Though it was black for mourning, it was in the latest fashion and becoming. She had removed the short jacket so that her shoulders were bare and the decollate plunge to her breasts exposed. Jet earrings graced her ears.

"Is true that a London tenor touring Victoria is performing this evening?" Jeannie pulled at the tops of her cap sleeves.

Gilly looked in a mirror nailed to the wall and pinched her cheeks. "So I heard. The finest right here! How very elegant." She picked up her wrap. "Are you ready, dear?"

"Yes." Jeannie smoothed down the front of her skirt as though it would smooth away the butterflies in her stomach. She was stepping out into society no matter how far-flung from the ends of the earth and of such peculiar arrangement. Two military forces on one lone island.

"Then let's go." Gilly swept her hooped skirt around the bedstead and opened the door to the tiny hall. Jeannie followed.

Out on the porch, Jeannie gasped at the venue for the ball. Soldiers were lighting the candles inside the lanterns so that the platform resembled a fairy ring at midsummer's eve. Beyond it, to the east the tops of islands and the mountains on the mainland glowed amber with the late summer light. The white picket fence around the grounds and blockhouse glowed too like the great white way she had seen once in Bristol so long ago. In front of the stage the officers gathered in their best jackets. Some of the men wore hats with plumage. In all, a civilized and yet unnatural scene.

When she finally arrived to take her place with the other ladies, she was given a dance card printed especially for the ball. It immediately started to fill.

"Ladies," Pickett drawled and then the first dance—a grand march —was announced by the American officer of the evening. Pierce, who was the first on her card, took her arm and led her to a folding chair where she sat. They watched couples line up behind Pickett and his companion and Bazelgette, the officer at the Royal Marine encampment and his escort. When the piece began, Bazelgette and his escort were invited to take the lead and the remaining couples promenaded behind them down the length of the wide stage. Turning, Pickett and his partner stood side by side. Bazelgette and his partner stepped up next to them. Then the two couples split, one to the left, the other to the right and led the way back down. The rest of the couples followed suit, boots shaking the boards and skirts swaying as they did so. And so it went, each time increasing the number of couples in the line until there were five couples in a line sweeping down, a grand procession if there ever was one. Everyone clapped gloved hands when it was over.

"Wasn't that splendid, Mrs. Naughton?" Pierce said.

"Oh, yes. A wonderful sight." Jeannie excused herself to join Gilly.

For the rest of the evening she found herself frequently alternating with Pierce and John Forrester and the large group of both British and American admirers who maneuvered for a chance to sit with her. It was like the races all over again, as the men jockeyed to get their names on her card. The night began to echo with the music and the laughter of the dancers, but at no time did she see Jonas Breed.

"Mrs. Naughton," a clipped voice said. Jeannie looked up. It was Cooperwaite. "May I bring you some punch?"

Jeannie put on her best smile. She was alone with no help from Gilly and Dr. Parker who were waiting for the next rill.

"That is very kind, Lieutenant—"

Cooperwaite bowed.

Jeannie dipped her head politely, "—but I have had my fill, thank you very much."

"Then a parley. You look very fine this evening."

"Thank you." Jeannie fiddled with her fan, causing the dance card to dangle off her wrist.

Cooperwaite fixed his eyes on her dance card. "I would beg to add my name, but I fear that would be pretentious."

Jeannie shifted on her chair. She managed to get her fan open without trembling. "I'm afraid it's full."

Cooperwaite stroked his mustache. In the lamp light he looked immaculate: white gloves tucked into his belt, his shoulder epaulettes golden. But something about him was cold. His drooping eyelid seemed more pronounced, the scar that caused it looked red.

Jeannie and Cooperwaite both turned their heads as the dancers started up again, making the boards clatter. "You do not dance?" he asked.

"It's not allowed." When he gave her a baffled look, she said, "I'm in mourning for my boy. He died of the variola."

"My condolences. I didn't know. "

"Thank you."

The assembly clapped hands muffled by their gloves as couples promenaded around their circles. The fiddle players worked to a frenzy. Before long, Jeannie was tapping out the time with her opened fan. How she wished to be out there among them.

"May I ask you something?" Cooperwaite's question startled her. She closed her fan.

"It's remarkable that we are both so far from home," he went on, "but I can't help admiring you. You remind me of a young lady—a Miss Jeannie Hackmore of Christchurch."

Jeannie's fan dropped and slid down to her knee before she could catch it. Her breath had been slammed out of her. Though she knew she had gone pale, she mustered her courage and said to the marine,

"What an odd coincidence to be associated with someone from that pleasant place. As I said before, I am from Bristol."

"Oh, I beg your pardon. She was quite the local beauty. Married an acquaintance of mine, Captain Harry Marsfield."

Jeannie slowly brought the fan back to her chest. The lights in the lanterns blurred. The music and laughter muted. "How interesting." She dared not respond further, but his knowledge was crushing her. She had been found out. "I'm sorry. I do not know the gentleman."

"We went to naval school together."

Jeannie swallowed and looked at him. *Had he truly known her husband?* She didn't recall seeing Cooperwaite at their wedding or the public reception. Had he been at the trial? "I'm afraid not."

"Excuse me, then." Cooperwaite pulled at his forelock and bowed. He opened his mouth to say something more, but John Forrester showed up to take his turn on the card to sit with Jeannie. Gilly and Dr. Parker followed. A quick click of the heels and Cooperwaite went away. Jeannie began to shake.

"Jeannie, dear." Gilly said as she sat down with a poof of crinoline and skirt. "Are you chilled?" When Jeannie didn't respond, she slipped her paisley wrap over her shoulders. "Such a shame for you. It's almost criminal what society rules. Do you want to go back to the bungalow?"

Jeannie looked for Cooperwaite, but he had slipped away. What was next? "Not yet."

At ten, there was a respite and the tenor was asked to sing. He obliged the company with American minstrel songs such as "Camp Town Races," "Oh, Susanna," "Nelly Bly" and the plaintive "Hard Times" which touched Jeannie's heart. His fine, cultured voice was the hit of the evening and he was asked to sing more. Jeannie clapped her approval, then excusing herself, slipped away from her flock of suitors. At last, she had seen Breed out on the grass and heading towards the officer's quarters. Putting on her shawl, she announced that she wanted to attend to her toilette. Adjusting her eyes she went in search of him, but aware that someone might see her, she restrained from turning her amble into a run.

The long twilight was finally over and a nearly full moon out, but as she got further away from the festivities, the buildings became dark as jet. The night air was sweet and intoxicating with a hint of the sea and the smell of sheep from Belle Vue Farm. For a moment she could not see much of anything until she saw the flash of a lucifer to her left, as someone lit a pipe. It was Breed. She walked around to the side of the officer's house where he was standing in the grass beyond the picket fence.

"You are leaving, Mr. Breed? You have not enjoyed yourself?" Jeannie asked.

Breed shook out the match. "I did enjoy myself. It's amusing watching a pride of officers and their ladies square off."

Jeannie grinned. "I suppose one is squared off, though I do freely admit there are other reasons. The ability to dance is often considered a necessity for improving one's station in life."

He took a puff on his pipe. "I've seen the ladies at Fort Victoria and Fort Steilacoom so driven. I'm afraid that I'm not a good catch at all—being so self-consciously awkward."

"You are not awkward—Jonas." She still wasn't used to calling him by his Christian name—"You are—oh, dear." Jeannie blushed. Breed took a puff on his pipe. She thought she heard him chuckle.

"And you?" he asked. "You didn't dance at all. That would have been amusing too."

Jeannie's smiled disappeared. "I'm sure you know that I am not allowed because of the death of my son, Jeremy. It's thought unseemly."

Breed raised his pipe in sympathy. "Ah, the sweet lad. But there are mourning rules."

"Yes. Rules for a husband. Rules for the death of a child, though not so long" She moved into the depths of the shadows alongside the building. *But no rules for my aching heart.*

"But your dance card is full?"

"No, I had to leave a little space for myself. After sitting so long and having to carry on conversations of unimaginable lengths, I had to take my leave before I could not rise again."

Breed laughed. "Perhaps a cooling off period is required."

"You make me sound like a horse."

"The race is done and the riders have gone home. Will you walk with me, Jeannie?"

Jeannie swallowed. It was rash to walk out alone with him without Gilly as her chaperone.

Breed waited patiently for her to answer. The tenor sang again another some minstrel song accompanied by a fiddle from the orchestra. The night was warm and close around her. Behind him, Jeannie said yes. He gave her his arm.

They walked through the gate at the western side of the picket fence and out onto a path that went alongside the back of the officer's buildings. As they followed the trail up, she could see down the hill to the Strait. Not far down, a sole candle in one of the windows winked in one of the Hudson's Bay farm outbuildings, a competition to the pale moon. The half-rutted, half-grassy path led up to a hill where a year ago, Breed explained, American soldiers from an engineering unit had been furiously working on a rampart for the thirty-two pounders taken off the USS *Massachusetts*. "They abandoned it with the joint occupancy agreement between Governor Douglas of Vancouver's Island and General Winfield Scott."

At the top, he helped her up on the earthen rampart wall. She gasped when she took in the extraordinary view lit by moonlight.

"Why, you can see forever."

"*Ah-ha*. It is even better than Mount Young to the north. I never tire of this view no matter the time of day."

Much like the prairie where the races had taken place earlier in the day, the scene here covered the islands and hints of distant high features, but it was also surreal because the moonlight distorted the hills and structures closer in. Down in the lagoon where San Juan Town was situated, several lights twinkled accompanied by the distant sound of music and rowdy laughter.

"Is the town so evil, Mr. Breed?"

"Just the goings on."

"How long has it been there?"

"Some say the buildings appeared like a ring of fairy mushrooms the day after Captain George Pickett arrived with his men during the conflict over the Hudson's Bay pig a year ago. A lot of the buildings are abandoned miner's shacks from Bellingham Bay settlements. Pickett calls it a 'perfect bedlam day and night' and I believe him. Not suitable for a woman."

Jeannie pulled her shawl closer to her neck, wondering if the "unsuitable" had to do with improper relations with loose women. She knew enough of that from the unsavory parts of Plymouth, the naval town where she grew up.

"Mr. Krill is associated there."

"*Ah-ha*. He fancies himself an American gentleman, promoting his business such as lime diggings in a not so gentlemanly way, but he has his admirers for his brashness against any British interest. I am not one of them."

Jeannie cleared her throat. "I never truly thanked you for the other day. Mr. Krill gave me quite the fright, though. I don't want you to think that I am always in need of rescue."

"I don't believe you are. You showed a great deal of courage coming down to Kanaka Town. Quite outside the bounds for a lady of your station. Mrs. Parker still gives me the stink eye over it."

"Stink eye?"

"Beg pardon. Her disapproval. You *are* her particular friend."

"Ah. Well, it's very kind of you to say."

"It's the truth."

Jeannie took a couple steps away from Breed and looked to the east. The moon in the cloudless sky provided enough light to suggest a large white headed mountain miles away. The view continued to astonish her.

"And Cooperwaite?" Breed asked. "Is he still worrying you?"

Jeannie hesitated and collected her answer. "Yes."

Jeannie paused. "He imagines that he knows me, but he is wrong."

"Truth," Breed said.

"He associates me with someone he knew back in England."

"And you do not wish to be associated with this woman."

Breed's perception cut to Jeannie's heart. It felt like it would thump out of her chest.

"You needn't answer. It troubles you, I see."

Jeannie swallowed. "She got into trouble. She was falsely accused."

Breed said nothing. He let her words disappear into the night air. Breed and Jeannie resumed their walk and made a turn around the rampart's edge. Lifting up from the parade ground, voice and fiddle wafted over them. Jeannie stopped, still shaken. She closed her eyes, a pensive memory stirring.

"Are you all right?"

"Yes, I'm all right." She sighed. "Just a silly memory. A country dance when I was a girl." Breed came close. In the moonlight, the features of his face were blurred, but the round earring in his left ear glowed.

Jeannie pulled her shawl tight. She stepped away. Her heart resumed its pounding. Her last country dance before her marriage to Captain Marsfield who swept her off her feet and promised her the world. How young she was and so naïve.

The fiddle was now joined by a flute. Together they weaved around the voice of tenor and floated up to them distinct and clear. Jeannie leaned in to listen, banking down the memory that haunted her. She was grateful that Breed didn't pursue any further inquiry. He seemed to listen to the music too, but after a time he cleared his throat.

"Better now?"

"Yes, thank you."

"Will you stay longer?" In the dark, Breed seemed close to Jeannie, the faint scent of cedar strong.

"Here?" Jeannie wondered what he meant, then realized that he might be asking about the Parkers. "Oh, here at Camp Pickett. Just for another day, then we shall all tromp back home to the Royal Marine Camp where my stay is extended indefinitely. In the meantime, I shall have this memory of a wonderful day."

He stopped at the last rampart, which faced out towards the Olympic Mountains and Haro Strait.

Here again, the moon illuminated a chain of rugged mountains to the west. Down below, the oily black water looked like it had been strewn with diamonds under the moonlight. It was so bright she could see the waves come onto the shore far below them. He pointed down to the left. "There's a traditional salt station down there. The salmon sweep through by the hundreds of thousands." They watched the waves silently for a bit, then he helped her down. They walked back towards the parade ground side of rampart and looked down on the festivities.

The tenor had stopped singing and a fiddle took up a rill. Her foot began to tap.

"Do you wish to dance, Jeannie?"

She put a hand to her throat and sighing, nodded quietly. "It's a silly thing, but I use to dance with my boy, Jeremy. In Toronto, there were several balls and gatherings. He wanted to play the gentleman." She frowned. "There are so many rules I have to follow about mourning. I hate them. I don't understand the half of them."

Breed looked down at the parade ground where the lantern lights twinkled and shadows circled on the dance boards. "No one can see us here."

"I thought you didn't dance."

"I didn't say that I didn't know how to dance. I've not really practiced. But I assure you that I won't step on your toes." He held out his hand encased in a leather glove. Jeannie hesitated for just a moment at breaking taboo, but she took it. When he placed his hand on her waist, she felt her knees go weak. They crossed arms and began to dance.

Awkward at first, they stepped into the soft strain coming up from below and they moved around the rampart swept by moonlight. She showed him how to hop, turn and promenade. It was only when they came back to where they started did she feel for the first time the strength of his arm around her. Her hem crashing against him. She was dizzy with joy. He seemed to be enjoying himself too for his face was all grin.

"Shall we go again?" he asked.

"Oh, yes, please."

The full orchestra was playing now and they could hear the shouts and clapping of the dancers below as they swirled and do-si-doed. Jeannie and Breed twirled and turned at every beat until they came home to the beginning of their exchange. By then, they both were laughing. Reluctantly, she slipped out of his hold and let go of his hand.

"*Mahsie*," he said making a bow. "Shall we go back? Don't want to cause alarm."

She opened her fan and cooled herself down. Her skin was prickling with perspiration and excitement. "Yes, we should go. Thank you. I haven't had such amusement since Jeremy died."

"Then I have served your dance card well. It's the first time I've heard you laugh. You should do it more often. I know you are saddened by your loss, but after someone goes into the forest, life goes on, even when you miss them."

"Into the forest?"

"An Indian way of saying you passed on. You must live now and fully for his sake and your own. Don't you have a promise you'll meet your son again?"

The walk back was hasty, not what she wanted, but she could think only of his arm around her waist and how it fit. Even now, she could feel its warmth and strength. She wanted to stay up on top of the ramparts, but she knew Gilly would be looking for her.

Outside the picket fence, it sounded like the dancing was continuing. It turned out to be the tenor singing again—a lively tune—and then there was applause. A pause followed, then a lone violin began to play and the tenor began to sing in a plaintive, sensuous voice:

> *I dream of Jeannie with the light brown hair,*
> *Borne, like a vapor, on the summer air;*
> *I sigh for Jeannie*

The song went on and hung like a thick scent of rose water in the dark. Jeannie and Breed stood transfixed alongside the walls of the quarters, unaware that they had stepped close to each other. When the song was finished, there was a break before the applause and the melody continued to stay suspended. Finally, Jeannie noticed that she had leaned against his chest. Embarrassed, she started to step away.

"You need not fear me, Jeannie," he said gently from the dark. "You are with a friend."

"I know," she said softly. She could see a light smile on his lips when he bowed.

"Your servant, Mrs. King George. Always."

"You are leaving?"

"I had my turn on your dance card, no matter how ill gained. *Mahsie*." With that he stepped back and disappeared into the gloom when the orchestra resumed its playing.

LIME KILN

A few days after the dance, Jeannie returned to Victoria to visit her uncle. The Parkers had extended their invitation to her for as long as she liked and she went to get more of her things.

"Are ye sure this is good purpose, kitten?" Uncle Archie asked after she told him her plans. "I can see your stay has restored you close to your ownself and I'm glad for it." He looked down at his teacup. "But I had hoped you would return to stay in Victoria."

Jeannie reached over and touched his arm. "Uncle, what can I say to the dearest man in the world?" She swallowed. "I'm not strong enough, as yet. Too many things here to remind me of Jeremy. And female society there is so restricting. Do this, don't do that."

"T'is true about the ladies. I cannot deny it."

"Having first publicly mourned for my husband only to be set in scandal, I prefer to mourn my true and deepest loss quietly. Gilly Parker is so kind and the island's nature a balm."

The old Scot sighed. "Well, I'll not impede, but will you promise me by summer's end, you'll come home?"

Jeannie rose and kissed him on his forehead. "Oh, dearest. Don't hold me hard to such a promise. I do promise to write every day."

Uncle Archie harrumphed. "When do you go back?"

"Not for four whole days, Uncle. Dr. Parker has come here for consultations at the naval hospital and will return on Monday's sailing to the encampment. He will be my chaperon. In the meantime, you will find it hard not to find me at your side."

"Hmm. Then we shall invite him to the company table."

On her return to San Juan Island and the Royal Marine Camp, Jeannie wondered what it would hold for her now. So much had transpired since she arrived with Jeremy over three months before. As she approached Garrison Bay for her third visit, the camp and its surrounding forested hills rose up to greet her like an old friend. Since then, her first impression of belonging in the Pacific Northwest had deepened. Despite the hollow grief that sometimes overtook her, she saw her way more clearly. What was new was her intense desire to belong on this island, but as an unattached female there was only one way: secure a post as governess or teacher—if such a thing existed—or marry.

She thought of the dinner Uncle Archie had arranged. The company table turned out to hold more than Dr. Parker. When Jeannie arrived, she was surprised to see Harry Ferguson and several other gentlemen from the trading fort and the town. One came with his sister, another with his wife. The other men were alone.

Such eager boys with dreams and grand expectations. Harry Ferguson was a pleasant sort. Uncle Archie said he had excellent business sense and he would prosper. All to the good. The other bachelors were pleasant too, but she felt a too-mannered sensibility behind their desire to secure a private interview with her. Nothing scandalous. She knew the men were meant to keep her distracted from her sorrow. Perhaps she might even consider marriage.

As the steamboat came alongside the camp landing, she saw Breed and her heart leaped for she knew exactly where it should be. He stood with a group of men that included Collie Henderson and three other gentlemen she didn't know. One man was Chinese. He was of medium height and lean built and though dressed in the typical clothing of a local *shipman*, had retained the long single braid of his countrymen. He listened with interest to the conversation and occasionally said something, but Jeannie thought him watchful and wondered what role he had with Jonas. The second man was a laborer of some sort by his canvas pants and rumpled sack coat.

The third man was small and wiry with a black hair and slightly bent wire-rimmed glasses. He had difficulty in keeping his sack coat on his narrow shoulders, but she was to learn that any impression about him being a banty rooster ended there.

Jeannie gathered up her valise and followed Dr. Parker down the plank

"Mrs. Naughton," Breed said as Jeannie approached. "I trust your voyage was pleasant."

"Yes, it was, Mr. Breed." She felt her face start to flush and willed it down, noting he meant to keep their familiarity a secret for now.

"Didn't expect you to be here, Jonas," Dr. Parker said as he came up to the group of men. "You're not keeping a regular schedule with deliveries?"

Breed chuckled. "The limestone occupies my time lately, though truth is, I'd rather someone else run it."

"Which is the point of the crew gathered here," Collie grinned. "We're here to occupy it."

Breed laughed, "Not too literally, mind you. The issue of who owns the island is not decided."

Collie winked. "All the more to shift with the wind. I believe there's an equal number of British and Americans among us for the undertaking."

Dr. Parker grinned and shook his head. "The thoughts of clever young men. I heard someone caught stealing a sugar cone and coffee grinder down in San Juan Town complain to Pickett that he could not be arrested as he was a British subject and got away with it until he did a similar offense at Victoria and claimed he was American. They got him then."

"And should." Breed frowned. "Order is not necessarily a bad thing." He turned to Jeannie. "It looks as though you are becoming fully entrenched here."

Jeannie laughed. "I hope my poor hosts don't think so. I rather not end my welcome."

"Then let me extend your acquaintances, Madame." Breed stepped aside. "This is Billy Po, one of my *shipmen* and advisors, Dylan Feemster, woodsman, and this is Neville Hector. Folks around him call him Doc-tin."

"It's Chinook Jargon for doctor," interjected Collie.

"You are a surgeon?" Jeannie asked.

"Not like the good doctor here," Doc-tin said in a distinct nasal accent, "but I read medicine back east in Philadelphia and have applied myself when the occasion warranted it. Without the loss of the patient I might add."

"Before the military camps brought their sawbones here, Doc-tin was doctor in these parts," Collie said. "Fixed many a broken bone and sawed off a limb when needed."

"He's a good farrier too," Dr. Parker said. "The few horses here he has seen to with equal skill. Excuse me, gentlemen, I think I see my bride coming down from our quarters and I'm sure that Mrs. Naughton would like to rest up after her journey." Dr. Parker called to one of the privates unloading the steamer. "Could see that my medical boxes are taken to the infirmary? And you, corporal, help Mrs. Naughton with her valise."

He nodded at Breed and his friends. "Good afternoon, gentlemen." With that he gathered up his own valise and medical box and headed off the wharf. Breed's men stepped aside and made room for Jeannie's hooped skirt as she swooped by them.

~

The following morning, Jeannie rose early and rode out with Gilly and her brother to see Breed's lime works at Farseeing on the northern side of the island. Wooded inlets wove in and out along the coast hiding silent coves rich with birdlife or harbors deep enough to hold several boats. Sometimes there were dangers as well, with surf that could crush a simple canoe into pieces against uplifted, honey-combed bluffs without warning.

They smelled the lime kiln before they saw it. When they arrived, Jeannie saw several men in Breed's employ, including Indians, moving crushed limestone rock into the tall brick kiln to make the lime. While Gilly and Forrester dismounted to talk to one of the workmen, Jeannie noticed a woman in a bowler hat going over the side of the hill. Curious, Jeannie urged her horse forward to follow. On the beach below, she could see where the men's families were camped out, their smoke fires pungent with the scent of alder and salmon where they smoked fish.

This is a more scattered arrangement than Kanaka *Town,* Jeannie thought. Canvas tents and cattail mats draped over frames provided the only shelter. Children played along the shore while their mothers in bright head scarves and calico dresses cut salmon or fed the fires. Laughter and chatter filled the air. It reminded her of dockside in her home in England. Jeannie watched them for a moment, then went back to the diggings.

At the nooning, they stopped to eat up on the ridge. Jeannie spread out a blanket with mats around it. On the blanket Gilly laid a picnic of meats, bread, cheese, and jugs of switchel made of vinegar and molasses and another filled with cider. Jeannie sat on a mat that Alani made for her and took food from the blanket spread out between them on the grass and sandstone rocks. The sky was full of clouds—though there was summer sun—and a cool breeze played at the ribbons on her bonnet. The view across the water to the next group of islands was wonderful. They were well into their meal, when there was some excitement up above on the steep hill and two marine officers in shirtsleeves appeared. One was Cooperwaite. Seeing him, made Jeannie's stomach sour.

"Good day, ladies, Mr. Forrester."

Forrester stood and shook Cooperwaite's hand. Before Jeannie could give warning, he and the other officer were seated on one of the mats as guests. The lunch continued and to her surprise, Cooperwaite proved a genial companion, but she did not trust him.

Then Breed and Kaui Kalama appeared. His very appearance stirred not only her feelings, but somehow Cooperwaite's.

Breed nodded to Forrester. "So you've come to the workings? I'm sorry I wasn't here earlier."

Gilly laid her knife on her butter plate. "Oh, yes, Mr. Breed. It has such promise."

Breed shrugged. "Who's to say? I know that there are better, but for now, this satisfies." He looked around. "I leave it to the others who have stomach for it. I'd rather work fish than this."

"But it is profitable already?" Forrester asked.

"*Ah-ha*. Enough to pay the others and then some."

Cooperwaite jutted out his chin. "What is that? Five blankets and a hatchet blade?"

Jeannie grew quiet as she watched Breed's eyes turn cold, curious how Breed would respond. "All my men are paid in coin and fairly." Breed said. "With all due respect to the HBC, I have not been so casual with the labor."

Cooperwaite drew himself up. "They are only Kanakas and Indians. They will spend it on whiskey and other illicit means."

Breed's mouth tightened. "Your views are narrow, despite the draw of San Juan Town."

"Your views are tainted by your love for them," Cooperwaite spat back.

"Gentlemen, gentlemen." Forrester spread his arms out between them. "This is not the place for such a discussion. There are ladies present. Now please, my sister has gone to rather great lengths to prepare a delicious picnic, which is going to waste. You will stay, Jonas, I hope. Your Kanaka friend is most welcome too. Lieutenant. Cooperwaite, you may do as you like."

Cooperwaite staggered to his feet and tugged on his jacket. "You're quite right. I've overstepped my bounds. I beg your pardon, Mr. Breed. And ladies, I do apologize." He cleared his throat. "I'll take my leave." He jerked his head at the other marine who, from his startled look, wasn't prepared to go, but made his bow and left. Cooperwaite brushed against Kaui as he passed. Jeannie didn't think Cooperwaite meant his apology too heartily.

Kaui Kalama. Jeannie hadn't seen him since she left Kanaka Town. Now after several weeks she could see that he was well recovered, though there were deep pox marks on his cheeks. If he had taken offense to Cooperwaite his warm brown eyes did not betray it. He did nod at Jeannie when he took off his hat, but stayed behind Breed as if he knew his place in this setting. She smiled back at him.

"Come, come, Mr. Breed. Do join us." Forrester motioned to Kaui, but Kaui excused himself and went past them down to the beach.

Breed sat down on the blanket. He accepted the cheese and bread offered him. "I won't stay long. I leave in the evening for Lopez Island."

"Will you be gone long, J—Mr. Breed?" Jeannie asked, astonished that she nearly said his first name.

A shadow of a smile touched his lips. "A few days at most. Kaui's coming, Dylan Feemster, and some others."

"More workings?" Forrester asked.

"No. A contract for lumber."

The picnic and talk continued, but eventually the food was gone and the empty stone crocks and tins put away into a hamper. They stood and helped shake out the blanket and mats. When they were put away, Breed asked if anyone would like to go look at the salmon being smoked on the beach, but Gilly said she was too comfortable after the meal and Forrester wanted to see the workings again.

"Mrs. Naughton?"

Jeannie felt a flutter in her chest. "Is it all right, Gilly?"

"Of course, dear. You are in excellent company." She gave Breed a piercing look and closed the hamper. "Help me up, dear brother."

Breed gave Jeannie his arm. She felt a shock of electricity pass between them. He must have felt it too for he gently squeezed her hand. She remembered their dance upon the ramparts. Through her black lace half-gloves, she felt his strength. For a moment, she felt they were conspirators in a tableau about manners in which to the outside world neither of them could show any emotion. As he helped her down the steep dirt path, he leaned in. "And how is Mrs. King George today, truly?"

"You tease me, sir."

"My pleasure." He gave her hand a pat.

Jeannie felt a delicious bubble of joy. If there wasn't the threat of being watched, she would have tapped him with her parasol.

On the beach Breed showed her the salmon smoking operation. The number of fish staked over the coals had increased since she first arrived. The women's faces flushed with the heat. He started to explain how they cut fish open through the back and then threaded the whole fish onto alder frames with cedar or ironwood withes, when two children ran toward them.

"Missus King George. Missus Jeannie!"

Kapihi threw himself on Jeannie just as Jeremy used to do, causing her skirt to swing. Jeannie kissed the top of his head. "Why Kapihi. Noelani. How wonderful to see you. Are you having fun?" she said as she enfolded both children in her arms.

"Oh, yes, Missus Jeannie," Kapihi said in a big voice. He looked up her with pure love that touched Jeannie's heart.

By now, several of the women gathered around them. One expressed interest in her blue muslin dress and admired her straw hat. Another her parasol.

A short woman wearing a braided cedar bark band on her bowler hat approached. "You like a band for your hat, missus?" She removed the band and offered it. "It nothing for what you give me. My Kaui's life. But maybe you like it."

For a moment, Jeannie was speechless. *What was her name? Sally?* The Indian woman had a smooth oval face and shiny black hair twisted into a braid. Her calico dress was shapeless from no corset and was stained with charcoal and fish oil, but she carried herself with natural dignity. Kaui's wife, mother of her young friends. *How could she not accept?*

"Why, thank you. *Mahsie.* How very sweet of you. Shall we see if it fits?" Jeannie unpinned her hat and placed the gift around the base of the crown.

"Aloha, Missus Naughton."

Jeannie looked and beamed when she saw her friend from Kanaka Town. "Alani. What a joy to see you again." *Victorian society be damned,* Jeannie thought and gave Alani a hug. "When did you get here?"

"This morning. Let me help you." Alani set the hat on Jeannie's head, then gently set it in place with the hat pin.

Breed had been silent during this exchange, but once Jeannie had her hat back on to approval from the women, he introduced her to Sally Kalama and the other women. They were a varied group. Some came from villages across the strait, some were Kanaka and some the Indian wives of the few white men among the people working there.

"Would you like to taste some smoked fish?" Breed asked.

"Oh, yes."

"*Klahowya,* Mrs. Fulson," he said to one of the women setting a stake near glowing burning coals. The woman straightened up, making the little bells on her earrings jangle. She put her hands on her hips and smiled, exposing a missing front tooth.

"*Klahowya,* Jo-nuss. What you want?"

"Some of your good work. *Mahsie.* For my friend Mrs. Naughton."

"*Hee-hee.*" She took a knife from a leather sheath and cut some pieces from a browned fish the color of a brick and put it on a hand-kerchief. Breed offered it to Jeannie.

"Be careful. It's hot, but tasty."

Jeannie took a piece. It smelled of smoke, alder and the rich sea. It was even better to eat. Though she had tried salmon many times at Uncle Archie's, this sample melted in her mouth.

"It's very good," she told the woman. "Lovely." There were invitations to try more smoked salmon and fresh spring water.

Sally brought Jeannie a canvas stool and invited her to sit. Kapihi and Noelani sat down at her feet, their chatter interrupting each other. Jeannie put a hand over her mouth as laughter and sadness overtook her at once.

Momma. As she visited with her young friends, Jeremy's little voice seemed to come out of nowhere as clear as the sun shining on the water.

After a time, Breed said it was time to head back. There were words of friendship and good-byes. Sally put some salmon in a huck-abuck woven towel and gave it to Jeannie. "Come again," she said.

Halfway up the bank, Jeannie turned around and thanked Breed.

"You're welcome," he said. Once again, he looked at her directly as he had on the dock the day before. His look carried no hidden meaning, no lewdness. Just a quiet interest like he was looking deep into her soul. When he took her hand, she knew in her heart that a silent declaration had been made between them. She kept the feeling all the way up to the top until she ran straight into Collie Henderson.

"Beg pardon, ma'am, but I need to see Jonas."

"Collie," Breed said. "What brings you here?"

"A family matter. *Tenas klootsman.* No time to lose."

Jeannie had no idea what he meant, but the tension on Breed's face gave her a hint of some trouble.

TROUBLES WITH SAN JUAN TOWN

Breed stood on the porch of *Krill's Mercantile* and checked the double doors. Behind him, lantern light from a dozen shacks groped its way through the thickening mist. A tinny piano played a throbbing tune. Voices and laughter sounded disembodied. The only light on the porch was a candle lantern on the store's post.

"They're locked."

"Use this." Collie Henderson handed him a picklock out of a leather case. Breed had to squint to see it. The sun had long since gone down, leaving the summer twilight to spread its shadows over the collection of twenty ill-formed buildings and tents that made up San Juan Town. Yet the reason he was here was urgent—the rescue of the twelve-year-old daughter of a Makah friend. He thanked the spirits for the mist softly drifting off Griffin Bay onto the main lane.

Breed jiggled the lock. "When's the last time Billy Po saw her?"

"About a half-hour ago," Sikhs said. He stood at the dark edge of the building holding a shotgun.

"Krill was talking about taking her out of the root cellar," Collie said. Wanted to bring her up into one of the rooms." Collie's voice was taut with anger. "Shhh—"

Two buildings down, a door opened and a couple of soldiers stumbled out onto the candlelit porch. One bumped into a post before weaving down the steps into the lane. *They'll be in trouble for sure*, Breed thought as he pressed up against the shuttered store. Pickett had to expand the boundaries of the military post to within a few feet of San Juan Town just to keep the soldiers in line.

One of the soldiers, his corporal's stripe nearly erased by the dying light, bent over in the middle of the street and retched. The stink mixed with the other smells of the settlement: wood pile litter, broken whiskey bottles, and barrels reeking of spoiled food and brackish water. Breed fought back the urge to retch too. They had so little time. Since he had learned of the girl's kidnapping, Breed had been on the lookout for her for the past two days.

Krill's place was more than a store selling civilian and soldier's needs. Behind the Chinese glass bead curtains next to the counter, there were several rooms that stretched back to the lagoon. Krill's boarders.

"Get on, Liam. Sarg's goin' to give us piss."

"I'm pissed. A shiny dollar for that swill." The soldier spit a final time, keeping his hand on his belly.

The two soldiers staggered off, this time off toward the high grassy hill leading back to the army post. Breed waited until they were out of range then went back to the lock on the store's double doors. The street was deserted now, everyone seemingly indoors, staying warm from the unexpected change in the weather.

He was about to jiggle the lock when a woman screamed. Both men swung around, Collie pulling out his sword from his scabbard on his back. But then the woman's voice changed into a squeal of pleasure and laughter. Breed almost missed the cry from the store on the other side of its doors.

"Jonas." Collie rammed his shoulder against one of the doors.

"I heard it." Breed signaled Sikhs to go around to the back. He gave the pick lock one more turn and they spilled into the store. Inside, the store was dark, the floor to ceiling shelves behind a thick counter displaying tins and wooden boxes like plaques in a mausoleum, but down the hall there was candle light.

136

A muffled cry and then someone spit out, "You little heathen."

"There!" Breed leaped over the counter and raced down the hall, kicking in the nearest door. Collie came behind him, slashing the bead curtain with his sword into smithereens. The little beads bounced and rolled down the floor into the room where a naked man and woman were stacked up against the headboard in a state of disarray and shock. Breed was gone and into the next room before the couple gave alarm.

The next two rooms were empty. Collie checked the beds and the hidey holes while Breed tore into the last room. Throwing his shoulder against the door, it gave away easily into Breed's worst fears. Some hairy brute had cornered the girl on the bed and was trying to ward off her flailing brown legs aimed at his face. Breed grabbed him by the shoulders and threw him against the wall.

"*Coolie, coolie,*" Breed shouted to her. Run! She obeyed, scrambling off the bed like a scared rabbit and out into the hall.

The abuser staggered to his feet, holding his bleeding head. He ranted and swore. Breed socked him again on his jaw and he went down for good.

"*Tot, elan, elan!*" The girl's desperate cry for help wailed from the hall. Breed drew his knife, wondering where Collie was.

The candlelight in the narrow hall flickered violently from a sudden breeze. Down towards the broken curtain a furious fight was going on in one of the vacant rooms. To Breed's right, Krill blocked his way at the half-opened door, holding the struggling girl tight in his big-handed grip.

"Your backup's down, Breed," Krill snarled.

"Don't count on it. Let her go, Krill."

"Says who? I told you to leave my boarders alone, you *siwash* lover."

"She's a child. A *tyee*'s daughter. Best give her back—unspoiled."

Krill yanked on the girl's shift. "This?"

Breed threw his knife. It cut through Krill's top hat and nailed it to the door. Breed charged. The burly man dropped the girl and met

Breed head on, throwing his bulk into him with such force that he was thrown against one of the narrow hallway's walls.

"*Ipsoot*. Hide," Breed shouted to the girl as Krill's meaty hands grabbed his ears. The pain was blinding, but Breed fought back, jabbing his elbow into Krill's throat. The man released him and staggered back to the other side of the hallway, then ricocheted back into Breed. Breed felt like he'd been hit with a sack of anvils.

For a moment, they fought hand and fist in the tight space, each drawing blood until Krill suddenly let go. Before Breed could react, Krill was at the wall, yanking out the knife

"You can have her. She's not worth the trouble," he said. "But don't you come in here and mess with my business." He took a swing at Breed and cut through his shirt sleeve, but his hand was stopped before it could cause further damage. Breed twisted the man's arm down until he cried out. The knife clattered to the floor. Breed kicked it away.

"Go to hell, Krill."

"You go to hell." Krill pulled out of his grip and threw open the door to escape. He didn't get far. Sikhs stood there with a shotgun aimed at his forehead. Krill backed in.

"I didn't take her," he said as he smoothed out his shirt sleeves. "Fella brought her. Sold her cheap."

Breed grabbed Krill and pushed him against the wall.

"You stinking bastard. You're in trouble now. If she was touched—"

Krill spat, careful not to provoke the Indian aiming the shotgun at him. "Aw, she's untouched. You made sure of that. Maybe we can make a trade. Got your friend cornered back there."

"I think not," said Collie as he emerged with the man Breed had interrupted in the first room." Collie held a Bowie knife at the man's throat.

Breed pushed Krill deeper into the wall so that he groaned. "Give me your purse."

"What?"

"I said, give me your purse."

"That's robbery,"

"That's insurance for your head, Krill. Don't you know they've launched their canoes already? That they'll be here in a matter of hours?"

"Pickett won't let that happen."

"Pickett will read about it in the newspapers. Your *head* will be someone's decoration by then. Now give it over. Then get me your best tobacco, axe blades and as many blankets as you can rustle up."

"You're a highway robber, Breed."

"You're in no condition to complain."

"I'll get you."

"You'll thank me." Breed released Krill to Sikhs's control. He nodded to the girl and spoke to her in her tongue. Her eyes opened wide, she came close to him for protection.

"Uncle, I make the *Boston* man knife sick," she said in jargon.

"You are *skookum tum tum*," Breed answered with a tight smile. He was knife sick too, the cut on his arm throbbing and bloodying his sleeve. It was hard to keep control. He would like nothing more than take Krill outside and beat the tar out of him in the cold waters of the lagoon, but time was of the essence. He smiled to reassure, then told her he would take her to her father.

Out in the store, some of Krill's men appeared, but Krill waved them back. "Rogers, get some blankets off them shelves and put them into one of them bottle boxes." Reluctantly he handed over his purse. Breed shook all the gold coins out and put them into his jacket pocket.

Krill sneered. "She's not worth it."

"That's the problem with you, Krill. You're just a cheap, cunning bastard. Now get that stuff so we can go out and meet the canoes. I don't have all night."

GENTLEMEN CALLERS AND A
BLACK BOAR

The days after the picnic at Farseeing moved irritatingly slow for Jeannie. After having spent time with Jonas Breed, she had hoped to see more of him, but he was elusive as morning mist. She had to remind herself that he said he would be going away for a few days. What comfort that was. To ease her incautious feelings she began to take regular walks alone with her sketchbook up on the military road and the woods on the hill behind the marine camp. After her scare with Krill, she didn't stray far.

One misty morning, Gilly accompanied her on her "airing," sometimes huffing as she gathered her skirts on the steep woodsy hill.

"Truly, Jeannie," she gasped when they reached the top, "They say it is healthy to take the air, but fashionable society has not made adjustments to what might be healthy to wear." She smoothed down her bodice, tapping her fingers on her corset.

Jeannie burst out giggling. "Perhaps we should take up the Bloomers and join that water cure."

When she saw Gilly's blank look, Jeannie hooked her arm through her friend's and began to tell her of Mrs. Jenkins, the woman at the American camp that had given her such trouble. Loose or no corsets were part of the Bloomer's philosophy. Soon she had Gilly laughing.

On their return to the Parker bungalow, Jeannie found two things waiting: a letter from Harry Ferguson and a *carte de visite* from American Camp, Andrew Pierce. She turned the card over. On the back was a picture of him in a dour-looking pose with his tie half-done which was apparently the fashion in the States. His reddish-blonde hair sailed off to one side like a dark gray wing.

"Mr. Pierce was here?" she asked the private who had delivered both communications.

"Indeed. About an hour ago."

"Is he still here?"

"I believe he is at the commissary, ma'am. A courtesy call, he says."

Gilly took off her bonnet and placed it on the entry table. "Thank you, Private Hollins. Would you like tea, Jeannie dear? I believe we have biscuits and clotted cream as well."

"Oh, yes."

"I should say." Forrester said peering over his *Gazette* from his seat in the parlor. "With such an armada of admirers, you need fortification. Allow me the honors to make a potion." He folded his newspaper with a flourish. Giving Gilly a peck on her cheek, he slipped off.

Jeannie took the pins out of her hat. She could barely look at Gilly. *An armada? Is that what this has come to?* Just in the few weeks since Jeremy's passing, the number of gentlemen "wishing to make her acquaintance" was on the rise. She wished they'd leave her in peace. Everyone seemed to think that marriage by the end of her mourning period would supplant the continual ache she felt for Jeremy, but how could they know? If that was their understanding would they understand her growing feelings for Jonas Breed?

She touched the satin trim of her bonnet and thought of the very simple plaited band of cedar bark now set on her straw hat. *Jonas.* He was simple and strong as that and equally undemanding. For the first time since the scandal, she was beginning to trust a man other than her uncle.

After tea, Gilly settled down to sewing and needlework. Forrester returned to his newspaper. Jeannie excused herself and said she wanted to go look at the progress of vegetable garden, but she really wanted to read the letter from Harry in private. Once out on the path to the stairway down to the parade grounds, she opened it up.

Mrs. Naughton,

I do hope this missive finds you well as the delightful weather we
have been having. There is nothing more grandiose than a clear blue skies
and mountains and forest to match.

The letter went on in the neat scrawl of a clerk, covering the whole page and on the sides. There was talk of Victoria and the latest social, news of her uncle and HBC doings, his observations chirpy as a winter wren.

Jeannie sighed. He was principled and a dear, but he was predictable. At the top of the stairs, she put away the letter and gathered her skirts. She went down the earthwork steps. The maples and alders to the right hid her descent. She was more than half way down when she overheard two men.

"Breed did what?" An English voice.

"Burst into Krill's whorehouse and rescued some native girl." An American voice. "Krill had the audacity to complain to Pickett about the Army protecting American citizens from hooligans such as him."

"Over the girl?"

"And damaging his establishment at San Juan Town. Krill took some punishment himself."

Jeannie gripped the handrail and froze where she stood. Jonas had not said one word about the settlement when they were up on the ramparts the night of the dance. Now she understood why. An indelicate subject.

"Ha." The British voice stepped toward the barracks and Jeanie recognized him as John Prettyjohn, one of the Royal Marines Dr. Parker thought so well of. A decorated veteran of the Crimean War and, according to the doctor, a friend of Jonas'. "Serves the bloody bastard right. He ought to be horse-whipped. I'm told nearly one hundred women were showing up at that place until a few months ago."

"One girl. Breed went after one girl. What was he thinking?" The

American voice stepped out. Jeannie was surprised to see that it was Andrew Pierce.

"I'm sure Pickett was amused," Prettyjohn said. "He abhors the trouble Krill brings to his men."

"Krill's hopping mad. Said Breed caused him bodily harm, but was glad that he took a bite of him in the fight."

Fight? Jeannie remembered the look on Jonas Breed' face when he challenged Krill after he had accosted her. Krill's face was no less full of hate. How badly had Jonas been hurt? The very thought of any injury to him made her ill.

The men conversed for a few minutes more, then seemed to depart. Jeannie decided it was safe to venture down. Overhearing two impassioned conversations of gentlemen in a scant week was bordering on voyeurism.

At the bottom of the steps, she found Pierce had not left. He was sitting on a log bench cleaning the toes of his tall brown boots. He was dressed in a dark green sack coat and pork pie hat, but the brown tie wrapped around his neck appeared hurriedly tied. He jumped when he discovered her.

"Mrs. Naughton! My apologies."

"Forgive me, Mr. Pierce." She waved her hands at the military buildings. "I'm afraid that I'm an intruder here."

"Not at all, not at all." He patted his tie and made a little adjustment. "I had quite a long sail up from Seattle. Got in at American Camp only late last night. I'm a bit addled."

"Did you bring goods for the sutler?"

"Yes. My monthly order. Now I must wait on the government to make good on the bill." He nodded toward the orderly tents on the parade ground and the barracks under construction. "You English are much more organized here. It practically takes an act of Congress to get anything at American Camp done."

Pierce went on to explain the politics of the United States Army and the remoteness of the military post on San Juan Island in relation to Washington City, the home of American governance. "We are an American territory out here. Our governor is appointed by the President. We answer to Washington City. To top it off, there are troubles back in the States that are becoming increasingly strident. Strong enough that cries to secede may very well become true. Getting bills paid on time may well prove more than items for conversation."

They engaged in small talk concerning the weather, the races and the fine dance. The topic of Jonas Breed came up when Jeannie asked if she might see Mr. Breed there as he was working on some lumber contract on Lopez.

Pierce opened and closed his mouth like he was trapping his thoughts. He cleared his throat. "I'm not sure he'll be there."

"Has something happened?"

"There was an accident. I believe he's back at Farseeing."

"Accident? Was he injured badly?"

Pierce seemed flustered by this turn of conversation. He fiddled with his tie, then cleared his throat. "Mrs. Naughton, I cannot say. It is only hearsay. I believe it is not serious."

Jeannie closed her eyes and opened them with a soft sigh. "Thank you, Mr. Pierce. For a moment, I was quite worried. I feel much better. Mr. Breed is an agreeable gentleman and I hate to hear any ill news of him."

"Indeed. Mr. Breed is not always the cup of tea for Americans, but I do trust him. I find him honorable in all our dealings."

Jeannie turned away. Where was Jonas? She didn't think he would come here. She wondered if he had gone to his lime kiln.

"Where are you going now, Mrs. Naughton?" Pierce asked.

Jeannie decided she would go to the stables. If Jonas was at Farseeing, she could borrow a horse and ride over there. She was sure she knew the way.

"I think I'll go to the stables. I hear there is a young colt there. They are so amusing."

"May I accompanying you?"

Jeannie said yes, but hoped that he would not stay too long.

∾

After chatting with Pierce on their walk to the stables and visiting with the marine on duty about the young colt's future training, Pierce departed. After she was sure he was gone, she secured a roan mare vouched by the marine to be gentle and rode out the trail to the lime works.

The day continued to be gray, the morning mist reluctant to lift and let in the sunshine. In fact, it appeared to be thickening. She rode on, regardless, her thoughts on Jonas Breed. As she rode, she made note of the trees and other natural features to help her find her way back. As the forest gave way to natural prairie, the mist lifted enough for her to see the brick surface of the lime kiln rising in the distance behind the low vine maple trees ahead. As she got closer, she saw that no smoke rose from its square chimney. When she finally reached the cleared-out grounds, they appeared deserted. Breed was not at Farseeing.

Disappointed she rode through the workings where large stacks of cordwood and raw limestone lay in neat order. The shack that had served as a tool station appeared locked. She rode down to the flat area where they had picnicked. Below, where the women had smoked the salmon, the beach was deserted. Across the water, she could barely make out a cluster of islands. She wondered if Timons Island was there. Jonas had said that it was to the north.

A breeze rustled her shawl and gently kissed her cheek with droplets of water. Mist crept through the trees. Where was everyone? Was work so easily abandoned? She felt chilled and began to regret her decision to come out alone. The sound of someone coughing caught her attention. Perhaps one of Jonas's colleagues was nearby.

She urged the horse forward along the low ridge covered with coarse bushes and madrone trees. The trail eventually narrowed as they entered the woods again. Jeannie sat up straight in her sidesaddle, seeking the source of the earlier sound.

There! Something grunted, the voice edged in pain. Her horse began to tremble and put its ears back. Jeannie looked behind her, but saw nothing. She tapped the horse with her riding crop and went forward. The trees thinned out. She could see the stony beach below where someone had pulled a small dugout canoe up on the shore. Water lapped at the canoe's stern.

Jeannie was so focused on the canoe that she missed the crashing black shape of a boar charging through the woods, its red mouth open with curled yellow tusks aimed at her horse's legs. By the time she heard its shrill squeal, it had hammered into her horse, knocking her off her perch. The horse neighed and reared, tearing her last hold on the reins away. A final buck and she was falling down the ledge, rolling over and over again. She screamed as she frantically tried to grab onto anything to stop her tumble, but it was over fast as she started when she landed hard on the ground. Dazed for the moment, she finally staggered to her feet. Her sleeves were torn, her skirt ripped so that she could see her mud-stained petticoats. Her hair fell out of its pins.

Gasping, Jeannie limped away toward the safety of the canoe. Above her the horse and the boar continued to thrash around. Suddenly, the low ridge exploded with broken branches and pebbles and the roan fell down just feet from where she had been standing. Close behind came the biggest black boar Jeannie had ever seen. As the horse and boar untangled, she saw for the first time that the horse was hurt badly. The skin on its cheek was torn, leaving patches of bloody flesh beneath; its legs were bleeding from gashes. Both horse and boar squealed with hurt and anger as they righted themselves.

A peculiar feeling of lightness came over her. The pit of her stomach became cold. She could barely think, but she knew she was in extreme danger. Shaking, she backed up against the canoe and pushed it out into the water, ignoring the chilly water of the channel soaking her boots and skirt. When it was afloat, she turned in time to see the horse separate from the boar and buck its way down the beach.

"Go, go," Jeannie shouted as she pushed the canoe back further, then realized that only the horse was making its escape. The boar was now trotting back, its little eyes trained on her.

There is blood all over its face and tusks, she thought. She hopped and scrambled into the canoe, her skirt catching at the gunwales. The boar charged. She threw herself to the other side of the canoe, causing it to rock.

The boar hit the side of the canoe with a loud thwak, its tusks splintering the edge. Jeannie screamed when it struck again, pushing the canoe sideways. A paddle with a tip shaped like an arrow slid against her. She wiggled the paddle from out under the plain wood bench and held it the way she had seen Collie Henderson hold his sword. Shaking, she willed to hold it steady as the boar backed to the edge of the beach.

Helplessly, Jeannie looked back up to the woods, but there was no hope there. She was alone. The boar shook its head and snorted, the muscles in its shoulders bunching for another run at her.

The boar was huge—over five feet long with long curling tusks at ended with knife-sharp points. It was also wounded. Sticking out of its right haunch was a shaft as thick as a man's thumb that moved back and forth when the boar pawed the pebbles. The boar snorted and plunged again toward her. She prepared to hit it over the head, but at last moment sat down on the bench and stabbing the long paddle into the water, pushed the canoe further out into the channel. When the boar struck the bow again, she pulled the canoe with all her strength.

She remembered Jonas saying he was puller, not a paddler. She pulled against the water again with the canoe floating steady with the increased depth of the water. The boar squealed again, enraged by the distance growing between them. Jeannie kept maneuvering the canoe backward, trying to remember how Jonas and the men had handled their wild ride down to Kanaka Town. She had rowed with her father and her sisters, a merry outing on a pond near their home. But this was a matter of life and death. Every decision she made could bring danger or safety.

Eventually, the canoe slipped back over the wave break. The boar trotted at the beach edge, snorting and tossing its huge head. Jeannie began to tremble uncontrollably. She pushed back some more, making the canoe turn parallel to shore. She finally got the courage to pull at the left side of the bow and head out into open water. The canoe responded easily and soon she was free of any further danger from the boar.

She looked up at the bank. "Help," she shouted. But the only answer was the call of a crow that flew from one branch to another in a gnarled madrone tree. The boar stood on the beach as if stupefied, its legs spread. It stopped to lick at the shaft, then looked back at Jeannie. There was no way she could return to the shore there. Her only hope was go out along the rugged shoreline and find a new landing place. She resumed paddling, remembering to switch sides as she pulled.

The canoe had no keel and she wondered for what purpose it had been carved out of a cedar log. But it did move smoothly once under way. Soon she was free of the pull of the shore and out in the channel.

Surely, there is another inlet of some sort, she thought. The shoreline, however, seemed to grow in height and forest, the beaches shrinking down to ribbons of pebbles and driftwood. Eventually, there was nothing. Only the cold water of the channel and the islands across it slowly falling under mist. The sun was not coming out today.

No one took alarm at the Royal Marine Camp until Jeannie was missed at the noonday meal. After Dr. Parker sent his steward down to inquire about her whereabouts, Gilly learned that she had gone out for a ride earlier in the morning. A couple of marines volunteered to go find her, but when they returned they had no news of her.

"Oh, Jeannie. Where are you?" Gilly said. She plopped down on the parlor settee, handkerchief at hand, then immediately jumped back up. She didn't dare look at her husband who was studying his pocket watch. She knew by the way the whiskers in his mutton shops quivered that was disturbed.

"Thomas, did Mr. Hollins say they will extend their search?"

Parker snapped the watch shut. "A mounted party is going out now."

Gilly cleared her throat. "I'm sure there is some explanation. She has always stayed close to the camp. Always says where she is going. You don't suppose one of the men... I heard some marines deserted for the gold mines on the Fraser River again."

Parker harrumphed. "No one would dare. She is our guest and your particular friend. Perhaps she has had a minor accident. She will be found." The doctor sighed. "I sometimes forget that she is young despite the hard life lessons she has experienced. I suppose she feels constrained and seeks adventure."

"She doesn't mean to cause trouble. She is just trying to find solid ground after the death of her little boy," Gilly said.

"Her uncle hopes she will meet someone and marry. That would give her solid ground." Dr. Parker froze when they heard steps were heard rushing up to the porch. When he opened the door, a young marine stood out outside.

"Beg pardon, sir. The search party has returned."

"Oh, thank goodness," Gilly said. "You found Mrs. Naughton."

The marine stood at attention and cleared his throat. "No, ma'am. I'm afraid I have rather bad news. They found no sign of the lady, but they did find her horse. It's dead, its legs torn to ribbons. They believe that the horse and rider were attacked, and possibly killed by a boar they found a mile away. Someone had speared it."

Gilly stepped back against her husband. She felt faint.

"Will you go again? Dr. Parker asked as he steadied her.

"Most of the search party is still out, but the weather is turning for the worse. A storm is coming."

TIMONS

Jeannie jolted awake to splatter on her cheek. She hadn't realized she had drifted off. After paddling for what she felt was hours, she could barely keep her eyes open. Instead of staying close to the shore, her canoe had been pulled out by a receding tide. Soon she discovered that the canoe that saved her from the boar had also put her in peril. It could not maintain any direction without constant paddling, yet the tide still swept her toward the small set of islands across the channel. If she didn't take care she would be pulled out into the larger channel, the Haro Strait. At one point she saw the distant sail of a schooner, but it disappeared behind the rising bank of fog.

Jeannie arched her back. She felt cold all over and having lost her shawl in her tumble to the beach she had no cover for her shoulders. She knew she had to get to land soon or she could die from exposure. "Heaven help me," she prayed and with that, resumed her paddling.

After fifteen minutes of paddling and straightening out her direction, the canoe came within the shadow of the closest island. A veil of mist skirted the cedar trees up on the hill, but it was clear on the small rocky beach below. She aimed her landing there, hoping that the canoe would hold steady enough for her to get out and pull it up on shore.

As she came closer, the waves rocked the canoe from bow to stern. She stabbed the paddle into the crystal-clear water to pull it through and eventually struck pebbles underneath. She was almost there. She stabbed again with what was left of her strength. The canoe shot forward and hit the beach, throwing her to her knees against the bow.

For a moment she braced herself, her arms shaking. She wanted to cry, but she was not out of danger yet. She needed to get on dry land, though by the looks of the thickening mist, damp land was more like it. She looked back from where she had come and found San Juan Island had disappeared, covered in fog. She pushed down the flutter of panic and concentrated on getting out of the canoe without falling into the water. She straightened out her torn skirt and petticoats and staying low, carefully put a leg over the gunwale and stepped onto the pebbly beach. Her foot was immediately drenched by a cold wave coming in. She gritted her teeth and holding onto the bobbing canoe, clambered out. Once up on solid beach, clear of the waves, she collapsed against a huge stump with white-washed roots.

I did it, she thought. *I'm alive.* She burst into hot tears of exhaustion exploding against the eerie silence of the cold gray wilderness. The past hours of terror passed before her: the empty grounds of Farseeing, the attack of the boar, and the tumble down the beach head; the wounded horse's muzzle; the canoe in the channel. All a jumble. The odd scenes became mixed up with her crying over Jeremy's rain-drenched grave. His little coffin. Her skin rose with goose bumps and became cold to her touch.

I could very well join him if I don't start using my head, she thought. She sat up and rubbed her arms to get warm. *I need to make shelter but how?*

A hand touched her shoulder. "Jeannie?"

She screamed and drew deeper against the stump, then gasped when she saw Breed standing over her. For a moment she thought she was hallucinating from her long ordeal, her rescuer only her heart's prayer.

"Jonas, are you real?"

"What in tarnation are you doing here? What happened?" His

151

voice was more puzzled and concerned than angry, but its strength confused her.

For a moment, Jeannie was too numb to answer, but finally, she blurted out, "B-boar. A boar attacked me and my horse. I was thrown. My only hope was the canoe." She began to fade.

Instantly, a strong arm enfolded her shoulders and lifted her as though she was as light as a maple leaf. Breed carried her back against a rocky face where sword fern overarched like a canopy. There he pulled her against him and wrapped her in his gray blanket coat. His warmth seeped into her and made her drowsy. She stopped shivering and dozed, coming awake with a jerk. She was entrapped in the coat, leaning against Breed's chest. Disoriented, she pulled away, only to be gently pulled back.

"Shh, shh," Breed said. "You're all right. You're safe now."

"Safe," she murmured. She relaxed. Tension ebbed away from her as she nestled closer.

For a long time, they said nothing. She was aware of waves breaking on the pebbly shore, a lone seagull lost in its mission and the steady beating of Breed's heart. Gradually, she felt warmth restored to her arms and core.

Eventually Breed stirred. "Feeling better?"

Jeannie sat up and slipped out of the coat. "Yes, Jonas. Very much better." Down the beach she saw a second canoe was pulled up further down the way. *His? Is that how he found her?*

"Good. Now tell me where the boar attacked."

"At Farseeing—"

"Farseeing. What were you doing there?"

"I heard that you had been hurt in some fight."

Jonas frowned. "It was only a graze." He cocked his head at her. "All this to find me?"

"Yes." She spoke in a whisper. "I must go back."

Breed chuckled. "*Toketie.* You can't go back tonight. The fog's too dense and a wind's coming up. I'm going to take you to a shack the other side of this island. It'll shelter us from any storm that blows up."

Jeannie staggered upright. She attempted to put her hair back into order, but she only made it worse, the weight of her long hair falling away from her last remaining pins. She felt herself crumbling again, but willed herself to stand up and act sensible. She was grateful when he put his coat back on her shoulders.

He gathered his things together, putting them into a tightly woven cedar basket, then put the straps on his shoulders. He pulled up the canoes behind some large rocks and before he covered them with cedar boughs, he picked up a rifle carefully wrapped in oilcloth from his canoe. Once he gathered his paddles, he pointed the way to the forest running along the spine of the island. Jeannie was surprised to see that he was nearly barefoot, wearing some sort of fiber sandals on his feet.

It was only a short walk, but by the time they reached the shack, Jeannie was exhausted. Her arms ached from paddling and her legs were stiff. Halfway there, she took Breed's arm again. Leaning into his shoulder, she thanked the Lord that it was he who found her. She stopped long enough to look at her surroundings. The shack was a simple affair with cedar planks for its sides, split cedar shingles and a chimney that appeared to be made of sticks and clay. It had only one window, covered with a large piece of parchment.

The shack faced northeast toward the giant mountains on the mainland, half-hidden by the purple-green islands rolling in front of them. Behind them the night crept across their showy heads. Beyond that, Jeannie was too tired to really notice. Inside, Breed set a fire in a fireplace made of smooth rocks and clay. He set a cedar bolt in front of it and invited her to sit. The flames jumped after he sliced some pitch wood into the fire. They felt warm against her knees. He put a kettle of water on an iron hook hanging over the fire. "I have tea, if you like."

"That would be lovely." Jeannie looked down at her clothing.

Breed frowned, then stood up. "I'll just go outside so you can repair yourself. Just let me know when you are ready."

Once Breed was out, Jeannie firmly locked herself in. She unhooked her skirt and four petticoats and draped them next to the fire which was now roaring. Wrapped in his coat, she sat in her chemise, corset, and drawers on the cedar bolt, her ears attuned to any sound outside. She could barely keep her eyes open, but the fire soon dried the bottoms of her petticoats. She dressed quickly, then let Breed in.

Resuming her seat by the fire, Jeannie drew the coat around her and watched Breed take a tin cup and a tin box marked "TEA" from a wood box set near the fireplace. Though drowsy, she was feeling more settled now. Her teeth no longer chattered. "Where are we?"

"On a small island some call 'Tenas Wawa' because it's little and a good place to take refuge and have small talk."

"Am I far away from the Royal Marine Camp?"

"You are a bit northwest. The tide was running out." Breed smiled at her. "However you did it, you were fortunate that you landed here. I admire your skills."

"All I remember is that you told me one pulled an oar, so I stabbed and pulled." Jeannie looked down at her hands tender from holding the oar. "I did my best."

"You saved your own life. That is good enough. When you are ready, I'll lay out a mat for you," he said. "First, tea to warm you."

Several hours later, Jeannie woke to the sound of rain driving down on the cedar roof above her. At first, she forgot where was, then remembered that she had lain down on the hard floor on a horsehair mat with his coat for a blanket. Its rough horse hairs tickled her nose.

It was dark in the cabin, but when she shifted, she saw the cabin door was open. In the gloom she could make out Breed. He was smoking his pipe, the bowl occasionally glowing when he took a draw on it. He appeared to be sitting with his knees drawn up. Stiffly, she rearranged herself in the coat.

He caught the movement. "Are you all right?

What could she answer? She was embarrassed that she was still wearing his coat and he had nothing to keep away the chill of the rain.

When he made no move toward her, she gave him the answer

she thought he wanted to hear, then closed her eyes. The rain was roaring down now, making large pools in front of the shack. It brought a cool freshness to the dank cabin. Then the wind picked up and she thought she could hear the trees next to them creak. Somewhere further out, something crashed to the ground. Breed eventually shut the door, plunging them into total darkness, except for the low flames making magic lantern pictures on the mantle and walls.

In some ways it was like her first night at Kanaka Town. Jeannie was overtired from the long canoe trip then, but this time she was ever more alert to Breed. The rustle of his clothes. His soft breathing and the draw of the pipe. Feeling totally safe, she went back to sleep.

She woke to the sound of flint being struck, then an exclamation when the tinder didn't catch. There was another hit, then satisfaction as the spark caught on the char cloth. A fire was soon leaping and crackling to life. Its warmth spread all over her as though it was caressing her. She sat up. With her back to Breed, she braided her hair.

"Morning. Soon as I can, there'll be something to eat," Breed said behind her. "I've smoked salmon. Some hardtack too. Military issue. Not bad if you don't mind the possibility of weevils. I'm making coffee."

Jeannie finally turned and faced him. "What time is it?"

"About seven in the morning. I let you sleep in. I'd give you more time, but I best get you to Timons. There's probably a party out looking for you, though they can't get across the channel in this fog."

"Has it stopped raining?"

"For the moment. It could start up again. Are you cold?"

"No, I'm fine," Jeannie answered.

"*Ah-ha*. Come closer to the fire."

She obeyed without protest, glad to get warm. Breed looked rested though she doubted he slept at all last night.

"I'm sorry," she said.

"What for?"

"My foolishness. I'm sure you would rather be elsewhere."

155

Breed looked directly at her. "I don't want to be anywhere else, Mrs. King George."

~

An hour later, Jeannie followed Breed through thick trees, coming out on to a rocky beach where a loaded canoe waited. Once she settled in, he pushed off and paddled her across another open waterway. The morning was fogged in. The air was sharp and moist. It was hard to identify anything in any direction. She was confused.

"Where are we now?"

"About three miles northeast of Farseeing."

Jeannie shivered. "I can't see anything. Will it lift?"

"Hard to say. Do something for me." Jeannie complied and took the other paddle from the bottom of the canoe as instructed. On command, he told her how to hold it and steer in the front.

About ten minutes later, the gray outline of shoreline appeared to them. Breed turned the canoe so that it followed well away from the beach, but Jeannie could make out the rusty trunks of madrone growing on the steep sides of the island that rose above it.

"Keep going," Breed said. "We've a little ways to go."

A little ways turned out to be another fifteen minutes, then the canoe cut across an open space and Jeannie realized that they were at the mouth of a deep cove. Breed guided them in and then jumped out to pull the canoe onto the shore. When it was on land, he said, "Nobody home."

"I thought you lived alone," Jeannie said as she awkwardly got out of the canoe. One of her feet had fallen asleep. Breed gave her his hand, lifting her to dry ground. She brushed down her skirt, her hand catching on a large tear in the cloth. It neatly folded down like a page in a book, exposing her petticoats underneath. Oh dear, she thought. I'm in tatters.

"Most times. Sometimes Kaui comes through with his extended family. And there's a traditional salting station for salmon on the northern side. People can camp for weeks."

"Do Americans come?"

"Rarely. Until a year ago the only white people around here were HBC people on San Juan Island at Belle Vue Farm. Griffin, the manager, has always been well prepared. I've stayed with him a few times." He shouldered the bulk of the gear and then led the way up a steep trail to the top of a wooded ridge. A rugged handrail gave some support. Sandstone cliffs jutted out one side, pocked by wind. A grove of madrone leaned out over them like a figurehead. When she reached the top, she saw a small cabin in the shelter of the trees.

What a difference from the rude shack of last night, she thought. His dwelling was neatly constructed of four-inch-thick cedar boards, fitted together by dovetailing the corners. Its shingled roof was doubled at its bottom and peak with a brick chimney. Adding to its elegance were windows with sashes.

Breed stood outside the solid fir door. "Do you like it?"

"Oh, yes, Jonas. Where on earth did you get the windows and brick?"

"Windows came from Victoria in trade. Bricks are ballast. They're good enough."

What a pretty place, she thought. And another intriguing piece to the puzzle named Jonas Breed. When she stepped inside, she began to imagine herself here.

The one room cabin was as neat and cozy as the captain's galley she had visited on her voyage from San Francisco to Victoria. There were floor to ceiling shelves packed with books, a simple rope bed with an orderly pile of blankets stamped with HBC on it, a table covered in charts with one chair fashioned out of alder branches to service it. A bearskin rug without its head and woven rugs scattered across the fir plank floor. A simple cast-iron stove with a barrel oven on its side stood on the windowless side of the room. An oil lantern rigged from the rafter hung over the table. Handmade rugs hung on the walls too, but they were of a design that she hadn't seen before—ovoid patterns of birds and bears in blacks, reds and faint turquoise.

"It's quite grand here."

Breed harrumphed. "Comfortable. Even in a storm." When she

157

rubbed her arms, he promised to set a fire in the cook stove. "I'll make you something hot. Please, sit." He offered her the chair, handing her a blanket, but Jeannie asked if she could look at his books.

He nodded that she could, then went about building a fire in the stove. Jeannie surveyed the titles on the bookcase. She was surprised at their depth. She pulled out one of them, a book of sonnets by Elizabeth Barrett Browning.

Breed looked up from his stove. "Do you like that one?"

"I do indeed."

"Keep it for your own."

"May I? Thank you. You have so many books here."

"Does that surprise you? I learned to read at an early age at the mission in Honolulu. My father and my foster father, Captain Godfrey, had many books aboard their ships. I remember liking *Robinson Crusoe* as a boy. After having actually been stranded, though, I can't say that it is my favorite any longer. As for my reading education, it came abruptly to an end at thirteen years of age and I started a new round of studies. These books are some I've rescued over the years." Breed stood up.

Jeannie didn't know how to answer. She knew he was talking about his capture. "How long have you lived here?"

"Since '55. Came first with a tent and then put this up."

"Who made the rugs?"

Breed pointed to the large one near his bed. "That one is Salish. The rest are from the north—Haida and Tlingit. They have mountain goat wool in them and cedar warp," Breed explained. "They are highly prized by the Indian peoples here. The one on the wall is even more special. It's very old. They used *ske-xe* wool."

"Skay-heh?"

"Dogs. Little woolly white ones."

Breed quickly prepared a meal of cabbage, onions and a slice of bacon, then set tin plates of food and a coffeepot on the table.

"Come, make yourself at home." Breed sat on a canvas camp stool next to her. "Eat up. I'm sure you are starved."

"Oh, Jonas. You have no idea. I haven't eaten real food in a day."

They ate quietly. At one point, she reached over and took his hand. "Thank you for saving me."

He squeezed her hand. "I think you saved yourself.

"But if you hadn't been there..."

"If you like, you can mend that skirt of yours. I have a housewife."

"Housewife?"

Breed laughed. "Mending kit. Every *shipman* and soldier has a housewife." He pointed to the cook stove. "If you need to, you can dry your outer clothes at the same time. All that fog."

When she flushed, he leaned in. "I'm no dangler, Mrs. King George. I don't give a young lady divers attention and false sentiments then take advantage of them. I'll be out. I need to collect wood."

The meal over and the dishes cleared from the table, Breed brought over a sandalwood box with carvings of fanciful birds and vines on its lid and sides. Inside were trinkets and a rectangular cloth bundle with twill tape to bind it. "My housewife," he said. He unfolded it. Inside, pins and needles were stuck in the cloth. A brass thimble and various colored threads wrapped around pasteboard in a pocket.

He set the thimble on the table. "This was my mother's. It was lost to me for a number of years, but when I came back from Haida Gwaii, a friend at the mission in Honolulu returned it to me."

She picked it up. "How lovely, Jonas." Lovely indeed. She wished she wasn't estranged from her mother. She would give anything to have something of hers.

"Well, then. Let's set to work."

Once Breed left and the closed door, Jeannie undid her skirt, draped her damp bodice next to the stove which Breed had pumped up. Sitting on Breed's camp stool, she took needle and thread from the housewife and set to work on the torn skirt. She worked quickly worried Breed would come back soon. She was fully dressed when Breed knocked and asked to come in.

"You may, Jonas. I'm ready." She threw the blanket over her shoulders and wrapped it tight.

Breed came in with a load of wood and stacked it by the stove. He stood up. His eyes lit up as he surveyed the mended skirt. Breed came close, making her skin tingle. She felt her face blush.

He cocked his head. "Are you alright?"

"I'm fine." But Jeannie didn't feel fine. She felt out of sorts. A strange rush of desire made her feel exposed. "Very well, I'm not fine. I feel—so foolish to put you to all this trouble. That you might laugh at me"

He took her hand. Skin to skin, it felt like sparks from a fire. "I would never laugh at a woman who came after me in a canoe."

"The boar compelled me."

"Then I'm eternally grateful to that side of ham." He tenderly adjusted the blanket that had slipped from her shoulder. *"Toketie,"* he said.

Jeannie didn't know what it meant but her heart started to pound. She wondered if he could see it beating out of her breast. She was floating, aware only of her breathing as her shoulders rose and fell against his hands. She closed her eyes when he kissed her cheek.

Jeannie laughed and sighed. "I think you are dangling with me, sir."

"Ah-ha."

"Jonas." He was maddeningly close, smelling of wood smoke, cedar and the wild things she loved about him.

He took her hands again. His fingers caressed hers. "I know you are stiff from yesterday, but it's best to work it out early on. You'll feel better in the end. Would you like to see my island?"

Jeannie nodded yes.

On the beach below, Breed built a fire and showed her how a plank of cedar could be bent into a box with four sides by cutting kerfs into it at strategic places and steaming them, bend the wood over the cuts. It was held together with wooden pegs and tar pitch. Then he brought out coned shaped baskets and put in bait. "For the crabs to eat," he said. He rolled up his pants and walked into the water to set them. Back on shore, he worked around the fire for a bit.

Jeannie sat on a rock, his Hudson's Bay Company blanket wrapped around her shoulders like the best paisley shawl. The air was moist and alive. They were utterly socked in, like they were the only people left on earth.

"Would you like to go for a walk, Jeannie? We might find a sun break."

"I should like it very much." She took his hand. The cove was still socked in, but on the northeastern side, they did find sun and could see over to another island lying like a humpback whale in the water. He explained that it was the beginning of the next round of islands going north. They belonged to the Colony of British Columbia and were not disputed. He sniffed the wind for direction, then pointed out the location of other islands and named them by what he knew of their plants and animals. Then the fog closed them in again. There was no sound except for the steady cadence of the surf and the muffled cry of seabirds finding their way across the fog-bound water.

In the shelter of madrone trees, they sat down on a blanket on the beach.

"Comfortable?" he asked.

"Yes, Jonas. It's so peaceful here. It's like we're peeking out a window into a different world, then the shutters closed."

"But it's nothing like Haida Gwaii." He looked off into the distance and began to tell her of his time in the north. "The Queen Charlottes, as they are known here, are forested islands with a thousand miles of coves and inlets each with great beauty and mystery. They have enormous, ancient trees. Moss so deep you sink into it up to your knees." His descriptions were fantastic, a world and place that she could not even imagine. He told of villages above the beaches with their tall, standing totem poles forty inches thick and forty feet high, carved with such animals as hooked-nosed eagles and bears eating frogs, exquisite beings sprung out of a fertile, imaginative mind and spirit. He spoke of potlatches—great giveaways of wealth and status—and shamans on spirit journeys, families working and gathering together; the birth of a baby and the death of an elder. "As a youth there, I would travel with my master and his family to different gatherings or work."

"Was it hard, that life as a—captive?"

"Ah-ha. But my master was much kinder to me than my first. My original capturer didn't care if I lived or died and was glad to get rid of me in trade. I was young and scrawny as a twig." Breed picked up a pebble and rolled it between his fingers. "My new master spoke some English. I think he was curious about my stories about the sea beyond their sea. By the time I was fifteen, he allowed me to sleep inside the door to the big house. He taught me how to make canoes and gave me more freedom in the village when I showed I was eager to learn. I had been at sea so young, they admired my sea craft, something they know so well."

"You have a great affection for the place and the people," Jeannie said. "You speak as if you regret leaving. How could you when you were a captive?"

Breed shrugged. "I think they grew on me—their art, their seamanship, the people themselves. I wanted to earn their respect. When I asked, they let me go."

"What about the older man with you? Seeks?"

"Sikhs?"

"Yes," she smiled. "I'm sorry. I'm afraid that I cannot quite get my tongue around the names of people and things here."

Breed made a clicking sound in the back of his throat. Another sound reminded Jeannie of rushing wind. "You have to get your tongue just so." He smiled. "Sikhs is from across Haro Strait. He is an old friend, more like a father than anything. He was the first to accept me when I came here and from the beginning has been my teacher. It is an honor for me because he is a respected elder and wise man among the Songhees and S'Klallam." Breed grinned. "For some reason he tolerates me. I'm much too slow for him."

"I rather think he believes that you are a very fine man."

"Humpf," Breed said. After that, the stories stopped and they returned to the beach below the cabin.

"Thank you, Jonas, for this day," she said as she sat on a log near the fire pit. "How do you say 'thank you' in the Chinook jargon?"

"Mahsie," Breed said as he built the fire back up.

"Maw-sy. Such a surprising, wonderful day. Normally, on a day like this, I would have taken a book and sat by the fire. Or mended. You've shown me a different way."

Breed's head was bent, but she knew he smiled. She handed him some driftwood near her, then got up and looked for pieces of cedar, which ignited better. Soon he had a strong fire going. He told her to fill the bentwood cooking box partway with water, then taking off his shirt and rolling up his pant legs again, waded out to the baskets.

She had turned for just a moment to pick up the water-tight basket when he left a loud "Aurgh!" Breed slipped on the smooth rocks and went down on his back. Jeannie got up in horror, but Breed came up soaking wet and laughing. In his hand, he held the ropes to the baskets. His long dark hair was plastered to his head, dripping on his broad shoulders. There were goose bumps on the solid muscles of his chest. Most of all, his deep blue eyes were alive with a joy she would always remember.

"Jeannie," Breed said, dragging his catch with him. "Where is my water?"

She snapped out of her daze and apologized. She finished filling the box a few inches deep as he instructed. He squatted next to her and added hot cooking stones from the fire with a pair of tongs split from slim cedar planks. Each time one hit the water, sizzling clouds of white steam rose around his arms. He arranged them around the wall of the box and soon the water was boiling, giving off the smell of fish and clams lingering from a past meal. He put the crabs in, then laid some cedar planks on top of the box for a lid to hold them down. Finally, he dried himself off with a piece of wool blanket, but not before she saw the long red gash on his upper arm.

"Is this what Krill did to you?" She traced the long red line with her fingers.

"Yes. And the reason you came looking for me. *Mahsie*, Krill." He sat down by the fire his leg touching hers. "You all right?"

"I am. I thought you hit your head."

"No, I'm fine." He ran his fingers through the wet tangles and squeezed some water out.

"You won't catch cold? You haven't worn shoes all day."

"Nah." He took a stick and lifting a plank, pushed a crab back down into the water and held it down. When he was done, he picked up the blanket scrap and ruffled his hair with it.

Jeannie stayed quiet, but it was hard suppressing her desire to dry his hair with her hands. "You are the first man I've met who wears his hair long. Most men I have seen wear their hair short—except for Captain Pickett. It seems the fashion of the day."

"I wear it so because I am free. Only slaves wear their hair short, so the people will know their servitude and position. This way I say to everyone I am no *mistchimas*. My status has changed."

"Oh." Jeannie would not have had guessed that. She brushed down her ragged mourning clothes, wishing she were free of the troubles that forced her to leave England.

Breed checked on the crabs. "You eat crabs before?" he asked.

"Not like this," she answered.

"When you are done, you say *mahsie*. In spring time, the first salmon caught is honored so that the spirit of the salmon will come again."

"I thought you didn't believe, Jonas."

He smiled at her. "I believe in many things. Don't you give thanks before you eat?"

"Yes."

"Well, then." Breed put the lid back on and sat back on his haunches. He tapped his stick into the dirt near the fire. Jeannie looked at his left hand. At the base of it near the wrist there was a tattoo she had never noticed before. It was brown and black.

"What is that design?"

"An orca. Killer whale. It's eating a seal. See? Mouth of orca here, head and flipper of the seal there."

"Did you do that?"

"No, it was forced on me."

She noticed another tattoo on his left ankle. It was an eagle sprung from the fantastic imagination of a native artist. "The other too?"

"No." Breed looked down at his foot. "I had that done. To honor my *tyee*'s family."

"Did it hurt?"

"Not like this." He turned his right wrist over. Underneath there were some scars made from burns. "There is a game boys play—how long you can hold a red hot cinder on your skin. I wasn't going to let anyone beat me."

"They look terrible."

"Not as bad as Kaui's. He was burned pretty badly, but he didn't make a sound."

Jeannie touched the scar and circled it with her fingers. For some reason, it made her feel sad. Her eyes began to well up.

"Jeannie, what is it?"

She shrugged. "I don't know. You went through so much as a boy. I can't imagine. Yet you seem whole. You go on." Jeannie swallowed. A tear strayed down. "I have a scar too. Only I have never shown it."

"Where is it?"

She put her wrist against his scar. "I can't say. You can't see it, but it's a scar nonetheless."

"Maybe someday you will show it to me."

Breed lifted the lid off the box and poked one of the crabs. Gingerly, he lifted it out by its large claw, but it was bright orange and cooked. He laid it into a tin plate and poured cold water over it to clean off any remaining sand. He poured the water off and took out his knife. In no time, he had split the crab open and the meat separated. He repeated the process with the other crabs, then they sat down on rocks to eat. This time he had drink other than water—a bottle of wine.

"Dr. Parker gave this to me at the races. Some naval officer left it." He poured some into a tin cup. "Here. It will take away the chill of the hour."

Jeannie sampled it; a red wine, surprisingly good. She handed it back to Breed who drank a mouthful. He sat back on a rock and picked at a crab leg. The cove was peaceful. There was a sun break. Evening sun. She could see across to the other side where there were more cliffs and trees. Out in the passage, the fog was lifting too, exposing the blue-gray top of the next large island to the south.

165

They stayed there until nightfall. Breed had dried out more or less and had put his shirt back on. It was chilly out, but neither really wanted to go up. It might be clear tomorrow and they knew that she must go back. She sensed that he wanted the day to go on just as she did. They sat by the fire and shared more stories about each other.

"Where is this place you come from?" he asked.

"It's to the southwest of London. My family lives near the sea."

"Why don't you ever speak of them?"

"You didn't ask. My life was rather tame, really. My father was involved in shipping. I was the second youngest of five girls. A rather frivolous world now that I think about it—dances at the assembly rooms, walks in the park of the nearby manor—but I was happy. We were schooled at home in the female arts, though I enjoyed the accounting books my father kept and learned to help him."

"Then you met Captain Naughton."

"Then I met Captain Naughton." Jeannie abruptly changed the subject. She began to talk about the most self-important people she knew at either the British and American camps. Breed joined in. The talk became light again.

"Captain Pickett is quite a study," Jeannie said. "When he walks into a room, a cologne I just can't quite name always seems to follow him. At the dance, he was absolutely bathed in it."

"Jamaican Rum. Good bear bait. They'd smell him a mile away."

"But I rather like the way Captain Pickett speaks. He makes ordinary words sound gallant."

They talked for a bit more on the subject of who was the most self-important person at either of the military camps. The wine began to disappear, Breed having drunk a good portion of it. Once, as he put another load of wood on the fire, he brushed against her coat. When he was finished with the fire, he sat back on the log and looked at her.

"You are *hyas toketie*, Jeannie Naughton," he murmured. "*Hyas toketie*." He thoughtfully tossed a pebble in his hand, then leaned over and kissed her full on the mouth. Gently, but firmly, Jeannie pushed him away.

"Please. Don't spoil it," she whispered, then pulled the coat as tight as she could as though it would give her protection from further action on his part.

"Forgive me," he said. "You know I would never hurt or shame you."

"I know."

"You know I care for you."

Jeannie nodded.

"Well, then."

A thick, heavy presence grew between them. Breed sat up. Jeannie shrank back.

"Are you afraid of me now?" he asked.

Jeannie looked directly at him. "No. I'm not afraid of you. I just think you have had rather too much wine."

"Maybe so." The firelight made gold patches on his face. It caught his eyes and she was surprised to see that they were glistening. "But, you are *kloshe tum tum* to me. You have grown on me. I will always care for you." He kissed her lightly on her forehead, then stood up and lit a tin lantern. "Take this and go sleep in the cabin. Everything is inside. Blankets, water. It's going to warm up tonight. Be more natural weather. I'll stay with the fire. You need not fear me. I'll sleep with the crabs."

He helped her up and pointed the way to the stairway. "Jonas—"

Jeannie felt sick. She wanted to say that she loved him, that it would be alright if he held and caressed her. But if she said she loved him, she'd have to tell him the truth about her scar. With love there must always be truth, but she couldn't bring herself to say it. Not yet. Because she didn't know how to tell him the truth about Captain Harry Marsfield's demise and all the things that went with it.

Jeannie did not see Breed until the next day when he came up and said that the passage would clear by afternoon. They would go then. He fixed breakfast for her and was polite and friendly, but avoided any mention of what had happened the night before. Jeannie would have liked to tell him that she was not upset with him, but she never got a chance. As soon as the dishes were put away, he asked if she didn't mind if he went down to the beach where he needed to tend to the canoe and some gear before they left. Jeannie let him go with a nod. She would set the cabin to rights.

Jeannie was outside sweeping the steps when she heard voices cutting through the mist. Going to the edge of the hill, she saw two high-browed canoes like tall-disembodied spirits suddenly appear out of the morning mist. They were filled with native men and a few women wearing conical cedar hats and blankets of exotic designs like in Breed's cabin. The men were either bare-chested or wore European-style clothing and held their paddles tip up while two others got out and secured the canoes. Jeannie quickly counted fourteen people.

One of the men helped a beautiful woman with long black hair out of her canoe. She was taller than the other women in the party. Wrapped in a Chilkat robe with fanciful designs in black and red, she carried herself like an aristocrat, with pieces of silver jewelry on her person and ears and vermilion paint in the part of her hair.

Suddenly Breed appeared on the shore. When the woman saw him, she raised both her hands to him and smiled. Breed seemed pleased to see her, though when he spoke to her in her tongue he sounded to Jeannie like he was scolding her. The woman laughed, her voice like a throaty bell. When she moved, the fringe on the robe swayed. Breed greeted the men with his hands palms up, moving them like he was weighing something. The men laughed and patted him on his back. They conversed several minutes before he invited them to sit down on the logs and rocks. He started to build them a fire.

For a moment, Jeannie stayed hidden, not sure what to do. Then she remembered what she had learned during her time at Kanaka Town: guests were always fed. She wasn't sure what Breed had in his cabin, but she knew where he kept his coffee pot and coffee beans.

Slipping away, she went back to the cabin. After filling the pot with water from his well, she put hardtack, coffee beans, coffee grinder, and a can of peaches into a basket and went down to greet them.

At the edge of the stairs, Jeannie paused. Down below, the fire was roaring. One of them had threaded salmon through sticks. The woman was sitting off to the side on the same rock Jeannie had sat the night before, laughing and chatting with Breed. Jeannie knew that she had done the right thing when he spotted her and smiled.

"Jeannie," was all he said. When she was down, he introduced her. Though they spoke no English, they welcomed her with open palms and chatter. Between introductions, Breed explained that they were Haida from the north, come down for trade and recreation. When he introduced her to the woman, he showed a particular deference.

"This is Shells Shining. It's the closest version of her name in English I can come up with. She and her retainers are from my former master's house."

"*Klahowya*," Jeannie said, not knowing what else to say.

"*Klahowya*," the woman said. Up close, Shells Shining's eyes were dark brown like a chestnut. Her cheekbones were high, but her round face was smooth as a skipping stone. On her lower lip was a labret about the size of a twenty-five cent piece. The plug was covered with abalone. Jeannie had learned that it was a sign of a high-ranking woman. Shell Shining's dark eyes were friendly, but seemed to appraise her intensely. Jeannie tried to relax, but felt she was seen as a rival.

They stayed down with the party all morning, Jeannie playing hostess to whatever Breed asked. Preparing the coffee as Breed had taught her at Kanaka Town, she roasted the coffee beans in a pan on the fire, ground them in his coffee grinder and threw them into the boiling coffee pot along with a slice of greed alder. When the coffee was done, she served the group using the china and tin cups they had with them. That seemed to warm the Haida to her, including Shells Shining. Once again, Jeannie was reminded that out here there was a different society from her home in England, but somehow more and meaningful.

At noon, the fog suddenly lifted. It revealed a bright, sunny day. As if on cue, the Haida took down their cattail and canvas shelters and loaded their canoes. When they were ready, they came to Breed and Jeannie with their hands raised.

"Hows dang king say," Jeannie thought she heard them say as they crowded around Jeannie and Breed. She assumed it was some sort of goodbye or well wishing.

Breed said something back. He shook hands with lead paddler, then helped Shells Shining into the canoe. As the canoe got underway, Shells Shining turned back to him and waved.

After they left, Breed put out the fire.

"Time to go, Jeannie. We must make use of the clearing weather." He straightened up and looked directly at her. "*Mahsie* for coming down," he said softly. "It was a fine thing you did."

They packed up the canoe and quietly headed back toward San Juan Island. Whatever disappointment Breed felt about Jeannie's rejection of him the day before seemed to have gone away. He showed her how to use the paddle again and pointed out features of the islands and the people who had lived there among them. By the time they came around the west side of San Juan Island to the Royal Marine Camp, their friendship was restored and in its proper place. When they came into Garrison Bay, the stars were out twinkling as brightly as a million campfires. It would be forever embedded in her mind: the islands like black forested bowler hats upon the water and Jonas at the back steering the canoe.

Even when she thought him shriveled up in his grave and gone to bones.

PROPOSAL

On the day of her return to the Royal Marine Camp, Uncle Archie greeted her in a state of disarray and angst. Jeannie soon learned that on the first afternoon of her disappearance, her poor horse had been found dead up on the prairie trying to make its way home. The marines immediately gave alarm, especially when they found turkey buzzards feeding on a boar with a staff in its flank. The puzzle of her vanishing only worsened. The search for Jeannie focused.

Uncle Archie became equally focused. She had never seen him in such a state, not even after Jeremy's passing. Soon after she arrived, he was scolding her in the privacy of the Parker's parlor.

"What were ye thinking, lass? Gallivanting across the countryside. Are ye out of your mind?"

"Uncle."

Uncle Archie put up his hand. "I'm not finished. I came immediately when ye didn't show up the first night. Thought the very worse, consider finding your horse dead, legs slashed to ribbons, and a boar with shaft stickin' out of its haunch." Uncle Archie sniffed, his eyes watering.

"The poor horse," she said under her breath, but Uncle Archie had gone on with his lecture. He sniffed again, his eyes watering.

Removing her wrap, Jeannie laid it on the settee. She thought, *It's now or never to make my case.* Uncle Archie was certainly torn between being angry with her and wanting to show his joy that she was found. She took his hands and decided to tell him everything. When she was done, he pulled her into his arms.

"Dinna ye know, I love ye lass? What if ye had drowned or the boar killed y'?" He rocked her bit, then let go, shaking his finger at her. "This is not Toronto or Christchurch, England for that matter. Ye are in a wilderness with wild things and a society that is small and as gossipy as a pack of crows. Kanaka Town, now this. Your past is hidden only so much. Should ye be exposed, it could hurt any chance of happiness. You were reckless going off."

"I promise you, I have done nothing shameful. And Mr. Breed was a gentleman."

Jeannie turned away when she said that, remembering how close she came to letting him have her.

"He's like any other man, though I thank him a thousand times for finding ye and bringing ye back. Ye can't go off without broadcasting your purpose. Did ye not chase after him to seek some attachment? And what are his intentions?"

Jeannie arranged her skirt and sat down. "He didn't say, but I think he loves me."

"Think?" Uncle Archie thundered. "He made no proposal?" His muttonchops puffed out like a bird's feathered cheeks.

Jeannie flushed remembering how Breed had kissed her. She had been in danger of returning it.

"No."

Uncle Archie glowered and stamped his cane on the floor. He shook his head, then with heavy shoulders, sighed. "There's too much talk about this already."

"I love him, Uncle," Jeannie said in a steady voice. "I heard that he was injured and only sought to find out how he fared. I only intended to see him at the Farseeing lime works and then come home. I didn't expect I would be fighting for my life with a pig and tossed on the sea in a canoe."

Uncle Archie frowned, then sat down next to her. "Then let us hope that he gives you an offer. He *must* give you an offer." He drummed his fingers on his knee. "It's the only way to save your reputation."

Jeannie grew quiet and twisted her fingers together. "I would love nothing more than his offer of marriage. He was so kind to me after Jeremy died. And so attentive to my opinions. But I don't know how to tell him about Captain Marsfield. How will I undo the lie?"

"Oh, I see. Yes, of course, of course." Her uncle looked downcast. He leaned on his cane. "I have to tell him, Uncle." She sighed. "But in telling him, I could lose him."

Uncle Archie patted her hand. "Aye. That is the very pickle we always have envisioned. But it must be done. The truth will out, they say."

~

"So what did she say?" Collie asked Breed as they threw brush on the bonfire. Along with Sikhs and Doc-tin they were clearing a quarter acre around the hastily put up shack Doc-tin was claiming. It was about a mile south from the English Camp.

"Who? Shells Shining?"

"No. Mrs. Naughton." Collie froze in his tracks and frowned. "When did you see the Haida woman?"

"The other day. They were coming through."

"To cause mischief or to say hello?"

Sikhs looked up, his body stiff with tension. Breed answered carefully, for the Haida and Songhees sometimes fought if someone took offense. The Haida were foreigners and raiders from the north who took slaves and goods from local people, though they often came down to work at British and American sawmills. Then they were perfectly peaceable.

"They were late coming through as it was the end of the anniversary of her husband's walking into the forest."

Collie threw a big alder branch onto the fire. Its sparks rose high above the trees. "You're a sentimental bastard. I don't know why you continue to meet with them."

"Maybe I am still a part of their household. I am certainly their friend."

"Bah." Doc-tin spat, pushing his wire rimmed glasses back on his nose. "Those northern Indians will ever be friends of mine. Not with Jacob being murdered, and them taking his head."

"Wrong people, Doc-tin," Breed said. "The people you speak of were from a place called Kake." Sikhs walked around the crackling bonfire, his bare feet muddy. The rains had stopped since Breed got back from Timons, but the ground was still drying out. Another day of sunshine would finish it.

"Be careful, Jo-nuss. I don't trust them."

"I'm careful, though there is no danger to my head."

"They cause trouble all the time," Sikhs grumbled.

Breed clapped him on the shoulder. "Not this time."

Collie dragged another branch over and with Breed's help, tossed it on the fire. He brushed his hands together to knock off some lichen. "You haven't answered my question. What did Mrs. Naughton say?"

"What are you, my wet nurse?"

Doc-tin laughed. "Nosy wet nurse."

"I never asked her."

"What kind of suitor are you?" Doc-tin drew on his pipe.

Breed wondered himself. She was so much on his mind lately that Collie said he was wont to fall into tomfoolery. Without asking, Breed knew Jeannie cared for him, but maybe she was beyond his reach.

Breed shrugged. His voice trailed off when he spoke. "I really don't know." Maybe he'd never know.

THE GO-BETWEEN

"Jeannie, dear. There is a young lad here to see you. He says that he is a friend." Gilly stood in the bedroom doorway with a book in hand. She had been napping.

Jeannie looked up from her needlework. "Where is he?"

"In the kitchen."

Jeannie went back to the small area where a stove was kept for plain cooking and heating. A few cupboards and clothing pegs finished out the space. As she opened the back door, she came face-to-face with Kapihi, Kaui Kalama's boy. He was a wild little thing, but she could see the care his mother took in dressing him in his knickers and an old linen shirt. His brown feet were bare. Jeannie was sure he had grown an inch since she last saw him.

"*Klahowya*, Kapihi. Are you enjoying the hot weather?"

The boy nodded solemnly, then leaped into what must have been rehearsed. "Come," he said. "My father's *kahpo* says that you must come."

"Mr. Breed?"

"*Ah-ha.*"

"And if I don't?" she asked, amused. She had never been commanded before.

"Jo-nuss will be very cross. And very sad. He has *hyas* love for you. He regards you very high."

"He has told you this?"

Kapihi shook his head, no. "But he didn't have to. He *kiawali sick.* Love, love in his eyes and talk." The boy rolled his head and body from side to side like he was seasick with love.

Jeannie suppressed the urge to giggle. "Then I suppose I must go."

She went back into the parlor. "Gilly, I'm going for a walk with a little friend from Kanaka Town. He has news of his father, the one I attended." Jeannie put her light shawl over her shoulders and put on her lace gloves.

"Do you think you can manage that? You will not get set upon by wild beasts again?" Gilly's voice sounded amused, but her eyes betrayed some concern.

"No, I think I am quite safe. I have my waist watch. I'll be very careful. We'll just walk up to the top of the military road."

"Very good. Do remember that we dine with company this evening."

Jeannie pinned on her straw hat and went out the front door. Off to her left, Kapihi waited. What did Breed call him? *Kolohe.* It meant rascal in Hawaiian. Breed said his double cowlick at the back of his head proved it.

"Which way are we going?" Jeannie asked.

"This way." Kapihi took her hand and guided her to a trail that took off into the wooded outcropping behind the bungalows. After a short ways it connected to the road.

The day was hot, almost humid, the kind Uncle Archie told her was the area's deepest secret—that summers here were pure heaven— little rain and skies that were clear and blue. A constant breeze kept the temperatures even.

As they walked or rather as Jeannie walked because Kapihi skipped and turned as they went up the road, the boy shared news of his parents and how everyone knew that Jeannie fought off a boar with big tusks and pulled a canoe across the water all by herself.

"My Papa Kaui say you make one good *klootsman.*"

Jeannie stopped and laughed. There was that jargon word again. *What does it mean?* "Where is Mr. Breed, Kapihi?"

"He's not far."

Jeannie looked across the forested road that now turned toward the southern end of the island where the Americans were encamped. There was no sign of him. Kapihi crossed in front of her and disappeared into a hedge of thimbleberries. When she didn't follow, he poked his head out.

"Come Missus Jeannie. Jo-nuss is up here."

Jeannie pushed aside the bushes. Behind them a trail led up through a lane of lush summer greens. Kapihi hopped ahead, pushing aside the velvety leaves as though he was swimming. Jeannie followed. Unsnagging her hat and shawl on the shrubs, she finally came out into a clearing surrounded by Gerry oak, conifer and fern. Breed was waiting.

Jeannie stopped to catch her breath, laying a hand on her breast. But she was not out of breath from the hike up the hill, but from the flurry of emotions and desire he stirred in her after an absence of several days.

"*Klahowya*, Jeannie. I wasn't sure if you'd come," Breed said as he stood up. "I didn't want to cause more gossip showing up at the Parkers. There's been enough." He turned to Kapihi. "*Mahsie, ow.* Could you skedaddle now and watch the road?"

"*Hee hee.*" Kapihi backed down towards the bushy path. "You *kiawali sick.*"

"Skedaddle. Get going." Breed grinned as the boy laughed and disappeared into the thimbleberry wall. The leaves continued to tremble after he left. He turned back to her. "I was afraid you wouldn't come after my behavior on the beach. I did drink too much, I'm afraid. I apologize again."

"You are forgiven."

Breed smiled at that, his face full of relief. He seemed to weigh his words before he spoke again. "I've missed you and wondered how you fare."

"I'm fine. Only a few scrapes and bruises from my wild journey

177

linger. I thank you again for helping me." She wrapped her shawl tighter, as though she could keep him out of her thoughts which were quite unladylike. Each time she met him, she discovered something new about him, but she was always drawn back to his form, his dark hair, and the way he moved. Was this how a love of her own choosing and not the desires of her parents felt? She felt her cheeks and neck flush.

Breed stepped closer. He smelled of that faint cedar again and sweet tobacco. "I'm glad of it. Being cold and wet can kill many a strong constitution. And you have a strong constitution."

"Hmm," Jeannie said. The clearing became quiet and still. Somewhere off she heard the hammering of a woodpecker. Or was it from the camp? She changed the subject. "That Kapihi. Such a sweet boy."

"*Ah-ha.*"

"He called you something. Key-wally sick or something like that. What does it mean?"

Breed snorted. "Well, if you want to know, it means lovesick. And that is what I am." He stepped closer. "I love you, Jeannie Naughton. I've wanted to say that for some time."

"Oh." This is what she wanted to hear from him since their journey back from Timons. Maybe long before that. She loved him too. She raised her eyes to him, wistfully waiting for him to go on.

"I've never met a woman so headstrong to risk her reputation to do something for others as you did when you cared for my friends at Kanaka Town. I can only imagine what that cost you in your society. Certainly, this last episode has caused more comment. I want to relieve you of any such gossip." He took her hand. "I want to marry you, to have you be my proper wife."

"Jonas..."

"I'm not as poor as you might think. I have legal holdings in the territories that can be used for cash. Collie and I have talked about several businesses that we could start. Shipping, for one."

He gently rubbed his thumb over her knuckles. A touch that was soft and sensuous. It was Timmons Island again. The image of him coming out of the water hit her with a fresh, flash of desire. More than anything else, she wanted to fulfill it.

"It doesn't matter that I was married before? That I had a child?"

"*Nawitcha*. It doesn't matter."

Jeannie beamed at him, pushing away her memory of her first husband's courtship of her. Captain Marsfield was older than her by fifteen years, but had courted her with respect, promised her many things. *So many things. But why didn't I see? You never came home from sea, Harry. But your ghost brought something.*

"Yes, I'll marry you."

The joy on his face made her feel guilty and happy at the same time. How could one person do that for another?

Breed took her hand and kissed it. "I'll speak to your uncle and ask permission to marry you if that is how it is done."

Jeannie pulled away and looked at him. "What does one normally do out here?"

Breed grinned. "Bring a supply of HBC blankets and pile them up. Throw in some smoked salmon and some copper."

Jeannie batted his arm. "Oh, Jonas. Would you do that?"

"No, we'll post banns. Contact a judge or sky pilot—a preacher." He wiped a tendril of hair off her forehead. "Maybe Captain Pickett can marry us. Whatever you wish." He grinned. "I'll throw in some otter hides." He reached into his coat pocket and took out the thimble he had shown her on Timons. "It's not a ring, but please take it as my promise to you." He slipped it onto her ring finger. "Till then."

"Oh, Jonas. *Mahsie*. It's beautiful. I will always take good care of this" She stood on her tiptoes and kissed him on the mouth. "I love you Jonas Breed. For some time now." She placed her hand on his tattoo and traced its outlines. Breed pulled her against him. She put her arms around, and they kissed with barely contained passion.

After a time they stood still, holding hands and listening to sounds of the woods around them. The woodpecker made its call and flew in closer. A squirrel complained. The air was warm. Sunlight streamed down through the trees. She could have stayed all afternoon for Breed seemed to bring nature closer to her every time she was with him.

Kapihi burst through the bushes. "Marines coming."

Jeannie blanched.

"Don't worry," Breed said. "Just walk out with him. You've been on a stroll with your little friend. I can send him again for you. Kapihi's mother is staying with her family at the old longhouse not far from here. I belive that Alani is visiting too."

"Will I see you again?"

Breed frowned. "Soon as I can. Might have to go to Port Townsend. I'll send word." He took her hand and kissed it. "Until then, Mrs. King George."

" 'Til then, Jonas." She followed Kapihi down the leafy trail. Each step she took felt light and airy with joy. The only problem was that she hadn't told Breed the particulars about her marriage to Marsfield. Would he love her then?

COOPERWAITE

True to his word, the next day, Breed sent a note through Kapihi. *"Toketie,"* it read, *"Collie and I do have to go to Port Townsend for business. I promise to be back in a few days. If you need anything urgent, let Kapihi know and he will get word to any one of my particulars. They will gladly help. If I can, I'll slip a message over to your uncle. Go with the spirits. Yours, faithfully, Jonas.*

Jeannie folded up the note

Jeannie wasn't sure if she needed anything urgent except for another fan. August was proving to be a hot month. She did feel the need for him, a powerful sentiment, billowing around her like the much desired breeze that came off the bay.

For the next several days, Jeannie's day settled into a routine: she would get up in the morning and have a light breakfast of tea and toast with the Parkers, spend some time helping in the infirmary or helping a marine write a letter home. After lunch, she would go for a walk to write in her new pocket journal or to read. Sometimes she brought the new watercolor box set Uncle Archie gave her and painted little scenes of the woods and fields further south. Once she was away from the camp and up on the hill, Kapihi would appear with the latest news on anything happening on the island, including what he had for breakfast, Breed's companions' projects and what his mother was teaching his sister.

"Noelani, she doesn't like makin' cedar baskets. She rather play teacher with her dolls or look at herself in the mirror."

"Don't you like your sister?"

"My sister is a girl."

Sometimes, Jeannie might walk a little further on the forested road and sit on the folding camp stool she carried on her back. There she read or wrote in the shade. Other times, she might read to Kapihi if he should appear early. If someone from the camp encountered them, there was her explanation why she was there. Once, Alani and Kapihi's mother, Sally Kalama, came up from the longhouse bringing along a sullen Noelani. Jeannie hadn't seen the women since the day she was smoking salmon near the lime kiln. Jeannie didn't know Sally like she did Alani, but thought again that she was a pretty woman. This time Sally wore the simple dress of a settler and a corset though her feet were bare. Her hair was pulled back in a bun. She wore a woven cedar hat. She carried a basket on her arm.

"Morning, Missus. How my boy Kapihi? He is behavin'?"

"Good morning, Mrs. Kalama, Noelani." Jeannie smoothed Kapihi's hair with her hand. "Yes, he's been very good."

"I hope so." Sally smiled. "I brought you honey for your tea."

"Why, thank you. *Mahsie*." Jeannie put the crock in her basket. "Where is Kaui these days?"

"He workin' down by American camp. I'll see him bye and bye. But first, I go Orcas to see my auntie." She put her arm around Noelani. "We'll be gone couple days."

Jeannie smiled at Noelani. "It sounds like a grand adventure. Are you excited?"

When Noelani folded her arms and frowned, Jeannie suppressed a smile. Apparently not.

"Is Kapihi going?"

"No," Alani answered. "He'll stay with me and Moki at the longhouse at Mitchell Bay."

Jeannie looked down at Kapihi who was looking at the mixed

colors in her porcelain paint dishes. "He's welcome to come by and see me at the Parker's."

"*Mahsie.* You are very kind."

No, you are kind, Jeannie thought. The boy, she suddenly realized, was very precious to her. Like sweet Jeremy.

Jeannie visited with Sally and Alani for a few minutes more, then taking the children with them, the women left for Mitchell Bay.

The following day Jeannie arrived at her usual spot and found no sign of Kapihi. She set up her stool and watercolor set and began to paint. The woods around the road were still. Dry dust motes filtered down through the green maples lining the road. She became so absorbed in her painting she didn't hear the lone rider until he was upon her.

"Mrs. Naughton, how charming."

Jeannie looked up with a start. "Lieutenant Cooperwaite." Instantly, she was wary as he pulled his horse up next to her. He was handsomely dressed in full uniform, the scarlet coat splashing against the greens of the woods. His studied appreciation of her left her cold and vulnerable. The scar next to the drooping eyelid looked enflamed.

"I used to dabble in paints, myself, in my midshipman days in Plymouth. Many picturesque scenes, don't you think?"

"I'm not familiar with the town, sir."

He shifted in his saddle and peered over at her effort. "Excellent rendition of the woods around here. You have an eye for nature."

Jeannie wiped her brush and put it in her case. She willed her fingers not to tremble.

"Mrs. Marsfield. You know, it doesn't become you to lie."

Jeannie straightened up. "I beg your pardon."

"I know who you are. You're Miss Jeannie Hackmore who married my friend, Harry Marsfield. He was an excellent sea captain, but I'm afraid he had a bad habit of falling in love and marrying the first young lady he met in every port."

Jeannie blanched. "I don't know what you are talking about. Please go away."

Cooperwaite shifted in his saddle. For one terrible moment

Jeannie thought he would dismount. "I knew his first wife, Sarah Packwood. She was a shrew. It was supposed to be a marriage made in heaven. Family money and all that, but it was all in the Caribbean Islands. Harry was glad when she was deposited there. Being gone to sea all the time, he'd come home long enough to make a new thing for her to suckle."

Jeannie snapped her case closed. "Stop. You are disgusting."

Cooperwaite chuckled, his shoulders shaking. "I didn't come to your wedding. He spoke of you before with some affection. Said he'd come into money with his new father-in-law and his business. Said you were a pretty thing and highly intelligent for a young lady of your age. Said he'd enjoy squiring you around on your honeymoon. Apparently, he did. That was Harry's son who died, I assume."

Jeannie blanched, hair rising on the back of her neck, but she knew she must stay calm. She was alone on the road. She picked up her stool and case and started down the road.

Cooperwaite clucked to his horse and began to follow. "Now there was nothing suspicious about old Harry's death. Died of typhus in port in Zanzibar. What was suspicious was the death of Sarah after she showed up at the reading of his will in Plymouth which I *did* attend. What a muckle that must have been for you. In an instant, you are not only the drudge of a bigamist but your child a bastard."

Jeannie put together all her courage to turn and face him. "How sad for that young woman. I'm sure as an officer in the Royal Marines you would have felt some compassion. I'm sure I would. Unfortunately, I have not heard of this. I am from Bristol, not this place of which you speak. Good day."

Jeannie bit her lip and kept walking, each step taking her back to that terrible moment when all the world knew her betrayal and shame. She put all her will into ignoring Cooperwaite, in hopes that it would confuse him. Behind her, she could heard his horse following. Suddenly, it took off. When she looked back Cooperwaite was barreling up the military road heading south. As soon as she was sure he was gone, she ran into the woods and straight into Collie Henderson.

"Oh, Mr. Henderson. I do beg your pardon."

"The fault is mine, Mrs. Naughton." Collie brushed his sea jacket down. The sword he always wore strapped across his back banged against him.

"Are you all right?" Collie looked at Jeannie curiously, his mouth tight.

"I'm fine. Is Mr. Breed back?" Jeannie struggled to gain her composure. Her lips trembled.

"He's gone ahead." Collie's eyes narrowed. "Do you need an escort back?"

"I'm—" Jeannie started to make up an excuse.

"I'll walk with you. I don't think Jonas would like you going out alone." Collie gave her his arm. "I don't like Cooperwaite one bit either."

～

"He said what?" Breed's voice was sharp. He scowled as he threw his haversack down on the floor of the half-finished hut he was helping Doc-tin build.

Collie took off his cap and slapped it against his knee to shake away the light rain that had fallen on them as they walked up through the woods. "He was implying that Mrs. Naughton's late husband was actually a Captain Marsfield. A bigamist, with a wife in another country, maybe more."

"Wah—" Breed grabbed a lantern from a chair, the one piece of furniture in the room, a chair, and lit it.

Collie worked his mouth. "Told you I didn't know any Captain Naughton in the South Pacific trades."

"I'm sure there was a reason why she used a false name."

"Maybe she's not even Archie Campbell's niece."

Breed ignored him and hung the lantern up on a nail in the low rafter. "What else did you hear?"

"Something about the first missus showing up at the reading of the will. She turned up dead a couple of weeks later, after Mrs.

185

Naughton was no longer Mrs. Marsfield and her little boy a bastard."

Breed stared at Collie. "That's an unkind thing, Collie. Poor little lad, but no cause for murder."

"I wasn't implying—"

"Cooperwaite was. Who the devil is he? He's not with the regulars. And what's it to him?"

"Don't know. It may not matter. There's rumor that he's resigning his commission or is being asked to. Some impropriety. I do recall something about a scandal back in England concerning a man named Marsfield and his heirs. There was a sensational trial of some sort. It was in all the English papers a couple of years back."

"Why would you remember that?" Breed rubbed his arm where the knife cut itched. Their trip to Port Townsend to inspect a schooner made their proposed venture promising, but he was tired.

"The age of the young widow. Barely nineteen. The real Mrs. Marsfield had sons in their twenties."

Breed looked out the window. Shadows gathered in the woods as light rain continued to fall. The hut grew dark. Jeannie had said she had a scar. Was this the scar? A sham marriage? A trial for murder? He couldn't fathom it. He remembered the look on her face when she traced the tattoo on his wrist. He remembered the hurt in her voice, her wish to be free.

"What will you do?" Collie asked.

"I'm going to bed. I'll sort it out later." With that Breed picked up his haversack and using it as a pillow, lay down on the hard floor and wrapped his coat around him.

186

THE TRUTH WILL OUT

Jeannie didn't wait for Breed to contact her after the encounter with Cooperwaite. She was positive Breed's friend had overheard everything. She wished to correct any false impression Collie Henderson may have related to Breed. But first she had to deal with Gilly who did not miss her distress when she returned to officer's row. Jeannie finally told her the truth about Cooperwaite's advances on the road, but not what she was distressed about.

The day after the incident, she approached Gilly and asked if she would walk out with her. She had seen Kapihi earlier in the day and from him knew where to find Breed. "I need to speak to Mr. Breed, but I want it to be proper. Will you do this for me?"

"Oh, Jeannie. What has overcome you?" She put her hands on Jeannie's shoulders to appraise her. She brushed a strand of hair back from Jeannie's forehead then noticed the silken throng about her neck that slipped behind her bodice. "Hmm."

"Would you like to see?" Jeannie looked outside the parlor window for any sign of Dr. Parker and John Forrester. No one was on the porch. She pulled the ribbon up and revealed a tiny linen drawstring sack with blue forget-me-nots embroidered on it. Inside was the thimble Breed had given her.

"Jonas's pledge to me. He gave it to me a few days ago. We won't make an announcement before he hears from my uncle in Victoria. So it must remain secret."

Gilly put her lacy gloved hands over her mouth in astonishment, but they could not conceal her wide smile. She beamed. "Oh, Jeannie, dear. You must tell me everything." She trembled in anticipation has she pulled Jeannie down to the settee. "Will you marry here or in a church in Victoria? Will you post banns? Jonas Breed. In my twenty-nine years, I've never heard anything so romantic. So many gentleman have asked after you. Dr. Parker said there was quite the flock at your uncle's table in Victoria." Gilly pressed her hands together. "But dear Jonas Breed. Did you know he is a particular friend of Dr. Parker? Despite what wags might say, he's not so wild. He is a very good man with prospects." Gilly patted Jeannie's hand. "How long has this been going on?"

Jeannie let Gilly go on and on, relieved that her friend approved of the match. Now she answered. "Since the races. And I assure you he has always been a gentleman."

"Has he made a good offer to you?"

"Yes. I'm very happy. We can marry once my mourning period is over."

"You like a sister to me—I always wanted a sister—but I must say, I'm feeling rather old. I can't quite follow how young people court these days. Particularly bundling. I'm not quite sure about bundling. You're not going to bundle, are you? But I am so happy for you. Since your boy's departure, I've seen your grief lingering." Gilly's eyes glistened. "In truth, your grief will always be there as my own grief for my Priscilla is with me, but it is right you move on."

Jeannie put the thimble away. She sighed. "Yes, but there has been a misunderstanding. I have to speak to him before he leaves again. Please."

"Alright." Gilly picked up her wrap. "Let's go out the back door as to keep the mystery going."

The walk was further than either woman intended, but they found the cabin as Kapihi described back in the woods east of the military road. Breed was in his shirt sleeves on the roof with Collie and Charlie Bone when they showed up.

"Mrs. Parker, Mrs. Naughton," Breed said. "This is a pleasure."

"Good day, Mr. Breed," Gilly said. "We heard of your venture through that young scamp, Kapihi. Is he around?"

"With his parents and the Kapunas who are visiting."

"Ah. Very good, very good."

Jeannie stepped forward. "I would like to speak to you, Mr. Breed." Collie and Charlie Bone stopped hammering and looked at him. There was an uncomfortable silence. Jeannie felt Breed's eyes on her. His mouth was tight.

"I'm afraid I'm busy at the moment." His eyes were cold.

"Now, Jonas," Gilly said, apparently tired of formalities. "Mrs. Naughton has asked me to come and she wishes to speak to you about some matter I don't know what, but I can tell it troubles her. It's not going to rain tonight. Flashing can wait. This may not."

Collie guffawed. "It seems to have come back to your corner, *kahpo*. We can rest a spell." He climbed down the rickety ladder and picked up his haversack. The other man joined him.

"*Wah*," Breed muttered. When he stared at Jeannie, she felt her courage sagging, but it had to be done. He had to know the truth.

"And I shall go off a ways," Gilly said.

Breed scrambled down. "All right. But let these gentlemen take you back to the camp, ma'am. I promise to bring Mrs. Naughton home after we speak. Collie, will you walk with Mrs. Parker?"

So it was done. After the party disappeared into the forest, Breed turned to her. "What is it that you wish to say?"

"Oh, Jonas. How can you be so cold? I know that your friend told you about my encounter with Cooperwaite on the road. You do not seem to care about my plight."

"I care," he said under his breath. "But I'm confused on the details, Mrs. Naughton. Or rather Mrs. Marsfield. Is that part true?"

"Yes. I *was* married to Captain Harry Marsfield. He was the father of Jeremy."

"Why the name Naughton?"

189

"To protect me and my son. My dear uncle devised everything. You know his character. He is an honorable man."

"You're his niece truly?"

Jeannie clasped her hands. "His devoted niece. I would never shame him."

Breed's voice stayed hard. "Collie heard Cooperwaite say that it was only at the reading of the will that the true Mrs. Marsfield showed up."

There was no escape. If Jeannie didn't tell him, she could go away, but would lose him and everything she wanted with him. If she told him, she could lose him anyway. She weighed the choices and their awful accounting; she measured their day on Timons Island, the look of love in his eyes then.

"'T'is true. I was so shocked. I didn't believe it. But she had legal papers and two sons older than me. All keening to get what was theirs." Jeannie's voice trembled. "I received no support from my family. My mother who had victoriously championed the match with Captain Marsfield now called me a drudge. My father took ill."

"Collie said he remembered some scandal in the papers back in England."

Tears formed in Jeannie's eyes. This was harder than she thought it would be. She felt exposed with no inkling about which direction this telling would go. "Yes, there was a scandal. A sensational scandal which everyone seemed to enjoy. I was in the newspapers daily like some blood and thunder novel. I was given a week to leave the house with what I owned, which was very little. Everything was in *his* name. I lived at a rectory while things were sorted out. There would be no money for me. Jeremy's good name was in ruins. And then Sarah Marsfield was found dead at the house, the day after she moved in."

Jeannie took a deep breath. "I had nothing to do with her death, but I was accused by one of her sons, complaining that I wished to rob them of their inheritance."

Breed stepped away from her. "And then?"

Jeannie felt chilled. This was the moment Uncle Archie said would be telling of Breed's measure, but it was not going well. "There was a trial that went on for weeks. In the end I was acquitted when suspicion next fell on one of her own sons. Still, my reputation was ruined. My father's business was failing. I couldn't stay. Uncle Archie happened to come on one of his rare visits to England. He proposed taking me away. He booked me and Jeremy under an assumed names and took us to Toronto. He found a place for us there. He returned to Victoria, and then sent for us six months ago."

"Why does Cooperwaite show such interest?"

"I don't know, Jonas. He says he and Captain Marsfield were friends. Oh, what if I'm found out? It could hurt my uncle." Jeannie put her hands over her face and wept.

Breed gently took down her hands. "Cooperwaite won't do a thing. I'll see to that." Breed cleared his throat. "I'm sorry."

"I'm sorry too. I should have told you when you asked me to marry you. But I was afraid."

"This was your scar?"

"Yes." Jeannie wiped a tear from her cheek. "Then, we're all right?"

"*Ah-ha*. We're all right." He smiled faintly at her, then looked down at his wrist where the tattoo stuck out from under his sleeve. "Sometimes," he said distantly, "things happen. We're either better for them or we're all *mistchimas*."

"Yes. Bound. I can never go back to who I was, but it does bind me."

The late afternoon sun lighted the tops of the trees. A Swainson's thrush made its dizzy call. Neither Jeannie nor Breed made a move. Finally, Jeannie asked, "How much more time until the hut is done?"

"Tomorrow." Breed spied the ribbon around her neck. "What's that?"

"Your mother's thimble."

"Jeannie." He took her hand and kissed it. "*Toketie*." The word was sensuous and still a mystery to Jeannie, but she knew it conveyed love and desire. Just as she felt. Suddenly, they were in each other's arms, kissing and caressing. He pushed her against the cabin wall and pressed into her, kissing away the last tears on her face. He whispered to her in languages that were foreign and full of clicks and rushing melodious sounds. She closed her eyes. How things had changed. She was no longer the child bride who married a sea captain nearly thrice her age. She had made her own love match.

Breed stopped kissing her and braced his arms on both sides of her. "I love you, Mrs. King George."

"I love you too, Mr. Jonas Breed." She slipped a stand of his long hair behind his ear. Her whole body throbbed. She felt alive, but eventually she pushed him away. She tried to bring her voice to normal. Slipping under him, she went into the hut. Breed followed her in.

"Does Doc-tin intend to live here?" The place was so new that the smell of the cedar shakes in the roof was strong. The only furniture was a chair and pile of otter skins in the corner. "I thought people couldn't claim a homestead."

"Military can't, but folks on both sides are determined to take a piece of the island, so they put down something. Still have to wait to see which nation's going to get it."

"Hmm." She put her arm around his waist and leaned into him. "Where will we go?"

Breed pulled her close. "I'll keep my place on Timons, but we can live here. Or over at Port Townsend if you like. I prefer to stay in Washington Territory. For the shipping business I have in mind." He touched her nose. "*Toketie.*"

She took his hand. "What does that mean?"

"Beautiful. Pretty. You are very pretty, Jeannie Naughton." He kissed her on mouth.

She kissed him back, then giggled. "I think you are Toe-ketty too,"

An hour later, Breed had her back at officer's row. Though still light in the Northwest summer evening, down on the grounds, the marines were lowering the flag. Bagpipes droned through the big maple trees. At the Parker's bungalow, he said good-bye.

"Think you can manage?" Breed asked.

"Well, having dangled with me, you must support any alibi I conjure."

"I promise. And I promise to get that letter to your uncle. We'll post banns in Victoria and in Olympia. In the meantime, hold on to that thimble." He looked around and seeing no candles lit in the officer's houses, he kissed her full on the mouth. "Good night."

WALKING INTO THE FOREST

"Oh, John, do hurry. Thomas is already down there." Out in the parlor, Gilly was in a swirl as a subaltern took the last of her valises out the door and down to the dock. Ribbons and straw hat, gloves and fan, all hallmarks of a splendid summer accoutrement, were in a full display. Her crinolines made her skirt sweep the room.

Jeannie watched Gilly with amusement. Jeannie was dressed for the afternoon, available only in bombazine mourning black. She wished for Jonas's sake that she could wear a soft teal, one of her best colors. She had just the lace for the neck and a tiny gold watch on a chain. Now her only jewelry were her jet earrings, the thimble and the mourning pin that held a snip of Jeremy's hair.

"Jeannie, dear, we'll be gone for a couple of days. Thomas is to look into the hospital at Esquimalt. John is taking the steamship to San Francisco."

Jeannie smiled at John Forrester. "You will be missed. You're a very fine fellow, Mr. Forrester. How I have enjoyed our adventures together."

"Or without me." He leaned in and winked. "My fondest wishes for you, Mrs. Naughton. He kissed her hand. "I hope to return with astonishing business prospects."

Jeannie laughed. "You'll charm them all, I'm sure. Safe journey to both of you. While you're gone, I'll have to find new ways to entertain myself."

Gilly started down the stairs then came back and whispered. "Do let me know how things are between you and Jonas. I can't wait."

"I promise."

After they sailed, Jeannie changed into her starched corded petticoat and black walking dress, packed her basket, box, and canvas stool and set out through the back trail to the military road. As they discussed the day before, she would meet Breed at two o'clock. Once on top she was to go further down the road to where the trees opened to the prairie. He would meet her a little ways beyond.

The air was hot and sunny, a stillness and sense of anticipation stirring in the trees. The only sounds were a little bird flittering in the brush and a raven cawing off in the distance. As she walked along the dusty road, her skirt stirred up fir cones and big leaf maple seeds. What a perfect place, she thought. No wonder two countries wanted it. Whether she and Breed would settle here or Timons was the question. They had begun to talk about that yesterday.

"Jeannie."

She looked up and Breed was there, standing next to a large cedar tree, its branches drooping like a subaltern's mustache. He was in his shirtsleeves, the cedar rope band around his neck showing. "Come this way."

She looked around and seeing no one, followed him into the trees. "Where is Kapihi?"

"The little rascal took off. We're on our own." He kissed her long and hard. "You look *toketie* today."

Jeannie's heart thumped. She smiled. "You mock, me sir, but *mahsie*. It's still the black dress of mourning, after all."

He took her basket, box, and stool and led her back into the woods. Eventually, they came around a large cedar tree, where a shelter of cattail covered with fern was set up.

Breed set the basket down. He put his hands on her waist and drew her against him. "I've missed you."

"In such a short time?" Jeannie grinned and brushed back his hair from his forehead. Saw the small scar again. "I missed you too." She stood on her tiptoes and kissed him on his mouth. In return, he kissed and hugged her hard. Tension was all through him, but not all of it from desire. She wondered what was amiss.

"Come into the shelter, Jeannie. I have water and some food. We should talk." He flipped back the edge of the cattail mat and exposed a tidy space inside with a small folding wood table and canvas stools. A jug was on the table along with a tin plate of cheese and bread. And books. Behind it was a cot.

"Have you been here long?" she asked.

"No. I've been off with Collie and Doc-tin. Finishing up that shack." He sighed. "There are other matters as well. Are the Parkers at home this afternoon?"

"I'm sorry, but they've gone to Victoria. The doctor is at the hospital in Esquimalt. John Forrester is leaving for California for business."

"Then we truly are on our own." His eyes twinkled, though his mouth was set.

"Is this where you sleep when you're on this island?"

"Sometimes. It's easily moved." At the table, he filled a mug with water from his jug and gave it to her. He raised his mug. "Here's to the future. Our future."

"Ours," she said and drank, scarce believing that soon it would all be true. "Did you write to my uncle?"

"It went out with the packet this morning. I look forward to his answer."

"What are you reading today?" she asked as sat down on a stool.

"An American— Emerson." He sat down next to her and cut some cheese and bread. He gave her a sampling.

She opened the book to an essay and read out loud, "Self-Reliance." He leaned over her shoulder and read a paragraph or two before they grew too conscious of each other.

"Self-reliance, indeed. More like wit's end," Breed said. "Something I learned at a young age." He kissed her on her shoulder. A crumb dropped from her mouth onto the pages. Breed picked it up and put it into her mouth. She closed her mouth down on his fingers.

"Did we come to read or talk?" he asked,

Jeannie laughed. "You undid me, sir, with your proposal. I can't contain my joy."

"You've undone *me*, Mrs. King George."

Jeannie closed her eyes as he lightly ran his fingers over her arms, his breath at her neck. She leaned into his shoulder and did not protest when he put his other hand on top of her corset where her breasts swelled. *My own choice.*

"I love you, He said. "You are *kloshe tum tum* to me. Gently, he pulled on the ribbon that suspended the thimble and drew it out. He kissed it. "*Toketie*. On my mother's grave, my pledge to you."

Sometime later, Jeannie woke with a jerk and removed Breed's hand from her waist. *Had she heard something?* The sun moved through the cattails, speckling the table, their lair with gold lights. The woods were still.

Breed woke up and rubbed his eyes with the flat of his hands.

Jeannie put her feet on the ground. Her back felt warm and sticky as she shook out her dress. "I think I heard mess call. It's getting late." She twisted her hair into a braided bun and put the pins back in. Breed moved behind her and sat up.

"I'll take you down right away," he said as he put his shirt back on. "First, can I show you something?"

Jeannie got up and buttoned up her bodice. The thimble lay once again hidden behind it.

Breed sat on the edge of the cot and spread out a map. "This is where we are right now—

San Juan Island—and these are the other islands the American and British are contesting, including Haro Strait." Breed pulled Jeannie to him. "Collie and I have been talking about shipping goods between Washington Territory, San Francisco and the Sandwich Islands. That schooner we looked at in Port Townsend a few days ago can carry either logs or goods. He feels that it's very sound."

"I'd like to help. I can do accounting. I have been keeping my uncle's records at the Fort Victoria. But I learned how in my father's office back in Plymouth some time ago."

Breed smiled at her. "You must favor the works of Elizabeth Gaswell. The strength of the independent woman."

"You know about her? I am not some foundling without education."

"All the more to admire you." He squeeze her hand. "Mahsie for you tender attentions," he said. "I'll sleep much better tonight, I think."

"Will I see you again?"

"Tomorrow. I'll see if I can find Kapihi. Send him."

He walked her back out to the road then gave her a long kiss, its heat smoldering.

"Aloha," he said. "Go with the spirits."

SHELLS SHINING

" **K** *ahpo.*"

Breed rolled over on his side and squinted at the face above him. Early morning light was hitting the beams behind him, in sharp oranges and yellow.

"Collie? What time is it?"

"It's nearly five o'clock. The rooster's been up for hours."

Breed sat up, disoriented for a moment, and then remembered he was at Doc-tin's shack. He had been dreaming about Jeannie. Jeannie with the light brown hair that smelled of cardamom and Brown Bess soap. Jeannie with the smooth white skin. He ached just thinking about her. His *klootsman.* "Something wrong?"

"It's Kaui. You see him? He came looking for you."

"When? Yesterday?" *If it was yesterday,* Breed thought, *I was with Jeannie.* Feeling guilty, he put on his linen shirt. The shack was cool, but the sun coming through the only window promised another hot day. "He say why?"

"I wasn't there. Just heard he was looking for you. But folk said he sounded urgent. Funny thing, he hasn't been seen since early last night. Brought your horse for you, in case you wanted to go down and see him for yourself."

Breed got up from the floor. He looked at the cold fire and wished he had coffee, but something told him that he should go down. Kaui just didn't worry around like that.

It was still early when Breed and Collie arrived outside of Camp Pickett, but the soldiers were already up and gathered around their mess tent. The sound of a braying mule and the blacksmith hammering on his anvil clanged through the clear morning air. They rode along the edge of the picket fence, eventually coming around to the officer's row. Breed dismounted and tied up his horse. It was hard to believe that not so long ago he had met Jeannie here and walked her up to the ramparts.

"Captain Pickett in?" he asked the soldier on duty at the gate. It was O'Malley again, this time sober.

"Yes, sir, Mr. Breed. He's in his quarters."

Breed and Collie passed through the gate, but before they reached his veranda, Pickett came out and called to them. He looked like he hadn't slept much. He had been eating breakfast. A large napkin was stuck in his shirt neck and his long dark hair flowed in greasy strands over the collar of his regulation shirt. He wore no jacket, but had put on his tall leather boots for the day.

"Thought y'all might be com' by, Mr. Breed. My sincere apologies for my appearance, but it has been an unnatural night. Did you find your Kanaka friend, Kaui Kalama?"

"He was here?"

"Came by late last night. The officer of the evening said he was looking for you."

Breed set his mouth. Something was truly wrong. Kaui had come all the way up to English Camp then back here. "He say anything?

"Only that there was some trouble you should know of."

Pickett pulled the napkin from his collar and wiped his hands. "Did say he'd been to see Griffin at Belle Vue Farm. As he left, he met some civilian and they took off down there." The Virginian nodded his head in the direction of San Juan Town far below the edge of the military reserve."

Breed straightened up, his stomach turning sour. "You said an unnatural night."

"The usual trouble with intoxication and fornication involving my men, but this time there was mayhem and murder in the town. Dead *siwash* found in the street and a whiskey ranch broken up. I wish we could be rid of the whole lot."

Breed turned to Collie. "We better go down and look for ourselves. I'm obliged to you Captain Pickett."

Once they were saddled, they rode along the west side of picket fence towards the ramparts. Halfway up, they ran into Moki Kapuna and two Hawaiian companions walking briskly from Belle Vue Farm.

"Jo-nuss, you see Kaui?"

Breed pulled up. "I was hoping you had. What's going on?"

Moki looked dumbstruck. He worked his jaw for a moment. "Kaui, he's been tearing around since early yesterday. I never see him, but he was at the farm." Moki took a deep breath. "I think maybe I know why. I think there some big trouble with that Haida, Comes Shouting. His party of warriors are down on the beach."

Breed frowned. He wondered if there was more fighting going on between the Haida and Songhees. Where did Kaui fit in with this?

Collie came up beside Breed. "Shall we take a look-see down at the town? Shouldn't be too much trouble. The citizenry most likely all passed out."

They made their way at a trot along the worn prairie path the soldiers used to get down to San Juan Town and Griffin Bay. Moki and his companions kept up behind the horses at a jog. The sky was still a dull gray with a promise of sun break by noon, but the water was clear of fog and the islands to the south and east of them were sharp, smoke rising from occasional homesteads hidden amongst the trees. Below them, San Juan Town crouched on the shore below like a collection of weathered box crates. When they stopped to let Moki catch up, Breed spat. The last time he was there, he'd rescued the little girl. That felt like a lifetime ago. He prayed to the spirits for his friend, but he felt a heaviness on his shoulder that gripped like the hand of Hades.

As they came down the steep hill, the path pointed its way down with no care for horse or rider. They met up with a road the army built for wagons to carry goods and equipment from the Hudson Bay's Company wharf and went on down to the beach where the settlement sat.

For the next twenty minutes, they searched the buildings and questioned those who were awake. They all knew of the Indian who was killed but none had seen the Kanaka.

"It was uncommonly rowdy last night," said a man sweeping off his bedraggled porch in the front of a large canvas tent. "Wicked."

"But you saw no one like the man we describe." Breed was frustrated that so far Kaui hadn't been seen.

The balding man shook his head dislodging a long strand that swept cross his pate. "No, sir." He wiped his hair back and resumed sweeping.

Breed looked back up toward the hill. Kaui came down with "a citizen," he thought. Why? What would bring him down here?

"*Mahsie*," he said. Discouraged, he walked back to his horse. A feeling of dread bit harder. The place stunk of vomit and the faint sweet smell of blood. He wanted to be out of the place as soon as possible. Collie joined him and they talked of what to do next.

Moki came out from between two buildings. "Jo-nuss. Got something. Feller say he saw a Kanaka come down with two white men. Then a fight broke out and that Salish man got rushed and killed. Everyone disappeared, including the Kanaka."

"Does he know who the men were?"

"If he does, he not saying." Moki went on, "But, he thinks maybe they went between the buildings and out toward the lagoon. It was dark—very dark."

Breed untied his horse. "Let's ride."

They galloped out along the lagoon behind the buildings and searched for boot marks. Collie was the first to find something not washed out by the rising tide seeping up through the muddy ground.

"Some tussle here," he said as he leaned over. Moki crouched and looked too. Breed rode over to inspect, careful not to destroy any other tracks. There were several sets of boot prints, but one was violently smeared from heels digging in deep. Water glistened in them with an oily sheen. A rock next to the boot mark was awash with blood.

Breed's mouth turned dry. He looked over to the brush and trees edging the beach. His heart pounding, he kneed his horse forward, the others close behind.

He found Kaui dumped behind some boulders and trees, a worn boot sticking out from the pile of cedar branches laid on top of him.

Moki pulled them away, and burst out crying, "*Auwē*, Jo-nuss. Your *ow* is dead. Murdered."

Breed felt like he had been punched in the gut. Dismounting, he yanked away the branches near his end and choked. Kaui's head lolled back against the bank, his body jackknifed in. His gray shirt was torn and stiff with blood congealed from several stab wounds on his chest, shoulder, neck and stomach. His nose had been bashed in. When Breed pulled aside the shirt, he found bruises everywhere. He leaned over and examined his friend's mouth and then his hands. After he finished, he gently stroked the hair still shiny in death, then straightened up.

"His mouth was bound, so not to make noise. They beat him, then knifed him. From the bruises on his arms, he was restrained, but from his hands, he put up a good fight."

He smiled sadly at Moki and the others. Tears filled his eyes. "He was my *kloshe kahpo*, my *ow*," Breed said thickly. "We will always be together."

An image of the two of them together during the starving winter, the year they met, came to him. They kept alive eating offal and telling stories of the warm Sandwich Islands. The trials they had been through in the north and the friendship they continued to share once they were down here sealed them as brothers forever.

"What we do next, Jo-nuss?"

Breed straightened up. He ached everywhere, like he hadn't slept in hours. "We'll have to take him to Griffin at Belle Vue. He'll want to know. Maybe he can have a coffin built for him. We'll have to get word to Sally"

"Should I get a wagon?" Moki's eyes glistened.

"There's no time. We won't get answers here." Breed nodded at some cedar saplings. "We'll make a travois for him." He wiped his mouth. "Collie, would you be so kind and go ahead and let Captain Pickett know. See if you can get a wagon there to take Kaui to Belle Vue Farm. We'll be along."

Collie put his hand on Breed's shoulder. "I'm sorry, Jonas. He was a good man and my friend too." He mounted his horse and took off at a gallop for American Camp, leaving Breed in a cloud of depression.

Pickett was in full uniform when Breed came by pulling the body of Kaui on the makeshift travois of poles and blankets. He met the mournful party as they passed behind officer's row. "My regards, Mr. Breed, as I know you have some affection for Mr. Kalama. We'll certainly look into the matter. I've already sent word to the manager at Belle Vue Farm. I believe that Griffin is having a coffin built."

Breed looked at him sharply. "Tell me, was Krill in San Juan Town?"

"I can't attest to that, but I believe I heard he was on the scene. Why? Do you suspect some foul play by him concerning your friend?"

"I suspect him of many things. Most of which are true."

"Now, Mr. Breed," Pickett drawled. "I would advise you to be cautious. No need to accuse."

"Who's accusing? The man will speak for himself." Breed was shaking with rage now, but he dipped his head and thanked the officer. "I'll be going now."

Breed got back into his saddle and headed down the path to the farm. He felt fury building inside of him, at the injustice that Kaui survived smallpox, but some species of larger vermin had done him in. Why in heaven was that allowed?

As they entered the main lane of Belle Vue Farm that pointed directly out to Haro Strait, he found Collie and a small group of

Kanakas and other employees of the Hudson Bay Company gathered at the first house. On the porch, one of the men raised his arms.

Breed dismounted. He began to choke up with grief when the Hawaiian wailed,

"*Auwē*, Jo-nuss. *Auwē*."

"Have you sent for Sally?" Breed asked Collie.

"*Ah-ha*. Griffin says you can lay Kaui out here in this house." Collie smiled wistfully at Breed, his hands in his pockets. *Not your usual demeanor, my friend*, thought Breed.

Breed sighed. "Well, let's get him inside." Breed untied the ropes holding Kaui's body on the travois. The death of his friend was still unreal. When he was done, everyone came to assist and carried Kaui into the front room of the little house. Once he was laid out on the table, his feet sticking over, Breed went back out to get a breath of fresh air with Collie. "What else did the manager say?"

"Not much to me, though he was grim-faced when he learned of Kaui's passing."

"All right. Wait for Sally. She'll want to tend to Kaui's body herself. Let me know what she decides about burial. I'll go talk to Griffin." With that, Breed sighed deeply and went out into the early morning sun to find the manager.

David Griffin was at his desk scratching an entry n his journal. "Breed, ghastly business, this. There's some great trouble brewing, I'm afraid. I sent a messenger over to Fort Victoria to warn them."

"Over Kaui? What does his death have to do with danger, other than my own wrath?"

Griffin straightened his sack jacket, then thoughtfully rubbed his bearded face. "It's more than that. A young Haida woman of high rank has been abducted from near the Indian camp down on South Beach. I understand that is why Kaui Kalama was out looking for you. I asked for your assistance as the woman was someone you know well. I'm terribly sorry. I liked Kalama very much."

"Tell me the name. The name of the woman." Breed could barely keep his voice under control. "Was it Shells Shining?"

"I'm afraid I can't recall the name, but she was in the party of the Haida Comes Shouting. Kalama said you knew her."

Breed nodded his head vacantly. Griffin continued to talk, but Breed wasn't listening. His mind was on the woman he had known since boyhood. She had championed him early on and unknown to her brother, had lain with him more than once. Now, though she hadn't been found, he already felt she was dead.

"They're amassing now. What will you do?" Griffin's voice finally broke through Breed's thoughts.

"Aid in the search. I'll go down now."

"Think it's safe? Emotions are running high."

Breed stiffened. "They are my friends, no matter how I came by them. Did they suspect another tribe was seeking revenge? With the troubles last spring..."

"They appeared to be searching quietly, as if it might have been only an accident, an occasion of her getting lost and hurting herself. She apparently went for a walk in the late afternoon and did not return. That was nearly forty hours ago."

"You didn't answer my question."

"They might, but I am wondering if it wasn't someone from American Camp above or from San Juan Town. Someone could have mistaken her for one of Krill's unfortunates."

Meaning prostitute, Breed thought. "Thank you." He prepared to go. "I don't blame you for what has happened to Kaui Kalama. I appreciate you trying to get word to me."

"And all too late. I'm sorry he didn't find you."

"I wasn't at the limestone diggings as he thought. When I heard I came immediately."

Griffin rose from his desk. "I wish you luck and my sincere gratitude for coming. If there is any great trouble—well, I did send word over to headquarters in Victoria. The marines have been alerted up island. Captain Pickett will know very soon."

Breed started to go out, then came back. "Do you have any idea why Kaui went down into San Juan Town?"

"No, I don't, unless someone told him you were there."

"Who?" It was a question that neither could answer.

Collie followed Breed down the open hill to the long beach, their horses making trail in tall, rough grass wet with morning dew. It was a windswept area with hidden stony hollows and occasional bushes. Further south, the hill became steeper, arcing back to become forested Mt. Finlayson. Lopez Island was close by. Halfway down, the men stopped briefly to survey the open expanse and to talk.

"Might be dangerous, Collie. They could be in full fury."

"Not leaving. You need some backup." He patted the sword on his back.

"Comes Shouting needs backup too. And I want to find Shells Shining."

They continued on down seeking Shells Shining's brother. The day was warming up and there was mist out on Haro Strait that blocked the lower view of both Vancouver Island and the Olympic Peninsula. Eventually Breed made out a group stretching out in a line going from the shore back up on the hill. Walking southward, the group was intent on the ground before them.

"Over there," Breed said to Collie and urged his horse forward. A few minutes later they were upon them. It was a band of men in all states of dress, Haida and European, but all warriors by their manner. One wore only a blanket, his brown-black hair held in place by a headband of bird skin. He carried a war club.

At first, the mood of the search party was so grim, Collie stayed back behind Breed, his sword ready to pull. Breed paid him no mind and went immediately to a short, aristocratic man wearing a conical spruce root hat over loose brown hair. Breed nodded to him and dismounted.

"*Klahowya,*" he said in Chinook Jargon for Collie's benefit, then launched into Haida. "*Gasán uu dáng gíidang?*" Breed said.

"*Gam díi 'láa'angang,*" Comes Shouting grumbled.

Of course, you're not fine. You're in some personal hell. He gave the man some words of encouragement and empathy, then waited for his response.

Round headed with a straight nose and small hooded eyes, Comes

Shouting's thin lips curved down like a classic Haida mask someone unfamiliar with him would mistake for cruelty. Above them was a thin mustache that drooped alongside his mouth. Breed knew him to be an honest man, though swift in his actions once he made a decision. Sometimes, he was harsh. More often, generous with a biting sense of humor.

Breed bowed low, then stood up straight and handed the reins of his horse to Comes Shouting, but Breed's former master smiled and returned the reins. *"Háw'aa"* he said to Breed. Thank you.

"What would you like me to do?" Breed asked in Haida.

"Walk with us or go ahead on your horse to find my sister."

An older man stepped up to Comes Shouting and shook a rattle made of mountain goat horn in Breed's face. "Go away. You don't belong here."

Comes Shouting told him to step back. "You are being disrespectful." Breed nodded to Comes Shouting, then walked back to Collie who seemed to have been contemplating the fight worthiness of his sword. Breed grinned at him.

"Don't look so worried, Collie. We're invited. I told him we knew the ground like the back of our hands."

"They friendly?"

"Comes Shouting is my friend, but he's an important *tyee* and I was once a part of his household. I owe him my respect. I may be a free man now and a friend, but there are others who would be easily offended if I slighted him. The gent with the rattle is a shaman. Doesn't particularly like me, but it'll pass." Breed nodded in the direction of the beach where it rose up toward the mountain.

"Comes Shouting wants us to walk. They'll continue the line for the next half mile, then break off."

It was a tedious process. After a time, they took to canoes and expanded the search to the straits and channels. At night, they stopped and gathered at the southern end of the beach to eat. A fog came in. They would not be going out that night. Restless, Breed took a torch and continued to search a while longer. The image of Kaui crumbled in a cranny reminded him of possible hidden places. He looked alone, until exhausted, he returned to the group and rolled up in a blanket on the beach.

They were up at first light, but nothing was discovered until around noon when a canoe came in bearing the form of Shells Shining. Immediately, there was an alarm when it was discovered she was badly injured. A keening went up. Breed recognized the sound and was tempted to stay back, but he went down close. What he saw struck him hard.

She had been brutally attacked. She was covered with a blood-stained blanket, but underneath her clothing was torn away. There were scratches and bruises on her face and throat. Her whole lower jaw was swollen. Worst of all, her attacker had torn the labret from her lower lip, leaving a large open, misshapen wound. Her eyes were closed and she appeared to be comatose. As people help lift her out, Breed was jostled back. He was subservient once again. He sought out Collie.

"Collie, ride back up to the farm and alert Griffin to what has happened. Have him send a runner to Pickett. I'm going to see about putting her into the fishing shack over there."

"What about you?"

"I'll stay back."

"Are you crazy? Don't you remember the Haida killed a Songhees last spring in Victoria when he came to make peace?"

"Ah-ha. Now go." Breed was well aware of that story, but for the moment believed that he was safe. He just wanted Collie away just in case.

Comes Shouting was beside himself when he looked at his sister. His eyes burned with anger and hatred. "Who has done this?" He looked straight at Breed. "Who has done this?" he repeated in English.

"We'll find out, I promise. Take her to that shack over there. No one will complain."

They laid her inside the rough building. Breed stayed around for a while and learned how she was discovered across the water on a rocky beach on Lopez Island. How she had come there, no one could tell nor would they ever know. Though she woke several times, she was too weak and distressed to tell them. Heartsick over the loss of Kaui and now this, Breed decided that he should attend to Kaui's family and then go north to see Jeannie. From the way things were progressing, he felt he might not get another chance to speak to her for a while.

TRIALS AND TRIBULATIONS

J eannie was on the front porch when she heard rustling from the side of the bungalow. At first she thought it might be Kapihi. She was startled to see Breed walking in with a horse.

"Jonas, you gave me fright," she said, her heart leaping. "What a joy to see you." Jeannie went to him, then stopped when she saw his face. "What has happened?"

"I'm sorry I frightened you," he said. "It's Kaui. He's been murdered in San Juan Town."

Jeannie gasped and clapped her hands to her mouth. She sat down at the top of the stairs in a heap of skirt and petticoats. "Oh, Jonas. I'm so sorry. The dear man. Is there anything I can do?"

"No." His voice bristled with bitterness. "Not at this time." Breed tied the horse to the porch.

"Do you know what happened?" she asked.

"No, but I have an idea. I only know Kaui came here to this camp looking for me." He sat down on the porch next to her.

"Do you know why?"

Breed frowned. "I believe I do now." He became quiet and sighed. His eyes grew distant and dull.

Jeannie put a hand on his arm. "Do you want to tell me?"

Breed came out of his thoughts. "Oh, it's not for you, Jeannie. Such an unpleasantness."

"I promise you, I won't be repulsed. And whatever you say will be kept to myself."

Breed studied her, his thoughts weighing candidly on his tanned face. He was all native again and so unlike him, unkempt, as though he hadn't slept for several days. Jeannie's heart went out to him. For the first time since they had ever met, Jeannie saw vulnerability. His eyes were unusually bright and he was subdued, as if he had mislaid his bearings and could no longer navigate through the waters of what he had been, had been forced to become and was struggling to be.

'It's Shells Shining."

"Has something happened to her?"

"The worst. She was abducted a couple of days ago. I think it was Krill who did the deed and why Kaui came here—he had word of it, then I suppose went to San Juan Town to find her whereabouts when he couldn't locate me. They killed him there, threw him out like rubbish. With no witnesses, it will be thought of as another drunken brawl with no suspects."

Jeannie put a hand on her stomach. "Where is Kaui now?"

"He's to be interred at a cemetery near the HBC farm. The pastor from over at Whidbey Island has been kind enough to offer a Christian burial."

"And Kapihi? Where is he?"

"Right now with his mother, but I'm afraid he'll bolt. I might take him on for the moment. Doc-tin's offered too."

"And Shells Shining? Was she found?"

"We found her yesterday, but it's too late." Breed looked down. Jeannie thought she had never seen someone so sad and miserable— except for herself when Jeremy had died. "She was molested," Breed went on, his voice strained. "Brutally used. Someone found her on a rocky beach on Lopez Island."

A chill came over Jeannie. *Brutally used.* Jeannie knew that meant. "Has she named anyone?" She laid a hand on his arm.

"She cannot. Her assailant tried to strangle her. She can't speak."

"Oh, Jonas. What does the doctor say?"

"That he can do very little. She is too hurt and with her exposure—the shaman will try, but I believe she wishes to die. Her death is certain." Breed sighed, then leaned forward to get up. "Forgive me. I have said enough."

"And I'm not repulsed. What a dear man, you are, Jonas—to care so deeply for friends."

"There have been some who have gone far enough to say unkind things—that she was my mistress. I'm no monk, but they don't understand."

"What will you do now?" Jeannie took the hand he offered and got up. She brushed down her skirt while he slung his haversack over his shoulder.

"I'm going away until I can find out what happened. Collie Henderson will be around if you need me."

"And if you find the murderer and abductor is Krill?"

"Justice will be done."

"Will it be American or British?"

"It will be right," he said tightly. He untied the horse. "I have to go back down to help get Sally Kalama's things to Kanaka Town."

"Will I see you again?" After the joy of yesterday, Jeannie felt he was pushing her away.

He took her hand. "Of course. Perhaps we'll hear from your uncle soon. Just let me finish this. If you need me, ask any friend—Collie, Doc-tin. Otherwise, I'll hear of it."

"I will pray for Shells Shining."

"*Mahsie.*" He leaned over to her ear and whispered, "Go with the spirits." His breath was as sensuous as a kiss. She felt its warmth long after he left.

When Breed returned to the beach, a day later, Shells Shining's brother came to him. "She has been awake for a while and is asking for you."

While Collie waited inside the door, Breed was ushered further into the hut, no more than a room, yet goods befitting her station were hung around her: a rare copper plate, carved bowls and masks and robes made of mountain goat wool. Her head rested on a woven pillow made of bear grass stuffed with merganser feather down. A richly woven robe was laying over her. Ermine pelts were around her head. She followed him with swollen eyes when he knelt by her bed. She could not smile, but she made a sound when he murmured her name in Haida, settled back into breathing short and rattled. Suddenly, he curled down into a ball beneath her, putting his hands on his neck. Comes Shouting raised his voice at Breed, his hand above him as if he would strike. Breed knew his move unsettled Collie as though he feared some sort of retribution. He heard Collie start forward, then get blocked by the burly Haida guarding the door. *Stay calm, Collie*, Breed thought. Their movements were only an act. Comes Shouting put a hand on Breed's shoulder and Breed stood up.

"*Háw'aa* , Jo-nuss. Thank you."

"*Huu 'láagang.*" You're welcome.

Breed turned to see Collie's keeper push him out the door and close it. Turning to Comes Shouting, Breed took his place by the woman's feet and prepared for the end.

At sundown, more canoes came. People flooded the shoreline. Their voices joined the keening of others as the fires were built up. The shaman came out briefly with his rattle and spirit boat, then went back in but to no avail. The woman was gone. The voices grew louder and more pitiful. The hard business would begin.

When the slow, steady beat of the drums and singing began, Breed sat outside on the steps and watched, a strange feeling of emptiness coming over him. As the night wore on, the voices grew louder, rising and falling above the noise of the channel's surf. Collie came closer to Breed, saying he wasn't sure about their safety, but Breed was beyond him. All of a sudden, Breed stood up and went down toward the drummers. For the moment, he stood outside the group and joined in the singing, but someone invited him in closer. Another put a blanket over his shoulders. He was to stay there until midnight. Then he came and told Collie they would go up to Griffin.

"I've made a decision," Breed said. "When this is over, I'm going to ask Jeannie to leave with me. We'll find a sky pilot when we get to where we're going."

"That's that? You howl for hours and you've come to that? What did Comes Shouting say?"

"They'll be leaving day after tomorrow. He wants to take his sister home, but the body will not make it on the long voyage, so tomorrow they will make a huge fire and burn it for her bones. Once her spirit has been sent on its way, they can go."

"Will there be trouble?"

"Not here. He has given his word."

Collie looked at Breed's drawn and tired face. "Where's your earring?"

"I gave it to her," said Breed without further comment.

Word spread quickly to Camp Pickett and a small contingent of soldiers was sent to watch on the hill. A rider galloped north to English Camp. Griffin must have been thinking the same thing. A small band of HBC employees joined them not far away. They were heavily armed.

At midnight, Breed and Collie climbed up the hill, leading their horses and carrying torches with them. When they stopped in front of Pickett's men, the sentry challenged them.

"Put away your flaming rifle, buck," Collie said. "We're just going over to see Griffin and go to bed."

"Those injuns to war?"

"What do you think?"

"Sounds like the gates to hell down there." The soldier looked at Breed who had continued walking past them like in a trance. "What's with him? He's bleeding."

Collie shook his head. Jonas had taken his knife and cut himself on his arm. It had bled freely until it stopped on its own. He had also cut back an inch of his hair.

"It's nothing. Go back to sleep." Collie clucked to his horse, then went past the patrol.

True to their word, on the day after they burned her body, the group got up silently and left, their long canoes heading north. They were gone as if they had never been there. Peace was gingerly restored. The soldiers and marines alike relaxed and resumed their duties. Kaui was buried in the little graveyard for Hudson Bay's Company employees and Breed and Collie went hunting for rabbit. Then, Engstrom Pratt, Krill's top man was found with his head lobbed off and the rumors began.

RUMORS

For two days, Jeannie waited for word from Breed, feeling increasingly troubled as rumors of Indian canoes going north were whispered in the Royal Marine camp. Then on the day after Comes Shouting left for the north with his sister's ashes, Breed sent Kapihi to the back door of the Parker's bungalow to seek Jeannie. The boy's clothes looked even more tattered than the last time she saw him, his eyes puffy.

"Come," the boy said. "My father's *kahpo* says that you must come."

Jeannie knelt in front of him and gently brushed back his hair. "Of course, I'll come, darling. I'm so sorry about your father. He was a very nice man. Are you and your mother and sister all right?" She squeezed his shoulders and thought he felt thin. "Are you hungry? I have fresh milk and biscuits."

Kapihi's eyes glistened. He nodded solemnly. Jeannie poured him a cup and gave him a tea biscuit. When he was done, Jeannie said, "Now we can go."

She put on her shawl, for the afternoon had turned cloudy. She let the boy take her hand and lead her up the wooded hill to the road. She found Breed where she had met him before on the trail to the lean-to. He sat astride a horse. She was shocked when she saw him, so great was the change. He was unshaven and his long black hair ragged on the ends like he had cut it with a knife. His clothes looked as though he had slept in them.

"Jeannie," he said. "Forgive me. I have not been myself these last days. I'm on my way home to Timons."

He dismounted and put the reins over the horse's neck. It stamped its foot and whinnied, pushing its nose against Breed's arm. Further up the trail another horse nickered back. "Collie's up there," he said when Jeannie looked alarmed.

Jeannie relaxed. She had been warned to stay close to the camp in fear of a raiding party passing by. Observers on the coast had watched the large party of Haida canoes go north and tension had been high.

"Is it all over?" she asked.

"They're gone. Kaui's been laid to rest. A parson from Whidbey was kind enough to come over and say words."

"Will there be an investigation into Kaui's murder? Dr. Parker thought there might be an inquiry."

"Mr. Griffin, the manager, is instigating such a one on the British side, as Kaui had been an employee of the Hudson's Bay Company, but the Americans have been slow. See it more of a brawl, than a murder. They are more concerned with the number of Haida and other northern tribes in the vicinity of islands. They have asked for the USS *Massachusetts*. Don't know what for. That old tub couldn't keep up with the canoes. They have also requested help from the Royal Navy in Victoria and New Westminster. Their ships, especially the HMS *Satellite*, are faster."

He ran his hand through his hair, stopping to rub the back of his neck.

"We have been told to stay close to the marine camp," Jeannie said. "There is concern that some of the party might peel off and take their revenge."

"Comes Shouting has given his word here. I believe him. I cannot say for any others, only that nothing will happen in these waters for now."

The leaves of a salmonberry bush rustled next to them and Kapihi stepped out. He had been exploring in the tangle of bushes behind the tall maple and fir trees. He came down to Breed and wrapped his arms around the man's waist. Jonas patted his shoulder and drew him in close.

"Kapihi's going to stay with me for a few days while his mother gets her possessions together. I think she will take Kapihi and Noelani back to her people near Sil-la-lish on the mainland." He roughed up the boys' hair and told him to go back up to Collie.

Jeannie waited until he was out of earshot. "What will happen to her and her children?"

"My hope is that her family will get the support that she needs, but I promised Kaui I would look after his family if something happened to him. We promised that to each other years ago. I'll help her with what I can. In the meantime, Griffin is giving her some money, a gift of blankets, and passage for her journey."

A soft whistle came down to him.

"I have to go. Collie's getting restless. There's the channel to cross."

"How soon will I see you again?"

"Soon. Unless, you want to go to Timons with us now."

She grinned at him. "No, Jonas. It must be done proper."

He came closer. "Then we shall be proper," he whispered. He leaned in and kissed her on her lips. "I'll see you soon, *toketie*."

Gilly said nothing when Jeannie came back to the bungalow where she was engaged in a hand of whist with Dr. Parker and some of his fellow officers. Nor did she comment the day when she caught Jeannie daydreaming on the verandah while the marines did formations on the parade ground down below. There were other things to be worried about.

It all came to a head one evening just after they came in for dinner in the officer's new mess hall. Jeannie was surprised to see the two women she had met at Gilly's tea months ago. She couldn't remember their names, even though she had seen them once on the muddy streets of Victoria. *Mrs. Stout and Mrs. Lean,* she remembered. *And as opinionated as Mrs. Jenkins at Camp Pickett.*

"They came over for the day," Gilly said under her breath as they sat down. "And will return to Victoria after the meal."

"There was no tea for them?"

"They came with their own party, led by the gentleman over there." Gilly nodded in the direction of a thin man with a high collar tied with a white tie to the point of strangulation. He sat near the end of the long table next to Captain Bazalgette, the camp commander. Gilly fiddled with her napkin. "I thought it selfish of them to come when things were so unsettled. I did go down and showed them how the garden has progressed, then returned home."

"Oh." Jeannie said. She dipped her head to the ladies sitting at the opposite side of the long, candle-lit table, then said no more, feeling unsettled herself. All her thoughts were with Breed.

During the meal, the captain of the HMS *Satellite* was announced. He went immediately to Lieutenant Bazalgette and spoke to him in confidence. The commander got up at once and apologized to the women.

"Ladies, will you excuse us for a moment? Dr. Parker, will you join us outside?" As the rest of the party sat adrift at the table, Gilly and Jeannie tried to speculate what was the emergency. Outside, there was considerable activity in the marine barracks and on the wharf, but no one came in to enlighten them. Eventually, Dr. Parker returned.

"Sorry for the mystery, ladies," Dr. Parker said as he sat down next to Gilly.

"What is it, Thomas?" Gilly asked.

Dr. Parker leaned toward Gilly and Jeannie. "There's been a terrible incident that has unnerved many at the south end of the island. An American by the name of Engstrom Pratt, a confederate of that character Emmet Krill, has been found floating out in the middle channel in a blood-splattered canoe. Headless. Though there were no signs of any northern Indians— they are believed to have been long gone—there is considerable anxiety as to what will happen next."

"What? Did you say Northern Indians?" Miss Lean stood up with her fan in a flurry causing the candle in front of her to waver. Mrs. Stout looked equally alarmed, slipping her hand under the table to a gentleman Jeannie assumed was her husband. Gripping hard, by the way he stiffened.

"There's nothing to fear, ma'am," Dr. Parker said. "You are perfectly safe here."

Lowering his voice again, Dr. Parker turned back to Gilly and Jeannie, his face grim. "This has led to speculation and rumor. Word has it that Jonas Breed is involved in this foul affair. Revenge for the death of Kaui Kalama and the Haida woman who was kidnapped."

"Thomas, how awful!" Gilly said. "What a scurrilous thing to say. It's not possible. He wouldn't do such a thing."

"I find it preposterous, myself, but according to the master of the *Satellite*, that is what many in San Juan Town and at Camp Pickett believe. There are calls for his arrest."

"Does anyone know where Mr. Breed is?" Jeannie asked.

By now, members of the Stout and Lean party were standing up. "I should like to know where this man is," Mrs. Stout said. "He's immoral and a danger to society." She nodded to her male partner for support.

Jeannie's hands clutched the ribbon that held the thimble as she stood up and faced the woman. "You do not know him, Ma'am and you are sadly mistaken."

"And you do?"

"Ladies," Dr. Parker intervened. "I believe that we should all retire. Mrs. Parker, Mrs. Naughton." He turned to Mrs. Stout. "Under the circumstances, Captain Bazalgette will have to find quarters for you and your party tonight. If you are so concerned about your safety, it's prudent to stay." With that, he gave Gilly his arm and escorted her and Jeannie out.

Within five minutes, Jeannie and the Parkers were ascending the stairs to their quarters. Halfway up, Jeannie paused to look back down on the camp. It was still light out and the waters of Garrison Bay were still, but on shore a group of marines seemed to be assembling by the block house. Jeannie pulled her shawl tight around her.

Gilly must have noticed Jeannie's action. "Dr. Parker, I fear you are not telling us everything."

Dr. Parker cleared his throat. "Very sorry, dear. I didn't wish to continue the conversation in the presence of such unsympathetic ears."

Jeannie turned. "You have news of Mr. Breed?"

"I did hear that someone put in at Timons to see him, but he wasn't there."

"I can't believe he has been accused of this horrible thing. What of Mr. Krill? Surely he is suspect in the murder of Kaui Kalama?"

"Mr. Krill is no gentleman," Dr. Parker said, "but no one has broached him in the murder of Kaui Kalama, let alone the woman. Besides, he is supposed to have a solid alibi."

"Has no one asked for an inquiry?" Jeannie felt her cheeks burn.

"What of Captain Pickett?" Gilly asked. "The manager at Belle Vue?"

"I believe Griffin has. Captain Pickett is disturbed, but then this is not the first time that someone has been murdered in San Juan Town. The whiskey ranches have always given him headaches."

Jeannie felt like stamping her feet. "So everyone is stirred up over one of Mr. Krill's associates. It is so unfair."

"All is not lost, dear," Gilly said as she put an arm around Jeannie. "Jonas has his friends here and at Camp Pickett, not to mention at Fort Victoria."

"But not in Olympia. He's their countryman. Why doesn't someone stop the rumors?"

"Excellent question, which I'm sure will be answered," Dr. Parker said. He took a couple steps up the stairway. "In the meantime, I would prefer it if you would stay close to the camp quarters. Just to be safe. The death of this young Haida woman has caused considerable unrest throughout the region. There was apparently an incident the other day over near Port William on the American side among some northern Indians who had come down to work at the mill. There was no serious bloodshed, but nerves all around have been badly frayed."

"Oh, Thomas, We'll be regular lambs, but," Gilly's shoulders dropped in a sigh of exasperation, "sometimes you are so thick. Don't you see? Our Jeannie cares very deeply for Mr. Breed's welfare. In fact, they are engaged."

"Engaged?" Dr. Parker's expression went from a smile to a worry. "I do congratulate you and understand the secrecy, but this does complicates things, doesn't it?"

Jeannie straighten herself up. "The only secrecy has been due to my uncle's reply. We are to post banns as soon as possible."

"And for your good reputation, I shall keep this to myself. Breed is a capital fellow, but it's best to keep this quiet until the situation is resolved." He stepped down to her and kissed her gloved hand. "I'll do all I can to help. Now let's get off these stairs before we topple off."

"Thank you, sir." "Jeannie almost said, "mahsie," her thoughts so focused on Breed. What if he had to go away until the crisis was over or worse arrested as Dr. Parker was suggesting some wanted? That frightened her more than anything. She had to see him.

"WAIT FOR ME"

T he chance came three days later when Kapihi once again came down to the back of the bungalow and asked for the Mrs. Naughton. Jeannie was in the parlor working on mending. A simple-minded task, it had nonetheless been the best therapy for the brain-numbing swirl of accusations and counter-accusations that had continued in island discourse for the past three days. Breed had found some powerful supporters in Victoria, including Jeannie's own Uncle Archie. A number of American officers at Camp Pickett and at Fort Townsend on the Olympic Peninsula were also vocal in his defense as well as an influential citizen in Whatcom. The murder of Engstrom Pratt was inconsistent with what they knew of Jonas Breed. Support remained, even after the mutilated bodies of some miners most likely on their way to the gold fields on the mainland were found on one of the islands north of San Juan.

Most of the personal attacks seemed to come from settlers staked out near the prairies near the American camp and the denizens of San Juan Town. They were extremely vocal and wrote daily missives to the territorial government to do something about Jonas Breed and all his Indian friends. Leading the attacks was none other than Garrett Tuttle, the American settler who had torn into Jonas at the horse races. Jeannie wondered if Tuttle had some connection to Emmett Krill.

Jeannie put down her needlework and went out to the small kitchen to put on the kettle for a pot of tea. It was early evening. The Parkers were gone, having accepted an invitation from Pickett to dine with him, Lieutenant Bazalgette, and some other officers from the English Camp. Much to Jeannie's relief, Cooperwaite had been included, so she felt comfortable in declining. She had a headache. The party had left just after breakfast under the escort of armed marines. The Parkers had left Jeannie in the capable hands of Sergeant Leech, presently down at the mess hall for dinner. For the rest of the evening she would be alone, though a sentry would be posted at the bottom of the wooded hill. She checked the fire in the firebox and added a piece of alder, then poured water from a pitcher into the kettle. It was overcast outside, the early fall evening darkening before its time. There was a breeze in the trees bringing the suggestion of rain before the night closed. A branch snapped not far off, nearly covering the slight rap at the back door.

Jeannie froze. "Sergeant Leech?" she called.

From the other side of the door there was a muffled answer, not the voice of an adult. Carefully, she picked up an iron pan and went to the door. "Who's there?"

Again a muffled answer and another rap. Taking a deep breath, she pulled open the wood door and peered through the screen. It was Kapihi.

"Kapihi!" she laughed nervously. "Is Jonas about?"

"In the woods. He says to follow me. There's is a sentry up there lookin' over the camp. He says to put on something warm. It might rain."

It took Jeannie ten minutes. She put on a brown wool skirt and blouse, warm cotton stockings and a woolen cape. A felt hat finished her outfit. She removed the kettle from the stove and put it on an iron trivet. A final check of the wood box and she was out the door.

The boy took her to the right, up into the woods and away from the main path. Behind her she could see the warm yellow lights at the backs of the other officers' homes winking behind the narrow trunks of the trees that covered the hill. Cautioning her to step carefully, Kapihi negotiated her past the lone marine smoking his pipe further down the main path. Soon they were deep into the forest of maple, cedar and fir that stretched up to the top of Mt. Young. Kapihi didn't take her there, but rather to a small animal trail that disappeared into a cluster of pokey, holly-leafed Oregon grape bushes and salmonberries. When she was close to breathlessness, he finally brought her into a fern-spotted clearing where Jonas waited.

"Did he tire you? I told him not to run." Jonas collared the boy as he tried to dash by and brought him back laughing. He swung him around his waist, then plopped him on the ground.

"He's like a little deer. So sure-footed," said Jeannie.

"Well, you don't have to run any more. Come, Jeannie. I have a horse for you."

"Where are we going?"

"Where we won't be watched." He brought a small mare down to her and helped her onto the sidesaddle. "It won't be far, but far enough from the camp's eyes. You're not afraid?"

"No, Jonas. I am not."

After getting her settled, he mounted his own horse and pulled Kapihi up behind him. Going into the trees again, he led her north from the camp sometimes climbing, sometimes going down rolling forested hills. It was early in the evening. Breed kept to shadows, hiding in them or keeping to the outside edge of the little prairies they sometimes encountered. Always alert, he engaged in little talk and kept her moving. Twenty minutes later they arrived at a little hut in the woods. Sitting out in front was Sikhs wrapped in a blanket up to his ears. Far off behind the hut, she thought she could see the water of some channel. She had no idea where they were.

"*Klahowyah*, Mrs. King George," Sikhs said to her. "You are *hyas toketie* tonight, I think." He got up and took charge of her horse while Breed got down.

"Fire ready?" Breed asked him.

"*Ah-ha*. Billy Po came by and made some tea. He wants to see too."

Breed snorted. "Tell him thanks and to skeedaddle." He helped Jeannie down, then invited her into the hut.

It was a simple, cedar slab construction as bare as the cabin she had spent the night in after drifting in the canoe. It was suitable for only shelter, not long term habitation. But it did have a table, chair and a simple bed hand-hewn from alder logs. Several Hudson's Bay Company blankets were spread over it as well as a large otter pelt. In the middle of one of the walls was an army-issued iron stove, crackling inside with a hot fire. Rubbing her arms, she came in and waited while Breed gave instructions to his friends. Kapihi came to the front of the door and ducked under Breed's arm, smiled at her until he was pulled away by Sikhs. Jonas told him to behave. He waved goodbye, then with gentle creak, shut the door. The windowless room became dark, lit only by a collection of tallow candles set on the table and lantern hung near the stove. Together they made little halos of flickering light that waved against the bare wood walls.

"Let me take your cape. The fire's warm and there is hot tea, if you wish. I don't have coffee."

Jeannie said quietly that it was fine.

"Are you alright, Jeannie?"

She shook her head and laughed. "It was the ride. I've never had to play at spies and soldiers before."

"Do you believe what they say about me?"

"No, Jonas. They are foul lies. I know that. A letter from my uncle came on the evening mail. He said that someone was spreading rumors." She smiled. "He has also given us his blessing."

Breed smiled, but his face was too serious. He set the chair before the wood stove. "Here. Make yourself warm." He pulled over a bench made out of an alder log split in half, the legs made out of thick branches peeled and jammed into the rounded bottom. After serving her tea, he sat astride the bench.

"They are looking for you, Jonas. Have they looked here?"

"Don't think they know about it. Most think I'm out on the water somewhere, raiding with the long canoes." His voice was harsh and bitter. "I won't be here much longer."

"Where are you going?" Jeannie tried to keep her voice level.

"Where things are calmer. Either into the interior of American territory or up the coast in British Columbia. Let things shake out."

"Will I see you again?"

"No, not for a long while." The words were flat and cold. Jeannie felt her face pale, her mouth slack in disbelief. His face softened. "Unless you go with me."

Jeannie flushed and looked down at her tea cup. When she left the comfort of the Parker home, she guessed that it would be his reason for sending for her.

He leaned over. "Say yes. Come with me."

Jeannie put aside her cup. "I'll go with you, Jonas." As soon as she said it she knew that to go with him would change her life forever, put her into scandal again that would surely follow their flight. And uncover her past. *Mistchimas*. Captive again. Slave to circumstances.

Breed kissed her hand. "Jeannie." The relief in his eyes touched her heart. "We'll move quickly. I'll take you back to get your things together. I'll come for you tomorrow night. We'll leave then."

"What about Gilly and Dr. Parker?"

"It's good they are away at the American Camp, but they must not know. A letter can be sent in a few days. By then, we should be married and safely hidden away until the ruckus dies down."

"And my uncle?"

"I'll get word to him."

When Jeannie was satisfied with his plans, she said, "All right. I'll pick out some things I need for now. I'll get the rest later." She paused, her heart racing.

Relief in Breed's eyes were touching. He pulled her to the bench and enfolding her, rocked her gently. "Mahsie," was all he said in answer.

The cabin was still, except for the crack of the alder logs in the wood stove. No words were spoken, but she could feel tension in his body. With their flight, she would have to be strong. She pushed back his sleeve and touched the tattoo on his wrist. In the candlelight, it seemed to have a life of its own.

"I love you, Jonas Breed." She let him take down her hair and stroke its ends. He kissed her on her mouth, opening it. Jeannie closed her eyes and breathed heavily as his thumb brushed the line of her cheek. His own breathing deepened.

Breed gently pulled on the ribbon that suspended the thimble and kissed it. "Toketie."

By the light of the candles flickering on the wall, he laid out the blankets and pelt, then they undressed each other. They made love on the bed and when they joined, it was the dance on the ramparts again: gentle teasing, passion unleashed and words spoken full of love and secret meaning. When they were spent, she lay against his glistening chest, her breasts pressed into him.

"*Mahsie*, Mrs. King George."

Jeannie's hands brushed the otter pelt. It was rich and silky to her touch. "How many of these for me?"

Breed laughed. "Too many, *toketie*. I couldn't meet the bride price. I'll have to kidnap you." He kissed her on her forehead, then grew serious. "Doc-tin said he'd help find a sky pilot for us, wherever we end up. I'll have a good sense by tomorrow's eve.

"*Ah-ha*," Jeannie said.

Breed kissed her again. "We should dress. Get some air. First, I'll get you some water."

After dressing, they walked hand and hand to the door, and sat outside on the doorstep watching the stars come out. Safely enclosed in his arms, his breath at the back of her neck, Jeannie decided she loved him more than anything else in world other than Jeremy. He had more depth and experience than anyone she had ever known and with him she felt utterly safe. They talked of his pressing troubles and how they would deal with them and when they talked of their pasts and of their future, she knew that they would make a good life together.

It was nearly ten when they left for English Camp. The sun was down behind the tall trees and the clearing in the woods turning dark. Kapihi was put up half asleep in front of Jonas on his horse. Sikhs picked up his war club and followed them on foot. There was a faint moon just appearing. It threw some light on the unmarked path, a leaf-covered trail through forest. They moved silently, without a word, listening to the sounds of night around them. A slight breeze had come up and what sky there was peering through the treetops overhead seemed clouded up. A change in weather was coming.

About a half mile out from English Camp, there was a sudden movement in the trees. Instantly, Sikhs and Breed were on guard, raising their weapons to face the unknown intruder. Moving with a fluidity Jeannie sensed came only from practice and experience, the two men visually searched the dark shapes of the maples and madrone, tense and alert. Though she had only imagined it before, she now had no doubt Jonas knew how to fight and would have no compunction to do violence. The thought both frightened and reassured her.

"Jeannie," he hissed. "Come here." She brought her mare next to him, going where he pointed so that his horse covered her. Sikhs planted himself to their rear, his face intent on the night sounds.

The movement in the trees grew closer, the steps of someone deliberately wanting to make himself known to them. Jonas began to relax. Soon they were rewarded with the appearance of Collie Henderson followed closely by Doc-tin and Moki Kapuna.

"*Klahowya*, Jonas," said Collie. "We've been all over the map and hard-pressed to find you." He nodded to Jeannie and seemed pleased to see them together.

"More trouble?" Breed said.

"I'm afraid so."

Instructing Jeannie to stay back, Breed urged his horse forward to the small party of men who continued to come out of the trees. When they were all assembled, she counted twelve.

"It's Krill," she heard Collie say. "He's been pushing his case with the territorial assembly about how dangerous you are. Trying to get them to arrest you, seeing the military is a bit reluctant to step in yet. But it'll take a while to get a sheriff out here. In the meantime, Krill's done his own underhanded campaigning—he's taken Kaui Kalama's *klootsman* and daughter. Wants to trade with you."

"What? Sally?" Breed's voice was like a growl. "When?"

Jeannie gasped when she heard this. She remembered Krill when he accosted her. He was dangerous and did not make idle threats. He had threatened Breed then.

"Tomorrow morning at eight out near the valley."

Breed's face was hard as flint. "We'll go sooner. Get all the rifles and weapons you can find."

He motioned back to Jeannie. "Could you take her back, Doc-tin? I'd be obliged."

"Sure, Jonas. Whenever she's ready."

"I'll say good-bye to her now. After this is over, we're leaving until things settle down. If it settles down..." He smiled sourly.

A beautiful evening ruined, Jeannie thought.

He said good-bye to her under the trees away from prying eyes. "Did you hear that? There's some trouble," he said, "but I'll be back. Get your things together and then we'll go."

"I love you," he said. "Wait for me." He leaned over and kissed her long and deep and then he was gone.

FIGHT AND FLIGHT

Breed gathered his men in a couple of hours, moving swiftly by horseback and on foot to the southern end of the island. Advancing quietly through the woods on old Indian trail, they came out onto the military road being widened from a trail that ran from Belle Vue Farm to north of Garrison Bay. Here the trees that crowded the road on either side were a dark and tangled collection of maple, Douglas fir and madrone. At the end of the alley created by the trees, the road turned and the forest opened up to prairie. It was already light out, but the sun had not climbed above the rugged mountains to the east, so the sky above the trees was weak and diffused, the color of pinks and grays—deathly still.

Once the party assembled, one of the Sikhs's Songhees friends went forward to scout. The men spread out, each looking into the trees and undergrowth for trouble as they advanced toward the increasingly bright opening at the end of the forest pathway. There was no talking, only feet moving silently on the slightly muddy and mossy road; all information was passed by hand signal.

They heard Krill's group before they saw it as they made the turn in the road. Immediately, Breed signaled and Moki Kapuna and three of Sikhs' companions slipped into the trees. Collie, Sikhs and Billy Po all went forward with Jonas as they would be the first to be missed and would arouse suspicion if not with him. The remaining four men walked behind. They moved casually, but were more intent on action than on parley. Arriving hour and half early, they planned to take Krill by surprise.

Sally Kalama was sitting on a downed log with Noelani next to her and an old blanket thrown around her shoulders. Her face was dirty with ash; her feet were bare. Breed could barely contain his anger as he stepped forward, his rifle aimed at Krill's neck.

"Come away, Sally," he said. "Just head up into those trees. Wait with Noelani and Kapihi. We'll be there bye and bye."

Sally picked up her daughter and swiftly hustled back behind them and off the road. When she was safe, Breed turned his attention back to Krill.

"What are you going to do, Breed? Hack us all to death?" Krill sneered.

"You've got a wild imagination, Krill. Now take off your gun belt and put it on the ground."

"Do it your own self."

"You're done. I'm taking you to Pickett for kidnap and murder. Bazelgette will know within two hours."

"And I counter-charge you with murdering Enstrom, you dirty, son-of-a-bitch *siwash*," Krill shouted back. He whipped his hat off and shook it at Breed. That was enough for Breed. In two strides, he was in front of Krill, batting the hat down with the rifle's tip.

"You'll wish I did it, Krill," Breed said in low voice as he poked the rifle's cold barrel against the man's throat. "You'd better hope. Comes Shouting gave his word, but I don't think the entire Native world's keeping it. You're being watched and not only by me. Soon you won't be able to stand a lick in the wind. Now put it down."

Krill began to waver. *Good*, Breed thought. He was glad when Krill blinked, though he had no choice with a rifle barrel to his chin. In the end, he surrendered, albeit a little too easily.

Krill put the gun down on the ground and backed away. Breed looked around to find out why, but saw nothing unusual. Collie and the others covered them well and the party was slowly disarming. Some of Krill's men were already kneeling on the ground with their hands on their heads. He looked to Collie and Sikhs, then up into the trees where Moki and the three Songhees were hidden. That gave Breed eleven men total. Krill had only eight.

Breed looked to the other side of the tiny fern-dotted prairie where the trees took up again like a solid green wall dabbled with mist. Krill looked at him, a subtle smile on his lips. There! A flash of white cloth of a distant figure. Then an explosion of flame like a red-orange flower, a disconnected roar, and shouting as six more of Krill's men came out of the woods like wild men.

Breed did not feel any pain when the first bullet struck him, nor the second, but his rifle went flying from his hands. From then on everything exploded into double time. Soon a battle raged. Sikhs raise his war club and howled his battle call. Collie swung his terrible sword like a pirate, splashing blood and mowing down anyone who came close. Behind them Billy Po blocked and fought with his rifle. Breed in the middle.

Krill rose up and plunged a huge Bowie knife in the air at him, but the force that took away his rifle had also pushed Breed back as Krill stabbed air and went past him. Breed knocked him away with his right arm and elbow. Krill came at him again. One of Krill's men raised his pistol. Breed leaped across the space and grabbed the man's wrist, and turned the weapon on him. The man screamed and fell against another man causing them both to fall down. Breed jumped over them, his face blackened by the powder and swung back, firing into the fighting where Krill had ducked and run.

One, two, three. The ammunition ran out. Breed threw the pistol away. He rushed in Krill's direction, dipped to pick up his rifle. He was surprised to discover that his left shoulder and hand were blood-soaked. A curious weakness spread out from his arm and chest. His hand had no feeling. He realized he had been shot straight through the middle of his hand. The blood flowed freely, but did not pulse.

Barely able to grasp the rifle in his left hand, Breed jabbed and smashed his way back into the center where Collie and Sikhs fought on.

All around him, the acrid smell of gunpowder hung like a foul curtain in the air. The sounds of the battle became distant. Krill's men began to fall under new fire coming from the woods. *Moki*, Breed thought hazily. In the close, unrestrained fighting, Collie and Sikhs had managed to stand their ground on the blood-soaked grass and now they had the advantage.

Breed felt weak. His breath labored and his head was light. All motion slowed down. Then Krill charged.

Krill came at Breed, wildly swinging a rifle he had picked up from the corpse of one of his men. Breed ran to meet him. The two men met in a jarring collision. They pushed and wrestled like rutting rams until Breed managed to get the rifle stock under Krill's chin and roughly push him away. Grunting, Krill fell back only to charge again with a knife. Breed answered with the rifle stock again and smashed it into Krill's shoulder.

They separated and stood face to face.

The fighting around them had nearly stopped. The five men left alive in Krill's party limped off toward the other side of the prairie. There had been enough noise to arouse the authorities. Soon they would show and each side knew that there would be serious trouble from both the American and British commands. They had to go, except that there was this one last thing: two men fighting to the death.

A nasty cut the shape of a tiny sickle opened on Krill's cheek. Blood flowed down his neck and onto his collar; a black welt swelled at the corner of his left eye. As bad as Krill looked, Breed knew he was worse. The wounds in his shoulder and hand bled freely. Blood soaked his front like glistening red sweat. Krill smiled at him crookedly. His eyes showed his growing confidence.

"Emmett, let's go," one of his compatriots hissed. "He's done for. We're done here."

"I ain't," Krill said. "Not until he's down for good."

Breed motioned for Collie and Sikhs to stand back. Sikhs tossed his war club to Breed.

Krill smiled again and waved his friend back.

Breed waited for Krill to charge. He felt tired. His head buzzed, but he stood his ground. The weight of the club felt good in his hand.

The rush came quickly, without warning. Krill feinted then slashed at Breed's belly and missed. Realizing his mistake, Krill half crouched and thrust again, but it was too late. The war club came down and smashed him on the back of his head. Krill's skull cracked open like a melon, spewing blood and matter. Krill grunted, then fell dying to the ground. Breed swayed over him, then slumped where he stood.

"Jonas."

Someone caught him under his arms and eased him down to the ground. He rested against someone's chest and lap. "Collie," his voice said from far off.

"Jesus, you're bleeding like a stuck pig." Something was wrapped around his wrist and pressure applied to it. Another hand tugged at his shirt. His eyes were heavy, blood blinding one eye. His head rang. He sought sleep and peace from that and the new sensation: a hard, relentless pain in his hand. The numbness had worn off.

"Is it over?" Breed wondered out loud.

"*Ah-ha*. It's over, Jo-nuss," another disconnected voice said. "Now we go fast. Be safe bye and bye." Breed nodded his approval and slumped over, glad someone else had made the decision.

Breed came to in the early afternoon. Lying on a litter and wrapped in Hudson Bay blankets, he felt safe under the swooping boughs of a cedar tree. Disoriented for a moment, Breed thought he looked down into an open, upside down green umbrella. The branches were its spines; the rough shaggy bark of the tree its handle. Then the pain hit and he moaned. Suddenly, two faces appeared in his umbrella and looked down at him. It was Sikhs and Moki. They sat silently next to him and shooed away little gnats that came near his face. Breed smiled stiffly at them, then asked for water. His mouth was dry as hardtack and the afternoon was hot.

"Jonas." Collie crouched down next to Breed and helped him drink. After he was done, he settled back.

"Where are we?" Breed asked hoarsely.

"On the southeast side of the island. Been waiting on Doc-tin."

Breed shifted his body and gasped. He hurt all over. "So. What's your opinion?"

Collie bit his lip. "I'll not keep the truth back, *kahpo*, for you'll not countenance it. You've been hit hard, as you can feel. I've cleaned your wounds as best I can and the bleeding's stopped, but the hand—Jesus, I don't know what to do about the hand."

"Show me."

While Moki supported Breed against him, Collie opened the sling, then gently unwrapped the linen piece that bound the hand and wrist to a narrow plank of thinly cut cedar. Though clean, blood had soaked through the bandage where the thumb and forefinger made the letter *C*. As Collie got closer to exposing the whole area, Breed stifled a groan. On the last wrap, he shifted uncomfortably. Underneath, a quarter piece of a tobacco leaf had been laid over the damaged wrist and hand. It was stuck to the skin and wounds underneath.

"Jesus," Collie said. "Would you look at that, now."

"Get it over with," Jonas said.

Collie exposed the hand.

"So that's how it is," Jonas said tightly through his teeth.

Swollen to twice its size, the hand looked as purple as a grape. On the wrist, stitching made from the white tail of Collie's horse tenuously held together a large, deep wound. A makeshift job made more gruesome by the evidence of cauterizing. A second, deep sutured gash showed where a bullet fragment had zig-zagged across the flesh.

"You've severed or torn tendons in the wrist, *kahpo*," Collie said.

Breed tried to make a fist, but it was a weak attempt. A groan exploded from his lips.

"I picked out all the cloth threads I could find, then sewed up and attached what tendons I could. I didn't think it could wait. Maybe Doc-tin can fix it," Collie said.

"Maybe." Breed laid back against Moki. Sweat broke out on his upper lip. His face was pale. "More water. *Mahsie.*"

Collie obliged, then felt his friend's forehead. He pulled away like it was burning hot.

"Anyone follow us?" Breed whispered.

"Sikhs's been keeping watch. Sent a runner not long ago. Bazalgette and Pickett both dispatched parties up to where the fighting was. They were investigating not more than a few minutes after we left. An alarm has gone out."

"And?"

"Your arrest has been ordered."

"And for any of Krill's men?"

"Now, we don't know that. The prairie was empty. No one wished to leave any sign. How could they know who the parties were? There was only the blood and weapons."

"How could they know about me?"

Collie couldn't answer.

Something rustled behind Breed. "Who's that?" His voice was tired and husky. He coughed to clear it.

"It's Kapihi," Moki said. "He was supposed to stay with Sikhs, but he ran away and followed us here."

"Where's his mother? Where's Sally?"

"We sent her to Kanaka Town."

Breed sighed. "Hey, *kolohe.* Come here."

The boy came around. He swallowed when he saw the exposed hand. Breed nodded to Collie that he should bind it up, then smiled. "You need to listen to your uncles when they tell you to behave. Your mother will worry."

The boy didn't answer.

"He saw everything, *kahpo,*" Moki said. "Hasn't said much since."

Breed smiled at Kapihi, then stiffly reached out and touched the boy's head. "You'll be all right." A tear spilled down Kapihi's cheek. "I'll be all right. Now skedaddle." Billy Po appeared and took the boy away. Jonas sagged against Moki.

"I'm tired," Breed said vacantly. "How long for Doc-tin?"

"He was sent for some time ago. We're thinking he's still near English Camp where he went with Jeannie Naughton. Probably has to be smuggled out past road patrols." Collie finished wrapping the wounded wrist and hand with a new cloth, then put Breed's arm back into the sling.

"Listen, Jonas. Moki thinks we should take you to the mainland. Maybe go up the Nooksack River and stay with Sally Kalama's folks for a while. 'Til you're stronger and 'til things get sorted out. You know, with the authorities."

"Not yet. Jeannie. We're to meet tonight."

Collie looked pained. "I know. I'm sorry, Jonas."

"I've got to get word to her."

"I understand that, but you're not thinking clearly. It's too dangerous now to get word to her. Besides, what could she do? She can't come here. It's impossible."

There was a long pause as Breed tried to get his muddled brain to think. "What if she were to go somewhere off the island and we send word to get her later?"

"Were would she go?"

"To the peninsula or Whidbey Island."

Collie shook his head. "None of us could go, Jonas. They're looking for *all* of us."

For a moment, Jonas said nothing. His breath rasped as he drew it through his mouth. Finally, he said, "Pierce. Andrew Pierce could do it. He could take a note, then get her away. No one would question him."

"When?"

"Now. Send someone now. When I hear that she is safely away, I'll go."

SWORD OF MERCY

Hours after the fight, Doc-tin caught up with Breed. Secretly summoned from near English Camp where he had left Jeannie, he had to go several miles around the patrols. By the time he reached Collie's makeshift camp on the southeastern side of San Juan Island rumors flew far and wide about Breed. The noise of the fight had startled the already nervous settlers near American Camp and San Juan town. Alarmed, both the British and American military were on the lookout for Breed and his men. By evening, there was also a rumor that Krill was dead and Comes Shouting descending down on the island with fifteen canoes each filled with sixty Haida warriors led by Breed.

"Where is he?" Doc-tin asked as he rushed into the camp set up on a forested ridge overlooking the water to the east. Sikhs took his horse while Collie led Doc-tin back to an old cedar tree. There he found Breed propped up on a slanted board covered with a cattail mat. He was bare-chested, his left arm in a sling and the hand heavily bandaged. Doc-tin did not need to know what might have happened. By the light of a candle lantern, the cuts and bruises to Breed's pale, strained face were visible. Dried blood stained his neck and arms.

"My God, Jonas," said Doc-tin. "What have you gotten yourself into?" He put down his medical box. Kneeling, he reached over and looked under the cloth bandage on Breed's shoulder.

Breed opened his eyes. "What took you so long?" He smiled, but it was weak as his voice.

"Patrols. They're everywhere. You've caused quite a ruckus."

"*Ah-ha*," Breed said. He breathed through his mouth in soft little pants, occasionally swallowing and licking his lips.

"Collie," Doc-tin said. "He needs water." He felt Breed's pulse. It was a little faster than he would have liked. Methodically, the farrier began to check Breed all over: feeling for broken bones, examining any wounds that needed attention, laying his head on Breed's chest to listen to his lungs.

"The bleeding has slowed," Doc-tin said to Collie when he came back with a tip cup of water. "There's some seeping."

Doc-tin put the cup to Breed's lips and let him drink. He handed back the cup and lifted one of Breed's eyelids and looked at his pupil. A couple of more taps and touching and he was done. He patted Breed on his good shoulder. "Can I look at that hand?"

Breed shrugged. "It's not much to look at."

"Bring some more lanterns, will you?" Doc-tin asked. "I'm a blind man here." When he was satisfied with the light, he began to unwrap Breed's hand. Collie came and sat down by the two men. "Is that Kapi-hi?" Doc-tin asked when he spied a small form curled up on the ground not far from Breed.

"Aye," said Collie. "Hasn't left Jonas's sight since the fight. Finally went to sleep, the little bugger."

"You feed him, Collie?" Breed asked sleepily.

Collie put his hand gently on Breed's good shoulder. "Never you mind, *kahpo*. The boy's looked after. I promise."

Doc-tin started the last wrap. Breed began to move his legs uncomfortably. "Hold on for a little bit," said Doc-tin.

"I'm not going anywhere." Breed gritted his teeth, then gasped when the cloth caught on the horsehair stitching and ripped the battered flesh on the wrist.

"Hold on, Jonas. Bring the light closer, Collie" Doc-tin ordered. He studied the stitches and the general state of the wounds on Breed's wrist and hand.

"Can you make a fist?"

Breed made an attempt, but the thumb and index finger could barely move.

"You fought like this?" Doc-tin wondered. "Hmm?"

There was no answer. Breed's eyes had closed and he slumped against the board, breathing nosily through his mouth.

Doc-tin touched Breed's forehead. It was hot.

"Damn," Doc-tin said, leaning back on his heels. "Have any whiskey?"

"Sure, Doc-tin." Collie called for some. When the little stone jug was handed over, Doc-tin took a big swig, then awkwardly got up.

"Jonas is right," Doc-tin said. "He's not going anywhere." Doc-tin got up and walked to the edge of the ridge. Collie followed. Across the water a faint light twinkled on the adjacent island. Hopefully, it wasn't some foe. In one day, the whole world had turned upside down.

"What do you think about the hand?" Collie asked.

"It's bad, Collie. I don't believe that I can do anything for it."

"What do you mean?"

"The hand should come off. It's already infected. The tendons are ripped to hell. You did the best you could, my friend."

Collie looked back toward his friend in disbelief. "You can do nothing?"

"I've got carbolic acid and laudanum. I can try to stay the infection from spreading and I can keep him comfortable, but in the end, the hand's so bad I think it will continue to fester until his whole body is filled with poison. I don't know how he did it. Fighting after he was struck. Charlie Two Bone said he was hit on the first volley."

Collie looked crushed. His mouth sagged. Something kept getting stuck in his throat. Swallowing hard, he stepped away. Doc-tin didn't blame him. His thoughts were pretty dark at the moment too. The thought of amputation sickened him, but he wanted his friend to live.

"How soon do you want to do it?" Collie asked.

"It's too dark now. Besides, I don't have my complete surgery, my saws or ether. With the patrols, I couldn't get back to my cabin."

"Jesus," Collie swore under his breath. "Well, never you mind, Doc-tin. When the time comes, we'll have what you need to do it, but maybe it's best for now. I'm not sure if he'd agree to do it just yet."

"What do you mean agree? There's no choice!"

"He wants to get word to Mrs. Naughton. Have Andrew Pierce take her away from here until it is safe for them to meet again. We've been waiting for sundown to send the messenger."

It was Doc-tin's turn to stare in disbelief. He looked back into the trees where he could see Breed propped up against the board and felt both a pang of fear and sorrow. All his plans to marry Jeannie.

"You can't, Collie. You can't wait on this,"

"You might have to wait anyway," Moki Kapuna said as he came through the trees. "Rider just came in. There's a patrol not far from here. American. They'll sniff us out. Should we get the canoes ready now?"

"Ah-ha," Collie said. "Tell the others to load now. You and Charlie Two Bone get Jonas set to move. We'll take five men in your canoe, the litter in the middle. I want the campsite cleaned of everything. Nothing is to be left behind. And Moki, send Feemster now to Pierce and get Mrs. Naughton away."

"It could take all night, kahpo."

"I know. But it's got to be done." Collie turned to Doc-tin. "We can move him, can't we?"

"You can move him. Make room for me."

"Even beyond that island over there? Plan is to get him to the Nooksack and upriver to Sally Kalama's people."

"It's a long journey and a terrible risk."

"I think at this point, we have no choice. If the authorities are going to look for him and treat him like some heathen criminal and his friends too, it's best to go until someone can speak on his behalf. He didn't bring this upon Krill and his gang. Krill did."

"Is it true he killed Krill?" Doc-tin asked.

"Ah-ha. There's no denying that."

Doc-tin sighed for the second time. "Well, let's move. How much fresh water do you have? He'll need it."

"It's been looked to already, Doc-tin. There's a small keg full."

Leaving Moki Kapuna and Charlie Two Bone behind to wait on word of Feemster, they found their next camp across the waters after successfully eluding the search party. Like gray ghosts, they paddled into the dark, their trail lost on the surface of the water. They made camp in a madrone woods up off the beach using cattail mats as cover in case it rained, but it had been hot and sunny that day and the weather did not threaten.

A guard was set up while the rest of the men slept. Breed had taken the voyage well, even showed renewed stamina, but it was obvious that he was very ill. By morning he appeared to have shrunk. He had spent a restless night. His eyes were unnaturally bright, the skin over his cheekbones tight and dull. Doc-tin got him to eat some broth made from desiccated vegetables and elk jerky, then changed his bandages. The shoulder was inflamed and tender, but at least the cauterized wound showed some improvement. The hand did not. Finally, Doc-tin sat down and told Breed the truth.

Doc-tin thought Breed took it well, but Breed would not agree to have it done until he heard news that Jeannie was away. As he struggled against the pain and fever, he focused on this one thing: he must hear that Pierce had taken her off the island.

At midday, they moved again, portaging across the forested island, then crossing open water again to another island on the other side. Here they set up a more comfortable site, well protected from any surprise attack. It was an exhausting trip. Breed went again in his litter, a helpless bundle as they scrambled over the rocky terrain to the other side. On the other side, he was nearly dropped down the steep slope to the beach. Loading him into the canoe was equally difficult as they fought incoming tide. There was a palpable tension among the men, the uncertainty of their future on their minds. Only Collie and Sikhs kept the men and Breed going. The old man spoke to Breed in Chinook and other tongues Collie couldn't guess at, joking and cajoling his friend to be *hyas skookum*. Breed was *hyas skookum* and more. His men began to wonder how he managed to hang on.

The day went on and still there was no word. Doc-tin became extremely fearful. How he would do the surgery had already been solved: he could not bear to saw through with his knife. The chance of further damage was too high and it would completely exhaust Breed. He would do it with Collie's sword. It was extremely sharp and would cut clean, even through bone. All he had to do was to get his subject to agree. Toward early evening, he could not stand it anymore and instructed Collie to light a fire and prepare the sword. By now Collie was alarmed at his friend's condition. He couldn't take it any longer, either. He ducked down to the makeshift hut and crawled in to where Breed was resting against his board.

"Jonas! For God's sake, let Doc-tin do his business. You can't wait any longer. You'll die."

Breed painfully shook his head. Collie watched him struggle to steady himself even in his propped-up position, but he was determined. "Not until she's away," he whispered hoarsely.

"Damn it, man. Have you no love for yourself?" Collie motioned for Kapihi to stand at the door and let them know the minute the canoe came, then put a cloth over his nose. The smell of sweat, blood and rancid flesh was getting to him.

Breed's head rolled back against the mat-covered board. It was hot in the makeshift hut, but he couldn't tell any more if he was smoldering or the air. The space felt dark and closed in, despite the gaps in the cattail matting. The late afternoon light from the irregular door opening was blinding. He stared at it with fever-filled eyes and fought the urge to rise, push his way through and plunge into the channel's cold water. The urge was like an itch he couldn't get to, but he wasn't going anywhere. He was too weak.

"Have some water, Jonas." Collie gently lifted his friend's chin and helped him drink before easing him back. "You look like shit. Don't say I didn't warn you."

"About women?"

"Yeah. Women." Collie scratched his whiskered face and grinned. He took a cloth and wiped Breed dry, then lightly patting him on his good shoulder, crawled to the opening to stretch.

"Don't go far," Breed said wearily behind him.

"I won't. I'll look to the fire."

"Make sure it's hot."

"It'll strike clean, I promise you." He looked back, his eyes pleading one more time. "Don't wait any more than you can. I'm afeared for you."

"When she's away," Breed croaked.

The minutes seemed to stretch out, each moment grotesque in its passing. Inside, the air was oppressive and heavy with a bittersweet stench. Flies buzzed lazily. Outside, the light decreased as it moved away from the door and slid down to the water's edge. Breed seemed to slip with it, his eyes closing, then shutting tight as he fitfully dozed.

Collie went outside with Kapihi and sat on a large rock with his rifle over his arm. The Kanakas and Billy Po had moved back under the sheltering trees. From their position, Collie knew they were safe. The evening was fast approaching, bringing its curtain of shadows and dark. The view across to the other heavily-forested islands was excellent. They could move with little warning.

He shook his head. He wasn't so sure that he would wait. Word could always be got out. But Breed, he knew, wanted to be sure. He might not survive the ordeal to come. He wanted to go knowing.

Collie stirred the fire and added pieces of wood. The sword would be hot. He started to sit back down when Kapihi said, "Look! *Canim!*"

Collie squinted into the low rays of the sun and saw the shape emerge against the backdrop of the island opposite them. It hugged the blue-gray shore, but further observation showed that it was well out into the channel where golden streaks of light bobbed on the water. Two figures were sitting in it.

"Come back in," Collie ordered. "I'll wait here."

"I know this one, Collie."

"You just wait 'til you see the whites of their eyes."

"It's Moki. His eyes are black."

It was Moki. Paddling with quick, precise strokes, the men brought the dugout canoe rapidly across the water. The Kanaka raised his hand in greeting, then took his paddle out of the water and rested it across the front of the cedar canoe. "We bring news," he said and let his partner guide them into shore.

A few moments later, Collie was back in the hut, scrambling across the matted floor.

"Jonas," he said, then groaned when he found Breed slumped over. "Jonas. Don't give up on me now. She's away," he yelled as he pulled him upright. "She's away!"

Breed opened his eyes. He had trouble identifying who was talking to him, then brightened. "Collie." He clutched his friend's shirtsleeve listlessly. "Who's come?"

"I have, Jo-nuss," Moki said. "*Mika kloshe tum tum*. She's away to Port Townsend. It's all arranged." The big Kanaka squeezed into the space and smiled broadly. "You look like shit, *kahpo*."

"I told him that already," Collie said. "Tell Kapihi to get Doc-tin and tell him to come fast. We've got work to do. First, let's get him outside. I can't do my business here." He put his arms around Breed's shoulders and under his knees and indicated that Moki should do the same. Together, they began to lift him forward.

"Wait... Who's with her?" Breed whispered.

"The *Boston*, Andrew Pierce, Jo-nuss."

"Good," Breed murmured. "Good..." He began to drift off, then caught himself and co-operated when they told him to move his legs.

They half-carried, half-dragged him to the opening. Collie called for help and Charlie Two Bone appeared along with another Indian man. They lifted Breed out and over to some blankets that Collie had set out hours ago under one of the drooping cedar trees. The fire crackled close by.

"Wrap him and keep him warm," Collie said to Moki after Jonas was set against the tree. Going to the fire he checked the sword laid in there a few minutes before, then the bentwood box where he had collected clean cloths. He looked across the water. The sun was down, twilight descending fast. He ordered one of the lamps lit, hoping varmints hadn't eaten the last of the tallow candles.

Doc-tin came out of the trees with the other Kanakas. He made a face when he saw Breed, then crouched down beside him. Breed's eyes were closed. The farrier sniffed the bandaged arm, then laid his head on Breed's chest. The heartbeat was strong.

"I'm not dead yet," Breed said unexpectedly as he opened his eyes.

"Thought you were trying to do just that. Waiting on this. You can't wait on something like this, Jonas."

"I'm ready. Just do it."

Doc-tin had Moki pass over a small, cherry wood box. Inside there were some surgeon's tools and some little glass bottles. He selected two of the bottles and a spoon. Opening the first, he poured a full teaspoon and ordered Breed to drink it. It was laudanum.

"I don't want it."

"You've got no choice. Now drink it and be done. I don't want you exhausting yourself any further. Everyone knows you're *skookum tum tum.*" He instructed Collie to open the other bottle and liberally pour some of it onto one of the cloths. Undoing the bandage, Doc-tin exposed the damaged flesh and cleaned around the infected forearm with carbolic acid. Breed whimper. When it was cleaned to his liking, Doc-tin checked for lines of infection coming from the tattered flesh and was relieved to see none. So far, the infection was contained around the wound and damaged tendons. They would have to move quickly. What they were about to do, he had never done before, but Collie had promised that the cut would be clean, including the bone. It would be as good as a saw.

Several lengths of cedar wood were splintered on the ends with a d-adze then bundled together before being laid into the fire to make a firebrand. A muslin bag was laid out on the blanket along with cloths from Collie's box. When everything was set, Doc-tin had Moki and some of the men come and sit behind Jonas, holding him into a sitting position. The wounded arm was stretched and laid across another bentwood cedar box, causing Breed to whimper. Doc-tin tied a tourniquet of India rubber above his elbow and tightened. When all was set, Collie brought the sword from out of the fire, its handle swaddled with cloths. Doc-tin inspected the hot blade. He knew that it was made of superior steel capable of cutting an elk leg bone as clean as slicing a butter cake. There would be no splintering. That was all that mattered to him. Without the necessary surgeon's saw with him, he needed a good substitute.

Doc-tin took Breed's hand and slipped the muslin bag over it, covering part of his still visible tattoo.

"I'm going to lose that?" Breed looked at the wide brown and black bracelet that had been a part of him for so many years.

"You're not a *mistchimas* anymore. You're a free man." Doc-tin gently but firmly took Breed's hand, making sure the arm was stretched out. He nodded to Moki to put a twist of cloth into Jonas' s mouth, then secure him at the shoulder and head.

"Know a saddlemaker up at Fort Langley," said Doc-tin. "Real good at making casings for things like this. Good piece of bent iron for a hook and you're all set. Saw a seaman once with a hook mend sail, comb his hair, and work an oar..."

Neither Doc-tin nor Breed saw the sword come down. Without warning, Collie brought it down full force, shattering the box. Moki and the farrier were left holding onto parts of Breed's left arm and hand. Then, before Jonas could even bite against the rag, Collie seized the cedar firebrand from the fire and thrust its flame against the raw limb. As flesh, bone and blood sizzled, Breed bit down on the cloth and screamed. His eyes rolled back in his head. Moki cradled him against his chest, his right arm around his neck. Breed's jaw relaxed and the rag began to slip out of his mouth. One of the Kanakas took it, while Doc-tin checked the cauterized limb.

"Looks good, Jonas. Gonna do some sewing and pull the skin over, then grease and cover it up. Then time will tell."

Jonas slumped forward. Mercifully, he was down and out.

ALOHA

Kapihi stepped out of the shadows and listened to the men talk. The boy knew that Jo-nuss was very sick and that the *Bostons* and the *King Georges* were all looking for him. He couldn't be taken to Port Townsend and he couldn't go into the British interior.

"You can't move him," Doc-tin said.

"But he'll had a better chance if we could get him to Sally Kalama's people."

The men continued to talk. Kapihi grew drowsy and went to sleep next to Breed's litter. He woke a couple of hours later. The men were moving around, with their lanterns masked. When he didn't see Breed, he panicked. "Where's Jo-nuss? Where's Jo-nuss?"

"Shhh, *ow*," Moki said. "They must get him away."

Straining to see past Moki, Kapihi saw them put Breed into a *salt chuck canim* and bundled him up in blankets. Kapihi went down with his candle lantern to look at him. He stood in the water and stared. "Is he dead? He looks very bad."

Breed was covered in sweat against the cool summer night's air. His face was pale and he seemed to be talking to himself. There was blood on his shirtsleeve and shoulder.

"Never you mind, Kapihi. He's just all mixed up and talking to the spirits. He'll be better bye and bye."

"I don't think so." He began to cry. To Kapihi the *canim* was like a coffin on the water. Breed was already laid out.

Breed opened his eyes. "Kapihi. Be good. Listen to your aunties and your uncles and especially, your mother." He spoke in a whisper, frightening the boy even more. Breed seemed to want to say something else, but the effort was too much. His eyes fluttered and closed.

Collie came over and put a hand on Kapihi's shoulder. Breed was asleep again. "Come and get ready to go. You'll be going with Sikhs."

Kapihi leaned over and breathed on Breed's face. "*Alo-ha*, Jo-nuss." He drew the last syllable out.

"What are you doing?" Collie pulled the boy back.

Tears streamed down Kapihi's face. "I am giving him *ha*, the breath of life, but I think it's too late."

Sometime later, the party loaded and left for the mainland. Kapihi was put in another canoe with his sister Noelani. They all went together for some time, then Breed's canoe separated from his, melding into the dark. That was the last Kapihi saw of him.

END OF THE WORLD

Jeannie waited all day for word from Breed.

"Wait for me," Breed had said.

But waiting was so hard. Jeannie saw how heavily armed and focused the men were. This was not simple trouble. This was an apex to a much larger event she didn't quite see. Her greatest fear was that Breed would be arrested.

Around her the woods were too still. The osprey that normally hunted the bay in front of the camp was gone. Even the Royal Marines seemed unnaturally subdued until they burst up the road behind the bungalows on a quick march with clanging weapons and creaking gear. As they passed they kicked up dust that dropped down through the trees to the bungalows like brown pollen. Going out on the veranda, she asked the officer next door if he knew where they were going.

"Not to worry, Mrs. Naughton. Some agitation down near American Camp. The marines are attending to it with their American military partners. The island has no civil government, y' see, with it being in dispute."

Jeannie's heart pounded against her throat. "It's not the Haida come back?"

"Oh, no. Nothing of the sort. A local disturbance. Don't y' fear." He straightened his uniform and hurried off down the steps.

Jeannie feared.

On the second morning after she had said good-bye to Breed, a subaltern knocked on her door. "I'm sorry to inform you that the Parkers are delayed at American Camp until it is deemed safe."

Jeannie clasped her hands so they would not shake. "For how long?"

"At least until the scoundrels are found. There are reports of causalities."

Jeannie put a hand on her throat and gripped the mourning brooch with Jeremy's lock of hair in it and the thimble on her neck. *Make me strong, Lord,* she prayed, as the man walked away.

She closed the door and looked around the parlor where she had spent so many happy weeks. Gilly had brought her back from the very edge of complete desolation after Jeremy died. Had shown her purpose, unconditional friendship, and most of all, made possible the way for her to meet and sustain her acquaintance with Jonas Breed.

She sighed. And now her stay must end. One could think she was taking leave of her senses, but she knew she had to find Breed. Something was terribly wrong, something delayed him from coming in close. If he was involved in the "agitation" and both the Americans and British military were searching for him, then getting away from the Royal Marine Camp was all more imperative. After struggling with every argument why she shouldn't go, she finally gathered all she could into her valise, found her bonnet and shawl, and put on her sensible shoes.

She took one last look from the veranda and ascertained that the camp was quiet. She only heard the normal sounds of the blacksmith clang and occasional shout of a marine hailing a friend. She closed the door and at the nightstand next to her bed wrote a note to Gilly and Doctor Parker, thanking them—very inadequately, she thought—for their kindness. She hoped to meet with them at a later date. And, she assured them there was in no danger to her soul or person. She folded and sealed the letter and left it on her neatly-made bed. One last look and she slipped out the back door and onto the trail she had taken so often with Kapihi.

She went through the woods toward the shelter. If Breed was trying to reach her, this would be the best place to meet. By now, people might know of Doc-tin's cabin and it could be watched. Their special place was hidden, known only to Kapihi. She pushed her way through the gooseberries turning color at the first hint of autumn and found her way back to the deer trail she had followed before.

The woods were already hot and still except for a pileated woodpecker testing a tree. His deliberate hammering echoed through the increasingly dense cedar and alder trees. Another turn in the trail and she was in the little fern glen. The shelter was still there, but now seemed forlorn. She flipped opened the woven flap and sighed. The cot and table with its folding camp stool were waiting for her.

Now what will I do? She put down her valise and sat down on the stool. Surveying the clearing, she wondered if she had brought enough things. She certainly had not brought a lantern, only a piece of adamantine candle. But then, a light or fire would be unwise. She looked up through the opening in the trees to find the sun's direction. It was nearly centered, though bent to the approaching change of season. She pulled her shawl around her even though she was near to perspiring.

The woodpecker's work continued for the next hour. Jeannie drank some water from a canteen and ate a bit of biscuit and listened for any disturbance on the road, but she was too cloistered in the trees to make much of. Finally, tired from a sleepless night, she lay down on the cot and fell asleep.

"Missus." A hand pressed over Jeannie's mouth as she jerked awake. Leaning over her was Alani, her dark eyes full of worry. "Shhh."

Jeannie bolted up. "Alani. What are you doing here?" She looked beyond the woman to a bearded man wearing big boots and a slouch hat. A haversack hung over his shoulder along with a rifle. She had never seen him before.

"We been lookin' for you." Alani stepped back. "This is Mr. Feemster, a friend of Jo-nuss."

Jeannie looked behind the man. "Where is Jonas?"

Alani bit her lip. "Oh, Missus, something very bad has happened. Jo-nuss, he kill that Emmett Krill. But Jo-nuss, he hurt so bad." Alani's eyes welled up. "He wants you away so he can find you later. I bring you *kokua*." She turned away as though she didn't want Jeannie to see what she really thought.

Jeannie felt as though she was hearing news from the end of a tuning fork. She heard the words that confirmed her worst nightmare vibrating in her head, but she couldn't make out what they meant. *How was he hurt?* "Mr. Feemster?"

He took off his hat. "I'm to take you over to the other side of the island, Mrs. Naughton. There you will go with Andrew Pierce down to Whidbey Island."

"Andrew Pierce?"

"Yes, Breed trusts him. He'll find a place for you to stay until it is safe. Jonas says that it will be proper."

"Have you seen Jonas?" Jeannie felt that dread again.

"Yes."

"Is he as bad as Alani says?"

Feemster kneaded his hat. "I'll not lie to you, Mrs. Naughton. He's gravely wounded, but we are all hopin' for the best. He's bein' moved as we speak, but it could take a few days to have you all safely together in good hands. There are patrols out lookin' for him. For all of us." He took her valise. "We need to go now."

With Alani following, he led her deeper into the forest. About a quarter mile from the shelter, the trees opened again to a clearing where three hobbled horses stood.

"We must move quickly now." Feemster tied her valise to his saddle then helped her up on her saddle. He spoke no further. Once Alani was up on her mount, they took off.

The ride through the forest was swift and solemn. Sometimes Feemster stopped to listen and test the air for what reason Jeannie couldn't tell, mostly it was move, move. It only increased her feelings of confusion and dreaded loss—the same apprehension she felt as she waited for her little boy's approaching doom. She gripped her reins so tight that after a time she couldn't feel them through her gloves. The horse eventually took the lead, eager to stay close to the others.

Eventually, they bolted across a prairie and down through a madrone forest overlooking a beach where a *salt chuck* canoe waited. Next to it was a crew of Indians and a rattled Andrew Pierce. He looked out of place in his black coat and hat and tie, but he greeted her with a sweep of his hand and the calming words, "At your service, Mrs. Naughton."

When he helped her down, Jeannie was sure he could feel her trembling—part exertion, part terror. She stared at the canoe and beat down the panicking image of being adrift in a smaller version not too long ago. But I am adrift already, she thought. I'm adrift without Breed.

"Where are we going?"

"To an American settlement—either Port Townsend or down to Whidbey Island. I have acquaintances in both places. Mrs. Kapuna is going as well."

Alani came and stood by her. Jeannie took her hand and clutched it to her breast. "And Jonas?" Her eyes filled with tears.

"He will be informed. Right now we must go." Pierce turned to Feemster. "Godspeed. I'll send word where we land."

"Wait." Jeannie straightened up. She asked Feemster. "Where are *you* going?"

"To let them know you are away. Then Doc-tin can do his business."

"Business?" Jeannie gripped Alani's hand tighter. Her voice squeaked.

Pierce looked hard at Feemster. "Best be on your way."

Jeannie pushed past Pierce to Feemster's side and put a hand on his horse's saddle. "I need to know."

Feemster cleared his throat. "Uh, Jonas— has been moved several times but –ah—Doc-tin needs to do some surgery." He smiled a reassuring smile that didn't quite match his eyes, but Jeannie had no time to assess it further. Pierce was taking her arm, gently leading her and her valise to the canoe. Feemster was off before she could protest. She stared at the canoe and wondered how she could do it again.

"Get in, Mrs. Naughton." Jeannie heard Breed's voice say, not Pierce's voice. She let the men settle her in with blankets and an India rubber ground cloth. At the last minute, Pierce asked if she would remove her bonnet.

"You need a disguise you see," He showed her a scarf and a cedar hat. "If we are watched from shore or ship, they will think you some native *klootsman*."

Jeannie accepted his explanation and exchanged her bonnet for the scarf and hat. All the men in the canoe smiled and approved.

"*Toketie*," one man said. It made Jeannie weep, a tear going down her cheek.

They went down the southeast side of the island, crossing over to Lopez Island and out towards Haro Strait. Jeannie looked back at the settlement of San Juan Town clustered near the lagoon. Smoke rose from one of the shacks, but the place looked unnaturally quiet. As it grew distant she could make out features at the American Camp further back on the bare hill. There the ramparts lay guarding the camp as it first was intended, but in her heart it held her secret of dancing in the moonlight with Breed. She choked up at the thought.

"Missus?" Alani sat behind her, wrapped in her own blankets.

Jeannie shifted around, and looked at Alani. "Are you warm enough?"

"Oh, yes. I'm always ready for the sea and wind." She smiled. "We will get there pretty soon."

Jeannie wondered where "there" was. Pierce still seemed undecided.

After another hour's driving run, they caught up with a steamer going down to Port Townsend and were loaded on. Jeannie was kept to the back with the men while Andrew made inquiries of the day. So far, no news had come of the fight up on the prairie as Pierce was now calling it.

"That is a good thing," he said. "It will give Jonas and the others time to get to the mainland."

He saw to her comfort, exposed as they were on the deck, but after they arrived at Port Townsend in the dark, Pierce had her put her bonnet back on and took her to a small inn for the night. The following day, he took her over to Whidbey Island where they stayed with one of his friends, Barman Kohl, until word came of Breed.

The Kohl homestead was set on a claim cleared of heavy trees only a couple of years before when the area was deemed finally safe after the area's first pioneer, Isaac Ebey, lost his head in a northern Indian raid. Beyond the field filled with huge cedar stumps, there were hills, shining water down below, islands and mountains. Chickens scratched in front of the door; a cow grazed behind a makeshift fence. An excellent place of respite in an excellent month—for September was proving bright and hot. It was a sharp counterpoint to the dread and sadness Jeannie felt when each day's end brought no news of Breed.

At first, she was consoled by the fact he was with friends. Though Feemster had said Breed was gravely wounded, she had hopes that he would recover and they could meet again. As the days passed, however, she became anxious for his return.

"Have you no word from Mr. Henderson or any of Jonas's friends as to why he is not coming?" she asked Pierce.

"Nothing new," Andrew answered, "though I did learn that the fighting on the island was hard. Krill wasn't the only casualty. There were deaths on both sides. That has caused an uproar among the military authorities and settlers on the island. Makes it difficult to locate him. They could be hiding on the mainland." Andrew said nothing more.

Jeannie found no comfort in that. As days turned to weeks, a new trouble rose before her.

Over the past week, she had awakened each morning aching in her body and sore in her breasts. Food disinterested her. Sometimes she felt too ill to get out of bed.

"What have you heard, Alani?"

The two women sat with Kohl's Swimomish wife, Mary, picking over bowls of green beans under a tree.

"Some people talk about the fight and say how glad they are Krill is dead. Some say Jo-nuss fight good with all his *tillicums* and friends. Some say he is still fighting." Alani cracked a bean in half and threw it into an iron pot front of her. "But others say—"

Jeannie put her bowl of beans down on her apron-covered lap and swallowed. She tried not to cry, but it was hard. She was so emotional lately.

"—Some say he gone into the forest." Alani slowly raised her eyes to Jeannie. They were full of tears. "Makes my heart sick, for Jo-nuss is a very good man. He never ask anything of anyone but goodness and *aloha*. He gives the 'ha.' He listens to people, asks their opinion and takes it. He never ask where you born or what you come from." Tears rolled down her cheeks, matching Jeannie's.

"What do you think, Mary?" Jeannie asked.

"Jo-nuss was one good man. So sad to think him gone."

Jeannie caught a sob in her throat. Alani took her hand.

"Missus."

"Not Missus. My name is Jeannie. You are the dearest of friends." She squeezed Alani's hand and hiccoughed back a little sob. "You too, Mary. I honor our friendship. For where would women be without such sisterhood?" All three women sat quiet for quite a time.

Jeannie finally sniffed and wiped her nose on a handkerchief. "We must have hope and wait. It is only rumor."

"Wait for what?" Pierce asked as he came into the yard with their host, Barman Kohl.

"Supper." Jeannie made her voice as light as possible. "The beans are nearly done." She broke the last one, ends and all and put them into the bowl. "Mrs. Kapuna has made a ham. Mrs. Kohl baked some potatoes." She stood up and wobbled, feeling faint.

"Jeannie," Pierce supported her under her elbow.

"Andrew." She allowed him that for all he had done for her. It was something Breed would want. Besides, for all his reserve, Andrew Pierce was a pleasant fellow.

The morning Jeannie woke and lost last night's dinner brought not only alarm to her situation—her monthly courses already late—but the news she never hoped to hear, confirmation that Breed was dead.

Jeannie had been drinking ginger tea by the stove in the Kohl kitchen, a lean-to separate from the house, when Pierce came in and said he had bad news.

"Jonas Breed is dead. He was mortally wounded in the shootout and did not survive." Trembling, Jeannie put the cup on the table next to her. "How do you know, Andrew?" She couldn't bear to look in his face.

"A fellow merchant reported it. Someone saw him in the islands a couple of weeks ago. Said he was near to death. Not expected to make it. Blood poisoning."

When she shot up to say he was wrong, he altered his tone. "I am so very sorry."

"I thank you for that. Jonas sent me with you because he trusts you, but do you know that we had planned to marry?" Jeannie began to weep and rage clasping her hands and pacing the little room. Alani came in from outside and stood in the doorway, her eyes wide.

"The rest of the world condemns him, especially your countrymen, yet he has done nothing, nothing but to protect those he cares about. Kaui Kalama was his friend, not his servant. The Haida woman was his better. Krill kidnapped Kalama's wife. Her children are fatherless and she has no protector. Shells Shining leaves a shattered people. Why doesn't anyone have pity for the Haida and Kanakas and their families?"

She knew she was making herself sick, but she just couldn't accept that Breed—her dear Jonas—was dead. She wrenched away from Pierce when he tried to console her. She threw her shawl around her shoulders and fled out the door, lightly brushing by Alani. She ran out into the yard and past the corral to the cleared field where a patch of corn grew by the rugged lane. She ran as far away as she could toward the forest at the edge of the claim, eventually slowing down as she approached an orchard of apple and pear trees. She stopped.

All across the orchard, the leaves were turning gold. On the ground there was scat from deer coming to eat the fallen fruit. The fruit trees appeared to be older than the log house itself, some past effort of an earlier settler. So beautiful. Plucking one of the red apples from a low branch, Jeannie shined it up on her skirt.

This impossibly beautiful place, the Pacific Northwest where she had vowed to stay the night she first arrived at the Royal Marine Camp, still beckoned. That was before she knew true love or the sting of deepest sorrow. For the first time she felt utterly alone. Not even her dear Uncle Archie could help her.

She took a bite of the apple, hoping it would calm her stomach and continued to walk on.

"Jeannie." Alani walked steadily toward her. "Wait." She hurried up until she was next to Jeannie.

Jeannie stopped and pulled off her shawl. She was too hot. "He doesn't know what he is talking about."

"I think maybe there is truth to what he said. It's been nearly five weeks."

Jeannie turned on her. "Do you really believe that?"

Alani looked at Jeannie, her dark soulful eyes peering at her heart. "*Ah-ha.*

Jeannie burst into a sob and started walking again, though she didn't know where she was going.

Alani caught up with Jeannie. "Jeannie." Her voice was soft. "You have more worries, don't you? You are afraid and you feel alone." Alani grasped Jeannie gently on her arm and stopped her. She paused and took a big breath. "You have Jo-nuss' child, don't you?"

Jeannie suppressed another sob. She touched her stomach, nodding numbly. "*Ah-ha.* How did you know?"

"I know."

"Do you think anyone else knows?"

Alani shook her head and put a hand on her shoulder. "No." She patted Jeannie's arm. "But this is a good thing. One beautiful thing to have his child."

"I want Jonas." Jeannie leaned against the woman's solid shoulder. "I want Jonas." She began to weep uncontrollably.

"Jonas is all *pau*. Gone to the spirits. That's what everyone say. I think that it is true. He has disappeared from us. More betta we care for his own."

Jeannie wiped her eyes on her apron. "Maybe I should wait until there is final word."

Alani put her arms around her and hugged her. "We have final word."

What shall I do? Jeannie stepped away. *Five weeks with child.* It had been that long since she laid with Breed. Soon she should show. An image of her standing the docket back in Plymouth, facing down the claims that she murdered Sarah Marsfield, people pointing fingers in her face. She was Captain Marsfield's widow even if the marriage had been declared illegal. Now there would be the rumor and shame of being a grass widow—a mother of a child born out of wedlock.

During a recent visit to Coupeville to shop for supplies, Jeannie had overheard two women in the mercantile talking about a young woman who had given birth to a baby out of wedlock. Their whispered condemnation behind their gloved hands and bonnets gave Jeannie chills, for the girl was young and would be forever shunned in this tight little society of white women who lived on the island.

Grass widow. The words stung and made her feel nauseous. She put a hand on her stomach. *I'll protect you little one,* she thought. *But how? Leave the Northwest?* Her uncle's reputation would be sullied too.

Jeannie spied Pierce coming up the lane, concern on his face and in the way he moved. The other day Alani said he looked at her like some sick cow even though he knew about her feelings toward Breed.

"If you need to go away," Alani whispered. "I will go with you."

"Where will I go?" Jeannie whispered back. "I can't go back to my uncle."

"Perhaps Mr. Collie can help you."

"Mr. Pierce implies that all Jonas's men are being hunted as criminals."

Jeannie watched Pierce stop to catch his breath before he came up them.

"Are you alright, Jeannie? What can I do to help you? It grieves me to see you so distressed."

"I should like to write to a letter to my uncle. Perhaps, he can find out for sure."

Pierce gave Jeannie a sympathetic smile. "I wish I could say that would bring Jonas back. My source is reliable."

Then I shall write to Uncle Archie and ask for his forgiveness and fall upon his good nature to help me.

Andrew gave her his arm. "Let me walk you back."

Jeannie took his arm. As she passed Alani, her friend lowered her head for just a moment, then looked up. Her eyes were on Pierce, her face in a frown.

Jeannie wrote a letter to Uncle Archie and then another, but didn't send them. Each time she dipped her pen into the inkwell and wrote, she considered the impact of her words. She would, of course, tell him the truth of her delicate situation, but could she say had secretly married Breed? No, that would be a lie and she would never lie to her uncle. She could only write of her confusion and broken heart. That letter was not sent either.

Another day passed, each hour sounded out by the clock in the parlor. Mary Kohl, sensing her trouble, joined Alani in keeping her secret. Pierce, on the other hand, thinking it was merely Jeannie's emotional state over her loss, was vigilant in fulfilling any of Jeannie's simple requests, including her request to be alone in her grief. After another day of this, he finally asked if he could join her on one of her walks. Jeannie, worn down by his attentions, agreed.

They walked out past the apple orchard in silence and took a path that led out toward the water. The late September afternoon sun was hidden behind a billowing white cloud. The air was crisp and smelled of cedar and fallen leaves. When they reached the edge of the ridge that looked down on Admiralty Inlet, Pierce cleared his throat. "I was wondering what your intentions are now? Will you return to English Camp or to Victoria? In either case, you shall be missed."

"I haven't yet decided. English Camp, though I have many friends there, is out of the question." Jeannie clasped her hands in front of her and sighed. "And as for Victoria—my son is buried there and my dear uncle is there—but I'm not sure if I am welcomed."

A long silence came between them. Jeannie listened for the Steller's Jay that lived in the big leaf maple at the ridge. She had become fond of the birds since coming to the Pacific Northwest, finding humor in the way they raised the crowns on their heads when agitated; the grating noise they made. This particular one greeted her every day with such a display. She smiled when it started in on its objections to her coming close to its tree. Or was it saying hello?

Pierce cleared his throat. "May I offer a solution? You are an unprotected woman with an association with Mr. Breed and his men. I know you do not love me, but I would honored if you would agree to be my wife."

Jeannie stepped away from Pierce in shock. She had never considered this. In her cloud of grief, she had not noticed his increasing solicitation of her. Now she saw for the first time his *kiawali sick* eyes —lovesick eyes—that Alani had spoken of.

"I don't know how to answer."

"Then take your time." Pierce cleared his throat again. "I have to say that I have admired you since I first met you at the dinner at Captain Pickett's lodgings." He turned and took her hand. "I would look after you with the greatest respect. And I have excellent prospects in Seattle for a good life."

Jeannie was relieved when he let go of her hand, still stunned by his offer. She tried to recall the few times she had spoken to him. There was the dinner party and the time that they had gone to look at the new colt at the Royal Marine Camp. She had been anxious then to take leave of Pierce to find Breed.

I could marry him and go with him, Jeannie thought. She had heard so many stories out here of lone women doing just that with no explanation. She used think that was dishonest, but now... *I can say my heart is broken, that I can't stay here anymore. I'll have to deal with the rest when the baby comes.*

Jeannie closed her eyes, acutely aware of Pierce waiting for some answer. All she saw was Jonas Breed coming out of the water with the baskets full of crabs, him canoeing her home after their stay on Timons, his ardor when he made love to her. She put a hand on her stomach as if she was brushing away some dirt, but it was to caress the one thing she had left of Breed.

"Would you mind very much, Mr. Pierce—Andrew—if I think this over?"

"Of course, of course."

Back at the house, Jeannie and Pierce separated. On the excuse to get water from the well, Jeannie went outside. Alani followed.

"What did he say?" Alani asked as she helped lower the bucket into the well.

"He has asked me to marry him. I had no idea." Jeannie felt a wave of nausea as she spoke. "What shall I do?" Nausea turned to grief. She began to weep.

"Jeannie. It is the only way to leave everything. Marry Andrew Pierce. I think he take good care of you and the baby. I think he really loves you."

Jeannie put a hand over her mouth as tears rolled down "But Jonas. Jonas." She laid her head on Alani's shoulder and sobbed.

"Shhh," Alani's voice was soft. "I will go with you and I stay until after the baby is born."

"*Mahsie.*" When Jeannie was calm again, she said, "He'll never know his father."

"Some day when he is a man you tell him. Now go and give Mr. Pierce the answer he wants to hear."

"I'll go only if he agrees that you can come too."

Two days later, Jeannie married Andrew Pierce in the company of Alani, the Kohls and a hastily summoned parson. The next day before their departure to Seattle where they would live, a small group was pulled together for a wedding feast. The region was still on high alert with rumors of northern Indians attacking lone travelers on the water and land and Krill's remaining men making trouble in San Juan Town. A few men stood guard outside the barn while the rest of the revelers danced to tunes and ate the food prepared from the late summer harvest. At some point Jeannie slipped away to hide her protesting belly. Andrew had already consummated their marriage the night before and was feeling buoyant. Jeannie was miserable and disappointed but for the yet unnamed baby, she would have to show more delight and enthusiasm. She would have to learn to love Andrew.

She looked up to the wide, nearly cloudless sky. To the west, the Olympic Mountains rose. To the south, huge white-headed Mount Rainier was visible. She would be closer to it when they moved to Elliot Bay down by Seattle.

Go with the spirits. How often she had heard Jonas Breed say that. Two eagles came into view, circling lazily in the sky. Their wing tips seemed to caress each other as they danced around their ramparts in the air.

"Tell him," Jeannie said out loud. "Tell him that I will always love him."

The eagles dipped their wings. A raven called.

There would be balance in her world again, but at its center, only she knew the terrible cost she paid.

Mistchimas. Captive once again.

BOOK II

THE NOTE

Seattle, 1880

The note lay unannounced alongside *The Intelligencer* and the day's calling cards. Sealed in a plain, off-white envelope, it jarred sharply with the elegant cards embossed with gilded formal script and strewn on the silver tray like expectant offerings.

Jeannie picked it up and turned it over in her hands. Thoughtful, she went over to the sunny window, the long folds of her black mourning gown crackling as she walked. She paused for a moment, staring at the light carriage and wagon traffic outside the wrought iron fence that encircled the mansion's elaborate grounds. She slit open the envelope.

He is the one and the same. Seen in the San Juan Islands.

Jonas Breed was alive. After twenty years.

Her hands trembled. As she closed her eyes, a flood of images rushed at her: the forested islands rising out of the water like the backs of slumbering whales; cedar and fir trees sticking up as straight as hat pins along the shore; the deep dark of the night on water and remembrance of him.

Jeannie clenched the note in her hand and knew that she would have to be strong because what she had believed as true all these years was as solid as candle smoke.

"Mother?"

Jeannie started. She had almost forgotten that her children were here. She smoothed out the envelope and with hands shaking, slipped the note and the cedar sprig accompanying it into the folds of her gown. She turned and faced her daughter, seventeen-year-old Jeremi-nah, a slim, dark-haired girl on the verge of womanhood.

"Another well-wisher?" she asked. Like her mother she wore black.

"Yes, Mina." Jeannie smiled as she turned. Her soft voice was soft, lyrical with her Devonshire accent, still pronounced after living so long with the colonials. "Just a note to say hello. Are you two ready to go?"

Beyond Mina, near the door, stood nineteen year-old Phillip, dressed in a black linen suit and silk tie and every bit a young gentle-man. He was tall and lean as Breed, had the same cut of the shoulders. The look on his face was full of concern and curiosity.

"Yes, Mother," he said. "Won't you come with us? You'll be left alone again."

"Don't you have to meet with Burgess later today?"

"That's tomorrow. Mother. We have a meeting tomorrow."

Jeannie rubbed her arms. She felt cold despite the warmth of the June sun through the glass panes. Outside, her butler, Mr. Rupert Wilson, stood in the driveway next to a buggy holding the horse's halter. With him was their groom. The groom and butler exchanged words then Wilson headed back to the front door.

She felt her children's eyes on her back, anxious and waiting for an answer. How should I answered? Say I can't come because my life is in spin?

Twenty years ago, she had left San Juan Island and all its sorrow, concentrating on the one thing that had led to her marriage to Andrew Pierce—the child she carried. Phillip was grown now, his origin safely tucked away like the many other secrets she was bound to. Jonas had been right. We are all *mistchimas*. Now Andrew was dead and Breed was alive. The irony confused and frightened her. *Jonas, why didn't you come?*

"I'll be fine. There is correspondence I must attend to." Jeannie had to respond to the detective Sims, but she must take care. It would be foolhardy and indiscreet to continue this. She well knew that the decorum of widowhood had its own rules and regulations and Andrew had been gone barely two months. Above all, the note told a history none of her children knew. Yet the news was driving her crazy.

Jonas alive! A rush of joy warmed away her earlier chill. Then she felt anger. *Jonas, where have you been? Why didn't you come?*

"No, you two go. I'll be fine."

Mina came and put her arm around her mother's trim waist and hugged her. "We'll miss you."

Jeannie hugged her back. "I know, but you mustn't keep your friends waiting!"

Later when Jeannie was alone, she retired to her bedroom, closed and locked the door. She sat on the edge of the high bed. The ropes under the feather mattress groaned. *Just my sentiment*, she thought.

Jeannie unlocked the compartment in her writing desk next to the bed. Among some cherished letters Jeannie found the wooden figure carved by a marine at English Camp and a tintype of Jeremy. She set them upon her lap and sighed. She remembered when the photograph taken in a studio in Toronto, Canada. He had just turned four. Jeannie kept it in a simple leather wallet-frame to protect it from the light. Twenty-one years later, she had to turn it to catch the silver image captured there, but he looked as he had that day: the serious face too big on a little body stiffly posed in a borrowed suit, the dark hair brushed to the side above eyes deep with understanding beyond his years. She had loved him the moment she had seen his wrinkled face as he cradled in her arms.

Jeannie pushed aside some letters and searched until her fingers touched the cool medal of the thimble. It was still there where she had placed it years ago when they first moved in this house. Phillip was four years old then.

It's not a ring, but please take it as my promise to you
She had kept Breed's token of love all these years.

On the desk there was a picture of her family as it stood a year ago: Jeannie seated on a chair next to Mina, the young woman a reflection of Jeannie at that age. Behind Mina, Andrew stood as stiff as a statue and important looking with his beard and mustache. The crow's-feet near his eyes were the only sign of humor. Yet he had been a good father, much better than some husbands of friends in Jeannie's circle. He had undertaken the schooling of Phillip in business and law personally and took interest in Mina's doings.

Phillip stood behind Jeannie, his hand on her shoulder. She sometimes looked for Breed in her son, but Phillip was fair with brown eyes, something that was a blessing. Neither Jeannie nor Andrew knew who he favored, though occasionally Phillip reminded her of her own father. He had been born late, after a difficult pregnancy and delivery. A bit undersized, Phillip gave no dangerous clue as to the timing of his conception. Andrew had been delighted in him at first look and that was enough for Jeannie. Phillip was doted on from the very beginning, as any son should be and ironically, was very much like Andrew in temperament. But now that Breed was alive, she wondered what exactly she should tell Phillip.

There was something else in the unlocked compartment—a kukui nut hat pin. Alani Kapuna had given it to Jeannie on the birth of Phillip. True to her word, Alani stayed with Jeannie until six months after the birth of the boy. Jeannie didn't know what she would have done without her. Near the end of her confinement, she had been very ill. Alani was there to nurse and encourage her.

"It's your heart, Jeannie," she said. "You so sad. Be happy for him."

"The baby's a boy?"

"Ah-ha. You see."

While Alani stayed with her, Jeannie made arrangements for Moki to come down and work on the docks for the shipping company Andrew was starting. Eventually, Alani and Moki left to go back to the San Juan Islands, which were still in dispute. The military camps were going strong, but by then Pickett was gone. Back in the States, the country was at war, having split itself in two. Pickett had deserted and gone back east to join the Confederate Army.

Jeannie turned the hat pin over in her hands. She had learned to love Andrew in his own way and adored her children, but now the past had returned and her world was out of balance again.

Wait for me.

Oh, Jonas. A deep sorrow welled up. What should she do? The kee-keeying call of an eagle in the cedar tree next to the house seemed to give answer. Hadn't Jonas taught her to listen?

Go with the spirits. Jeannie decided to go look for him.

PHILLIP

The following morning, Jeannie was up early. She found Phillip in the dining room eating toast and drinking coffee. For a moment, she stood in the doorway and watched him, wondering where the years had gone. He had been a sweet baby and easy to please, but sometimes she longed for Phillip to have some of the qualities that she loved in his real father. As he grew, Phillip became more rigid like Andrew and though kind, had high opinions that she did not always agree with. Still, she encouraged her son's interest in the natural world and his curiosity about the various nations that worked on the docks where Andrew had ships. And when he was a stubborn and snobbish child, she reminded him of how lucky he was to the all the comforts Father provided. *Because you're true father had nothing at your age. Just his wits and the ragged clothes on his back.*

Now as Phillip leaned over the day's paper, Jeannie saw more of Breed in him. He had the same way of studying things. She wondered why she hadn't noticed it before. He was only nineteen so maybe he would grow into being more like Breed.

"Won't you have more than that, dear?" She sat down next to Phillip and reached for the silver coffeepot.

"I'm off in a bit. Burgess wants to show me something he found on the books."

"Oh?"

"He just wants to make sure all the accounts are settled, so that you will be well looked after. The company is fine." He put a hand on her arm. "Are you all right?"

Jeannie took his hand and squeezed it, trying hard not to betray the clash of emotions roaring around in her head. "I'm fine. One must take each day as it comes. It's the only way to do it." She patted his hand, lightened her voice. "Are you taking your horse?"

"Yes. I'll leave it at the livery stable near the office." He kissed Jeannie's cheek. "I better get ready, Mother."

Later she watched at the window as he mounted up. As Phillip bantered with Wilson, she wondered if Breed would approve of his upbringing. "I did my best," she said out loud.

Several hours later, Jeannie stood outside the downtown office of Pierce, Campbell and Waddell located on the first floor of a tall brick structure housing several businesses. Stepping lightly down onto the raised, planked sidewalk that negotiated the dirt, mud and dung of the city street, she gave Mr. Wilson a nod and gathering her skirts at the firm's glass-etched door went in.

"Mrs. Pierce. Good morning." From behind the walnut desk in the main foyer, a young man as thin as a weedy cattail rose and greeted her with a stiff bow. It was not Mr. Burgess, but Mr. Frederick Howell, a legal assistant in the firm and a persistent brass polisher. She supposed she tolerated him because he was young and eager and because Andrew had hired him not long before he passed away.

"Is Mr. Burgess in?"

"I'm afraid Mr. Burgess has been called away unexpectedly and won't be back for some time."

"Was my son not with him?"

Howell cleared his throat. "I believe Master Pierce was going to see him off."

"Well, then," she said, trying not to show her disappointment, much less her irritation. "I should like to see the mails, if any." She lifted up her black net veil and laid it back on her small felt hat.

"Ma'am," Howell said. He showed her the small sample set out on a silver tray and after she collected it for later reading, he bowed and asked if there was anything else. Jeannie refrained from assigning him the polishing of the brass doorknobs on the first floor.

"No, thank you. Please leave word for my son that I have come."

"Indeed."

Wilson was waiting outside at the carriage, his nose in a book. He jumped to attention when he saw her.

"Everything satisfactory, ma'am?"

"Actually, no. Mr. Burgess is out. I didn't know. I thought Phillip was meeting with him."

"What would you like to do now?"

Jeannie looked at the envelopes and package in her hands. "Would you be so kind, Mr. Wilson? I should like to have a cup of tea and read my correspondence at Warner's for a bit. I shan't be long."

Mr. Wilson closed his book and put it under his seat. Stepping into the traffic, he helped her cross the busy street to the door of Warner's, a local eating establishment of good reputation. On the window gold letters spelled out the name in an arch.

"If you don't mind, ma'am, I'd like to walk down to the docks," Mr. Wilson said once they were across. "If you wish, I can inquire about Master Phillip, see if he came with Mr. Burgess to check on cargo for your ships. I'll be back in half an hour and call on you."

"That should be lovely. Thank you, Mr. Wilson. Enjoy your stroll."

Inside, Jeannie found a private room and a solicitous waiter who met her every need, then left her alone. After taking a sip of the hot brew, which passed for English tea, she reached for the object that had caught her eye at the firm—a thin volume wrapped in brown paper and tied with string. Slipped under the smooth tan cordage was a small note with "For Mrs. Andrew Pierce" on the front. It was Burgess's handwriting. She opened it up and read:

Mrs. Pierce. Sorry for the inconvenience, but urgent business has sent me away. I found this in Andrew's effects and have sent it along. Mr. Howell has been working on the rest of the papers and should have an accounting shortly. Will contact you as soon as I return. Your servant, Burgess.

Jeannie carefully lifted the string from around the package and undid the wrapping. Inside was a small account book, battered and water-stained. The dark green marbling on the face of it was faded and the amber-colored leather binding cracked. A single leather cord tied the book closed. Jeannie ran her hand over the cover. She had briefly seen the account book long ago in what seemed a different plane of life. Sighing, she untied the cord and opened it.

It was an ordinary accountant's book, its columns of blue and red lines marching up and down the pages like stripes in a counter pane quilt. Andrew had used it for a diary. In the middle of the very first page, written in fine script, he wrote his name and his intentions for keeping it: "to record my passing in this strange and wonderful place." The year was 1859 eight months before she had first visited San Juan Island and the year the troubles began on the island over the wayward pig.

She stared at the writing, the edges of the pen strokes fading to brown. Had her memories gone brown too?

On the next page was the first entry. It began on October 1, 1859. Andrew was in Olympia, the capital of Washington Territory, arranging for goods to be taken to San Juan Town on San Juan Island. Then Jeannie found something else.

October 5

Weather fine. Crossed the waters to Camp Pickett to see Muggins. Landed at San Juan Town and walked up to the camp. View of Mt. Rainier and Mt. Baker spectacular. Along the way, had the occasion to meet a Jonas Breed, an American of exotic nature. A guide and shipman *of considerable skill, he lives near S. J. Island where he has a small homestead. When inquired of at the camp, I was apprised that he was the one and same fellow who has lived intimately with the Northern tribes, having been captured as a youth and enslaved. I found him a vigorous and forthright fellow. His sobriety on this island of sot is refreshing. I hope to meet him again.*

Jeannie smiled. "An American of exotic nature." Is that what people thought of Jonas? She found another entry:

October 10

A disturbance at Kanaka Town reached both the American and British authorities, but by the time any military was put forth, the affair was blown over. Was interested to see J. Breed again. He was instrumental in settling the dispute, apparently having some sway over the Kanakas and Indians alike. Muggins says he is a confounding man in his predilection toward native folks, but I suppose once a wild man, accustomed to the wilderness as he has been, it would be difficult to change.

Jeannie brushed the entry lightly with her hand. "A confounding man." It was strange to read her dead husband's words. She remembered her own first reaction to Jonas Breed and held it secret in her heart.

Jeannie read a few more of the entries, then flipped through some more pages. She started to close it when she noticed that the account book didn't lay flat. Curious, she opened to the offending page and found a folded note jammed against the center.

What is this? Thinking it some ancient bill or invoice, she discovered to her surprise that it was a note addressed to Andrew. There was no date, but its contents chilled her.

Per our arrangement, if you try to alert the authorities, I will expose your supposedly virtuous wife as a sham to all. The Marsfield incident is my guarantee that you will comply.

Covering the note with her fingers, Jeannie pressed her hands against the table to keep them from shaking. *Someone threatened Andrew with her past? Who and why?* She picked up the note and read it again. Andrew had been tense the past few months before his accident. She put a hand on her chest, drew her breath in sharp. "Oh, dear Lord, not Cooperwaite?" she gasped

"Mrs. Pierce. Excuse me. Mr. Wilson's looking for you. Shall I send him in?

Jeannie looked up so sharp from the note it put a crick in her neck.

"Yes, of course," she replied to the waiter, then rubbed her neck when he was gone. She looked at the little watch pinned to her dress. Oh, heavens, she thought. She'd been reading nearly an hour. And she had told Wilson it would only be half that. She gathered the letters, then after laying the note between the pages again, she tied the account book back in its paper wrapper. Jeannie had them all stacked when Wilson entered the room.

"I was worried, ma'am."

"I'm sorry. I got quite caught up. I do apologize." She reached for her cape and gloves. "Any word of Phillip?"

"No ma'am. Shall I take your mail?"

Jeannie assured Wilson she would be all right with them. "And thank you. You've been most patient."

Wilson bowed at the compliment and then helped her into her cape when she stood up. He was a quiet, be-whiskered man in his late forties who moved with an efficiency that spoke of pride in his work. She never knew him to be tardy or smelling of masculine habits that other friends fretted about in their male servants. She smiled at him after she was done buttoning the collar. "Thank you, Wilson." She slipped on her black gloves and started for the curtained door.

"The bill's been taken care of," he said then pulled back the curtain.

After he had her situated in the buggy, Wilson tended to the horses. Jeannie leaned back against the seat and closed her eyes. She felt absolutely drained.

I'm all mixed up with grief and memory, she thought. *And now this note. I must go soon.*

She watched Wilson take the reins. He had been the one constant in her life besides the children these past weeks. She was so grateful for him. He was courteous and devoted. Once she heard that one of the more influential families had tried to hire him away, but he had declined. He wasn't in it for the money, so she was told. He was to serve the Mrs. Pierce and that was that.

Wilson turned back to her. "Any other plans for the day?"

"Yes. Please take me to the booking agent for the Puget Sound steamboats. I should like to take a trip to the islands. I think it would do me good to step out."

"Will you be going alone, ma'am?"

"No, I think I shall take Mina. We'll have an adventure."

Mr. Wilson allowed that it would be one. "And Mister Phillip?"

"I assume that he wants to stay and make sure the accounts are in order."

"Very good, ma'am."

Wilson urged the horses forward. Jeannie thought him unusually quiet as they drove away.

～

"She's booked passage, *kahpo*. Leaves for Port Townsend on the morrow." The speaker, a tall blonde man in his mid-forties was dressed as a businessman, but the years at sea and on the waters of the Pacific Northwest had left its mark. His tanned, weathered-lined face above the stiff white collar said "sea captain." He crumpled the telegraph in his rough hands, then smoothed it out when he thought better of it and handed it back to the man sitting behind him. He didn't turn around at the clumping sound on the wood desk. It was only the steel hook smoothing out the paper.

"What will you do?" the blonde man asked.

"I can't hold her back," the man behind replied. "See to her protection and keep me posted. In the meantime, I'll pay my respects to Annie and let her know I've brought our daughter home."

"What if Jeannie Pierce comes here?"

The voice behind him sighed. "I'll deal with it then."

"Then I may go?"

"Use your discretion. I'll send someone if you need it."

"*Mahsie.*"

"Go with the spirits.

The discussion was over.

JOURNEY

Jeannie ordered tickets for the *Lily T*, had their clothes cleaned and pressed, and their valises and trunks packed. She would go to Port Townsend and from there would be able to go in any direction she wished. Though not informing Wilson of any of her real intentions she was able to get information on additional schedules and boarding houses should she wish to travel in the area, Victoria included. Mina would go with her, but only as far as Port Townsend on the Olympic Peninsula where she would spend time with an old school chum. Once having boldly made her decision, Jeannie realized that she needed her daughter along. There was less to explain about two women making a trip during bereavement. It would be more acceptable, even if Mina was dropped off from time to time while her mother did business.

Once, Mina worried about them going on their own. "Lucy Rhoades says that there are smugglers out in the San Juan Islands. Not too safe for women to be traveling alone."

"We'll be on the *Lily T*, sweetheart. I doubt whiskey smugglers will commandeer it. Mr. Wilson has reviewed the travel plans and says that they are most sensible. The journey will be a pleasant diversion for us both."

There was one hitch that nearly wrecked Jeannie's plans: Phillip was missing. At first Jeannie thought her son was with friends when he did not come home the night after Jeannie went to the office to pick up her mail. But when he did not appear for lunch the next day, Jeannie began to worry.

"I'll look into it, Mrs. Pierce," Wilson said. A few hours later, he came back with unsettling news.

"It appears that young Phillip never returned to the company office. And after checking with his circle of friends, they have not seen him either."

Jeannie frowned. "Where on earth is he?"

Wilson cleared his throat. "Well, I did confirm that he was seen with Burgess on Front Street about the time you were taking tea."

"Do you think he's in trouble?" Sitting in Pierce's leather chair in the parlor, she willed her hands not to shake.

"Well, given the circumstances of Mr. Pierce's untimely death, I would urge caution for your trip until he is found. Burgess has always been reliable." Wilson's voice tightened up with that pronouncement making Jeannie wonder if he was telling her everything. "But we should have it figured out soon. I have some colleagues looking for the young master."

The matter was cleared up that evening when a note in Phillip's hand arrived. He begged her forgiveness for not informing her but he was well and accompanying Mr. Burgess to visit the company office in Victoria. He would report to her once they arrived.

"Shall I go now, Mr. Wilson?"

For a second, her butler's face stilled as in deep thought. He normally was not so transparent. "I would prefer that I went along."

Jeannie looked away. She had to go on her own. This mission was not ready for the light of day. "But do you think I'll be safe if I go on my own?"

Begrudgingly, Wilson nodded yes.

They left early the next day. Mr. Wilson took them down to the busy harbor cluttered with tall square-rigged ships from San Francisco and China and side-wheeler and sternwheeler steamships for local waters. He escorted them out onto the wharf, up the gangway and the stairs to the upper deck of the hundred foot long side-wheeler where the more genteel class spent their time. Inside the large deck house, men in bowler hats and somber topcoats, women with children, and women alone, dressed in capes, skirts, and form-fitting jackets with bustles to match their station in life filled the space with their voices and busyness. Wilson located an empty wood bench to their liking and set down their valises and picnic basket. Then they went out to the open deck.

It's going to be warm and clear once the mist burns off, Jeannie thought. Already the Olympic Mountains rising up behind the heavily forested islands across from the blue-gray waters of Elliot Bay loomed in the haze like jagged pale-blue triangles topped with white. Laughter came from groups around her. There were several families on board as well as tradesmen. Leaning over the rail, Jeannie looked toward the bow, where a Port Gamble Indian and his wife crouched around two large cedar baskets and other possessions. Next to them, a solemn little girl in a calico dress held onto her little dog, a skinny black and white runt with black bug eyes.

Directly below, she watched some laborers come up the ramp and board the ship. One of the late arrivals was a tall young man with wavy brown-black hair. He looked up as he came on board and stared directly at her before lowering his dark-as-coal eyes and moved away. He was brown-skinned, but his face had the features of an aristocrat. The nose and sensitive mouth could only be that of a Kanaka from Honolulu or perhaps someone from old Kanaka Town.

The memory of her time there stabbed at her. *Alani and Moki Kapuna. Kaui Kalama. The children, Kapihi and Noelani.* Jeannie found herself smiling at him.

"Did you know him?" Mina asked.

"No, but he reminded me of someone I knew a long time ago on San Juan Island. There were Kanakas working for Belle Vue Farm. They tended the sheep there."

Mina grinned and gave her mother a hug. "I wish you'd tell me more stories from there. Promise me you'll show me the places you went when you first met Papa. That Camp Pickett..."

"Closed. Ever since Kaiser Wilhelm decided in favor of the United States over the ownership of the San Juan Islands eight years ago. The Royal Marine Camp too. They're all gone, turned into homesteads. You were a little girl in grammar school when it was settled."

"It sounds so forlorn, yet romantic."

"Romantic? Camp Pickett was quite barren and windy."

"Didn't you say it was named after the American captain who faced down the British Navy on Griffin Bay with just a handful of men?"

"Yes. He was later at Gettysburg. It'll be all changed. I've heard the camp is a homestead now. No soldiers there."

Jeannie wondered about San Juan Town down below. She had heard its reputation hadn't changed in twenty years. Having enjoyed playing off both British and American authorities for twelve years while under joint military occupation, the islanders continued to be an independent lot and in some cases outside the law. San Juan Town was the only settlement of any consequence on the island. As for the old Royal Marine camp on the north end of the island Mr. Wilson said that if she truly wanted to see it, she should ask for an escort. He gave her a name of someone in Port Townsend. The old wharf was intact. A boat could put in there, if one wished.

"I think you'll find all your tickets and papers in order, Mrs. Pierce," Wilson said. "If you need me, telegraph and I'll come."

"Thank you. You're indispensable, Mr. Wilson."

He dipped his hat to her. "My pleasure. Miss Mina."

As he went down the gangway, Jeannie almost wished she had asked him to accompany them after all.

The *Lily T* left fifteen minutes later to the thunk-thunk of its large paddle wheels set amidships on the boat. Though old, it was a worthy vessel for its schedule. They would be heading north up through Admiralty Inlet stopping off to pick up passengers along the way. As they headed out into the middle of the channel between the bay and Bainbridge Island, Jeannie looked back toward the town she had called home for twenty years. Seattle didn't look like much—just a brave frontier settlement of wood and brick structures stacked on the hills above the bay, each crowing about whom had the biggest false front. The tide was in, so the stinky mud flats weren't exposed. Further back behind the town and all around were stands of enormous fir and hemlock trees. Gulls dipped and swooned, filling the clear, crisp air with their cries. To the south, the huge white head of Rainier poked above the mist.

Jeannie took a breath and turned toward the direction they were heading. There were signs of settlements along the edges of the islands they were heading toward, but she knew that she was heading back in time when she saw a *salt chuck* canoe cut in front of them. Paddling swiftly, the paddlers raced across the water and into an isolated patch of mist.

I want to be a siwash, *Mama.*

You can't, Jeremy. You're English.

Can't I sit in the canoe?

Some other time. We'll ask uncle.

Oh, Jeremy, she thought, *I'm coming.*

Like clockwork, the side-wheeler made its way up the Inlet between the islands. It stopped just about anywhere, sometimes at little wharves where the draft was deep, but that was rare. Generally, it stayed anchored out a ways and let canoes take passengers and gear back and forth. There was an informality to the schedule. If one wanted passage, all one had to do was stand on shore and wave something. The *Lily T* obliged and heaved to. Sometimes, Indians in bright colored shirts or loose-fitting dresses would come out in their dugout canoes to sell smoked salmon or cedar baskets which could be had for a coin or two.

The passage was a maze, an empty trail upon water between what were larger islands and little skerries of no consequence. Douglas fir, cedar and hemlock with their scraggly tips bent over dominated the earth and sky while in clearings cattle and sheep grazed, but except for some lone hand-hewn cabin, more often than not, rocky cliffs and trees were all that greeted the boat. It was green, green, green.

"Was this how it was?" Mina asked as they stood on deck.

"In many ways. I first went to the Royal Marine Camp on San Juan Island from Victoria with my Uncle Archie in 1860. I had full view of the mountains which was quite spectacular."

"Did you meet Papa then?"

"No, not until later." *But I met Jonas.*

The progress of the boat was slow. At noon, they joined their fellow passengers in a salon for lunch. Polly, their household cook, had packed food for several days. Sitting on a hardwood bench at a round table, they began to assess their companions. Open only to those who booked staterooms, the rougher crowd had been winnowed out and what were supposed to be respectable folks filled the benches and tables.

Mina politely worked on her tea sandwiches. She was wearing a dark green traveling suit that complimented her hair and fair looks. In many ways, she looked like Jeannie. At seventeen, she was a beauty.

But without the falsehoods that went with it, Jeannie thought with pride. Mina was honest and sincere and not given to airs that many of Jeannie's best friends' offspring had acquired. Jeannie could claim credit. She had raised her children to be respectful toward people of all classes and not to worry about material things which were fleeting. While several of Mina's friends had marriage proposals to consider, Mina would continue her studies at the new female academy and would start in the fall. Still, here in the confines of the paneled room, Jeannie noticed she was attracting the looks of many a male admirer. One of them finally figured out a way to meet her.

"Excuse me. Mrs. Andrew Pierce? Beg pardon, George Coward, here. I believe my mother has come to tea at your lovely home."

Jeannie looked up. *That was nicely done,* she thought. "Indeed?"

The speaker was a good-looking man in his twenties, dressed in a suit made of expensive linen. Fair-haired with a pleasant round face, he reflected wealth, but on inspection, Jeannie thought there was a bit of hardness about the eyes he hid well.

"I beg your pardon. My mother is Sarah Bonnier Coward."

"Ah, Mrs. Coward. How do you do. This is my daughter, Miss Jereminah Pierce."

"Miss Pierce. Ladies." The young man bowed deeply to them, but aimed himself more in the girl's direction. He gazed deep into her hazel eyes, then jerked up when Jeannie started talking again.

"How is your mother? I missed her at the women's social last month. She's not unwell, is she?"

"Quite well. There was an inconvenience."

"Oh, the weather. It was rather misbehaving at the time." Jeannie laughed. "Five feet is quite a lot, one of greatest snowstorms I've ever seen. So, what brings you on this outing?" Jeannie kept him pinned in his place, not sure if she would invite him to sit down.

"A trip to Whatcom on Bellingham Bay. But first to some holdings at Port Townsend."

"Really?" She glanced at her daughter.

Eagerly, he pulled a chair over, then discreetly looked over his shoulder to a group of men sitting in a corner underneath the windows. He gave them a slight nod, then sat down. Jeannie smiled politely at him, but she hadn't missed the exchange.

They talked for several minutes about his interests in Whatcom, a settlement of around on hundred and fifty souls north of them. It was enough to impress Jeannie.

"You seem to know your investment well, Mr. Coward."

"Oh, yes." He folded his well-manicured hands on the table and smiled. "I aim to make a profit. How about you, Miss Pierce?" he asked Mina.

"I'm going on an adventure," she replied.

"Adventure?"

"I'm going to see an old school mate for a couple of days. Mama is going to see the progress on one of our father's concerns."

"The late Mr. Pierce. I'm so sorry."

Jeannie accepted his condolences. Mina leaned in closer and began a lively discussion with George Coward. Jeannie began to wonder if his desire to speak with Mina was more than an act. That it had some other purpose.

Easing back against the bench, she took a sip from the bottle of sarsaparilla Polly had put in the basket. She hadn't any idea why she was suddenly so edgy, but the tension of the past few days had been considerable. Its only relief was the note from Phillip. *I will have words with you, young man.* Jeanie knew her plans had left the household in a tizzy, but she had to go. Too many memories good and bad tugged at her, but nothing hurt her more than Jonas Breed's reappearance. *Why didn't you come?* After seeing Mina off with the Garretts, she would make her supposed trip to look at the family's holdings and slip quietly over Victoria.

She turned her attention back to the young people, then over in the direction of the party to which Mr. Coward had nodded. They were a quiet, sullen-looking group. They could have been university boys but they weren't as well-mannered as Mr. Coward. In fact, she thought them a bit too quiet and conspiratorial. Someone caught her eye outside the window behind the group. The Kanaka she had seen earlier was looking in. His eyes searched the salon. When he saw her, he looked away and left.

"Mama."

"Uhmm?"

"Mr. Coward has asked me to walk around the deck with him. May I?"

"Yes, of course. I could use some air myself." Mina would have a chaperon no matter what Mr. Coward was hoping for.

Outside the air was warm and bright exposing open water full of all sorts of watercraft: schooners, rowboats and dugout canoes. The islands were more cultivated, some from ancient island prairies that rose up from the water. Farmhouses, little cedar-slab salt boxes under the high, wild blue sky, dotted the area. This was a day when the Pacific Northwest revealed a secret—it didn't rain all the time. Just part of the time.

Coward leaned against the rail. Mina followed, holding onto her straw bonnet. A gull was flying close to them looking for food.

"Fearless thing," Mina observed. "Take this." She threw a piece of bread towards the bird, but it dropped into the water. The bird dove down and came up with the bread in its beak.

Jeannie looked toward the bow. The Port Gamble family was still there, grouped around their possessions. The man wore an old felt cap. The woman had a bright red paisley scarf covering her head and tied under the chin. In between them, the little dog was tied to the rail while the girl slept in her mother's arms. The couple looked old and weathered, but they probably weren't that old, just reflecting the hard lives they led.

They reminded her of the fishing camp Breed showed her up at Farseeing. She remembered Sally Kalama and other women smoking fish. Noelani and Kapihi. How long ago that seemed though at the moment the memory was as real as a pin prick. She remembered the dense runs of salmon sweeping through by the hundreds of thousands and how Breed said that the San Juan Islands had been used by many Indian people, traditionally the Lummi. But that was before the raids from northern tribes and the smallpox.

Smallpox. It made her shudder. She rubbed her arm and bit her lip at the memory. Oh, why were the memories were so strong? What was wrong?

"Port Townsend. Coming up," a steward announced as he walked along the deck. He had to nearly shout over the sound of the paddle-wheel thump, thumping as it cut through the water.

Mina turned to her mother. Her face was flushed with excitement. "We're almost there!"

"Yes. We're almost there. How about you, Mr. Coward? Will you be disembarking?"

"As a matter of fact, yes. I have some business here. Will take a steamer out for Whatcom at a later time."

"That's nice," Jeannie said, hiding the misgivings she had about him.

"I think we ought to go and get our things together," she said to Mina. "I would like to freshen up before meeting your hosts. You will forgive us, Mr. Coward?"

He bowed to them and offered to escort them back in, but Jeannie thanked him and said they would be fine.

"Miss Pierce," he said, tipping his hat to Mina. "It's been my pleasure."

Mina took her mother's arm and smiled back at Coward. "If we don't see you again, have a safe journey."

In a settlement under one hundred and fifty souls, it would be impossible not to, Jeannie thought. She wondered what she would do about that.

They disembarked and were greeted by the Garretts, a couple in their mid-forties. The father was a former merchant now trying his hand at farming. Their daughter, Sara, had boarded at Mina's school in Seattle until finances got a little too difficult. Sara was going to a school in Port Townsend, a customs station, and was being paid seven dollars a month to help teach the younger children. Mina and Sara remained fast friends and wrote twice a month or more to each other.

There was a short wagon ride out to the Garret farm. They unloaded at the farmhouse, a handsome two-story cedar-slab house set on a gentle hill. There was a barn and other outbuildings. What passed for fields and pasture were dominated by enormous stumps, some five feet high. There was barely room for the cattle to get around. Still, it was a beautiful place, totally enclosed on three sides by a dense forest of Douglas fir and spruce. The fourth side opened to the water and the mainland and islands rolling on in blues and grays miles away. From far-off across the water to the east, white-headed Mount Baker rose in the clouds. Jeannie spent a pleasant afternoon, strolling down to the beach to collect driftwood and shells.

They went back into Port Townsend for dinner at the best hotel in the town where elk steaks and bear paws were on the menu. Jeannie had insisted on repaying her daughter's hosts for their kindness with dinner in a fancy place. It was enough prestige to be an acquaintance of Mrs. Andrew Pierce, but an evening out would increase the cachet and give the family a much-needed balm for their hard labor. The Garretts, she knew, were respected. She was glad to hear that Mr. Garrett was considering accepting a job of manager at a sawmill. It would help him as he proved up his homestead claim. Lumber sales to California were doing well.

At nine, they said their good-byes. Jeannie would be staying in town, hoping to do business. She might even go to Victoria to see Phillip. She hoped to meet up with the Garrets in a few days.

"Good-bye, dear," she said to her daughter as they stood outside on the hotel stairs. "Have a lovely time."

"Oh, Mama, I'm already having a wonderful time." She gave Jeannie a kiss on the cheek, then climbed onto the second wagon seat and pulled her skirt around her legs. Mrs. Garrett climbed in next followed by Sara. While the women waited, a lantern was lit and hung up on a pole next to the driver's side. There was still over an hour of light, but in the woods, it would be dark. There was a final wave from Mr. Garrett and they were off.

Inside the brick and sandstone hotel, Jeannie gathered her keys in the lobby and went up the oak staircase to her room on the second floor. Her valise and other packages had already been taken up hours before by a clerk and placed on a luggage stand. It was a well-appointed room with high ceilings and drapes gracefully looped around the tall window that looked down into the street. The bedding had been pulled back and fresh flowers set by the ornate walnut bed. Kerosene lamps had been lit sending a soft glow around the room. Jeannie removed her wrap and hung it up on the coat stand, then proceeded to undress. It had been a long day. It didn't take long to fall asleep.

~

"Mama. I'm so hot. So hot," a little voice wailed. Get them off! Get them off!"

"I will. I will," a voice soothed.

It was suffocating hot in the hotel room and rancid with sickness, but the windows had been nailed shut and the door locked. There was no way to get out.

"Mama!" The pitiful little voice wailed its misery, believing that a mother could cure anything. This was something that was not cured and could only run its deadly course. Sores covered his little body everywhere. The shiny light brown hair was dull, the eyes swimming in fever.

290

"I'm here, sweetie," the voice cried out

"Where Mama? Where?" the boy moaned. "Don't leave me!"

"I'm here, Jeremy!" The woman suddenly screamed in terror for the boy had disappeared from the bed he lay on. Frantically, she searched the room, pulling off the covers to the floor and overturning furniture. Finally, she looked outside the window where a little soul fluttered against the window-pane like a moth at lantern light.

The moaning increased and it began to scratch to get in. "Mama! Mama!" Then tiring, the words became a whisper and with a bang vanished into the stormy night.

"Jeremy!" Jeannie gasped as she sat up in the dark. Fumbling for the lucifers at the bedside table, she lit the lamp and looked around the room. There was nothing out of place, though this room had been in the dream. She looked toward the window. Fueled by some draft, the drawn linen curtain under the drapes shivered lightly as it tapped the window. Summoning what courage she had left, she got out of bed to investigate. It was black as coal outside, but she could tell that the window was slightly up, causing air to come in. During the night, a wind had come off the Inlet. She pushed the window down and the whining stopped. Shaking all over, she hopped back into bed. It was cool in the room, but she knew that it was the breath of death come visiting. She pulled the covers tightly around her and stared into nothing.

A draft came under the door and caused the candle to flicker. Jeannie wrapped herself deeper into the blanket and leaned back against the headboard. Never had she felt so absurdly small and powerless. Not even after Andrew's sudden death. *Am I going mad?*

She had always kept a special place in her heart for Jeremy all these years. Sometimes when Phillip and Jereminah were small, a strong memory was evoked when they did something similarly precocious or silly. Jeremy had died so long ago and was only a shadow, like a brilliant flower pressed into a book and faded to gray. She had been able to keep the grief contained. But now the possibility that Jonas was alive had also rekindled the life of Jeremy, for there was a time when they were closely entwined.

VICTORIA

"Did you sleep well, Mrs. Pierce?"

Sitting in the hotel dining room, Jeannie guessed she had fallen asleep at some point. It had been an odd night, full of ghosts and strange whisperings. She felt stiff and light-headed from lack of sleep.

"Yes, thank you." She smiled at the waiter, then asked for coffee.

The dining room was quiet. Jeannie and one other patron in the corner were the only customers. Except for the customs house and the maritime trade that brought, Port Townsend felt like a frontier town, but had grand plans to get the railroad terminus here. Sitting by the window, she looked out into the street. Most buildings were two-story wooden affairs, but a few were brick. Not far away were the docks and mud flats that stretched far to the south where she knew there was an Indian encampment.

The waiter returned with coffee set on a tray with a pitcher of cream. Jeannie thanked him. On an impulse, asked if the customs house was open for the day. She added, "There's a ship I'm interested in. It may have dealt with my husband's firm."

"No, ma'am," the mustachioed man said. "But if you wish, Captain Wise, the gentleman over there, may know. May I inquire of him?"

Jeannie flushed. She didn't feel so bold, but the sea captain must have overheard the conversation and turned toward her.

"Madame, may I be of assistance?" Captain Wise folded down his paper.

Jeannie tried not to fuss with her napkin to show her nervousness. She hadn't expected to make any public inquiries. Despite big ears with white hair sprouting out of them, Captain Wise appeared every inch a mariner with his trim white beard and high collared blue captain's jacket. She decided that he was reliable.

"Oh, a curiosity. I saw a ship the other day in Seattle. It was quite handsome and unusually marked with gold and red trim. I wondered if it came here often."

"What was her name?"

"*Klose Tum Tum,* I believe."

"Hmmm. Did she have a figurehead?"

Now that was something Jeannie hadn't seen. It was facing the other way.

"Unfortunately, I didn't see one." She swallowed. "Someone told me it might be a foreign ship."

Captain Wise looked thoughtful. *Probably wondering how I might know that bit,* Jeannie thought.

"That's doubtful, ma'am. Not with that Chinook Jargon name. But ships come in all the time from the points in the Hawaiian Islands—Honolulu, Lahaina. Come for the timber, you see. Could be local."

Jeannie pretended that this was news, but she was fully aware the firm of Pierce, Campbell and Waddell had a bark that regularly made the fourteen-day run between the Hawaiian Islands and Port Townsend monthly.

"—did see a schooner that might match what you're looking about the two weeks ago. Just came back through customs.

"Had a mixed crew of Chinamen and Kanakas."

"Do you know where it was going?"

Now the Captain did look at her curiously as though a woman really should stick to the kitchen, then he chuckled.

"Beg pardon, ma'am, but you're as beam-bright on the subject as my wife, God bless her. After ten years at sea with me she knows the goings of all ships between San Francisco and Port Townsend and more." He winked. "Your ship was headed to Victoria."

The captain got up. For the first time she noticed that his right hand was missing two fingers. She flinched but caught herself.

"Not to worry, dear lady. I'm quite capable." He tipped his cap to her. "Good day." He put his newspaper under his arm and headed out to the hotel lobby.

Jeanie leaned back in her chair. She felt buoyed with this intelligence, but her task to find Breed was overwhelming. She finally decided that upon arriving in Victoria she would seek out their capable agent, Cyrus Simpson, at their Canadian office. He might have ideas on how to locate the ship and arrange a meeting with its owners.

It was still misty out and chilly, but promised a bright day. As she finished her coffee, she wondered what Mina was doing. Jeannie felt a pang of guilt for the ruse, yet her daughter had been devastated by her father's death and she needed some cheer. The trip and stay at the Garrett's would hopefully provide that. As for herself, she often felt numb. Andrew could be difficult, but he had provided and, really, he had been a good husband and in the early years, an affable companion. She had even learned to love him. In the last year, however, he had been moody and grim. Her feelings of grief that he died so young and unexpectedly mingled with conflicted feelings of long-lost desire. She studied her wavy reflection in the window pane. She looked drawn and sad. *Of course, I am*, she thought. *I'm in mourning. But I am also seeking.*

After breakfast, she turned over her keys and one of her valises to the proprietor, promising to return in a few days. Outside, the settlement was waking up. Wagons were coming into town with produce and other goods. Underneath the painted canvas awnings just opening up in front of businesses, men in sack coats and derby hats were gathering on the porches. On the stairs, some blanketed Indians were sitting with cedar baskets and other wares for sale. She bought a tiny basket with a lid and canoes woven around its side from one of them, then walked down to the wharf. At a wood slab building built precariously at the start of the long walkway, she located the agent and secured her ticket for the steamer to Victoria. Settling down on a worn wooden bench, as she waited for it to come, she became aware she had been followed. She couldn't tell who he was from a distance, but he seemed to have followed her from the muddy street, slipping into an abandoned building once she bought her ticket. From time to time he looked out, pretending to check his watch or the weather, but she was sure he was checking on her.

At seven-forty, the side-wheeler came thumping into view and made its landing a short while later. Several travelers disembarked along with a dozen cartloads of goods. When the vessel was ready, Jeanne boarded. Buttoning her cape she stepped out onto the deck and watched Port Townsend recede as they moved out, putting her further away from the man who followed her. Whoever he was, he had unnerved her. She didn't feel safe until they were upon open water.

They approached the islands known now as the San Juan Islands. Green and heavily forested, they crowded together like gate heads to the straits of Haro and Rosario to the left and right. The wide open prairie on San Juan Island where the horse races were held was easy to spot, splaying out on South Beach like an apron, but anything beyond that she struggled to name from where she stood on the throbbing deck. She had not come this way in many years.

Wait for me.

For an instant she was on another boat, the insistent drumming of the side-paddle wheels pounding in her head as they moved further down toward the Olympic Peninsula. She had been miserable then, full of anguish and confusion.

He had not come.

Jeannie stiffened her shoulders at the long-suppressed memory and brought herself to the present. They were further out into the strait now surrounded on all sides by forested mountains. Everything else was dwarfed, even the tall ship with its sails billowing like squared pillow cases passing in front of the steamboat a mile ahead.

Jeannie wondered if it was heading off to San Francisco or to the far north. A *salt chuck* canoe, braving the crosswind and current as the tide went out, came in view. It held ten Coast Salish men paddling in fluid motion. Like her, it was headed north toward Victoria.

As the boat turned toward the Vancouver Island coastline, Jeannie looked back to San Juan Island and squinted to seek out features of Kanaka Town where she had nursed Kaui Kalama, but could not find anything. Yet memory was stronger than geography.

Once the steamboat landed in Victoria, the boat's captain sent for a carriage to take Jeannie where she wished. How things have changed, she thought. It was hard to believe twenty years before, she had stood at this same spot, penniless and with only Jeremy for support and friendship. It was her good fortune her dear Uncle Archie had extended his loving hand to her across a continent and ocean and brought her here. And for that she would always bless him. She suppressed a sudden sob. He had been dead for some years, her last known relative from her past.

After checking her valise and trunk at the best hotel in the town, Jeannie instructed her driver to take her out to the old cemetery. The day had shrugged off the early morning clouds and was embracing the noon sun breaking high over the wooded hills beyond the town. The air was sweet with golden, summer warmth. It reminded Jeannie of other summer days here.

They arrived sooner than she expected.

"I shan't be long," she said, her English accent strangely stronger than normal. As if to re-establish herself here. "I think it's just a little ways away."

Of course, the grounds had grown. And trees around the picket fence when Jeremy had been laid to rest had been cut down to make way for widening of a planked road. For a moment, she was disoriented. She looked for the trees further back, half expecting Jonas

Breed to come out, but all she saw or heard was a Steller's jay making its way to a higher perch.

I must do this on my own, she thought. *What would the driver think?* Memory guiding her, she ventured into a stand of headstones casting short shadows on the grass, looking for names. Before she left for English Camp with Gilly after Jeremy's death, Uncle Archie had placed a small headstone on his grave. Jeannie looked for a headstone with a little angel carved above Jeremy's name. When she couldn't find it, she began to panic. *Where are you, sweetie?* A long suppressed nightmare of being down on her hands and knees in the mud and rain at Jeremy's newly made grave, pierced her heart. *Where could he be lain? Who moved him?* She hugged her arms and looked around.

Eventually she oriented herself to a little knoll higher up on the slope and walked toward it. There encased behind an iron-rod picket fence was a tall granite obelisk stating ARCHIBALD CAMPBELL.

So this is where her uncle was laid, she thought, knowing that Andrew had arranged for the monument. She had been unable to come to the funeral as the children had been ill and she could not leave them. Andrew had come instead. Her uncle and her husband had been partners for a time, up to Uncle Archie's death from pneumonia. Strong, sensible Uncle Archie. She felt the stab of sorrow in her breast. She missed the old man terribly. She looked at the obelisk. There was more writing underneath. She read it eagerly, but halfway through, she stopped, her heart pounding. Under writing about his life: "Trader for Hudson's Bay Company. He served his country well," there were some other words.

"Beloved nephew, Jeremy. 1855-1860. Rest with Sweet Jesus."

Jeannie's bouquet of flowers dropped from her hands and slid down on the inside of the fence. At first, Jeannie felt relief. Jeremy had been moved to rest with her beloved uncle. The nightmare from a few moments ago dissolved into a sense of peace. She read the inscription again and then put a hand on her heart. A tear rolled down her cheek. "Thank you," she whispered. For once, Andrew had done something right. For that, she was grateful, but why didn't tell her.

Andrew.

Anger sliced through her memory. Privately, their marriage hadn't always been sweetness and light. Andrew could be so controlling, especially in the last few years. As she searched for a gate into the enclosure, a terrible idea came to her head. Did Andrew know something about Jeremy and Marsfield? In anger, Andrew had once told her she was secretive as a cuckoo slipping her egg into an unsuspecting nest. He apologized later, but she was so hurt, it took weeks for him to gain her favor again. Yet... was he thinking about Jeremy and the Marsfield affair or Phillip?

Jeannie knew she had been dishonest, but never having the courage to tell Andrew the truth about Breed, she encouraged her husband's affection for Phillip the moment he was born. Andrew truly was mesmerized the moment he held the baby. "We'll name him Phillip after my father."

Jeannie didn't know what would hurt Andrew more, the Marsfield scandal affecting the good name of Pierce, Campbell and Waddell or Phillip's parentage. She picked up the bouquet and laid it on the square ledge going around the moss-tinged obelisk. She murmured the names of Jeremy and her uncle, then shut the gate. The Steller's jay called again, its annoyance at her growing, but Jeannie didn't hear it. Grief unacknowledged for years reopened and for several minutes she quietly wept.

Now what to do? Coming to the old cemetery and the strange dream of the night before drained all energy. But she had be resolved in this undertaking to find Breed. First, she must go to the local offices of Pierce, Campbell and Waddell and look at the accounts. Since Andrew died, the company was in a state of flux, and faced an uncertain future. Except for Waddell, all the partners were dead. Burgess, the solicitor, had said the Canadian office might close. On that note, the head clerk would know about ships coming through Victorian customs. She also would find Phillip. He needed to explain himself. It was not like him to be discourteous, to cause her worry.

After refreshing herself at the hotel, Jeannie walked down to Wharf Street where the offices were located. The afternoon was warm, drawing a good portion of the town's respectable citizenry out on the planked sidewalks.

"Mrs. Naughton—forgive me—Mrs. Jeannie Pierce, is it not?"

Jeannie turned, startled that someone here would recognize her. The gentleman was British by his accent, but he was dressed in clothing more suited for a settler in town on business. Jeannie thought he looked familiar, but could not place him.

"Royal Marine Camp, Mrs. Pierce. Summer, 1860. My sister was the wife of the assistant surgeon there. Mrs. Gilly Parker."

Jeannie's lips parted in amazement. "John Forrester! I thought you lived in San Francisco. Are you here on business?"

Forrester smiled. "Oh, no, I live here. Have for almost a year. I run a cannery outside of town."

Jeannie put a hand on her breast. "What a delightful surprise." Her grim assessment of her day vanished.

Forrester looked around. "May I take you to tea? I can't wait to let Gilly know. She'll be most happy."

"Gilly? She's here?"

"Yes, but not in Victoria. She has settled on San Juan Island near the old English Camp. She has only been here for a few months, alone."

"Alone?"

"Dr. Parker has passed on."

"Oh, dear. I didn't know. What a lovely man." Jeannie blinked, pushing away tears. She had lost contact with the Parkers about ten years ago. "How does she manage alone?" Jeannie often asked herself that question too.

"A nephew runs it for her, though my sister is a game and able lady,. Ah, here's the place. Excellent tea."

"Tell me of your life in Seattle," John said after they sat down in a little corner in the tea shop.

"I've had a rather good life, I should say," Jeannie removed her gloves to serve the tea. "Andrew did well from the start and though Seattle was frontier society then, it was not lacking in some culture." Jeannie went on to tell him anecdotes of her early years in the little settlement and the growth of her family. When her narrative ran out, she asked, "What about Gilly?"

"Quite well. She's had every intention to contact you once she was settled, you know. She learned of Andrew's passing through the newspapers, but she has been engaged in the task of bringing her home to bear. She may still be unpacking." They continued to talk pleasantly about Gilly and some of Forrester's endeavors. By the time their teacups were filled for a second time, it felt as though they were once again on the front porch of the surgeon's bungalow at the Royal Marine Camp, twenty years melted away.

"What brings you to Victoria, really?" John asked.

"Old ghosts, I suppose. My uncle for one. He died eight years ago." She looked down at her delicate china teacup. She listlessly stirred the caramel-colored brew with her demitasse spoon. "And then, there are others. Coming here certainly has rekindled old memories. Sometimes, when I look around here, I feel it has never changed. Then I wonder how I ever lived it. No one remembers those times as we do."

"Those certainly were difficult years," John acknowledged. "After I left here, Gilly often wrote about the troubles with some of the settlers and their trade at San Juan Town. It continued long after you left. Mr. Pierce, your husband, would have probably been aware. Didn't he still have some involvement with the sutler at the American camp?"

"Yes."

"Gilly said both officers from English Camp and American Camp had their hands full with the whiskey ranches and the other unsavory business in San Juan Town. Wild times, indeed." Forrester looked kindly at her. "And then, there was that ugly business with the American *shipman*, Jonas Breed. You remember him, I'm sure."

Jeannie's heart skipped beat. She felt a catch in her breath. "Yes, I do remember him."

"You know, I'm not supposed to repeat this—so I ask your discretion—but I've heard that he's alive."

"Alive?"

Forrester could see the news stunned her, but not in the way he thought. "Quite extraordinary, isn't it?"

"How do you know?"

"From Gilly. That's all I know."

Delicately, Jeannie brought her napkin to her lips, hoping he didn't note her trembling hands. What she hoped for was true—another confirmation of Breed's resurrection—but with that truth came tortuous questions. Where had he been? Why didn't he come? This news was making her sick. Just like Uncle Archie's monument with Jeremy's name on it, it seemed there were important things in her life she had no control over. She dabbed at edges of her lips to hide her disquiet and shock.

"Did Gilly see him?" Jeannie tried to sound non-committal. "I recall that she and Jonas were on good terms."

"Not sure." Forrester leaned back against the fir wood wall. "If you are free, you should go see Gilly." He smiled at her. "She'd be over-joyed. She has talked of nothing else."

Jeannie looked out the lace-curtained window. Some of the businesses were getting ready to close even though it would be light for several hours more. She watched a store proprietor start to roll up his canvas awning and have barrels brought inside. Her mind drifted. She knew Forrester was waiting for her to say something, but all she could think of were images, not words.

Forrester would be shocked for all she saw was Breed coming out of the water, stripped to the waist and pulling the conical cedar net full of crabs nipping and clawing each other. At that time, she could not have loved him more.

"I can arrange a boat over," Forrester continued. "A side-wheeler still goes to the old Hudson's Bay wharf at San Juan Town, but I'd put into Garrison Bay. The buildings at English Camp are part of a homestead now. She doesn't live too far from there."

"I don't know. My daughter is in Port Townsend. My son Phillip is here on business with our solicitor." She started to draw back her eyes back in again to him when she stopped. Across the street leaning against a post was George Coward. He said nothing about coming here. She felt the blood drain out of her face.

"Is something wrong?" Forrester asked.

"That man. The one leaning against the post. Do you know him?" Jeannie asked.

Forrester peered out the window. "He has come to Victoria on several different occasions. The most recent about three weeks ago. An American, I believe."

"Yes, he is. I met him on the boat to Port Townsend, yesterday. Didn't see him today."

"I wouldn't be surprised if there were another means of getting here. He runs with a suspicious crowd. Illegal goods, etc. And yet, I've seen him at the office of Pierce, Campbell and Waddell."

Jeannie stared at him. "It can't be. The man's father has a respectable shipping outfit in Seattle. Perhaps, you are mistaken."

"Perhaps." Forrester smiled reassuringly. "But respectability goes only so far when two and two make three."

"What would he want with the company?"

"I wouldn't know. Perhaps you ought to ask the head clerk."

Jeannie watched Coward change his position against the post, then offhandedly wave at someone out of her line of vision. "Funny, I was going to do the very thing when I ran into you."

Forrester checked his pocket watch. "Why don't you do it now? I'll escort you and then get a telegram off to Gilly."

Jeannie looked outside again. Coward was gone. What did that mean? While Forrester beckoned the waiter and paid the bill, she thought back carefully to the trip up to Port Townsend and everything Coward had said. She hadn't paid too closely to his conversation with Mina. Now she wished that she had. Her initial dislike of him seemed more rational. Had he followed her intentionally?

"Come, Jeannie," Forrester said. "We'll slip out the back door. I know the proprietor."

Jeannie grinned at him. "Now we are the conspirators."

Forrester led her out through the back of the false-fronted

building and down a muddy lane littered with wood chips and apple peelings.

"Raccoons," he said as they went around a barrel lying on its side. It was peppered with long-fingered tracks.

They made it to Wharf Street where the office of Pierce, Campbell and Waddell was located. It had a discrete, orderly brick face and well-swept boardwalk in front of the large maple door. Forrester peered through a round, curtained window on the door and announced that someone was in despite the fact that the sign in the main window said CLOSED. He pushed on the door knob and the door gave way. Inside, a bewhiskered gentleman in his late forties, came forward to protest. Then he saw Jeannie.

"Mrs. Pierce. I had no idea you were coming."

"I apologize, Mr. Simpson. Lately, I have had questions about the firm I felt only you could honestly answer me. I didn't want anyone to know that was my purpose for my trip." She took off her gloves hoping that her explanation would suffice. Simpson was truly someone she trusted, but she would say nothing about her real impulse to come to Victoria.

Cyrus Simpson locked the door, pulled down the shade. The front room was well appointed with fir wainscoting around the wall and paintings depicting early scenes of Vancouver Island. Behind the large oak desk was an oil painting of Uncle Archie. Dark and formal, his black coat blended to some dim scene of timeless forest and the old fort when Victoria was a new settlement. His beard and hair were white, but though the years were in the lines of his face, he had a ghost of a twinkle in his eye. He had sat for it not long before his death.

Simpson invited her into the back, nodding to Forrester when he was introduced. "We have met. Christmas, 1878, I believe. Do come, Mrs. Pierce. The gentleman is welcome."`

"Tell you what, Mrs. Pierce." Forrester was formal again. "Why don't you speak to Mr. Simpson in private? In the meantime, I'll compose my telegram to Gilly."

Jeannie thanked him for his consideration, then followed Simpson upstairs.

At the top of the stairs, Simpson led her down a dark hall to the front of the building. He opened a door to a room with overstuffed chairs, knick-knack cases and a heavy oak table. In one of the corners, a large sword fern spread its green plumes. Jeannie went to the window which overlooked the harbor. The harbor was busy with every sort of sailing craft: steam paddle boats, schooners and smaller craft necessary for travel between the shores of the great inland sea and the islands. In the west above the forest hills and mountains around the harbor little clouds the shape of stepping stones promised a glorious sunset.

"Beautiful."

"Yes, it is. Mr. Campbell especially enjoyed the view." Simpson pulled out a chair for her. "I'm so glad you're here. I've been trying to arrange my schedule so I could go to Seattle and deliver some papers to you."

"You needn't have bothered. Mr. Burgess left word some days ago he was traveling out here. I assumed he was coming to the Victoria office as it might be closed down. My son Phillip is with him."

"Mr. Burgess said that?"

"Yes, he told me himself. Said since Andrew's death, the office might not be so profitable. Now with both partners dead…"

"He did, did he?" Simpson stroked his short beard thoughtfully. "I wonder if he considered Mr. Waddell's feelings on that part."

"I was under the impression Mr. Waddell is a silent partner, only a formality in name."

"Tell that to Mr. Waddell." Simpson frowned. "Excuse me, Mrs. Pierce, for my sarcasm. I know you've been present at many of the board's meetings. My hat is off to you. I do not think, though, you've been told everything. Mr. Waddell is indeed real. As for Mr. Burgess, I've had no word from him."

Jeannie gasped. "Mr. Burgess is not here?"

"No, ma'am. I have not seen him. Were you expecting him?"

"Very much so." Jeannie's knees went weak, but not wishing to appear a fainthearted female she steadied herself with a hand on the table. "My son said he would be with him."

"Perhaps his ship has been delayed. I'll have someone look into it right away." Simpson opened a leather satchel and set a water-stained package tied with string in front of her. "About a month ago, I found this under the flooring of an old house once used by the firm in its early years. We were preparing to tear the building down. I think it was quite forgotten. It must've been of some personal importance. You can see Mr. Pierce's writing on the front."

Jeannie studied the faded black ink on the package's face. It was so like Andrew to exaggerate the shape of the "I" and the "E". She read: "In the event of my passing, please give to J____Pierce." The first name was almost obliterated.

Simpson cleared his throat. "Did Burgess ever tell you about a break in to the office?"

"No."

"An American came into the office looking for papers belonging to the firm. Said he was acting on Mr. Burgess's orders."

"Was he?"

"Never saw him before in my life. A few days later, someone broke in, but apparently didn't find what he was looking for." He tapped the package. "I decided to keep it hidden when someone tried to get into my own quarters. I think something is seriously wrong. Have you spoken with Mr. Wilson about it?"

"Mr. Wilson? My butler?"

"Yes. Mr. Pierce had great confidence in him. Wilson often had first hand at arranging schedules for him among other duties outside the family. That included firm business."

"I had no idea."

Simpson smiled softly at her. "Not your fault. Burgess's more like."

"You are not happy with Mr. Burgess." Jeannie was anxious to see what was inside the package. It reminded her of the other papers Burgess had given her.

"I know he's a trusted solicitor, but he has acted strangely the last few months. It's his duty to keep you informed. Especially with Mr. Pierce's sudden passing."

Suddenly Jeannie remembered Coward. She gave the best description of him she could manage. When she finished, Simpson made a face.

"The American. Sounds just like him."

"Mr. Forrester says he has been seen with a 'suspicious crowd.'"

"Perhaps I should talk to your friend." He waved at the package. "You can read here if you like. If it's a legal matter, I'll find some way to secure the package. Since this is an international office of the firm, I can perhaps ask for help from the American consul." Simpson stepped away from the table. "I'll only be gone for a moment. I can arrange a search for Phillip, if you like. See if he came in one of the morning's steamships."

"Oh, please."

Simpson bowed and left, leaving Jeannie to her thoughts and the harbor view. It was easy to get distracted. She stood up and walked over to the window. Down below, the shops and other businesses were closing for the weekend.

Where are you, Phillip? Her growing dread of days before was back. What Simpson said about Burgess was unsettling, but she knew Simpson could be trusted. As a young man, Cyrus Simpson had worked for her uncle. One of Uncle Archie's great gifts was judging people correctly. She wished her uncle was here now. She couldn't put her finger on it, but she knew her presence in Victoria was somehow dangerous. She had upset something. She decided she would take Simpson's advice and send a telegram to Wilson and have him look after Mina.

A noise downstairs brought her attention to the table. She should open the package here, then give it back to Simpson for safekeeping. She had no idea what was in it, but putting it under the floorboards of an old residence was peculiar. She read the writing again. "In the event of my passing…"

Oh, Andrew, she thought, *much has gone on since.*

She removed the strings and unwrapped the paper. Inside she found a pile of documents and a small pocket journal. She separated them into two groups and looked at the journal first. It was Andrew's, the entries hurriedly scribbled in pencil and dated from 1870. It noted a few things—mostly lists of merchandise for one of the company's steamboats.

About five pages in, though, he left a couple of days' entries. As she read, her face grew hot.

Oct 8, 1870

I am suffering from a most devastating encounter. Met with Waddell on his instructions. It is one thing to have to beg for assistance. It is another to be taken advantage by a ghost. Waddell is none other than Jonas Breed.

Jeannie gasped, but she had to continue reading.

I thought him dead years ago. He is most insistent that he become a partner as certain properties of his were misappropriated some time ago. He has no leg to stand on. He gave up his rights in becoming a murderer and fugitive. It will be folly to pursue this.

The anger and confusion she had felt at the graveyard returned. Andrew had not been truthful. Worse, neither had Jonas Breed, the man she had loved so passionately and whose death and resurrection was hurting her deeply.

October 9, 1870

Met with Breed and his cohort, Collie Henderson again. What a murderous pair they are! To think we were once friends.

October 10, 1870

Have met with the rogue J. B. again. He certainly has me cold. I have no other offer and without him, I face ruin. He has made up the terms and I will sign tomorrow. He has promised immediate capital. As long I keep to his terms, he says the company will be not only solvent, but highly profitable. He will remain in the Sandwich Islands for the time being, but has his own men to see to his interests and that of the firm. I am to use the name Waddell in all matters, including correspondence. No one is to know, but that is much to my relief. I do not trust the pirate for his old feelings toward my Jeannie. His manhood is in ruination for his dalliances with his brown-skinned consorts. He's not fit to be with a white woman.

There were several more entries, but Jeannie read. Picking up the documents in the other pile, she could see that the name Waddell was an important factor on all of them. For ten years, Jonas Breed had been a partner in the shipping firm of Pierce, Campbell and Waddell. Had her uncle known? She had never questioned why the Campbell name had remained after his death—she thought it a nice gesture—and she had never asked who Waddell was.

Betrayed. That was what she felt. She closed her eyes to hold back the tears, but she couldn't hold back the image.

Wait for me. He had kissed her passionately, buoyed they could be together as man and wife. It would only be a short wait.

Where were you, Jonas? Why did you come ten years later? If you were to come at all, why then? A whole life without me. And I—I bore your child.

Shaking, she put all the papers back and folded the brown paper wrapping back in its place around the pile. She looked at the writing on the pocket journal cover again. She took the whole package over to the window. In the late afternoon light, two more letters appeared: an "e" and what appeared to be an "r". Could it have been Jerad? Andrew had a cousin somewhere back in New York State by the name of Jerad. The package was never intended for her. More betrayal.

Deeply hurt, Jeannie tied the package up tightly and pushed it away. It must have some great importance. Perhaps it was the only record of the relationship between the three men. Was this what Coward was looking for? She decided she would have Simpson secure it. She walked over to the window, wondering what to do next. It made no sense that Breed would suddenly reappear and enter into a business arrangement with Andrew. Andrew had never spoken of any financial difficulty. What could have led him to such secrecy? And such bitterness and hatred toward Jonas Breed.

Out in the harbor, a large schooner began to unfurl its sails and prepare to head out of the harbor. She watched the men clamor around the mainsail and begin to haul the main sheet up. She wondered where it was going. Wherever it was, it had a purpose. Jeannie wasn't so sure about hers any more. What had started out as a wistful search for someone she had loved a long time ago was turning out to be a hard look at her life of the last twenty years. Without the children, she wondered if any of it was real. What right did the men have to plan and plot without her knowing? Who were they to decide? Neither man had been honest, but Jonas's betrayal hurt the most. Of all people, he should understand what betrayal meant.

Jeannie was standing at the window when Simpson returned to the boardroom.

"How did you find the papers, Mrs. Pierce?"

"I would like to know more about Mr. Waddell. Have you ever met him?"

"No, but I have carried on correspondence with him all these years. I came into the firm in 1871, about a year after Waddell joined the partnership. After your uncle's death, he sent a representative from Honolulu, a Mr. Colin Henderson. He's one of his captains in his fleet of ships. Henderson makes regular visitations whenever he comes to the Pacific Northwest."

Collie Henderson, she thought. *Oh, what a web we weave.*

"Mr. Waddell is in Honolulu?"

"Yes."

"After my uncle died," Jeannie said, doing her best to suppress her fury at her discovery, "the Campbell name was retained in company and his portion put into a trust for my children. I have always appreciated this gesture on my uncle's part, but I have never inquired how this was carried out."

Simpson looked surprised. "Didn't you know ma'am? Burgess never told you? It was Mr. Waddell. He insisted. You see, your uncle's will wasn't quite up to snuff. In short, beyond the minimum, it was missing. Your uncle was in the process of changing a portion when he contracted the pneumonia that took his life. When he died, there were no provisions on record for anything. Mr. Pierce would have preferred the money be divided equally, but Mr. Waddell was the majority owner and he insisted your uncle's third be kept intact."

Jeannie's face fell in confusion. "If my uncle and husband were partners, it was equally divided before Waddell joined."

"It was never equal, ma'am. The house of Pierce owned two thirds. Waddell bought out more than half of the house of Pierce."

"Oh," she said in a small voice. "I see." No, she didn't see. Wills, secret agreements, cemetery monuments. She sighed, thought about joining Forrester, and then took on a different subject.

"Did you ever hear of a man named Jonas Breed?"

"Yes, I have. Quite a legend here in these parts. He was killed in some trouble twenty years ago, but in the Saanich village across the way they still speak of him as if he lived."

"Really? Did my uncle ever speak of him?"

"Yes, he did. Hours before his passing," Simpson said. "He was rambling in his mind and spoke of Breed on a personal level as I had not heard before. Was calling for someone to exonerate him. Later, when I inquired of the charges against Breed, I was told that a commission in 1865 had done just that."

"My uncle never spoke of him before?"

"Only once in passing. Less than a year before the English camp on San Juan Island was closed down and given over to the Americans, we stopped by to visit. He told me then about Breed and the troubles that had gone on there in the vicinity. Spoke right fondly of him and always felt Breed innocent. Did you by chance know him?"

Jeannie swallowed and looked away. She could not answer.

"He was certainly an interesting personality," Simpson went on, "and has been remembered in curious ways. At Saanich, I once saw a small totem carved for a potlatch. On it was the likeness of a Boston man—an American white man—with tattoos one might find on a slave. I was told that it was meant to be the likeness of Jonas Breed. Heard he was spoken of up in the Queen Charlottes as well. The *Boston mistchimas*."

Jeannie put a hand on her breast to keep her heart beat down. "I think these papers should be put in a safe place, Cyrus," she said. "They are important to the company and in particular, Mr. Waddell, since he appears to be real after all. They seem to document the original signing of the partnership with him and why. I also ask that they not be reopened until I have had the time to think about what they mean."

"I'll do it, ma'am. I know just the place."

She smiled softly at the clerk. "Thank you. My uncle trusted you. That I know. So I am going to seek your advice. Do you trust this Mr. Waddell?"

"Without exception. In the nine years of my contact with him through his representative, he has been honest and has served the company well. His business decisions have kept the company solvent in bad times and in profit during the good."

"And Mr. Burgess? What is your honest opinion?"

Simpson scowled. "Well, I've been troubled about him for some time. Even warned Mr. Pierce. I think Burgess has been tampering with the books and shipping lists. I fear Mr. Pierce may have found proof, but didn't have time to tell me before his unfortunate accident."

Jeannie gasped, but it seemed her only reaction to one bad revelation after another. She brushed the package. She had to make a decision what to do now. She wasn't sure if she should return to her hotel.

"Did Mr. Forrester tell you I may have been followed here?"

"Indeed, he did. What do you want me to do?"

"First, could you go to the American consul and have a search made for my son? I think he is danger. Then, I should like you to contact Mr. Waddell's representative, if it's possible. If it's not, then for the moment, I should like very much to have you continue to try. In the meantime, I'm going to San Juan Island to see my old friend Mrs. Parker, Mr. Forrester's sister." She gave Simpson the package. "I am wondering if I should have cause to be concerned for myself and my daughter. If that is the case, I want to be prepared. Could you please send a telegram to Mr. Wilson, my manservant, in Seattle?"

"I'll see to your requests immediately," he said. "I can arrange to have both the American consul, customs, and the local police look into Phillip's whereabouts. In the meantime, I'll consult with Mr. Forrester on what is the best way to visit your friend. I'll have your things removed from the hotel without notice and take you to another, comfortable place, then in the morning, put you on a ship to

English Camp. Or, if you are truly adventuresome, I can arrange for a *salt chuck* canoe. It would the quickest and least observable as we can put in north of here."

"All right," answered Jeannie. Ten hours later, she was in a canoe going across Haro Strait to a place she hadn't seen in twenty years.

REUNION

The dugout canoe slid onto the stony shore, grinding the dark gray sand and wave-weathered stones as men caught and secured it. While the other pullers helped to bring the canoe ashore, a young man at the bow got out, his brown legs buckling from his long hours at the paddle before he gained some sense of connectedness to the ground. Once assured that he wouldn't fall flat on his face, he headed for the trees and the interior of the little island. There were tall reeds and grasses at the edge of beach and weathered logs tossed up by last year's winter storms, but he was able to find the opening to the trail that led through the stand of madrone and big leaf maple. Punching through the forested center of the crescent-shaped island, he was soon rounding a cove and heading west along its steep embankment. Coming out high on a ridge, he sought out a second party of men standing around a camp fire several hundred feet away on a small, open prairie. Stopping to catch his breath briefly, he hailed the party as soon as he resumed his climb up to them.

"*Klahowya*," he shouted as he came up next to them, then bent over his knees.

A dark-haired man stepped away from the fire and came quickly toward the bowed runner. At forty-five, Jonas Breed was still a commanding figure. Tall and lean as when he was young only his face seemed changed with the addition of crow's feet around his eyes from years in the sun and wind. He was beardless, except for a little dab on his chin, his only concession to fashion. "What's wrong, *ow?*"

"Nothing, *kahpo*. The water was plenty rough. I had to fight it the whole way." He blew out his breath like he was spitting out seeds, then stood up laughing. "Maybe I'm lazy. I like the steamboat too much." He nodded to the other men as they came across the knee-deep grass towards him. "But I brought messages." He displayed a short stack of papers.

Breed took them in his right hand and sorted through them with his thumb and fingers.

"*Mahalo*, Kapihi. Excellent work." When he found one that interested him the most, he tucked the rest under his left arm. He held up a telegram.

"Anything of interest?" one of the men asked as he lifted a coffee pot off the tripod over the fire.

"Wilson sent this, Collie. Confirms my suspicions. She was followed. Coward apparently went all the way to Victoria."

"Who told Wilson?"

"Cyrus Simpson, the company's clerk there. He sent it at her request. At least she had the sense to request protection." The man nodded to the telegram. "She asked Wilson to send someone to watch over her daughter. She has guessed some connection between Coward and trouble."

Breed folded the telegram, then put it into the right pocket of his coat. He brought out the other papers and sorted through them again with his right thumb and fingers. While he read them, he asked Kapihi what he had heard in Victoria.

"She's taking a *salt chuck canim* to the old English Camp. She is going to see the Mrs. Parker, *kahpo*."

"*Hwah*," Breed said in disbelief. He shook his head and sighed. His companions looked down and shuffled their boots in the damp grass. They were a motley group of *shipman* gathered from every corner of the earth—Hong Kong, Sandwich Islands, Scotland, England, and the

Pacific Northwest—but they could understand this universal feeling of exasperation. Women. Unpredictable as ever. Always mucking up a man's game. "Why she doing this?"

"Maybe she knows." Collie poured coffee into his tin cup. "Simpson could know. Maybe told her."

"He doesn't know. At least not the whole truth." The man shook his head again. "You think she's going to be there a while?"

"I don't know," Kapihi said. "I followed her all the way from Seattle to Port Townsend, then to Victoria by *salt chuck canim* when she took off. I got there not long before she did. I could go to English Camp, if you wish."

"Yes, you could. I think I'll send some others as well. Stay close, if she should take a notion to go off again. But first, you and the others get some food and rest. You don't have to go gallivanting immediately."

The young man smiled, dimples forming in his brown cheeks. "Not me, *kahpo*. I never gallivant. Just run pretty hard."

The men straggled over to the cook fire. Collie stayed back.

"What are you going to do?" Collie asked Breed.

"I'd like to be alone a little longer, then we can decide what the next step will be." He looked over by the trees. There was a small fenced-in area formed by a picket fence. Behind the unpainted boards were granite headstones. One of the graves was recent.

"She's asked Simpson to locate Waddell's representative," the man said. "That means you, Collie. We'll see what happens after she meets with Mrs. Parker. Just might set it up. I do want a continued watch over her."

"I think Andy Po is doing that now, Jonas," Collie said. "Do you think it's all right that she sees Gilly Parker?"

Breed stepped away. He moved with his old grace, his mouth set hard at his friend's concern. "It's too late to turn back. Perhaps it's best this way—to let things just come out. Gilly knows what is appropriate. I told her so myself."

"It could also be dangerous. Both for you and Jeannie if she finds out the nature of Andrew Pierce's demise. Your role in the company. She's likely to hate your guts."

Breed shook his head. "She shouldn't have come. Why didn't she just let things lie as they were?"

"As I recall," Collie said, drawing out his words as he spoke, "she once cared for you. Powerful drive in a woman—lost or thwarted love. Not withstandin' her being a recently widowed woman. It's the stuff of novels."

"Damn it, Collie. This isn't some blood and thunder novel."

"No, it's not, but she's coming, *kahpo,* and she will come with hurt and curiosity and wondering-whys. A powerful enemy if not treated right. She's seeking justice too. Only she doesn't know what for as you do."

"She shouldn't have come," Breed murmured in frustration.

"Aw, you can't help that, *kahpo.* Unnatural as a homing pigeon not going home."

Breed closed his eyes and sighed. "Sometimes, I'm so tired my hand aches."

"It's the *skookum* in you wanting to take hold. Just a little while longer and we'll get them. Then justice will be done."

"Then what?"

Collie clapped a hand on his friend's shoulder. "The spirits will tell you."

Breed swallowed hard and looked back toward the cove. It was still early morning and there was a patch of mist around the edges. A blue heron was in the marsh at the beach's fringe, standing like a poker stick. The peeling bark of the madrone trees looked rusty in the yellow sunlight already grabbing hold of the day. The islands were especially beautiful on mornings like this, he thought. They made him long for many things.

Breed cleared his throat. "Sometimes I dream of going north and putting into one of the old villages. They say many are abandoned and falling down because of the small pox scourge so long ago. Now it's the lure of the canneries and hops down here that causes the Haida to leave the villages. I'd like to see them again, one more time. I'd like to sit on the beach and build a fire and listen to the stories. When I was a *mistchimas*, an *elite*, I dreamed of being free. Now that I have been free, I think that maybe I was freer then—for I have been bound to yet another master all these years."

Collie spit at the ground. "You can't cheat a man and get away with it. It might take a lifetime, but there's justice. You were cheated, *kahpo*."

"Tell that to Annie and my daughter. I'd like to be alone now."

317

GILLY

Going back to a beginning was harder than she thought, Jeannie mused as the canoe rounded Henry Island and the old blockhouse came into view. In some ways, the Royal Marine Camp didn't look as if it changed much in twenty years though it was now a homestead. Many of the old buildings were still in use, perhaps for the cattle and sheep dotting the hill behind what used to be the commissary and barracks. The woods beyond the old military post were green and lush with Douglas firs, big leaf maple, red alder and madrone. *It's still beautiful*, she thought. And certainly in a much better location than the old American Camp, the United States military post to the south. She held on to the gunwale and braced herself for landfall, but the Songhees men brought her in smoothly across the beach and were springing out before she let go.

Carrying a basket on her arm, Gilly Parker rushed down the damp grass to the beach, her curled hair was tinged with the color of raspberries underneath her bonnet. *She's kept a good figure too*, Jeannie thought. *Even clothed in a simple settler's dress of gray calico cotton.* Gilly set the basket down and came into Jeannie's arms after Jeannie struggled to get out of the canoe.

"Jeannie! Oh, Jeannie! You look so lovely, my dear. I can't quite believe it."

"Twenty years."

"Oh, has it been that long?" Gilly stepped back and admired her openly. "The same spunk I saw so long ago. A *salt chuck* canoe. How are you, dear?"

"I'm fine." Jeannie smiled wistfully, then burst into tears.

"Oh, dear. I think tea is in order." Gilly offered the Songhees men a jug of water and sandwiches in a basket, and then paid the lead puller in coin. "If you would be so kind, have one of your men take Mrs. Pierce's trunk to my buggy to the road. *Mahsie.*"

"Oh, you shouldn't have," said Jeannie. "I could have paid."

"Never mind. My cook, Mr. Chang, has prepared the sandwiches and I insist the men be paid." Gilly took Jeannie's valise, then linking arms with her, followed the Songhees men up past the old barracks and up a woodsy trail where a buggy was waiting on a new planked road. By then, Jeannie was composed as best she could be.

"My condolences for your loss of Mr. Pierce," Gilly said as she put the valise behind the seat, "Widowhood is something I know full well, but my brother intimated in his telegram that there has been trouble and that you needed some respite."

Jeannie put a hand on her chest as if to catch her breath, but in truth she was trying to sort out where to begin to say what the trouble was. "Gilly, I dare not burden you so soon after reuniting after all these years, but I have just learned of the most awful deceit in our firm. On top of it all, my son Phillip is missing."

"Oh, dear."

Jeannie paused. The thought of Phillip in any danger made her ill. "He was supposed to be with my barrister in Victoria. He sent me a note to tell me so."

"Surely, there is a misunderstanding."

"Well, neither of them showed up in Victoria. Our Canadian agent has alerted customs as well as the American Consul in Victoria." Jeannie grew quiet. "Gilly, there is more. I came here not only to see you, but for safety. I believe that I'm being followed."

"Do you know why?"

Jeannie paused, scenes of the past weeks rushing past her: *Andrew's unexpected death to her discovery of that ten years ago the company was in dire straits only be saved by purportedly dead Jonas Breed; the threat of exposing her involvement in Marsfield scandal; the disappearance of Phillip.* A chill went up her arms.

Gilly patted Jeannie's arm. "Let me get you to my house. As I said before, a good cup of tea should help me hear your accounting."

"What a beautiful place," Jeannie said when they pulled up to a large cedar plank cabin with a dormer in a cedar shake roof. *Miles from where I have lived these past twenty years,* she thought.

"Why, thank you, dear," Gilly said. "It's amazing what one will do for something that is of the heart. And all the years Thomas served with the Royal Marines. But I'm not ashamed that I became an American citizen so I could do it. The British have a right to this place as any other. Besides the manager of Belle Vue Farm over by the former American Camp has done just the same. And he is a Hudson's Bay man if there was ever one. Thomas and I always planned to return to the island."

The house sat on a knoll overlooking down into a quiet cove. Big - eaf maple and hemlock peppered the woods that ringed it. As they pulled up in back, a brown dog came out to greet them followed by a wiry Chinese man dressed in work day clothes local settlers wore.

"This is my cook, Mr. Chang."

Chang nodded at Jeannie as he tied their mare's reins to a ring on a cedar post, then picked up the trunk and took it around to the back of the house.

"Your place is so lovely," Jeannie said. "How do you manage such a property?"

"With the help of my nephew James Stacy. He was stationed in Valparaiso for the last ten years and has retired here with his wife to help run the place. They have forty acres and the little house you saw on the way in."

Gilly smoothed out her dress. "Do come in. I have been waiting for this moment ever since I came back to Victoria. I surely thought that I had lost you after we returned to England. All those letters I wrote and not a word."

"Letters?"

Gilly could see that this was news, so put it aside and led the way in.

Tea is truly an elixir, Jeannie thought. It restored her to some sort of equilibrium, her first in days. Sitting on the verandah overlooking the cove, she finally felt at home somewhere other than her own. After discussing the mystery behind Phillip's disappearance and how they might be vigilant in case whomever was following Jeannie arrived on the island, Gilly and Jeannie began to address their lives in the past twenty years.

Then there was Jonas Breed.

Jeannie took a deep breath. "John said that Jonas Breed is alive, but I already knew that."

Gilly stopped her teacup in mid-air. She put her teacup aside to listen.

"Several months ago, before Andrew's accident," Jeannie went on, "I went down to the shipping office to pick up some papers for him. On the dock, I saw someone who looked like Jonas. It was only a glimpse, but there was something about him that struck me. It haunted me for days. It was silly, really, a romantic lapse. Perhaps, I had been thinking of him." Jeannie blushed. "I did sometimes. It would just come to me. A memory of someone I loved long ago. After Andrew's death, I finally decided to hire a detective to inquire about the man I saw."

"Did you tell anyone?"

"No, no one. It didn't seem proper. Oddly, I thought that I should be cautious, that there was mystery to his presence in the Pacific Northwest and he wouldn't want it known." Jeannie bit her lip. "But oh, how the thought grew on me. To think he was alive." Her voice broke. "All this time, I thought him dead. Now, I think his return has upset some balance in the world."

Gilly reached over and squeezed her hand. "I'm so sorry, so very sorry. I know how much you loved him. I was glad for you. When you left the note saying you were going to find Jonas, I was at first apprehensive and a bit scandalized, but I did understand. Then word of the fighting... we heard it, you know. We were staying at the American Camp with Captain Pickett and could hear the guns' reports. We thought there was a riot in San Juan Town but the sounds came from the opposite direction." Gilly put a hand on her breast. "Such a tragedy."

Jeannie brushed the rim of the teacup with her fingers. "I thought I would die. First Jeremy, then Jonas. I couldn't be consoled. I finally gave into Andrew's wishes and married. In time, I adjusted. For a long time, I was content. Andrew was good to me, you know." Jeannie didn't say how controlling he was, though she knew in his way he did care for her. She sniffed. "Now, I don't know what to think. Is it absolutely true that Jonas is here?"

"Yes," answered Gilly.

"John thought you might have seen him. Did you?"

"Yes, dear. Only a week ago."

"Did he stay long?"

"For the evening. Then he went away. I have not seen him since nor know where he is."

"I wish I could find him," Jeannie whispered.

"I'm sure you do, but do you think it wise?"

Jeannie got up and went over to the railing. On a snag, a pileated woodpecker was tearing out rectangular patches in the dead wood. Out in the cove, some ducks had landed and were making their way to shore. If Jonas had been here, he would have pointed out things about woodpeckers and ducks and told a story about them, too. She hugged her arms. "That's why I've come. To find out why."

"Find out why?"

"Why he didn't come. To think him dead all these years, then learn that he has lived his life somewhere else and, according to John, with another!"

Gilly wiped her mouth delicately with her napkin and got up. She put some teacake into a handkerchief. "Let's walk down to the garden. I have roses and lilies. Can you believe it?"

They walked down to the garden set behind a picket fence to keep deer out and went in through the gate. It was a round formal garden with a bench in the middle. They sat down on it and look out to the water beyond the fence. The ducks had come on shore and were nibbling in the rough grass. Gilly stood up and went over to the fence. Taking the handkerchief out of her skirt pocket, she fished out pieces of teacake and threw them to the birds. The birds flapped their way over and gobbled the cake up before she threw some more. She amused herself and Jeannie until she ran out of cake.

"When did you hear that Jonas was dead?"

"A few weeks after I left with Andrew." Jeannie turned to Gilly.

Gilly made a face like some social etiquette had been overlooked, but Jeannie saw that she was deeply troubled.

"Jonas was alive," Gilly went on. "He was dangerously ill, but he was alive. Hidden by friends among the Nooksack and Stolo until he was strong enough to travel. There were very few whites there. Of course, none of us knew at the time. Not for all this time, really."

"Why there?"

"The wife of Jonas's Kanaka friend, Kaui Kalama, had family there. It was considered much safer than staying in the islands with the British and American militaries looking for him."

Jeannie sniffed back a tear.

Gilly took her friend's hand, then leaned over and kissed her on the cheek. "Poor dear."

Jeannie looked down, but she couldn't stop the tears spilling down her cheeks. "I'm so confused."

Gilly sighed. "Let's go back to the bench and I'll tell you what I know."

Once they reached the bench, Gilly said, "Jonas was on his way to see Captain Pickett" when they were attacked. He was severely wounded during the fighting in which Krill was killed, then both sides retreated from the fear of the authorities. When Thomas went out with some of the soldiers, they found the ground blood-soaked from a terrible battle."

"And then I heard he was dead."

"Jonas was alive, but unable to contact you. I don't think he was lucid for several weeks, hanging on by the simplest of threads. And his men were being sought after, so it was difficult to get word out. When he finally was awake, he learned that he had supposedly been killed. Then, he learned that you had wed."

Jeannie looked down at her hands and bit her lip. It upset her every time she heard that he'd always been alive. But what could she have done? She was with child. She had to marry.

"How did he get out?" She tried to keep the tremor out of her voice.

"He couldn't travel for nearly four months. Collie and some of the others made the arrangements. He was smuggled on board a Russian ship going to the Sandwich Islands."

"John says that a young woman went with him. An Indian girl."

Gilly cleared her throat. "Part-Indian. Her father was Scots, a trader at Ft. Langley. Her mother was mixed. Kanaka, I believe."

"They married."

"Now what else could he do?"

Jeannie nodded miserably, then wept.

Gilly patted Jeannie's hands and sighed.

"You'll make yourself sick, Jeannie. You've been through quite enough with Andrew's passing and now this."

Jeannie blew her nose on a handkerchief from her pocket. "It's all right. Ever since I first learned that he was alive, I wanted to know why he didn't come find me. Now I do." She looked up. She wanted to tell Gilly what she had found at the office in Victoria, then decided not to. She would tell her later.

"That is all I know," said Gilly as she played with a cedar twig she had picked up from the ground. "I have wondered, though. Who told you that Jonas was dead?"

"Andrew."

"When he came to take you away, did he ever say anything about Jonas being hurt and unable to come?"

"Yes, I thought he tried to hide the extent of Jonas's injuries from me. Later, after the end of the first week, I learned men died—then nothing."

"Didn't you think it odd?"

"I don't know. When we parted, Jonas warned me that there could be trouble. Things had been very tense between him and Emmett Krill. You well know he had been accused of the foulest deed. When I didn't hear anything, my fears grew worse and then came true."

"Andrew should have told you there was a delay. Surely, he knew your feelings about Jonas."

"He did. I told him, but he insisted that Jonas was dead." Jeannie looked for her handkerchief. She sniffed, then blew her nose. Composed, she asked what else Gilly knew about Jonas now.

"My brother John says that he is quite wealthy. Does shipping and other business throughout the Pacific, including here."

"Has his wife come with him?"

"She's dead. For ten years now. Died of consumption and left him with two small children. He has never remarried and now has come with the mortal remains of his daughter to rest beside her mother. Poor man. Very tragic, don't you think?"

"Yes... yes, it is..." Jeannie looked into the distance. Ten years. Ten years ago Jonas had become Waddell, a secret partner in Pierce, Campbell and Waddell. Had it happened after his wife's death? If so, what did that mean?

"He's looking well, if you'd like to know, though much saddened by the death of his daughter. I found him congenial and very well mannered. Not so wild anymore, but still a very manly gentleman. He's"— Gilly paused. "—well."

"What does he look like?"

The older woman laughed. "His hair is still dark and full without a hint of gray. He wears it shorter now. Favors frock coats. I'd say that he's very well appointed."

"Where did you see him?"

"He came here. Of all things and as silent as a ghost. Gave me quite a start. All his men, you know. From every corner of the earth and devoted to him."

Jeannie smiled. She saw Billy Po, from Hong Kong, Kaui Kalama from Hawaii, Neville Hector, the one they called Doctin—half-farrier, half-doctor—from a little village in upstate New York State and Sikhs from the Songhees tribe. What Gilly said was true. It was one of the things that fascinated her about Jonas—his ease with people of all nations and the loyalty he inspired.

"Do you still want to find him?"

Jeannie flushed, then laughed tightly. "It is unseemly, isn't it? Acting like a sixteen-year old taking off into the wild on her own when she should be in mourning. I just want to talk to him. To hear from his own lips...."

She looked away, her feelings suddenly very strong. She wanted to be angry at Jonas, but all she could think of was their secret bower and the thimble he gave her. As she recalled them spooning on the cot, the way he made love to her the evening before they departed forever, she felt her pulse rise. Even though it had been years, it dawned on her with cold, hard realization that she had never experienced any depth of passion close to theirs with Andrew. Realization brought shame. She hadn't waited for Breed.

"Jeannie. Jeannie, dear. You're so absolutely lost."

"Hmm?"

"I'm going to have Chang pull back the bed covers for you. You should rest now."

Jeannie looked across the cove. She must have fallen asleep. The strain of the last few days were finally getting to her. She seemed to flip in and out of the past and present, the memories sometimes so real. She looked at the retreating afternoon light. Clouds were forming, hinting at rain.

"Forgive me. I have had so much on my mind."

"You have done nothing but travel in the last few days. Please stay for as long as you like. Consider this your home away from home."

Up in the house, the covers were pulled back on the high rope bed and a window left opened ajar. Some roses were on the table next to it. Outside, a raven chattered with a Steller's jay, their argument continuing as they flew away. Far off, she could hear a sheep bleating. It was still light out.

"I won't wake you, but if you feel hungry don't hesitate to call me." Gilly smiled and closed the door. Jeannie lay back on the pillows and sagged into the feather bed. She didn't bother to undress and soon she was fast asleep.

Sometime later, Jeannie woke to rain, the cool sound driving against the eaves over her window. The lace curtain billowed out and in. For a moment she lay in the dark, forgetful of where she was, then remembered she was on San Juan Island at Gilly's homestead. She looked out the window to her left, but there were only shadows on shadows in the dark. The room was no better, though she could make out the shape of a bureau and a chair. There was another shape there, gray and shimmering. It seemed to rise and face her. She blinked.

"Kaui," Jeannie said out loud. The shadow in the corner wavered, then disappeared.

WILSON

Rupert Wilson read the telegram one more time, then put the last of his things into his leather satchel: an extra woolen shirt for the boat and his double-action revolver. He supposed this day would come for as long as he had served in this house, but it did not make him feel any less satisfied. He had grown fond of the family, especially the children, Mr. Phillip and Miss Jereminah.

It had been an odd assignment from the start. The family paid him well enough, but his real employer had been Jonas Waddell.

He met Waddell after the War of the Rebellion. As a Union soldier, Wilson had seen duty in some of the worst battles in the east. A war-shattered veteran he fled to the west. He found odd jobs in the territories and eventually ended up in Oregon, then on a bark to Honolulu. He had been an educated man, but seeking a less public life, took on work clerking for one of the leading shipping firms in the town. A quiet, reserved man, he performed his duties with aplomb. One day, he simply got up and walked away.

Waddell had found him in one of the rough waterfront saloons serving the international crews that came into Honolulu Harbor. They got to talking and Waddell offered him work at his firm. Wilson told him he hated doing numbers. He liked directing daily operations, though, and greeting people. To his astonishment, Waddell said he could go there.

Wilson looked across the table at the man he had only heard of from talk. The candle on the wood table reflected a soft light on the handsome tanned face.

"You don't know me, sir," Wilson said. "I'm grateful for the offer, but I didn't end up so low by accident. 'Twas my own doing that I should leave my last employment."

"And why was that?"

"It's the melancholy, sir. I was injured in the war, you see. Not physically, but the damage is there." He put a fist over his heart.

"What if I said I did know you? That I'm aware of your difficulties? I wouldn't have come down here otherwise." Waddell laid his left arm on the table. The hook tapped the candlestick. "I was injured once myself, but have made a new life beyond what I could imagine. You can do the same. What do you say?"

Wilson mused briefly. "That I think I should join, sir," he answered.

Wilson joined the firm and proved himself in no time. When Waddell's wife became ill a couple of years later, Waddell called on Wilson to handle the scheduling and security aspects of the company. Waddell left Wilson in charge of the main office as Waddell sailed for the Northwest with his dying wife.

Waddell came back alone and gave Wilson a new offer: a position in the house of a man by the name of Andrew Pierce in Seattle, Washington Territory. It wouldn't be as demanding as his position in the front office of the firm, but it would require the greatest loyalty in exchange for a comfortable, guaranteed salary for life. When asked for particulars, Waddell told him his responsibilities would be honorable.

"Pierce has run into difficulties. His partner, Archibald Campbell, is a particular friend of mine and I wish to see the company solvent for his sake. The woman of the house is a fine woman," Waddell said. "There is nothing more than to insure the well-being of her and the children as expected of a trusted retainer."

"And the husband?"

"He has been informed of my insistence that he keep a man of my own choosing in the household. Advise him, Wilson. He will listen. I am buying out over half his shares in the company. No one else will know your connection to me or me to the company."

Wilson had been uncomfortable at first. A moral man, he did not like indiscretions.

"Perhaps it is a lot to ask," Waddell said. "But you must trust me."

Wilson did trust Waddell because he was no hypocrite and employed only the best in his firm, regardless of their background. Waddell was also known as a courteous family man, a defender of the Royal Hawaiian Kingdom and its people. It was hard to find fault with him. Wilson worried that had changed.

"What connection do you have to Mrs. Pierce and this Seattle?"

"Mrs. Pierce is Campbell's niece." Waddell said. "That is all you need to know."

"Will you come too?" Wilson asked.

"No. Not at this time. My children are here and their welfare my utmost concern. But someday, I may return. It's important that this woman and the children are protected. It's good for her and it's good for the firm."

Wilson accepted. He had spent ten quiet years with the family. Now things were changing daily.

A knock came on the door. Wilson stiffened. Waddell had promised him a stress free life. For the most part, it had been that except for the last year. There had been growing trouble in the last eleven months, brought on no doubt by Andrew Pierce's business dealings. Wilson had become wary, then alarmed, since Pierce's untimely death. Now he was being asked to look after Miss Mina while customs agents and the police in Victoria were looking for Mr. Phillip. Things are coming to a head, he thought, and someone would pay.

"The coach is here, sir," the housemaid said when he opened the door. Wilson thanked her. Buckling his satchel, he went downstairs.

ANNIE

"We're ready, *kahpo*. Whenever you say."

Breed shook Kapihi's hand and clasped it. "*Mahsie, ow,* for following Jeannie."

"My honor."

Breed picked up a bouquet of foxglove he had gathered and leaning over the fence, laid the flowers high on his daughter's newly-made grave.

"I'm so sorry," Kapihi said. "Hannah was like a sister to me."

"I know. She thought of you that way too."

"You have always been good to me, *kahpo*."

"Your father was my friend. I'll never forget him. And you're like a son." Breed smiled faintly, then sniffed the wind. "Rain's coming again."

"It was wild last night," the young man agreed. "It might make for a wild passage again."

"When do you expect to get to old English Camp?"

"By evening, I think. You will go to the place we've chosen?"

"Yes. We'll wait it out there. We'll see what the others are doing. In the meantime, stay low. I don't want her to see you."

"She has seen me, *kahpo*. On the boat to Port Townsend—twice. After that, I was careful."

Breed grunted, looking thoughtful.

"Do you wish to know what she looked like?"

Breed looked up sharply. The young man was grinning widely.

"Kapihi, you are *kolohe*. My wife is sleeping here."

"She will not mind, I think. After ten years, wouldn't she want you to be happy? Jeannie Naughton Pierce is still very pretty." Kapihi went on to say more about his impressions of her.

Breed's eyes flicked with interest, but he said nothing.

"I'd better go," Kapihi said mischievously.

"I think you should too." Breed laughed. "Be careful."

After Kapihi left, Breed stood at the fence and mused over how Jeannie Naughton Pierce had been described. He had wondered how she fared over the years, sometimes following the social accounts of the Pierces in the territorial newspapers. He was pleased she often did charity work for the Coast Salish people. After Annie's death, he felt free to think of Jeannie and not feel guilt.

Annie McDougall, the daughter of Scots trader at Fort Nisqually and a Kanaka-Coast Salish woman had befriended Breed while he was recovering from his wounds in a remote Indian village. She had tended to him in the dark weeks of pain and weakness. She encouraged him to live after he discovered Jeannie had married Andrew Pierce and gone to the settlement of Seattle. The discoveries of his purported death and the charges against him were surprises, but Jeannie's marriage had hurt him the most. There was nothing he could to do to defend himself. Forces at work were beyond his control. He was too sick to fight back. So when Collie suggested they could get him out safely when he was strong enough to travel, Breed had agreed, leaving behind his possessions and shattered good name, in hopes that in time he could reclaim them.

Annie had a strong curiosity to see the land of her Hawaiian grandfather. Despite her father's disapproval, she had gone, asking nothing from Breed in return, except to continue to nurse him. In the dark of winter they left secretly. After three weeks at sea, they arrived in the Sandwich Islands.

He lived with Annie openly in Lahaina under a false name until the birth of a son. Born too soon, the baby died after an hour, leaving Annie bereft and Breed shaken. Like coming out of a bad dream, Breed came to his senses, aware of the ruin he was causing. He moved out within the week, putting Annie in the care of a Kanaka woman and joined Collie who was not as shipwrecked as he was. They formed a partnership and began to take on the lucrative trade in the Far East and South Pacific.

A month after he left, he came back. After asking her forgiveness, he began to court Annie McDougall. He could not have Jeannie Naughton, but Annie had been faithful and he owed her respect and in time, his love.

Two months later, they were married. He used his new name, Jonas Waddell. It had been his mother's maiden name, long since forgotten in the islands and not known in the Pacific Northwest. He had found this true of many things. His father's passing, his time with Captain Geoffrey, and his years with the Haida had erased many things. He was free to start over.

The company grew steadily, growing quickly from one ship to three and both men involved in the piloting. Collie liked being unfet-tered, so Breed took on most of the business duties. Eventually, he bought a majority of the business, leaving his friend content with the profits and the freedom to be at sea. It was an exciting time to trade and explore. The friendship of the two men—always strong—grew even more solid. So did the partnership.

During this time, Breed's family also grew. Annie gave him another son, Ransom and a daughter, Hannah, whom he adored. Flush with money, he built Annie a beautiful Victorian home in Lahaina that soon became a focal point for the social life of the whaling village. That was more her doing. As the daughter of an important trader at Fort Langley in British Columbia, she was used to hosting people from all stations in life. Breed tended to stay in the background, amused by it all. He had become content with her and could finally admit he loved her very much. In 1866, he learned that his name had been exonerated and everything began to change.

Looking back, there was no one time that year when the restlessness set in. One evening, Annie found him on the *lanai* staring off to sea. It wasn't his usual tension before he sailed to Hong Kong.

"What's wrong, Jo-nuss?"

"I don't know. I had a dream last night. I was walking along the beach right out here, but when I looked up on the hill, there were no palm trees and *keawe*; only cedar and fir growing up right before my eyes. Moss was hanging everywhere, dripping down like the hair on *Dzonoqua's* mask. When I looked closer at the trees, a village sprang out and great totem poles rose up like spears to the sky. A voice called out to me. I think it was *chak-chak*. I could see his white head as he flew away. I felt so lonely. I was homesick, Annie."

"For the Northwest coast?"

"*Ah-ha.*"

"So am I."

They walked down to the white sand beach holding each other, talking far into the silver-moon night. They made love on the sand to seal their decision about returning to the Northwest for they had grown into a couple who instinctively knew each other and cared deeply. A month later, Annie was on her way to Victoria and New Westminster, taking the children with her. He did not go, but he did send Collie on the first of many trips to the Pacific Northwest to explore business and investment opportunities that included salted salmon, limestone, and timber. When she returned five months later, she brought news of her father and events on San Juan Island that increased his restlessness. She brought something else.

There were no signs at first, but during the second winter after her return, she developed a persistent dry cough. Confined to the drafty house when the winter rains came, it grew worse to a point that Breed became alarmed. They consulted a doctor in Honolulu and the worst was confirmed: she had consumption. Given the medicine of the time, it was a death sentence.

It was then that Jonas Breed knew how deeply he loved her. For her, he fought the battle of his life. He moved their family to a house on Maui where it was drier, hired extra help, and made her follow the diets and medicines prescribed including wearing loose-fitting *mu'u-mu'us* and taking salt air walks. He no longer traveled for great periods of time, but confined business to the islands. For a time she seemed to improve, then at the onset of the winter rains in 1869, she worsened, coughing blood and sputum.

The end came near in late February, 1870. Called away from business in Honolulu, Breed hurried down in one of his company's schooners and found Annie sleeping on a rattan chaise lounge out on the *lanai*.

From where she lay, he could see the white heads of the surf as they methodically rolled in from the brilliant turquoise ocean. The sun was high, a breeze teasing the palm and *ti* leaf hedgerow around the house, and the planters hanging from the porch ceiling. It was light out with brilliant greens and blues and a madness of perfumed flowers—like an ending and beginning all at once. He couldn't believe it was happening. He crouched down next to her and taking off his straw planter's hat, stared out beyond the stairs.

"Don't be sad, Jo-nuss," Annie said faintly from the chaise, so soft he almost didn't hear her.

He looked at her quietly, his eyes tearing. She was lying in a cool white chemise, a light cotton Hawaiian quilt laid over her. Her hair had been combed and curled in ringlets around her cheeks. There were dark rings under her eyes and her face was gaunt and pale.

"Don't be sad."

Breed swallowed. "Can't help it." His jaw clenched.

"You mustn't. You're free now." She smiled at him. "You don't belong here, Jo-nuss. Not for a long, long time. Maybe you never did."

There was a pause. Neither one said anything. Finally Breed spoke. "I love you, Annie McDougall."

"I know that. Now go and find the other."

"Forgive me for not loving you first."

"It doesn't matter. I have been so happy."

Listlessly, she reached over and laid a hand upon his head. With effort, she stroked it.

"You are a great *tyee*, my husband. Once long ago I heard of you— the Boston *mistchimas* who lived with the Haida. Then I saw you when you first came to Fort Langley. I thought you were so beautiful. *Hyas skookum, hyas toketie.*"

Breed snorted and leaned his head wearily into her hand.

"I was a little girl, but you talked to me. I have loved you ever since. When I saw you so deathly ill at *Sil-latus*, I knew what I would do."

"You never told me this."

"*Ah-ah.* I know."

"You saved my life."

"And now you'll save mine. I don't belong here either."

Breed shot his head up.

"Take me back to the San Juan Islands, Jo-nuss. To the place where my grandmother's people caught the salmon and smoked it. I want to see the islands again and I want to stay there forever."

"They still haven't decided whether it's British or American."

"It doesn't matter. My mother's people were there long before."

He took her hand and kissed it. Weakly, she squeezed it back. "Take care of the children, Jo-nuss."

She didn't die that day nor the next, but held on for days. She always asked that he take her back to the Pacific Northwest. Finally, he had Collie outfit their fastest ship and brought her into the captain's cabin. Good wind and good weather pushed them along and two weeks later, a lookout sighted the coast of Washington Territory. They sailed past Cape Fear and up the Strait of Juan de Fuca, passing the mouth of the harbor to Victoria.

Breed brought Annie up on top when the weather cleared. Sitting her in a chair bundled in blankets, they rounded Vancouver Island and crossed the open Haro Strait. San Juan Island was before them. He could see smoke rising from where the Kanaka settlement had been. To the south, the prairie and beach below Camp Pickett where they had held the horse races. To the north was English Camp. Craggy rocks, trees, and water. The sharp March air pungent with fish and trees. Dolphins running near the bow. Annie died sitting there.

As promised, he buried her on the forested island of her childhood. Mine too, he thought. I should never have left. Not in secret then nor in secret now. He knew that for the present, however, he would probably have to continue to do so. Lawlessness was still in the islands, but once the military occupation of the island—now ten years old—was over, he could come and reclaim the things that belonged to him.

Breed looked at the graves of his wife and daughter one more time, then said goodbye. There were people waiting for him.

SIKHS

Jeannie woke to crows cawing and the barking of a dog. The dog was shushed down, but the crows continued their dialogue a little further away from the window. There was movement in the hall and then a polite knock on the door.

"Jeannie? Are you proper?"

Jeannie looked at herself. She was as proper as she was going to get. After another night of tossing and turning in another strange place, she had managed to get out of her dress and corset and put on a lace shift over her under things. Sitting up, she straightened her hair and invited Gilly in.

"There you are. I thought you had fallen in between the feathers in the bed."

"I must look like it."

"I don't think you ever would, dear. As long as I can recall, you have been the 'Belle of the Royal Marine Camp.' The American encampment too. All the men were quite taken with you, Jeannie Naughton Pierce, including Dr. Parker." Gilly came to the foot of the dark walnut bed and leaned on the heavily carved foot post. "Breakfast is waiting. Would you like some? The coffee is fresh roasted."

Jeannie smiled. "It sounds wonderful. I should like to freshen up, though."

"I'll bring you a pitcher of hot water," Gilly said

The day was cool and overcast. Outside, the woods near the house looked closed in and subdued. Going to the window, Jeannie raised the sash and peered out towards the water where mist hung along the edge of the shore like smoke. The air felt wet and fresh. It had rained pretty hard during the night. On the ground next to the house, there were little puddles of water trailing across the rough grass like lily pads. She started to duck her head in, when she heard the sound of chopping to her left. Craning her neck she caught a glimpse of Chang working at the wood shed. She pulled her head in and drew the cloth blind down.

A few minutes later, Jeannie entered the dark paneled dining room refreshed and changed into a new mourning outfit of black bombazine. She found her seat and put her napkin into its place.

"Well, what shall we do today?" Gilly asked as she poured coffee into a cup and passed it to Jeannie. "Though it's cloudy, my nephew says that it will turn out well. Perhaps we can go for a walk. Or if you wish, do nothing. That might be the best thing to do."

Jeannie sipped her coffee. "Perhaps it is. I have taken on too much in so short a time. Besides, there may be a message from Mr. Simpson. I hope to learn that my son is found," She smiled over her cup. "Then maybe a walk later. To the limestone fields, perhaps." She put her china mug down thoughtfully. "Whatever happened to the ones at Farseeing? Jonas Breed had a small operation there."

Gilly looked uncomfortable. She fussed with her lace cap, then fussed with a loose curl around her face before speaking. "I believe that was used up a couple of years ago and has been abandoned. A more lucrative operation has begun not far from here."

Jeannie frowned. "He lost all of his claims, didn't he? He had several, I remember, including a homestead on Timons Island."

Gilly sighed softly. "Yes, he did. I'm afraid that he was cheated out of them."

"Cheated?"

339

"Apparently, friends made secret moves to hold onto his claims not long after he left for the Sandwich Islands. Do you remember Neville Hector, the one they called "Doc-tin?"

"Oh, yes," said Jeannie, smiling widely.

"After Jonas was thought dead," Gilly went on, "Doc-tin appeared with papers, granting him the right to prove up the property. It had been signed by Jonas and recorded in Olympia not long before the fight with Krill. He also gave him right to the limestone quarry. Of course, the islands were still under joint occupation, so any ownership was subjected to scrutiny. It was not assured who would get what. When the decision came turning the islands over to the Americans, Doc-tin filed the papers. They seemed to be fine, but at the last minute, someone stepped forward and filed an objection. It appeared that about three years before, this person had contested the original claim of Jonas' on the grounds that he was a British citizen and that should the islands go to the United States, he could not own the land without being an American citizen. Jonas' estate as it was, was invalid."

"But Jonas' father was an American. He was born in Honolulu on an American ship."

Gilly shook her head. "But his life after that became so complicated. Some thought he'd lived in British territory too long."

"But it's not right. Not when he was still alive and filed properly."

"No one knew that. By all accounts, he was dead in 1873. Doc-tin continued to pursue the claim, but it was not honored."

Jeannie swallowed hard. "Who told you this?" she whispered.

"I heard it from some of the locals when I first settled here, but I also heard it from Jonas himself when I asked if it was true."

Jeannie stood up and in a distressed voice, said, "Oh, I can't bear this. Did Jonas say who the party was who stole his claims?"

Gilly swallowed. "Andrew."

"Andrew?" Jeannie went to the bay window and leaned her head against the long lace curtain that covered it. She closed her eyes, but she couldn't stop the images. Jonas coming out of the water with the nets of crabs. Jonas in his *salt chuck* canoe bent in a maddening sprint across the strait. Jonas, his eyes full of laughter. How could she have been so foolish? So content in her little world all these years and not think of others? Now her comfortable life seemed all a sham.

Timons Island. A dream world place if there ever was one. "Why?"

"I don't know," Gilly said gently.

Jeannie shook her head and thought of the diary Simpson had given her. *Misappropriating some property of his.* That's what Andrew had written.

"Jeannie? What are you thinking about?"

"Everything. My whole life. I'm so confused."

Gilly nodded her head, the lace above her forehead floating like a cloth feather. She reached across the table. "You still love him, don't you?"

"Yes," Jeannie whispered, "though, God's truth, I have been faithful to Andrew all my married life. I've thought Jonas dead all this time." Jeannie twisted her hands together. "Except for one deceit. Oh, Gilly, I must tell you something so secret. You mustn't say a word."

A door inside the house opened and closed. Both women froze. Then there was movement from the kitchen. Chang had come in with his wood and was loading the cook stove. Gilly went over to the door to the kitchen hallway and closed it. Together, the women sat down. Then Jeannie told her about Phillip.

The schooner *Toketie* dropped its sail and came silently into the long forested cove. A short while afterwards the anchor was thrown. A rowboat put into the water and made for the rocky gray shore half hidden by mist. When it wasn't far from shore, a man came out of the woods and hailed it as he walked down to the beach.

"*Klahowya!*" he said, raising his palms up towards his face in greeting.

"*Klahowya!*" Breed answered back, then slipped into a local tongue much softer than the old trade jargon. "Sikhs."

The older man was now some sixty years of age, his shoulder

length hair was streaked with gray. There was stubble on his chin. Dressed in canvas pants and a sleeveless cotton shirt, his copper-colored arms appeared flabby until he grabbed onto the rope thrown to him and pulled. The rowboat came in like a paper boat on a string.

When Breed was ashore, he patted him on the shoulder. Breed grinned. They walked up to a downed weathered tree bristling with roots and branches and found a smooth spot to sit down. Breed opened a pouch of tobacco and put some into a clay pipe. After it was lit, he took a puff and handed it to his friend.

"Was wondering where you were, Sikhs," Breed said in English.

"I saw you in good time, Jo-nuss. You were so noisy I heard you back there. You've been away too long." The man grinned. "Scared my great-grandson, though. He never saw a Boston *shipman* like you."

Breed laughed. "He the one who hightailed to the trees?"

"*Ah-ha.*"

Jonas laughed. "What kind of tall tales have you've been saying about me?"

"I told him you took heads."

"Now, you know I never did."

"But you have always been a warrior, Jo-nuss. Everyone knows that you are *skookum tum tum*. That you have a brave heart. For that, everyone wants to buy you for *mistchimas*. Two, three, maybe five canoes. Maybe even a copper. You are very good to have." Sikhs affectionately clapped Breed on his shoulder. "I'm sorry, Jo-nuss. That was a poor joke. Such *cultus hee hee*. Everyone knows that you are a great *tyee*, not a *mistchimas*. What I don't understand," he said, "is why you don't have a *klootsman*. You're still young." He poked Breed in the ribs.

Breed smiled wryly. "You talk too much."

"*Ah-ah.*" The older man made a face. "I think I know why. You're still love sick for that *King George* lady, Jeannie Naughton."

Breed took back the pipe. "You're talking like an old woman, Sikhs. I'm here for other business."

"*Ah-ha.*"

Breed swore and the older man broke out chuckling again. Breed tamped the pipe vigorously, but he was grinning.

342

"Where do the smugglers put in?" Jonas asked. He jammed the pipe into his mouth and took a draw.

"Here sometimes, but there is another place," Sikhs said. He pointed to the north. "Good cover. They come in from Vancouver Island and hide in the honey comb caves. You remember them. Near the *chak-chak* tree."

"Those eagles still there?"

"Does the wind still carry rain?"

Sikhs got up and wiped some sand off of his pants. "You think they come?" He walked barefoot over the pebbles and sandy gray beach to the water and splashed some on his face.

"They'll come. They're wondering who the hell Waddell really is, but they like the thought that the partnership just might go on."

"I think they just want to kill you." He slipped into the Straits language, some words accented by occasional clicks and clucks.

Breed answered back in that language. It had been a long time, but he remembered.

All those seven years, when Breed returned to white society, Sikhs had been a constant friend and mentor. He was with him at the fight with Krill and stayed on, watching him struggle against his injuries and heartache until he was strong enough to take a boat going to the Sandwich Islands. And for ten years Breed knew he waited for word of his adopted son who was dead to the rest of the world. When he hastily returned to the Northwest with his dying Annie, he sent word to Sikhs ahead of his arrival. They had met secretly out near Neah Bay at a Makah village. When Sikhs saw him, it was as if he had just been away visiting.

"You are *hyas skookum*, Jo-nuss," was all Sikhs said and then wept. "*Hyas skookum.*"

He saw Sikhs secretly a few times after that in the north, but now after a long absence, Breed was back in the Pacific Northwest to stay. He knew his tongue didn't work quite right and he was slow on his manners, but both Sikhs and he knew what he wanted.

"You hear what I said, Jo-nuss."

Down at the cove's edge, Sikhs found a sharp clamshell and began to scrape at the stubble on his chin.

"I heard you," Breed said. "Collie's in charge of that department. He's put some men together."

"I want you to be safe. I'll get *tillicum* for you too."

"*Mahsie.*"

Breed got off the log and walked down to the water. On the schooner, a second load of men was preparing to come over. He raised his hand to Collie who was standing near the bow. "Your grandson's back in the trees."

Sikhs squinted his wrinkled face in that direction. "Hey. Maybe you not so *chee chako*, Jo-nuss. You can see things pretty good in the back of your head."

Breed laughed. He was at home again and despite the dangerous game he played, happy to be back.

GHOST

"What do you mean, she's gone? Damn it! You were supposed to watch the woman! What's so fucking hard about keeping an eye on some petticoat?"

"We'll find her, Gutterson," George Coward soothed from his padded bench. "Paddy Theibold saw her with a man going into the café. I waited around until the place closed, but she never came out. Soon as we find out who he was..."

"There isn't time. Jesus Christ, do I have to paint a picture? Everything is coming to a head and Waddell's gone cagey on me again." Anders Gutterson got up and slapped his cap across Coward's shoulder. "I didn't come here to hear this. Damn it." He paced the tight confines of the captain's cabin, then spit into the nearest container available—a shaving cup. The action stained an already soiled blonde beard even deeper.

Coward looked like he was going to gag, but said nothing.

That's better, thought Gutterson. *You fancy pants. Little gambling shit.*

At thirty-seven, Gutterson was near to a copy of Emmett Krill as a half-brother could be, except for the thatch of dirty blonde hair that ringed an otherwise bald head. He also lacked his half-brother's discipline, being quick to explode and easily confusing dictatorship with leadership. He did not lack, however, the love of smuggling, having been a part of that persuasion since he was in his youth. Which made Emmett a hero to him, someone taken early in his time.

Gutterson had heard the stories of Jonas Breed and Emmett's trouble with him, but Gutterson tended not to take Breed's skills as *shipman* and fighting prowess too seriously. *There were a number of present-day old-timers who could claim that.* He looked sourly at Coward. If he didn't shut him up, he'd probably start talking about Jonas Waddell being Breed again. It made him want to spit nails instead of tobacco.

Just because my ma was a Swedish whore and my pa an alcoholic gambler with the morals of a tomcat, don't make you my better. I know as much about the shipping busyness as your family does.

"Where do you intend to meet this Waddell?" Coward asked.

"Somewhere in the middle channel, more like, and away from pryin' eyes."

"Why does he want to meet you?"

"Must have learned something during that internal stuff."

Which would be Gutterson's lucrative smuggling enterprise involving whiskey and other forms of hootch, opium, cheap Chinese labor, and a long list of other illegal activities that Washington Territory custom authorities fought against.

Goods were brought into the islands in a variety of ways, but Gutterson found a way to bring them in the cargo of reputable outfits and taken directly to the ports. It required having someone on the inside or an outright bribe, but sometimes, a vulnerable company might be convinced not too subtly to take on illegal goods.

There was a time that the firm of Pierce and Campbell had been ripe for such an arrangement, but a new partner, Waddell, had put an end to that route. Still, a foundation had been laid with one of Pierce, Campbell and Waddell's trusted employees. After the military camps closed for good on San Juan Island in 1872, small shipments of whiskey and opium were carried on legitimate vessels and transferred to hideaways for future distribution. All went smoothly until last fall, when a small cache was discovered in one of the warehouses in Port

Townsend and an internal investigation had begun. "Do you think he knows about Pierce?" Coward shifted on his seat.

"He couldn't. Far as I know, he's never been in the Northwest. Let's his agent handle everything. Just as greedy as the last." Gutterson sat down on the edge of his heavy teak desk. He got the juice in his mouth under control, then went on. "Cuz, he wants a piece. The lads and I are going to meet with him, set some terms and reel him in a little a bit. After a couple of months, he'll be in so deep, I'll have him."

"No disrespect, but it gives me the creeps," Coward said.

"What tell for?"

"There's that old tale about Breed going through the islands looking for the heads of those who killed him. I've heard that tale down on the docks countless times."

"That! Old island lore. Them days is long gone."

"But I heard something else the other day. That Breed *is* alive, right here in the straits. And that he's not a *shipman* anymore, but a great *tyee*. Owns lots of sea-going vessels. What if that *tyee* is Waddell? What if Waddell *is* Jonas Breed?"

"And who told you that?"

"Like I said, something I heard. Some *siwashes* were talking."

Gutterson laughed so hard he nearly lost his wad of chew, the juices spraying on his beard. His eyes stung from the tears. It took him a couple of minutes to get under control. Finally, he spit into his cup and wiped his mouth on his sleeve. "Now that's about the best bull I've heard in a long time and from such reliable ree-sources. Hope you didn't pay for it, cuz you've been had. Waddell is a coat-tailed businessman. Nothing else. Besides, if it were even a bit true, who cares? He wants in. And once he's in, I'll get what I want, then I'll kill him."

"You're not listening, Anders. If he's Breed, he doesn't want money. Maybe he's looking for you and the others. Settle old scores."

Gutterson laughed. "You rummy or something? What could he possibly want? He got his pound of flesh long ago out of my dear old brother."

"Your head. Maybe he's put it all together." Coward made a sour face. "You're laughing, but my father had an acquaintance who survived an attack on his boat by northern Indians in the 1850s. Said there was nothing more horrifying than the savages' thirst for revenge. Their patience is legend."

"What exactly is Breed looking for? He's a white man, for God's sake."

"But more *siwash* than *Boston*. He lived with them and he's looking for the one killed Kaui Kalama and stole that Haida woman."

"Weren't me. It was—"

"Right. And for the last five years you've been sitting on that knowledge. For five years, you've known that this was the very thing that led to your brother's death." Coward leaned over form his cushioned seat against the wall. "It doesn't matter if you were there or not. Only that you know. And me and some others know and protect the knowing." Coward swallowed when he was done, rubbing his hands back and forth on this thighs like he was trying to wash something off.

For a brief moment, Gutterson's thin mouth and brown eyes flared up with wicked amusement then his expression changed.

"Thing I like about you, Coward, is that you take things so serious. You're such a pretty boy. You've never had to live the way I have, but you've got street sense like a wharf rat and it pays to be cautious. You've done your part with your daddy. I'll take everything you said to heart." Gutterson made a fist over his heart and tapped it. "I promise." He got off his desk and opened the drawer behind him. Taking out a bag of dollar coins, he tossed it to Coward.

"I want you to find that Pierce woman, seeing it a more fitting line of work. Keep her at her female pursuits while I tend to the real business of the day. I'm meeting her solicitor at noon. He's bringing along some extra insurance. You probably know him. Phillip Pierce, her son."

"Phillip?"

"Yeah. Since you couldn't find any papers on the partnership at the office here in Victoria, we'll assume that for the moment Waddell is Waddell. Now get out of here. Paddy Thiebold can row you over. He can stay with you for all I care."

Reluctantly, Coward got up. "If I don't find the Pierce woman, I'll send word."

"If you don't find her, I might send you back to Port Townsend to watch the girl. I don't want that Pierce woman coming close to this, but if she's onto something and goes to the authorities, I'd like as much insurance as possible. Understood?"

"Understood. I'll go now." Coward made a face as he stuffed the bag of coins into his coat pocket. Just don't say I didn't warn you." Coward backed off and went up the ladder to the top deck.

As soon as he was out of sight, Gutterson drool-spit into the shaving cup.

"Course you did," he said to the empty room. "Trouble is you're seeing things, Coward."

There was no answer. Only an eerie vacuum, devoid of sound. He wiped his mouth and self-consciously looked around the cabin to see if he had stirred up any dead spirit.

"You hear that Waddell? If you're Breed, I'll kill ya for my brother. I'll kill ya, ghost or not. You won't be ambushing me."

AMERICAN CAMP REVISITED

"We must have a plan if you are to find Jonas," Gilly said. They had been closed up in the dining room for almost an hour. During that time Jeannie shed tears as she told Gilly everything —from her discovery she was with child, her decision to marry Andrew when there was no hope for Jonas's return, the birth of Phillip. How Alani Kapuna had stayed with her after the difficult pregnancy. When the boundary decision was made in 1872, Alani went north with Moki to Salt Spring Island. Many former HBC employees had to go to British Territory because Kanakas could not become American citizens.

When Jeannie finished, Gilly sighed. "What we women do to protect the ones we love. I'm sure you loved your son even then," she said in a soft voice.

Jeannie wiped her nose with her handkerchief. "I sought to survive, that is all. To keep my baby from scandal. I have had enough of it in my time. I loved Jonas so."

"You said Andrew was overjoyed."

"From the moment he saw Phillip. He was late to the event as he was to Jereminah's coming, his true offspring, but he was a good father." Jeannie put away her handkerchief. "It was business, always business that kept him away."

"Jereminah, so like Jeremy's name."

"I know. We never forget the little ones we've lost, do we?"

"No, we don't." Gilly poured more coffee into Jeannie's cup. "Is there more you want to tell me?"

"It seems Andrew kept some business matters from me." She told Gilly who Waddell was.

"Now we must doubly plan." Gilly said when Jeannie finished. She was going to say something more then froze when Chang dropped a pan in the kitchen. "Let's go outside."

Putting on their shawls against the cool morning, they walked down the path to Gilly's rose garden. Their skirts brushed the stinging nettle and salmonberry bushes as they passed through the narrow space.

"Surely, there must be someone to talk to." Gilly stopped to pick an orange salmonberry and plopped it in her mouth before they continued down the hill. "You said that your solicitor may not be trustworthy?"

"Simpson thinks so. And I do trust Simpson. My uncle selected him a long time ago."

"But you didn't tell him about Andrew's dealings."

"No. I told him to guard the papers, though."

"Well, I must say that I am quite out of sorts. Jonas said nothing about this. What a mess. Everything is so tangled, I don't know where to start."

"I guess I must start somewhere," Jeannie said. "I asked Simpson if he trusted 'Mr. Waddell.' He said that in all the years of doing business with him, he had been honest and had always worked for the best interests of the firm. My question now is, what is the firm? If Andrew took some of Jonas's property, did he keep it and then have it taken back by Jonas when he became majority owner or did he sell it?"

"A good question. Simpson should be able to answer."

"I don't think so. I'm sure he didn't know about the secret agreement. My uncle would have told him."

"Maybe your uncle didn't know."

"Maybe Jonas didn't want him to know." Jeannie sighed and found a place on the edge of the wooden bench in the middle of the garden. The mist had come in again, obscuring the smaller features of the hills and water. It was hard to see out into the cove. The ducks were out there, but beyond their calling, she couldn't see them either.

"Now what?" Gilly said.

"I think after the fog lifts, we should drive over and see the former manager of the HBC farm. Your brother John told me he's now an American citizen homesteading on the southern end of the island, but had been at Belle Vue Farm since the early '60s. He would certainly know much of the island's history from the British and American accounts. He might be able to say one way or another about Jonas and the ownership of land on the island and nearby." Jeannie did not think that the firm owned any, but she could be wrong. As she had been about a lot of things lately.

"But you're so tired!" Gilly protested.

Jeannie won out and in a half-hour, they packed the buggy. "We can get there by eleven, stay for a few hours and make it home by evening," Jeannie said as she climbed aboard. "You've told me yourself the road is only five years old."

Gilly nodded that it was. "It connects the settlements around the old English Camp to those at the southern end of the island." Gilly got into the buggy. "It passes by a telegraph station, another sign of change." Gilly picked up the reins at her seat "Today, they can get a message over in a matter of hours."

They were not quite a half-mile from the old military reserve, when they encountered a local farmer and learned that the former HBC manager had gone over to Vancouver Island for the weekend. When they asked about anyone who might have been at Camp Pickett in the summer of 1860, they were informed that a former sergeant had a small homestead not far from where they were.

"Goes by the name of Jim Higgins, he does. He was here with the Army the whole twelve years of miserable occupation. The day the islands became American, he resigned and filed a claim close by."

"Did the camp close then?" Jeannie asked.

"No, it remained open until the end of 1874, but he'd seen enough. You just go down the road that way," the farmer said. "Saw him working his fields earlier today just past that stand of fir. He'd be pleased to see you."

"Were you here back then?" Jeannie asked.

"No, ma'am. Not until the rule of law was settled after '66 when Captain Allen came to the post."

Gilly said "Good day" to him, then clucking at the mare, turned down the rutted dirt lane toward the Higgins homestead. About five minutes later, they found the man out in the field cutting hay with his new mower. Tall and lanky as a reed and perched up on the wooden seat like a hawk on a post under the handmade umbrella, he looked like he was half-asleep as his tawny-colored horses plodded methodically up the width of grassy prairie. When he finally noticed them, he brought the big animals to a stop and wondered aloud who had come calling.

"It's Mrs. Thomas Parker, late of the old English Camp," Gilly answered, "and my friend, Mrs. Andrew Pierce. We would like a word with you if we may."

"Why, I heard word of you, Mrs. Parker. How you've come to settle here." The man removed his straw hat. "It's a pleasure to have you in our midst again, ma'am. I most certainly remember Dr. Parker. I'm sorry to have learned of his passing. Good man, your doctor. Treated me once for a broken arm when our own surgeon was away. As you can see, I'm whole." He twisted in his seat and looked curiously, but politely at Jeannie, like he was trying to place her. "And Mrs. Pierce? I'm sorry, but were you not at the ball?"

"Why you are so right, Mr. Higgins." Gilly smiled at Jeannie. "She was Jeannie Naughton then. Hasn't time not so much touched her as enriched her?"

Higgins beamed when he recognized her. "Indeed, it has. Jeannie Naughton. I was on duty that night at the ball, serving punch and joining in on the music when called upon. What a grand affair that was. Begging your pardon, but there wasn't a soldier who didn't wish he were Captain Naughton, though we were shamed when we learned you had been widowed." Higgins cleared his throat. "I would be honored if you would accept some refreshment at my home. My wife would be pleased."

"Thank you," Jeannie said. "That's very kind."

Jeannie and Gilly were received warmly at the farmhouse. Mrs. Higgins, who was English herself, was delighted at the sudden company, as it wasn't often two ladies of such esteem came into the district. After curious looks at Jeannie's fine clothes, the Higgins' boys were hurried out and the parlor door opened. There was English tea and bread with blackberry jam, served on a silver tray whose lace doilies that had not seen much service. From where Jeannie sat, she had a fine view of Haro Strait across to the blue-gray torpedo shape of Vancouver Island.

"It's beautiful," Gilly said.

"It is indeed." Jeannie took a sip of her tea. She was glad when Gilly carried the narrative of their visit forward for them both. Coming back to the area stirred such powerful memories of happiness and loss. She hadn't expected to be so unsettled by them. She looked off to the left and saw an eagle flying in the direction of where she thought the ramparts might be.

Jonas Breed.

"—Why the company of Pierce, Campbell and Waddell, is well known in these parts," Higgins said. "My deepest sympathies, Mrs. Pierce."

Jeannie, coming back into the conversation, dipped her head at Higgins. "Thank you."

"Occasionally," Higgins went on, "some of their boats come into the wharf at San Juan Town, though the buildings there are largely deserted. They've a new town site laid out on the eastern side of the island six miles away."

"What about Camp Pickett?" Gilly asked.

"Oh, you mean, Camp Steele," Mrs. Higgins said. She was a plump woman with pink cheeks and wispy brown hair that wouldn't stay pinned. "After Pickett left to join the rebels, the name was changed," she explained. "Camp San Juan, Camp Steele. Of the original quarters on officer's row, one house remains, used now by a settler and his family."

"What happened to the other buildings?" Jeannie asked.

"When it closed, homesteaders took many of them down board by board and moved them to sites throughout the island. But the laundress hut remains. Mr. Higgins and I raised our family there."

"Who else has settled in the area?" Gilly asked Mrs. Higgins.

"At the present, the population of the island numbers close to over hundred or so. Let's see—there are several former soldiers from the camp in the vicinity. Down by the old Kanaka Town there are a few Kanakas left. They work at various trades around the island."

Jeannie looked up at the word Kanaka. "Do you know any of them?"

"Sometimes I put them to hire." Higgins took a bite of his crumpet and chewed it like a bull eating grass. "They did the sheep runs in old days."

"Speaking of which, do you remember Kaui Kalama?" Jeannie asked.

"I do recall him," Higgins replied. "Saw him once at the camp with that *siwash Boston* Jonas Breed. Kalama was a tall man, I recall, handsome-looking like those Sandwich Islanders can be. His children and Indian wife eventually departed for the mainland after he was killed."

Higgins took a big sip of his tea, then took his kerchief and wiped his mouth. "There's someone else around these parts you might remember. Was from English Camp. Didn't move here until about five years ago when he became a citizen. Thaddeus Cooperwaite."

Jeannie felt a chill at Cooperwaite's name.

"Thomas Cooperwaite?" Gilly exclaimed.

"Indeed. He's got business with the new lime diggings up at the northern end of the island and connections in Victoria, but keeps a farm down near here. Rents it out. Heard he had holdings on Timons Island in the 1870s, but it's haunted, you know."

"How is that?" Jeannie asked. She couldn't imagine it being haunted. *Except with my own memories.*

"Cooperwaite, I'm told said it wasn't safe. Indians still go there to fish and smoke their catch, so he let it go. Anyway, he's fairly well off, but has never been lucky in love. First wife died in childbirth. Second one just left."

"Mr. Higgins," admonished his wife.

"Beg pardon, ladies."

"I remember Mr. Cooperwaite," Gilly said. "He was briefly with the Royal Marines when we were here, but he resigned early on." She shook her head. "He was rather full of himself. I think my husband was the first to suggest that he could rather do better elsewhere. Our little society was so wonderful—really—some of my fondest times were there at that beautiful place at Garrison Bay. But it was too small for Mr. Cooperwaite. I think any place on the whole of the Pacific Northwest coast was too provincial for him. He was still in Victoria when we were transferred. I saw him once. I was always surprised that he stayed on at Esquimalt as long as he did. And to return here."

While Gilly talked, Jeannie thought of the note threatening to expose the Marsfield scandal. *Did Cooperwaite write it?*

"So San Juan Town is at its end," Gilly said. "What a wicked place it sometimes was."

"Well, it was the only place close by for the men," Higgins said, "It was a long pull of the oar to Victoria or Port Townsend. I went to San Juan Town myself, time to time, I admit, but the lawlessness some-times got too much." Higgins grinned suddenly, his thin lips catching on his uneven teeth. His pale blue eyes twinkled.

"And I did state my objections, Mr. Higgins," Mrs. Higgins said.

"The town was eight hundred and fifty yards from the parade ground." Mr. Higgins went on. "The reserve was eight hundred, but that couldn't keep the men from making the last fifty. Knew a man or two who kept gaining and losing his stripes for his time in the whiskey ranches."

Jeannie and Gilly nodded in agreement. Higgins warmed up to his subject entwining his fingers like a vicar in prayer. "I came over with Company D during the first confrontation with the British. I don't think we were there two days when tents were set up along the lagoon. Soon there were permanent buildings, about twenty in all, I recall, though not all used. When our ranks swelled to five hundred that summer, there was plenty of opportunity to ruin a man's constitution. Vexed Pickett something powerful and all the other commanders after that."

"You said you saw Jonas Breed at Camp Pickett." Jeannie asked. It was hard to pay attention. So many ghosts were racing in her head.

"Aye, I did. He came to Camp Pickett from time to time. Got along fair with the officers and enlisted men, I recall. Spoke to him once or twice myself and found him an intelligent man of little pretension. A pity that some were so easily turned against him. Folks were suspicious, you know, him being captive of a northern tribe. Weren't his fault. It was that Emmett Krill who had business with both camps and their sutlers, but did a good back room trade in whiskey and other unsavory business. Him and Breed had no love for each other. When one of Krill's top men was found minus his head—"

"Now, Mr. Higgins, that is quite enough. The ladies didn't come here to hear this sordid business."

"Yes, yes, dear".

"It's all right, Mrs. Higgins." Gilly opened her fan and used it to fan herself. "I remember those times most clearly," she went on. "I look upon them with as much sentiment as sorrow, but we are at peace now and only those who lived them could understand."

Gilly pretended to sigh, but Jeannie smiled inwardly at the ruse. Her old friend had always been very clever at getting information out of the most discreet persons.

"Mr. Breed was not unfamiliar to me," Gilly went on. "He came often to the Royal Marine encampment where he was an intimate of my husband. Thomas and I both thought the stories were unfair and have grieved many a time over his untimely death. It was so unnecessary. The authorities should have had more control, even in the matter of properties." Gilly put her fan into her lap and looked thoughtful. "After we left the island, we lost touch with acquaintances here. I was quite astonished to learn that properties that were held by

Mr. Breed had fallen into the hands of men with a less sympathetic nature."

Higgins looked surprised. "Are you thinking of Mr. Pierce or Mr. Cooperwaite? I believe Pierce and Campbell assumed the properties in '72, then sold outright at a loss. I remember that. Mr. Cooperwaite held Timons Island for a time, as I said, then let it go around '73. I do not think that Mr. Pierce was any adversary as he was friendly to Mr. Breed. Mr. Cooperwaite, I know, was another matter. A most disagreeable fellow." Higgins gave a sidelong glance at Jeannie, but she remained still.

"Have you seen Thaddeus Cooperwaite?" Gilly asked. She reached for her cup of tea.

Higgins looked at his wife. "As a matter of fact, I did. About a week ago. Came up from the wharf at old San Juan Town. Said he'd come to look at his holdings. We chatted for a while which was a bit unusual for him, you know. Wanted to know if I had seen anything peculiar as he put it. Strangers in the area."

"Have you?" Gilly asked after politely taking a sip of her tea. Information gathering was an art after all. Jeannie had done it herself.

"Now, you must know how these islands are. For twelve years under the joint military occupation, no one paid taxes, could do as they well pleased with the civilian courts so far away. A kind of free-wheeling life. Oh, the howl and protest when the islands were assessed several million in taxes when they became American. Folks refused to pay. No, ma'am. It hasn't changed. There are comings and goings all the time here in the islands. We're still a tiny community overall, so you notice things. In the past year, there have been more unidentified vessels in the area than I recall. Especially on the east side. I go there from time to time to visit a friend who lives there. Help him cut wood for fuel. I've seen the boats."

"Did you tell Mr. Cooperwaite that?"

"Decided not to say anything specifically. I repeated rumors, but he was interested in persons and I couldn't help him on that."

Gilly looked at Higgins wryly. "But you have seen someone..."

Higgins laughed. "Aye. I weren't about to tell him though. Not him. He drools over my land like a spider over a fly in its web."

"Who did you see?"

"Collie Henderson. Breed's right-hand man of old. Hadn't seen him in these long years, though I've heard rumors of him around. I know him because he came to Camp Pickett frequently in the old days. Was friends with one of the officers. A congenial fellow, I recall. You couldn't forget him with that sword and that blonde hair like yellow field corn."

The samurai sword. Jeannie could see the sunlight on its polished blade as Collie slashed it through the air at the races.

"You saw him?"

"Aye. Came on shore to speak with someone who homesteads there. That was curious too. He was with another man who was here back in those days—a man by the name of Neville Hector. Maybe you remember him. Known by the name of Doc-tin."

"Doc-tin lives on the island?" Gilly was so surprised that she almost spilled her tea.

"Oh, he doesn't live here. He left years ago. But over time, I've seen him."

"Where do you think he lives now?" Jeannie asked.

"Over near Orcas, I heard. There's a small store over there, though he's not connected with it. Prefers the quiet life."

Higgins laughed. "Don't give up on San Juan Town yet. There's still life in it. The old sutler has tried to make the new place at Friday's harbor the county seat, but there are few takers. The establishment down at Katzville—as they are wont to call it—is still well attended. They still hold elections there and other town meetings of importance. As for the whiskey trade, it still goes on. I suspect the boats go to Vancouver Island for it and other things."

"Is there anyone there now?" Jeannie asked.

"Most of the buildings are vacant. The goods they keep there are as little as possible. I prefer to go to Victoria or Port Townsend, myself. The shopkeeper is known to get an unwary man drunk, then talk him into buying more than what he needs." He looked at her curiously.

359

"You're not thinking of going down there? It's not fit for a lady. What population there is contains only drunkards and scalawags."

Jeannie bit her lip. "Perhaps to the road and look down. I have thought on it of late. You see, I knew Mr. Kalama."

"Then you know what happened the night of his murder?"

"Unfortunately, no." Gilly rested a hand on Jeannie's lap to still her from answering. "I don't think any honest person knows." And with that, Gilly brought the interview to an end.

COWARD

George Coward swore as he watched Simpson come out of his house alone. The Pierce widow was not with him. In fact, Coward was beginning to suspect that she wasn't in Victoria. Scouring the town all through the evening with Paddy Thiebold—who complained about the condition of his boots the whole time—her name had not come up at any of the respectable establishments. Before closing for the night, they had returned to the first hotel he had inquired at. Coward was able to weasel a peek at the register with the help of a woman he knew there. He was not pleased to discover that Jeannie Pierce checked out around six in the evening. Coward didn't like this new addition to his growing list of why he should probably just bag the whole enterprise and get himself to San Francisco far beyond Gutterson's clutches. Why was Gutterson so keen on following this woman?

Ever since Anders Gutterson had first showed up at the staid dark office of his father's shipping line in Seattle, Coward had tried to find a way to get out. But Gutterson had discovered that he owed several thousand dollars in gambling debts. Gutterson only turned the screws tighter and threatened to make Coward's debts public to his father, so Coward had to obey, getting deeper into the smuggler's attempts to control of the company of Pierce, Campbell and Waddell. One of the errands Coward was required to do was to go to Vancouver Island and meet an associate of Gutterson's—Thomas Cooperwaite.

How to describe that first meeting two months ago? A proud, imperious man, Thaddeus Cooperwaite at fifty-one on the surface looked the gentleman, but like the rapidly thinning hair the ex-Royal Marine tried to keep secret under his soiled silk top hat, Coward detected a distant decadence that he couldn't quite put his finger on.

Coward had met him at a little plank cabin on the southeast corner of Vancouver Island. A wild and uninhabited place, it was accessible only by water as no road came from Victoria town.

"I've brought papers from Gutterson," Coward said.

"Of course you have. He said I was to expect you." Cooperwaite scooted in closer to the table and opened up the package Coward gave him. Cooperwaite read silently while Coward did his best to make himself comfortable at the lantern-lit table. When Cooperwaite was finished, he said, "Balderdash," and tossed the papers to the side.

"Trouble?" Coward asked.

"Someone in the firm of Pierce, Campbell and Waddell has taken as notion to inspect the books against the warehouses. Some materials have been exposed."

"Who?"

"An unexpected member of the partnership. Waddell."

"The paper partner?"

"He is quite real and is making himself known. He wants to buy in."

Feigning ignorance, Coward asked, "Who is he?"

"I don't know. He has connections in the Far East, Hawaiian Islands and San Francisco, etc."

"But nothing of an illegal nature?"

"What are you getting at?"

"Why does he want in?"

Cooperwaite looked at him like he was daft. "Why the money, of course. And that's all you need to know. I'll write up something for you take back to Gutterson." The look he gave Coward convinced him to not to press his luck. "Anything else Gutterson wants me to know?"

Coward shrugged. "Not at this moment."

"Good. Help yourself to the whiskey, but when I'm done, get out of here."

"This time of night?"

Cooperwaite was suddenly on his feet. He grabbed Coward by his collar and pulled him across the table. "You impudent bastard! Do what I say or else—"

Coward was glad to be gone. Two months later, Andrew Pierce was dead. Coward thought it was no coincidence.

~

"George?"

Coward came out of his daydreaming and stamped his feet against the cool morning air. "She's not here," he said to Paddy Thiebold.

"Now what?"

"Need to find out if she's left the island altogether." Coward smirked. "Why don't you take the trail to Haro Strait and see if a ship has recently sailed off from there. I'll snoop around the harbor here."

"And if she's gone?"

"Gutterson won't be happy, but he's got his hands on her son. He'll have to send someone out to look for her. In the meantime, I guess he'll send me to go back to Port Townsend. The Pierce girl is there."

TILLICUM

"Hey, Jo-nuss. You better come up. While you were resting, a messenger has arrived from Andy Po.

Breed sat up in the bunk on his schooner and rubbed his tanned neck. It was dark and cool in the salon despite the opened skylight propped up above him. The sun outside was bright, its rays glancing off the brass trimming of the window's edge with eye-shattering flashes. From the corner furthest away from him, he could see the blue pants belonging to one of the deck hands.

"Where's Collie?" Breed asked as he swung his legs over onto the floor. In the center of the room, there was a heavy table, now full of books and papers. A large yellow cat lay curled up on the closest pile, its tail twitching in its sleep.

"He's with Anson Chong," Sikhs said as he softly came down the steep companionway. His bare feet were as quiet as the cabin cat's. He squinted into the dim room and watched silently while Breed expertly put his boots on, then adjusted the strap on his left shoulder and at his shirt sleeve.

"You all right, Jo-nuss?" he asked softly.

"I've no complaints." Breed smiled at the older man, then grabbed his cap off the table. He ruffed up the cat's fur affectionately, then stood up in one smooth action and waved his friend on. Sikhs didn't move.

"You worry," the older man said after a time. "I can see that."

"Maybe so. Nothing a little action can't take care of. Is Kapihi with Andy Po at Mrs. Parker's house?"

"Better talk with Anson. I heard him say that Kapihi went to San Juan Town. Those women went there this morning."

Breed frowned. "Why?"

"They went down to see the old manager from Belle Vue Farm."

"Whatever for?"

"Anson says they were talking about your holdings."

Breed pitched the bridge of his nose. Keeping an accounting of the two women was becoming exasperating. *Why would they want to know that?* Unless, Jeannie was trying to sort out what she knew about the holdings of the firm.

"I didn't tell Gilly about Cooperwaite being on San Juan," Breed said. "Figured she'd find out for herself through island gossip, but she won't know the whole story. No one knows."

"Except that Anders Gutterson. Maybe some others." Sikhs's face grew bitter, like he had swallowed a sour Oregon grape. "All these years. They think they're pretty damn smart."

"*Ah-ha.*" Breed's voice trailed off, lost in thought. He wished he'd known right from the start. Would have prevented a number of heartaches, which included his. Then again, perhaps it was bound to happen anyway. Back then, Emmett Krill had been itching for a confrontation.

I just didn't see how much you wanted Farseeing, he thought.

"I hope Kapihi will be careful," Breed said out loud. "I don't trust anyone there. As he well knows."

"He knows. It is of such long standing." At that, the men climbed up on the deck.

"So what do we have?" Breed asked the assembled group topside. It was late afternoon. The sky was clear blue with high white clouds clear to the east. They had been at anchor for a couple of hours, waiting for word from any of their men sent out to watch the movements of Gutterson and his allies. It was quiet in the forested cove, but the little breeze playing on the lines told of a change of weather again.

"Some of Gutterson's crowd was at the lagoon at San Juan Town again, *kahpo*. Tenas John says two, maybe three days ago." Collie acknowledged the Lummi man sitting quietly on the deck carving with his knife. His face was invisible under his cedar hat, but the way his sea-roughened brown hands worked the stick of yellow cedar said that he was listening closely to the unfolding conversation. Collie sat down on the doghouse and lit his pipe. When it was underway and glowing, he pushed the dead match into a clamshell filled with sand.

"What did they want?" Breed was restless, but they couldn't move without information.

"Just asking if any one strange had come around. 'Course, Cooperwaite asked the same thing of some of the settlers on that end just days before."

"That what you brought, Anson?" The young Chinese man he addressed was waiting patiently against the bulwarks. He was one of Billy Po's many nephews and a close companion to his cousin Andy Po who had a position with Gilly Parker. She had not guessed the family connection to Breed's old company factor. Unlike his uncle, he wore his hair cropped.

"I think there may be some trouble."

"Explain." Breed took the mug of cold spring water Collie offered, then sat down on the captain's chair set out for him.

"Someone has been asking questions about Mrs. Pierce's whereabouts in Victoria." Anson went on. "Whoever is interested may figure to come over to San Juan Island."

"Jeannie Pierce knows nothing of my partnership with *Pierce and Campbell*."

Anson shrugged. "Andy thinks she does. He heard her mention the name Waddell several times at Mrs. Parker's house. She knows."

Breed scowled. "How?"

"I think there were old papers, *kahpo*. Andy says Mrs. Pierce acted as though she knew what she was talking about." Breed looked at Anson Chong. He had known him since a small boy playing in the great warehouse of Waddell and Company in Honolulu. Though younger than Kapihi, he was another orphan he had taken in. Breed never forgot where he came from nor who his friends were.

You're my family now, he thought. *Mine's so sadly depleted.*

"That barrister of Archibald Campbell's—Simpson," Anson went on. "Everyone says he is pretty damn smart. Found something that Gutterson's men wanted. The office was broken into at least once. After Simpson and Forrester talked to her, Mrs. Pierce left for the Parker homestead. I think they were concerned for her safety."

"So Gutterson is having her followed to see if she knows what he knows."

"Something like that."

Breed looked back at the slight, gray-haired man who had just joined them. "What do you think, Doc-tin?"

Doc-tin looked at Breed through his wire-rimmed glasses. "Not much longer for Krill to make his move."

"As we wished for."

Doc-tin looked worried. "Not with her in the line of sight. We didn't think on that."

"No, I—we didn't. We'll have to prepare for that eventuality."

"Kapihi will take care of that, *kahpo*." Anson stood up. "He's staying near her and will follow every move. I'm going back over there as soon as I can. One of us will keep you informed."

Breed nodded his appreciation.

Anson cleared his throat. "My cousin overheard one other thing."

"What is that?"

"Phillip Pierce is missing."

Breed frowned. "Since when?"

"Well, Andy said that Mrs. Pierce became alarmed after she arrived in Victoria. Her son was supposed to be there with Burgess."

"Burgess? That's doesn't sound right." Breed stroked the little tab of beard on his chin. "OK. Anson, I need you to find a volunteer to take a message by my hand to the company office without alerting Mr. Simpson to our current endeavor. I wish to be apprised of

Phillip's whereabouts and what action is being done to find and protect him."

"Sure, boss."

"Where's Cooperwaite now?" Breed asked.

"He was last seen down near Lopez Island."

"Someone will have to watch him."

Tenas John looked up sharply from under the wide sloping brim of his hat. "I'll go, Jo-nuss. Be my pleasure to watch him. Maybe get some others."

"Take as many as you think necessary, John. *Mahsie*." Breed turned to Collie. "That meeting place and time been confirmed?"

"*Ah-ha*. We'll be sure that it's covered."

"Anyone notify the sheriff?" Doc-tin asked.

Breed grinned wryly at him. "Oh, he's been forewarned, but you know how anything can happen. Foul-up, bad weather. He'll get his notice. When it's appropriate. That's why you're so important—agent of customs that you are."

"I still don't like it, Jonas. You're taking a big chance. Anders Gutterson is from the same pool of muck as Emmett Krill was. I think Cooperwaite is even worse."

"*Ah-ha*. But he's an egotistical bastard and as predictable as rain."

"Jonas, please. His secret is out and when he knows you know, he will become desperate."

"And make a mistake." With that Breed slapped his leg and stood up. "Collie, if you would be so kind and get all boats away. As for the rest of you, we'll meet again at the appointed hour tomorrow."

"Aye, aye, captain." Collie nodded at him sharply then began to issue orders. After twenty-four years together, their relationship was symbiotic.

WICKERY REVISITED

"Oh, Jeannie, dear do you think it wise?"

"I only want to look. I don't mean to go into it."

"Merely to go close gives me such a qualm. It's not a proper place for ladies."

"Then we shall drive down as far as the rock on the knoll."

"And what if we should be approached?"

"We shall be proper ladies," said Jeannie. "It would be unconscionable we should be molested. We'll say that we've blundered and retreat."

"Posthaste, as my Thomas used to say." From her perch on the buggy seat, Gilly fanned herself with the flurry of a small windstorm.

They left the Higgins homestead just after one o'clock, took in the spectacular view of Haro Strait, then drove out to the old military road. Now with just an hour to spare, Jeannie wanted to go and look at what remained of old San Juan Town. The fan picked up speed.

"Ever since I read those papers in the Victoria office," Jeannie explained, "I have thought often on it."

"On what, dear? Surely not this place?" Gilly paused mid-stroke and waited for Jeannie to go on.

"But I have. I have felt the need to see where it happened—where

Kaui Kalama was murdered. After all these years, I have never been able to make sense of it. Oh, I knew of the whisperings of murder and mayhem at San Juan Town in those days just as I'm sure you did. After all, a royal marine can be indiscreet as any other man. Only I never thought it would actually happen to someone I knew. Kaui Kalama was a sweet and gentle man. No one's enemy. His death was so senseless."

"Yes, it was senseless. It won Jonas' undying hatred." Gilly abruptly put her fan down in her lap. "Tell me, did Jonas come to tell you that?"

"Yes." Jeannie looked away. The clouds to the west were bunching up. The sky was still blue, but there were changes in the weather coming again. The clouds were coming from over the Olympic range, dragging a solid gray underbelly. "He was very upset."

"I'm sure he was. Did he think then that Krill had killed Kaui or at least had ordered it?"

Jeannie nodded. "What I have never understood is why did Krill do it? To what purpose? It would only get him into trouble."

"I don't think Krill had any intention of getting into trouble. There were no witnesses or at least, any forthcoming. But it would be easy for people to assume that Jonas in his grief and rage could be capable of doing something inhuman like taking a head of that American."

"It still doesn't answer why Krill would take such a risk."

"For the properties. It must have been worth it. Jonas's properties would be for the taking. In particular, Farseeing, the lime site."

Neither woman spoke for some time. Jeannie only moved when Gilly leaned over to make sure the reins were properly set on its post. "Jeannie?"

"Hmm?"

"You said that Jonas came to see you. When was that?"

Jeannie turned. "Just a day after we heard of the dreadful beheading. He did not come up to the officer's housing where we were staying. He waited until I went on a walk in the woods."

〜

The side-wheeler made landfall in the afternoon at Port Townsend, but Wilson had disembarked into a small canoe some time before and headed south along the mudflats and low-lying bluffs thickly covered with madrone and fir. His S'Klallam companions were quiet, their attention on the rhythm of the paddles as they cut through the water just beyond the tide's pull. As they rounded a point sticking out into the water like a jib sail, a small beach came into view. They made a run for it, turning around at the last minute and coming in stern first. As soon as the cedar canoe struck the edge of the beach, the men jumped out and brought the canoe safely on shore.

"How far is now from here?" Wilson asked when he was on the gray sand.

"To the south, by less than a quarter mile" said the most senior member of the group. He was a man in his forties, a handsome man whose parents had foregone head flattening as a child. He was dressed in a wool coat and canvas pants coated in wax so that they were waterproof. He wore his long brown-black hair short under his felt hat. A cedar rope encircled the brim.

Wilson picked up his satchel and looked up the narrow trail that cut up through thickly forested ridge behind them.

"Thank you," he said.

"It is nothing. If you need us, we will be close by."

Wilson nodded. "I'll speak to the girl and the family first, then make inquiries in the town."

"When you are ready to go, all you have to do is signal. We'll get you in as quietly as possible."

Wilson reached into his coat pocket. "Thank you. I'm to give you this." He handed over a small bag of coins and a richly embroidered travel pouch made of otter skin. "And I am to say, 'Go with the spirits.'"

"And with you. May the Lord bless you."

Wilson saw the large silver cross on the man's neck and nodded. "Well, I shall be off. Good day, sir."

"Good day." They watched him go up into the trees, then Lakit,

Sikhs' son-in-law, turned around and gave orders for the canoe to be brought up and hidden.

~

Breed spent the morning with his crew, going over maps with Collie. Anchored away from the schooner, Andy Po directed the loading of a small steam-powered boat. Doc-tin watched the movement of men and materials from the edge of the low "doghouse" that covered the salon below decks.

"You cold, Doc-tin? Or you just daydreaming?"

Breed came over and sat down on the edge of the doghouse.

"Well, I'm no spring chicken, Jonas, but I can hold my own. I keep forgetting I have twelve years on you." He rubbed his close-cut beard, then pulled on one of the mostly grey hairs sprouting out of it like a steel wire brush.

"I wanted to keep you out of it until necessary."

"But you couldn't have kept me out of it, Jonas. Not for the world. No, I was thinking about the time I first met you and Sikhs. How it all was a marvel."

"You were one scared *chee chako*. Never thought you'd go back to homesteading here."

Doc-tin grinned. *"Ah-ha.* And there we were again in a year's time —*kloshe sikhs.* And never looking back."

"You've been a good friend, Doc-tin. Took up a lot for me when I couldn't defend myself. Never felt I have truly thanked you for it."

"Oh, you have, Jonas. Countless times. I've never regretted it. Made me the man of property that I am today."

Breed grinned. Outwardly, Doc-tin didn't look like much, but he owned a fair amount of real estate and had managed territorial properties for Breed as well. He always had a fine head for figures and a natural understanding of the law in all its intricacies. He preferred the life of a quiet homesteader and kept to himself on Orcas Island with his family and books. Contrary to his remarks after his first serious encounter with northern Indian folks, he had taken a young Sikkegate woman as wife a few years back and they had couple of boys. He was known for his generosity to stranded travelers and was the occasional doctor in emergencies. He had been named a customs officer in the islands a couple of years before.

Doc-tin looked out over the water to the forested shore of the island. Sweeping his hand over the scenery, he said, "Most beautiful place on earth. I've never regretted my years here. Yet sometimes when I look at it, and remember the struggles and friends who were lost. Wonder at the injustice of it and if there could have been anything done differently. If Kaui hadn't gone into San Juan Town. Funny, though. I still come up with the same answer."

Breed's eyes grew distant. "I know what you mean. Sikhs says you cannot change what the spirits see. I'm more optimistic, but sometimes I wonder that for all my maneuvering, things will just go the way they're going to go anyway. The what-if's are often very hard to accept: Kaui would die whether or not he found me; Shells Shining would be lost forever on a shoal."

"And love—denied?"

"You forget Annie."

Doc-tin's face reddened. "Forgive me, but ten years is a long time to be making up any guilt over her untimely death." He cleared his throat. "What does Sikhs say now?"

"The spirits will go with me..."

Doc-tin beamed at that.

"...still a hard pull before it's over, though." Breed grinned, "Just my luck."

"Just you give it a no never-mind, Jonas. Things are going to work out."

Breed nodded, but he didn't feel convinced. "What possessed Jeannie to come looking for me?" Brand asked suddenly. "What am I going to say to her if she should find me?"

"Jeannie? I don't know, *kahpo*. Let's pray she doesn't. Not before we settle with Gutterson and Cooperwaite. But if you do meet by chance, I'm sure you'll find something to say."

Yes, Breed thought. *Sorry, but I killed Andrew.*

~

The buggy came to a stop two-thirds down the rough dirt road to the town. From where Jeannie sat, the single story buildings looked ill-used and weather-beaten. Some of the storm-battered, hand-split cedar boards on one of the buildings were missing, leaving a tall, dark screaming mouth in the middle. On another, the moss-encrusted, gray cedar shingles had worked their way out of their rusty nails and were sliding down the rough peak exposing the skeleton of the rafters. Only one or two of the shacks looked inhabited, but they were at least cared for. Overall, there wasn't much to the place, even under the blue summer sky. How could such middling-looking scraps of wood construction be so evil? Jeannie wondered. Maybe it was the stench that came up from the treeless lagoon where the tide had pulled out and left the mudflats exposed. Or maybe it was just her imagination. Not everyone who had gone there had been evil—many an honest man found his way looking for provisions. It was more from reputation and the truly boisterous days as wild as the western dime novel.

Jeannie put a hand over her eyes. She could see the figures of people walking down there and although Griffin Bay was empty, there was a small sloop tied up at the old wharf used years ago by Hudson Bay's Company ships. Gilly opened her little silk parasol and twirled it on her shoulder.

"Well, I'll know where *not* to get provisions," she sniffed. "Victoria, Port Townsend or Whatcom for that matter, will do well enough."

"It is a little sad looking," said Jeannie. "Yet didn't Higgins say they hold court and elections there?"

"Only a formality. Once the county seat is removed to the new site. I shall certainly recommend it."

Jeannie continued to stare at it, rising out of her seat. After a time, she sat back down again. Her face was still and pale. "Have you not wondered, Gilly, that if Jonas had been there, the tragedy would have been averted?"

"For Kaui's sake? Perhaps. I don't know about the other matter.

374

There still would have been the outcry and unrest among the native population over the Haida woman. There would still have been the killing and blaming, all of which involved Jonas. On all accounts, Krill was quite set against him."

Jeannie looked down at the buildings. "Do you know where it happened? Where Kaui fell?"

"Oh, hush, why do you trouble yourself so?" When Jeannie continued to look at the row of buildings, Gilly sighed. "I heard he was found near the edge of the lagoon."

"Over there..." whispered Jeannie and became silent. Gilly took her hand and together they stared thoughtfully down at the collection of buildings, totally unaware that they were being watched.

The boulder-strewn hill where they stopped stretched out like a wide and green open fan that sloped lumpily down to Griffin Bay and the expanse of the wider channel and islands beyond. At both tip of the fan, the land rose and was covered with fir and other trees. Grass browned by the sun and windswept by the early summer storms that came frequently off the straits to the west of Griffin Bay covered the entire area. Here and there the occasional bush grew. Through it all rambled the road on its descent down to the town west of the lagoon.

They sat transfixed when suddenly the mare startled out of some reverie, jerking the buggy forward into an uneven dip in the road. The delicate left wheel bounced heavily, then rolled off over the edge into a rock. The buggy tilted and instantly, one of the spokes snapped with a sharp crack. A picnic basket fell against the side of the buggy's black hood, then spilled out and tumbled down the hill.

"Jump, Jeannie. It's going to go over." Gilly pushed against Jeannie, forcing the weight away from the damaged side of the buggy. Jeannie scrambled out. Gilly came quickly after with Jeannie's help. At the last minute, the now panicking mare pulled herself away, taking the lightened vehicle with her down the hill.

"Whoa!" shouted a man's voice behind the women. They both turned to stare at the rider who galloped past them to the mare bolting down the road on a tethered rein. He seized its bridle and brought the animal under control. The broken buggy was moved safely back to the center of the road, but at a cost. When the mare began to limp, the man dismounted and went to look.

Jeannie hurried down, coming to an abrupt stop when she realized their rescuer was Thaddeus Cooperwaite. Gilly continued on without apparently noticing.

"Good day, ladies," he said as they hurried down to him. "You've got a tender fetlock here," he said as he stood over the horse's leg. "She won't be able to pull any more today."

"Oh, dear," Gilly said. "And at a perfectly awful time. I do thank you for stopping her, sir, before the damage to everything was worse. It looks as though the hub might need the assistance of a wheelwright..." Gilly's voice trailed off as she realized who the man was.

Cooperwaite took off his bowler hat and smiled expectantly at them. Though his hair had thinned, he still cut a rich figure. He was meticulously dressed as a gentleman: tweed coat and pants, silk vest, practical but expensive boots. He smelled of lavender oil and the faint scent of cigars. *Much like a lord out in his fields for inspections*, Jeannie thought. *Except for that scar next to his left eye.* Over time the scar had caused the lid to droop further down over the end of his light green eye.

He spoke to Gilly first. "Why, aren't you Mrs. Parker, late of the English Camp, is it not? What a co-incidence. Perhaps you remember me, Thaddeus Cooperwaite, at your service." His British accent was proper, his solicitude dripping with formality. They could have been at the Governor's Christmas Ball in Victoria waggling over the dance card.

At first, Gilly seemed too shaken to say anything other than her gratitude for his fortunate arrival "Why, how wonderful," she finally said, fully aware that Jeannie was stiffening up behind her. "It *is* you, Mr. Cooperwaite." She elbowed Jeannie to behave. "I can scarcely believe it. How fortunate we are. You're a sojourner here?"

"No. How do the Americans say it? Homesteader? I have a claim not far from here. Run a few horses and stock. I heard that you were settled near the old Royal Marine camp. At the Dunwaddie place, I believe. An excellent location." He smiled, then turned and looked at Jeannie.

"Mrs. Jeannie Naughton, is it?"

"Mrs. Andrew Pierce," Gilly corrected.

Jeannie seriously doubted he had made a mistake. He knew exactly who she was.

"Yes, yes. I remember now. The American factor at Camp San Juan who parlayed his business into quite a fortune. Are you here on holiday to see the old camps?" Cooperwaite sounded almost jovial.

Jeannie wondered how far they would have to carry this charade. She looked to the west, worrying about the clouds drifting their way. It wouldn't do if it rained. "Mr. Pierce passed away."

"I beg your pardon, Madame. No offense. My deepest condolences. But how long has it been? Twenty years hence I saw you last? You are as beautiful as ever."

Jeannie had no intention of acknowledging his compliments. "Thank you," she said tersely. "And thank you for stopping our horse." She came forward. "We'll have to take the mare back to the Higgins homestead." She resented the fact she might have to rely on him and was not about to let him control their difficult situation. Twenty years did not erase her memory of him hating Jonas Breed nor lusting after her. Revulsion hid her fear of him.

"May I suggest down below?" Cooperwaite held the mare by her bridle. "It will strain the mare less. It's only a few hundred yards more."

Jeannie stared down at the collection of buildings. Common sense told her to leave everything and run. The mare, however, was a valuable animal. If they could get the wheel repaired, they could get perhaps the loan of a horse to go back to the northern end of the island before it grew dark. The mare could be cared for and at a later date Gilly could arrange to bring it home. That gave them only a few hours for even though it stayed light at this time of year to nearly ten at night, it would be dark in the forest along the road.

"Please allow me to help you," Cooperwaite went on. "It has been years, my good friends. A hot cup of tea or coffee, bite to eat while you wait. If you have any fears about the place, there is no need for them. The proprietor is a gentleman and will see to your wishes. I will be your gallant."

Gilly started to say something, but Jeannie for once spoke first.

"I'm sure you'll make a proper gallant, Mr. Cooperwaite, but only if you can guarantee a wheelwright."

"I'm sure it can be arranged. In the meantime, you will be out of the elements." He pointed to the west. "A slight change in the weather again. Should blow off by tomorrow."

"Oh," said Gilly, her mouth making a little "o."

"We have no intention of staying longer than necessary," Jeannie said, "I should like every much to have a message to Gilly's nephew to let them know there has been an accident." Jeannie waved back up the hill. "Perhaps one of the Higgins boys."

"A capital idea. A delay might worry them and we don't want that!" Cooperwaite put his bowler hat back on. "If we're fortunate, there might be a spare at the store. You never know!"

Cooperwaite rubbed his hands together in anticipation. He was very cheerful, sounding as though this was the most serendipitous thing to happen to him a long while. Jeannie felt more like a fly in a trap. She squinted down at San Juan Town. Someone was moving up onto the road and she wondered if they had seen the horse bolt. Perhaps there wasn't any need to fear.

Help came in the form of a buck wagon and two idlers from the store. The women were helped onto the seat smoothed from many a ride and the green and yellow painted wheel with its hub from the buggy loaded into the back. The mare was led down by hand. As promised, they were treated with respect. The unexpected arrival of such fine ladies was a treat and the men—not scallywags as Jeannie and Gilly had anticipated—did their utmost to make them comfortable.

There were discussions about the wheel and the spoke. The off-set hub required a more delicate hand. Who had the tools? Would they like more refreshment? Inside the cool, cedar plank walls of the store that offered only a meager selection of goods, they were given chairs at a table and cups of hot tea. A fire was set in the woodstove. The only window, a large many paned affair, was wiped of dirt so that they could see outside to the channel and the islands beyond. As the men rushed around to please them, Cooperwaite stepped out. Jeannie only missed him when she realized that time was ticking off to the clock's steady beat of the schoolhouse clock behind the counter.

WILSON

The rain hit just as Wilson arrived at the edge of the Garrett homestead. Seeking shelter underneath the shaggy stand of cedars guarding half the perimeter of what purported to be a pasture, he studied his surroundings. From all appearances, the rustic farm was not under siege.

It was peaceful as a Currier and Ives print. There was no activity on the roughly cut road that threaded back to the equally rough main house nor was there any living thing other than a cow and horse calmly grazing next to some tall stumps sprouting huckleberries in their crowns. Beyond, the tall fir trees that grew like a high green curtain to the back of the house were silent; there were no other alarms from any bird other than the crow calls that first announced his arrival. They had died away, leaving behind only the splatter of the rain on drooping, wet cedars.

Wilson looked for any sign of his charge, but didn't expect to see her. He could hear the tinny sound of a piano drifting through the rain-charged air. Mina, most likely. She liked to play "I Dream of Jeanie with the Light Brown Hair," with great exaggeration as it was a song she felt old-fashioned and melodramatic. To Wilson, a genera-tion and a half older, the song spoke of a more genteel time when sentimentality put love on a pedestal. Love for someone like Jeannie Pierce. He was very fond of her.

Wilson flipped open his pocket watch, checked the time, then checked the road again. It was beginning to rain quite hard now, but he'd have to go see this through. Go with the story he had been inventing since he got off the steamboat. He had no wish to alarm the girl or the family, but would offer some professional support as family butler. Garrett, he knew might not always be on the farm as he was pursuing the possibility of work at some mill.

Mina was at the piano. Wilson saw her through the laced curtained window as he stood on the porch. Other than her friend, there appeared to be no else in the room. He shook to get the rain off his cloak, then knocked on the door.

A prim middle-aged woman answered the door.

"Ma'am," he said. "I'm Mr. Wilson, from Mrs. Pierce's household. She has asked me to come and wait on Miss Pierce while she is away."

"Away?

"She has found it necessary to go to Victoria on business." He reached into his cloak and gave her a folded telegram. "I came as quickly as I could manage." He waited while Mrs. Garret read it silently.

When she was finished, she folded the telegram and looked up. "There is alarm, Mr. Wilson?"

"There is no alarm. She thought that you might wish some help while Mr. Garrett is in town. My presence here will help expedite her business up north. It will kill two birds with one stone."

She looked thoughtful, then brightened. "There is a room in the barn, Mr. Wilson. You are welcome to come through and get something warm to eat and drink in the kitchen. You'll catch your death. And your presence is most appreciated. I have been having some difficulty with the pump in the kitchen."

"I'll see what I can do, ma'am." He wiped his feet and followed her into the narrow hallway. Outside, it began to pour.

～

After Andy Po had loaded his steam-powered boat and slipped away to toward the southern end of San Juan Island, Collie and Breed prepared the schooner to go to the northern end of Spenser Island where they would put in for the night. They wanted to be away from the meeting place, but close enough to keep an eye on any traffic. In the meantime, Andy Po would head west along the end of San Juan and put into an inlet not too far from Griffin Bay. From there, he could send out runners to look out for Kapihi and see if he needed assistance. Tenas John had gone too, pulling his *salt chuck* canoe behind the sloop until the time he needed it.

"You hungry, kahpo?" Collie unrolled a piece of smoked salmon from butcher paper and placed it on the doghouse. "I've got salmon and hard tack."

"Not particularly. Please yourself, Collie."

"You're been pushing yourself hard."

"It's been a hard couple of months."

"Ah-ha. All the better to be prepared and rested."

Breed smiled at his friend. "I'm all right. Tomorrow, we'll get Gutterson and if we're lucky, we'll get Cooperwaite too."

"And if we don't?"

"I don't want wholesale murder. I want justice for Shells Shining. But I don't think this can be kept quiet too much longer. If we can't get Cooperwaite fair and square, then I say he's a dead man."

Collie nodded. Jonas was right. Things had a way of snowballing until they had a life of their own and no one could stop them. Shells Shining may be long dead, but for some, twenty years was nothing.

TRAPPED

G illy looked at the rain slashing the window panes and sighed. She joined Jeannie who was looking out onto the open space between the store and the opposite row of buildings and the socked-in bay. The afternoon was becoming early evening. "We're stuck, dear. Let us hope our hosts will continue to be well mannered. If only Mr. Higgins would respond."

"I wonder if he shall," whispered Jeannie. "I'm sure he would come if asked. Only I don't think he was asked."

Gilly leaned in. "Really?"

"Cooperwaite may have sent someone, but not to the Higgins, I'm quite sure. He didn't look like the sort of messenger one would send."

"You saw him?" The women kept their voices low, even though they were presently the only ones in the store.

"Yes, an ill-kept man. He returned just a moment ago."

Gilly stared through the window. "Truly?"

"He met up with Cooperwaite right out there. Oh, dear. I think we should sit down and act like sweet little lambs."

"Really, Jeannie," Gilly said as she obeyed. "Your imagination is quite at work. We are not in the wilds any more. These are civilized times. You've lived too long in the comforts of Seattle. Oh, I know what I said early, but really nothing has come to pass."

Jeannie sighed. "I don't believe that we are in danger. There are honest men here, no matter how rough their lives. But something is not quite right." She turned and looked at her friend. "You forget I left Victoria in quite a hurry. Perhaps Mr. Coward has said something."

"To whom? On this island, who could possibly be interested?"

The door opened and Cooperwaite came in followed by the earlier occupants of the chairs by the woodstove. Their slickers were wet from the rain.

"Ladies, I hope you are well. There's been a delay. The weather, of course. Mr. Baker has, however, offered rooms to you, free of charge. There is a pleasant meal as well. There is a place for you to clean up and make yourselves suitable."

"What has happened to the wheel and hub?" Jeannie asked.

"Being taken care of, Mrs. Pierce, I assure you. I've sent for someone who has the proper tools. Should be here before nightfall. It will be fixed, then you can leave in the morning."

He went over to the window where the rain continued to slash and rattle the glass. "The weather will break, but not before the light is lost."

"Are you sure? Do you divine weather, Mr. Cooperwaite?" Jeannie kept her voice light and musical as if she were leading the monthly tea.

"This island is well known to me, ma'am. Its quirks and particulars."

Jeannie sighed. "Then we are at your mercy."

Cooperwaite laughed. "How charming you are, Mrs. Pierce. You have not lost your ability to parry with a man and make him hope he will never be banished from your sight."

Jeannie smiled brilliantly at him and hoped she didn't look as nervous as she felt.

She must have said something right. A palpable tension that had entered the room, diffused instantly. The hangers-on removed their rubber ponchos and slickers and made themselves as presentable as possible with such ladies present. Cooperwaite ordered up some hot soup and bread with the promise of more substantial food in the next hour or so. In the meantime, they could take their basket and inspect the room.

Cooperwaite led down them down a narrow hall behind the counter. There were several doors on either side. At the end, a door on the right was opened to them. It revealed a plain but clean room with a maple bed and a highboy. Prints cut from *Harper's Weekly* were framed and placed about the whitewashed walls. There was only one window, a lean shape blocked by a heavy velvet curtain. By the bed there was a commode. "I'll see someone brings hot water."

After Cooperwaite left, they closed the door and pushed the lock home. They sat down on the high rope bed.

"It's not as bad as all that, though it is more adventure than I hoped for," Gilly said as she took off her gloves. "I certainly didn't intend to spend a holiday here." She ran her hand over the blue and white summer-winter coverlet with its crisscross lines and squares.

"I'm sorry, Gilly. I never expected—"

"Well, I think we'll survive."

Jeannie hugged her arms. She wasn't so sure as she looked around the room. She had an odd feeling. An old memory stirred about the girl rescued by Breed years ago. The unsavory business that went on in San Juan Town. Was this such a place? She didn't trust Cooperwaite at all.

She lifted the curtain at the window. Outside was the long, lone expanse of beach and prairie sweeping to the east where they reached a curtain of timber and undergrowth. The lagoon, a shallow pond-like body of water, jiggled under the rain's gray onslaught. There were more trees and what she thought was a house further up the bare hill.

Someone's claim, she thought. The sky was quite gray now, and peering back toward the lagoon, she saw dark, menacing clouds bunching to the southwest.

"About the same as in front of us. It's either rather bare or completely enveloped with trees."

"I thought as much. We're quite marooned."

As promised, there was a good meal and even pleasant conversation. The main room was warm and comfortable, a haven from the weather outside that continued to throw as much water against the window panes.

"Does it ever flood here?" Gilly asked.

"Sometimes in winter," the storekeep, Mr. Baker, answered. He was congenial man with well-cared-for mustaches and balding pate. His girth matched his good humor. "What is even more astonishing are the winds. They can be frightful. Last year, it blew so hard that twenty trees were toppled up on Mt. Finlayson and a roof next door was ripped off. A good blow that was."

He poured them more coffee, then went behind the counter.

"Have you been here a long time, sir?" Jeannie asked.

"Since the islands became American. It was a wild place before that. I suspect that you knew that, Mrs. Parker, with your officer husband and all."

Gilly's look implied she did.

"What will happen to it now?" Jeannie asked. "I'm told they're continuing to build on the other side."

"Who's to say? I'd say that it's being platted with high hopes. Not exactly new. In fact, it's five years old or more, but it has not blossomed as the proprietors had hoped."

"Oh, heavens, no. He has a fine farm not far from here, though it is presently run by a Mr. Clancy. I see the manager from time to time."

Gilly looked at the wall opposite the store counter front where chairs had been pulled up close to the wood stove. There, scattered across the wood panels, was a collection of Indian masks of every variety and nation. Some were of mythical beings: half-orca, half-man, lightning birds and wolf spirits, painted with black and red details and sometimes blue-green. They had fantastic lemon- shaped eyes with inlay of shell or copper. Others were of real animals, highly stylized, but of their essence.

"Do you admire them, Mrs. Parker?"

"The masks are quite fine. Are they old?"

"Aye, they made for the trade with the sailors who came in the 40's.

The old *shipmen* of all nationalities —English, Russian, American— they liked buying them.

"That mask looks so real." Gilly referred to the most striking mask, one of a beautiful woman with a labret made of abalone and whale bone. The rich cedar wood was lustrous and smoothed with seal oil, the high cheeks of the woman round with real human hair hanging down.

"Aye, that is the oldest one. Got it in trade myself. Thought it quite fine, though others felt a labret in the lip of a woman was hideous. The mask is of a high-born woman. Ever seen a *siwash* with one?"

"Once," Jeannie answered. *Shells Shining.* "A long time ago."

Mr. Baker smoothed his long brown mustaches. "Them were the old days for sure. Times have changed. More and more those northern tribes come down for the logging mills and canneries. A man need not fear for his head—I think." The man chuckled. "In some ways, I miss it. Life is so ordinary now." He looked around the room and seemed to acknowledge that he had come into hard times and the store's days were numbered. He started to say something more, when the door opened and Cooperwaite came in. Cooperwaite hung up his slicker.

"Good news. The wheelwright is here and will begin work on the hub and wheel immediately. He assures me that all will be well in the morning for your trip back." He looked at the shopkeep and then at Gilly. "Are you being taken care of?"

Gilly assured him they were quite fine.

Cooperwaite rubbed his hands together. "Well, the worst is over. It should clear up soon, perhaps even favor us a moon. You should have no difficulty getting home tomorrow."

"The hard rain must have been too much for our messenger. The rider is so long returning," Jeannie commented.

"Rider? Ah, the rider to Higgins. I chose not to send one after all. The nervous strain you had been under—I didn't want to inconvenience you with another move. I hope you will forgive me."

Both women were stunned. Jeannie couldn't maintain a proper ladylike facade for her feelings. "I'm sure we shall forgive you, Mr.

Cooperwaite, but is it not for us to decide? You ought not to assume anything."

"I beg your pardon," Cooperwaite said. "I thought only of your comfort." He pulled up a chair.

"I commend you, but please consult us next time." Jeannie looked straight at him, though it took all her courage to do so. Something warned her to be cautious, to feign geniality. She decided, however, she ought to be friendly toward him. She leaned over. "You are forgiven."

Smiling wryly, Cooperwaite kissed her hand. "Thank you." He sat down opposite the masks.

Gilly seeking peace said they had been discussing the masks. "I like the lightning bird. Kwakiutl, I believe. Jeannie likes the woman."

Cooperwaite studied it for a moment. "It's well-wrought. Almost lifelike. The cheeks. The mouth. Down to that thing they called jewelry."

"It reminds me of her, "Jeannie said.

"Who?"

"Shells Shining. The Haida woman Mr. Breed knew."

"Breed? Ah, Jonas Breed. I confess I nearly forgot about him. It's been a long time since I've heard that name."

"A different time," Jeannie said wistfully. "I saw her once. She was quite beautiful."

"Do you think so?" Cooperwaite asked. He thanked Mr. Baker for the teapot he brought on a tray and passed the cups and saucers around the table. "I wouldn't know. I don't remember seeing her. I was at the Royal Marine encampment. However, I'm afraid I wouldn't have been a good judge of beauty there. There were a few who were of merit, those fair skinned northern women especially, but I thought most of the native woman too swarthy for me. If you will excuse me saying so."

Jeannie quietly waited for Gilly to pour the tea. Cooperwaite made her feel uncomfortable.

He had chosen his words carefully. He was lying about the woman, about remembering Jonas. She wondered if Cooperwaite knew that Jonas was alive. It would be so easy to turn the conversation that way to find out, but then she thought better of it. Gilly had said Jonas had not wanted people to know that he was here in the islands. Not yet."

"Mrs. Pierce?"

Jeannie looked up at Cooperwaite.

"Your thoughts are far from here."

"I am rather tired. It's been a long day."

"I should say. I'm sure the last couple of months have been difficult. How is your family?

"As best as can be expected."

"May I ask if the firm is in good hands?"

"Yes, I think we are. There is myself and Mr. Waddell. My uncle died some years ago."

"My condolences. Waddell. I'm not familiar with the family. A local personage?"

"No. Mostly he has attended to business in the South Pacific." *And how did we get on this subject?* Across the table Gilly frowned slightly. A further shake of her friend's head warned her to change the subject.

Cooperwaite leaned back and sipped his tea. He appeared not to have noticed the shake of Gilly's head, but Jeannie wasn't so sure. His face was still, but his eyes were straying uncomfortably in her direction. The scar burned red. The name Waddell had disturbed him.

"I think you're blessed," he finally said. "To have such comfort in the knowledge that you and your children have been properly cared for. It honors your husband's name. Is the partner well-versed in the local economy as well as international?"

"I should say he is, Cooperwaite."

"These are booming times. Such promise for those of a business inclination. I should like to meet him. Is he in country?

"I don't believe so," she lied. "Mr. Burgess, our solicitor, has not been forthcoming about his whereabouts." For the first time since she had encountered Cooperwaite on the road, she sensed more than the need for caution. He had never been a friend of Jonas. She knew that. Cooperwaite was fishing for information about Waddell, and there was the danger. Until a day ago, Waddell had been a silent, paper partner.

She turned to Gilly. "Will you call us when the wheel is ready? I'd like to retire."

Cooperwaite sat up and put his cup and saucer on the table. If he was sorry for the end of conversation, he didn't show it. "I most certainly shall." He snapped his finger at Baker.

At half past eight in the evening the ladies retired.

KAPIHI

Once safely in their room, Gilly lit a lantern. Sitting next to each other on the bed, Jeannie and Gilly stared uncomfortably around the bare space. The room was less appealing now than the first time they had seen it. The bed felt damp and the smell of the lagoon wafted in, fishier since the tide had retreated further out. Jeannie wondered if something wasn't dead under the dusty floor boards.

Gilly removed her hat and set it next to her on the coverlet. "The men were all gentlemen. Cooperwaite was a gentleman. But God's truth, he was most inquisitive about Waddell while having no real emotion about Jonas. I found that quite odd. That's why I didn't think it should be discussed any further."

"I agree," said Jeannie, shaking her head. "There is something peculiar is going here. Cooperwaite never had an ounce of good feelings for Jonas, but why pass him over like he never existed? I thought he was searching for something about the name Waddell too. I cannot say what. What could he possibly know about the firm?" She fidgeted with her over-blouse, then stopped, remembering the note tucked away in the account book back in Seattle. *The Marsfield incident is my guarantee that you will comply*. Had Cooperwaite made that threat?

There was a deep well of silence. Gilly broke it. "And we won't be able to fathom anything further if we do not get some rest. Look, dear, you stay to the side you're on and I mine. I think I will only undo my stays, and sleep with the covers o'er. At first light, we shall ask for the buggy and leave." She proceeded to lie under the covers.

Jeannie followed her not long after, but once the light was extinguished, she lay awake staring up at the wood paneled ceiling. Outside, she could hear the faint rush of the waves on shore. Down the hall, the main room of the store appeared quiet. The hangers-on had apparently left. Staring through the gloom, she tried to make out the lock on the door and hoped that it would hold.

"Are you awake?" she asked Gilly.

"Just. I'm afraid the day has had more excitement than I have enjoyed in some time. You'll forgive me if I drift?"

"No. It's all right. I'm afraid I'm just the opposite. So much has stirred my mind. So many memories broken open."

Gilly pulled her hand out from under the covers and patted the top of the coverlet. "Don't distress yourself so much. Perhaps my brother John or Mr. Simpson has been able to contact Jonas's representative. When we get back, I'll see if a telegram can't be sent over. Many of your questions can be answered yet."

"What do you suppose he'll think?"

"John?"

"No. Jonas. I'm beginning to feel like a fool."

Gilly turned her head on the musty pillow stuffed with chicken feathers. Her face was a black oval in the dark. Jeannie sensed she was smiling.

"I'm sure you'll find the words. You have come out of friendship."

"Since Victoria, I have come out of guilt, I think."

"Why do you say that?"

"Because I did not wait for *him*. I thought only of myself, my sorrow thinking him dead."

"Lord, let us not punish ourselves over things that cannot be helped. Over decisions made long ago and newly regretted. Jeannie, dear. You just didn't know. All these years."

"But I believed Andrew."

The coverlet rustled as Gilly shifted onto her side. "But he played on your weakness, and then manipulated it for a long, long time." Gilly sighed. "It's possible that you'll never know his first intentions, yet don't you think that he truly loved you?"

There was a long pause. Finally, Jeannie said that for all the deception, she thought he did. "Still, it wasn't right. Not for either of them, for that matter."

"But you were happy all these years?"

"Most of the time."

"Then it's settled. We have no idea what passed between the men. Andrew cheated Jonas out of his lands. Jonas took over the firm. What all that means is in a man's world, but I'm sure if you saw Jonas, he would be most forgiving for anything on your part. If you see—when you see Jonas, it will be for friendship. What an opportunity you have, dear. You are both bereaved. There is much to talk about—with no obligation on either part to the future. You have only the past to mend." The ropes below their mattress creaked as Gilly turned on her back again and moved away. "Now sleep, Jeannie. We will be gone from here in the morning. Goodnight."

"Goodnight."

Gilly cleared her throat a couple of times and fidgeted with the coverlet. Despite the urge to sneeze, she soon settled deep on the hard dusty straw mattress. At length, she began to breathe deep and regular.

Jeannie continued staring at the ceiling.

The room was still, buffeted gently by a light wind outside the window. Further out, came the steady wash of waves as they ran over pebbles; further still, the tide as it pulled out into the bay. She turned her head toward the wall, past her friend's shoulder. The picture frames were ghostly shapes suspended in the gloom. The highboy was a tall box. She could have been anywhere other than this. Like the Kohl's log house on Whidbey Island where she had gone with Andrew. Like her hotel room in Port Townsend. Like her attic room in her father's house near Portsmouth, England where she had lived as a girl. Night shades were all the same and so were the ghosts that came with them. Like Andrew. Suddenly she was remembering her first night with him.

After the ceremony at a parson's home on Whidbey Island, the couple had taken a secondhand buggy out to a cabin owed by the preacher's family and spent their honeymoon. It was not what she had envisioned. Andrew had come to bed in his nightshirt. She had nothing beyond a borrowed nightgown.

"What a beautiful bride you are," he had said as he settled in next to her on the hard straw bed.

"If only I could have reached my uncle in time," Jeannie had answered as she lay against the feather pillow. She held the covers high.

"Come, come. I told you that things were unsettled. Didn't the parson intimate that himself? There is still unrest on the waters. We'll send word as soon as we are in Seattle." He stroked her lightly on her cheek, then without warning rolled on top of her. He hurriedly tugged his nightshirt above his soft belly.

"Andrew..."

"Don't be afraid. It's quite natural." He yanked up on her gown and when Jeannie began to protest, he tried to soothe her even as he pushed apart her exposed legs.

"Shh. Shh... Nothing to worry about." He stopped momentarily. "Oh, Jeannie, I have admired you so from the very first day I saw you at Camp Pickett. To think you are mine is beyond all my imagining I love you, Jeannie Pierce. I love you." And with that, he came into her like a flaccid rod. It was over in moments, leaving Jeannie betrayed and numb. He did apologize, later, saying that perhaps he was up not to Captain Naughton's attentions, but he would be considerate. Oddly after that, he was. But there was never any real passion, just affection. After time, she grew used to it, as a proper wife was expected to. Three years after Phillip was born, she had Jereminah. She loved them both, but as time went by she announced that she wanted no more children. Andrew could come to her, but he would have to shield himself.

~

The fluted-glass gas chandeliers burned low, spreading soft light around the room and on the men's faces. While Collie laid out the charts on the large salon table, Breed listened to the low conversation of his men. Some had worked for him for nearly three decades. There was a mild tension, but with their years together, it was only the energy of impending action. They were attuned to it all. Breed had experienced life at sea since he was small boy under American, British and Haida masters and been in action with Collie on numerous occasions both in the Pacific Northwest and the South Pacific during his exile of the last twenty years. Collie was a first-rate captain and had seen action in the South Seas on several occasions over their years of trade in that sometimes pirate-infested part of the world. Their leadership was practiced and experienced amid an easy camaraderie. While they both ran tight ships and were favored by the mariner community, it was Breed who led and inspired deep devotion in his men. Many were with them now.

The ship's cat stretched its length to the ends of its front paws, then delicately negotiated the book shelves and bunks behind the men's backs to the desk where Breed sat. It tried its master's thigh tenuously, then stepped down and settled into a thick coil of yellow fur on his lap. Jonas stroked it with his right hand, using the hook to pull papers and books toward him. In the middle was an account book. He made a face at it and crudely flipping it to the last section of its pages, opened it to a series of notes and figures.

"See what comes to wrought, Casper?" he asked the cat. "Sums and figures that don't add up." The cat was unimpressed. Only the tip of its tail across its nose showed any interest in its master's voice.

"That the list of numbers?" Collie asked as he brought a roll of charts over and sat down the captain's chair next to the desk. While he waited for Breed's answer, he unrolled the smallest, a survey chart of the waters around the islands.

"A veritable sleight of hand."

"You have to give Pierce some credit for its discovery. It made all the discrepancies in the Port Townsend warehouse inventories make sense. Things were hidden in plain sight."

"*Ah-ha*, but it cost him his life." Breed looked at the page, then shut the book. "Now all we need is the good solicitor."

"He was supposed to be in Port Townsend, then Victoria. That was the official word."

"I doubt it. I think he's with Gutterson. Something that Wilson said about him leaving everything so abruptly despite what the office said. I think he smelt something."

"His own stench, for one."

Jonas grinned sourly. "I think with Andrew's death, he got spooked."

"Why would he go to Gutterson? He could be found out and exposed."

"Protection, perhaps. Or maybe to negotiate. Probably feels that he's the social better, therefore can control the situation. Some help that will be." Breed brushed his hand over the numbers. "Would have been better to have gone to the authorities openly and take the consequences. I don't think Gutterson will be up to any double-cross. Even the perception of it."

Collie put down the chart thoughtfully. "Then it's a somewhat poetic justice, don't you think? The pen being mightier...."

"Not mightier. Arrogant. A thief is a thief."

Breed reached into his drawer and brought out a Colt .45 set in its holster. He placed it on the desk and carefully examined it. "Are all the firearms checked and conditioned? When we go to meet with Gutterson, I want to be covered. Gutterson's not going to know me, but if Cooperwaite's there—which is what I hope for—things could get dicey."

"We're just about done, Jonas. Everything's been cleaned and ammunition distributed. Just need some work on any personal equipment."

"Good. Sikhs will be there too, though not in obvious attendance. I've given my word to Doc-tin that this shall be done properly. Once there is a handshake, all the material evidence will be his. I think the list of parties involved is complete, including that little prick, Frederick Howell, in the Seattle office." Breed finished the check of his firearm and put it back into its holster. "Kelly will make breakfast, then we will be off. All we need now is word from one of the boys about Kapihi." He pushed back from the desk and stood up. "In the meantime, I'm going to retire for a few hours. Maintain regular discipline with the usual change of watch." He smiled at Collie. "Get some rest yourself, old friend. Tomorrow will tell us exactly how twenty years have weighed upon us."

Collie laughed. "Speak for yourself, *kahpo*. This old pirate is not about to retire. However, it's a thought well taken. The rest, I mean."

The rest of the room looked up at the laugh because Breed had responded with a hearty one of his own. It rang of old times, not the present where grief and anger had muted much of their conversation in the last few weeks.

"What are you looking at?" Breed grinned at the beaming faces tucked around the little crannies of the salon. "You look like a bunch of gossipy army laundresses."

"Minding our stitches too, *kahpo*," answered one of his men as he finished putting his rifle back together.

Breed chuckled. "Well. I've no answer to that except that you will see action soon enough. These smugglers are a crafty, bold lot, but I think they will see an end to their business." He shook his head in amusement. "See you in a few hours."

After Breed had retired to his cabin, Collie went topside to see to the end of first watch and other matters. Doc-tin followed him up into the chart house where Collie was putting away the maps.

"Want to come?" Collie asked.

"It has been on my mind."

The two men took a turn on the deck, stopping at the bow where a crewman was keeping watch. They talked with him for a couple of minutes, then walked slowly back towards the helm. Amidships, they stopped near the main mast. It was dark out with no moon visible except for a suspicious yellow haze to the east. A high bank of clouds had slipped in again covering part of the night sky. The features of the cove were obscured, leaving only an impression of land. The air hinted of cedar. Somewhere out there they could hear waves lapping the boulder-strewn shore.

"What do you think about this news about Jeannie Naughton being on the island?" Collie asked. "I find it unsettling. I hope that she will treat him well."

"You think they'll meet?"

"I think it is inevitable." Collie patted his shirt pocket, wanting his pipe, but dared not. The windows below and all lamps had been banked, even though the likelihood of anyone coming upon them was highly remote in this wilderness of water and forest. It was discipline that kept them to their tasks.

"So you do not think that it will be a happy occasion? My memory of the lady was of one who was empathetic and caring. A very charming spirit."

"You sound like Kapihi," said Collie. "He worships her."

"Kapihi was a boy. He's allowed that. I know times will change a person but over the years I've heard nothing but that she is a genteel woman, well loved and respected." Doc-tin made a face. "You honestly think she will do harm to him?"

"He's very low right now. Hannah's passing has been hard on him. He wasn't there when she died because of this bloody business with Pierce and Gutterson."

"I can see that. It pains me terribly."

"He loved Hannah so much and though he knows it is the right thing, he is torn with his son Ransom so far away. Family has meant a good deal to him. And after all this time, he still loves Annie. Probably always will. She grew on him, you know. He told me once she taught him patience. He could go to her with any problem. But most of all, she kept the Northwest alive in him and the things that he held most dear about it and could not let go: its people and its land. In the end, she was a very good mate for him."

"Funny," Collie went on, "but I'm glad that things went the way they did. I think it was good for all, only I regret all the suffering he went through. And I'm sorry for Jeannie Naughton. I have no doubt that she loved him and would have stood by him during those times had not things gone so sourly. It must have been heartbreaking to have learned, however erroneously, that he had died—"

"I have imagined that myself..."

"—however, I don't think she has the understanding to see what he has done for her these past ten years. Even if she should know that he is Waddell, she will not be able to fathom the depths to which he protected her interests. He not only strove to guard her uncle's affairs when they were being recklessly used, he sought to give her the life he thought she ought to have. As if she could appreciate it."

"So you think that she is a spoiled, frivolous woman who cares only about her position in society now?"

Collie didn't answer, so Doc-tin took it as his answer.

"Hang it all, Collie, how can you say that? I know you're wrong. That young lady loved him, was not afraid to go away with him even with the charges against him. We both know Pierce engineered what happened after the fight." Doc-tin cleared his throat. "I think Jonas has grieved long enough, has obliged long enough. It's time he breaks free. And I hope that they will meet."

"I hope that she will appreciate him."

Doc-tin snorted. "She appreciated him then. When I took her back to English Camp, she held herself well, but she was afraid for him. I'll never forget the look on her face as you all drifted into the trees. It was as if it would be the last time she would see him. And it was."

Collie said nothing. There was a light sigh, then he turned and headed down to the helm.

~

Collie and Doc-tin retired about twenty minutes later. Doc-tin slept on a cushioned bench in the chart room, his mouth open and emitting irregular bursts of snoring deep in his throat. Collie went to his bunk next to the galley.

After tossing and turning several hours, Collie woke suddenly to a slight noise outside his cabin door. Reaching for his gun, he carefully got out of the bunk and crept over to the door. Outside in the salon, the room was quiet. Only the occasional mutterings of some of the men deposited around the room like black lumps of laundry in the recessed bunks and benches marked their positions. Looking back to the galley, he noticed a faint light and followed it through. The area was deserted, but the light continued up the stairs to the chart room. Silently, he hurried forward through the sleeping quarters set in the bow and climbed nimbly up the ladder. Just as he thought, a figure emerged and came out on the deck. A cloaked lantern was set on the doghouse. From Collie's vantage point, the watch did not appear to notice. The figure stretched and went over to the side of the boat. There was a slight stir on the stairs and giving a plaintive meow, Casper bounded across the deck and up on the rail next to the figure. The figure stroked the cat, then picked it up. The dark shape leaned over the side and looked to the south. The clouds had burned off and a new moon was advancing to the bottom of the sky. Its sliver of a light tinted the island across the channel with a thin halo.

"No need to hide, Collie," the shape said.

"Jonas. What are you doing up?"

"Couldn't sleep."

"Neither could I." Collie joined him at the rail. It was chilly out, the first breath of dawn not far off. He suddenly realized that Jonas had his wool jacket on. He did not. "Something on your mind?" he asked.

Breed released the cat. It trotted behind the ropes and rigging, then jumped down to the deck.

"Nothing spectacular. Just the old restlessness, only this time memory has been abroad greatly."

"Do you expect an ambush?" Collie found a halyard out of order and tighten it.

"No. I think Anders Gutterson wants this to be legitimate. After that, he expects to manipulate me."

"Not like his brother. Emmett Krill was a piece."

"Not like his brother."

"Jonas?"

Toward the mouth of the cove, the long shape of a *salt chuck* canoe with its highbrow was gliding across the complacent water.

"Looks like we have company and from all appearances not what we were expecting."

Jonas squinted at the canoe coming toward the schooner in the morning mist. Kapihi and three companions were paddling, but the others were two women.

"I'll be damned," said Collie when he recognized them.

Jonas felt the same way.

FLIGHT AGAIN

Jeannie's inability to sleep grew worse as the night progressed. From her back to her right side and then to her left, the damp confines of the room offered no peace or rest. There were too many ghosts roaming. Finally, she got out of bed.

The building was still. Whoever had remained in the store earlier had retired. The only sound was the light night wind against the frame of the store and its add-on. Stocking-footed, she carefully crossed the creaky wood floor to the curtained window and looked outside. It was still cloudy out, but behind the vast sky cloak, the suggestion of a new moon was giving enough light to see some ways out onto the dark beach before it stretched off into a dense, black forest coming down to the water. There were no flickering lights from any settler's home on the hills above the beach. It was far too late.

She let the curtain go, intent on returning to bed and sitting upright until her eyes drooped, then decided to try a different tack. She would take the night air and see if that would tire her enough to sleep. Slipping into her button boots, she put on her blouse and skirt, then her shawl. A quick glance at Gilly's shape in the dark, and she was out in the hallway.

At the end of the hallway to her right, she had earlier observed a doorway. To the outside, she hoped. Perhaps a privy. At the opposite end of the hall were the swinging doors she knew led into the main store area, but she could only sense them. There was no light anywhere at that end. Cautiously, she went the few short steps to the wall and feeling with her hands, located a doorknob. Its round metal shape felt cold to her hand, but she was more wary of any complaint it might make than discomfort and turned it gently to see if it was locked. It was not. It opened readily and soon she was outside.

It was cooler outdoors than she thought and dark, the air sea-weedy and heavy with moisture. Yet, when she breathed it in, she was instantly refreshed and alert. Not the sort of thing she had planned on, but she was committed now. Afraid that someone would find the door opened, she closed it. Then wrapping her shawl tighter around her shoulders, she tested the slimy, ancient steps and stepped down to the ground.

On this backside of the store she could look up the dark shape of the hill where the old road came down. She supposed if she strained her eyes long enough, she could make out some feature where the buggy had broken down, but it would have been more of her imagination than fact. Only closer in, could she make out in the gloom a small, boxed-shaped building that was most likely the privy down to her right. She started to walk out to it, then suddenly flattened herself at the corner of the building when she realized that there were riders out front. There was a jingle of a bridle and a horse's snort and the voices of men. They carried quite clearly.

"The devil, you say. I want that woman watched until we're away."

"It's under control, Gutterson. I've got her blithely contained. She'll be off in the morning."

Jeannie gasped.

The voices stopped abruptly. Had they heard her?

There was the sound of boots crunching on pebbles and sand, but they were apparently walking around a horse or horses. They stopped at the corner and resumed talking, their voices even louder in the night air.

"And once this deal is made," the same voice continued, "you can continue to damn well watch her all you want. In fact, I might watch her all I want. She's still the lady fair and it might well do some good to have a presence in the firm other than your flunkeys."

"What about Burgess?"

"Well, he was a fool to leave Seattle and come here. I wouldn't eliminate him yet. He's still useful."

The men moved out from the corner, pebbles and sand unevenly grinding under their boots. Jeannie stayed where she was, terrified and in disbelief. The speaker had been Cooperwaite and they had been talking about Burgess, her wayward solicitor. It appeared that he was far more wayward than she had imagined. But all those questions Cooperwaite had asked about Waddell. Did he know Waddell was Jonas? And who was this Gutterson?

"Listen," Cooperwaite continued. "They'll be gone in the morning. I'm having someone personally escort them back."

"You had better. You're coming with me."

"Oh, no. I'll have nothing to do with this meeting. You are on your own with Waddell."

"Why? You haven't been listening to Coward, have you, the little brat?"

"Not at all. I just don't want any part of your end of the business. Just because I let you use my property, doesn't mean I agree to murder and kidnapping."

"He's as safe as a kitten in a basket. He'll be returned."

"You know what I mean. You didn't have to do it. I had him cold."

The voice named Gutterson laughed. "You mean Pierce? I don't recall you ever taking the high road. You have a way with the ladies, I hear."

"Don't play games with me, Gutterson." There was a shuffling sound and swearing, then it ended as abruptly as it began.

"OK, OK, you've made your point."

"I hope that I was perfectly clear."

From out in the muddy space that served as street between the false-fronted buildings, someone else joined them. There was a discussion, then someone went inside the store. Panicking, Jeannie started back to the steps when it sounded like someone was coming down to the back. She was relieved when he stopped.

"You going back to the farm?" Cooperwaite asked.

"No, I'm staying here," Gutterson replied. "I'll stay at Dailey's." They went on discussing their next moves for a few moments longer. Jeannie made it to the stairs and reached for the door, when one of the men passed the building and came out into the open space that was at the edge of town. He was carrying a lantern, holding it high to his face. Jeannie suddenly felt faint. His features were very clear. Though he was very much a man of this decade by his clothes, he was a reflection of another time and man—Emmett Krill. The resemblance was so striking she began to tremble. Something was terribly wrong. They were to meet with Jonas and they had spoken of murder and kidnapping. They had spoken of Burgess and of—Andrew.

Jeannie was trapped. She couldn't open the door and go back in without being noticed. She could only go back down and slip away to the side of the building. Carefully, she backed down. At the bottom, she backed away from the steps.

"Where are you going?" Cooperwaite asked from the front of the store.

"None of your damned beeswax. I'll be back in a moment."

He's going to the privy, she thought.

Gutterson lifted up his lantern up toward the hill and then down. When he found the privy, he started forward, the light swinging back and forth against the black space and the wall of the add-on. Three seconds and she would be seen and it would be all over. At that moment, she was utterly sure.

She felt her way back, when someone clamped a big hand over her mouth and lifting her off her feet, carried her around the corner like a suckling pig for market. The lantern light swept harmlessly by. There was a crunching of feet and the whine of a rusted hinge as a door opened and shut. Then silence.

For what seemed the longest time, Jeannie was kept muffled and enclosed in the stranger's grasp. Though not cruelly held, his intent was for her not to move or speak. When her fear made her mouth press against his hand, he relaxed it a little and spoke for the first time.

"Just a little wait, ma'am. Please be still." The whispered voice was rich with an accent she did not recognize, but told her nothing other than that he was neither British nor American. He smelled of seawater and cedar.

A little cry broke in her throat.

"Shh.... please. He will come here. Do you understand? Please nod yes."

Jeannie nodded. True to his word, after what seemed another long time, the door whined again and slammed shut. Lantern light splashed past their feet and out towards the beach. It swung back and forth like a clock's pendulum, started to go away, then paused. Boots crunched and Gutterson came over to the steps and stopped. He had found the door ajar.

"Damnation," he said. He stomped up the stairs and closed it and then came down. For one horrible moment, the lantern light painted the side of the building where Jeannie had been initially taken, but no one was there. Her abductor had nimbly carried her around to the beach side of the add-on and held her there. The light hung for a second then resumed swinging again. It became dimmer as it made its way back to the front of the building. There were bits and pieces of voices, then the sound of horses being led off. Finally, there was silence.

Again there was an interminable wait. The stranger did not move or speak nor would he let Jeannie. Only when it seemed that the night had been restored to its sounds and silences, did he speak.

"I'm a friend, Missus Pierce. I'm going to take away my hand, ma'am," he whispered. "You'll not scream? It would be very bad if you screamed."

Jeannie shook her head, no, she wouldn't. He released her and stepped back. Waiting briefly, she finally found the courage to turn around and look at him. In the gloom, she saw a tall dark-skinned man with high cheekbones and a long, straight nose that flared softly at the nostrils. His lips were gently bowed and his eyes dark, for only his whites showed. He was dressed as a laborer with boots, felt hat and a heavy flannel sack coat for the night air.

"Forgive me, Missus. I didn't mean to scare you. He was close to finding you out." He came out from the shadow of the wall and stood in what light there was. Instantly, she recognized him.

"Why, you were on the steamboat," Jeannie said in a low voice. "You've been following me!"

The young man proudly answered in a soft whisper. "*Ah-ha.*"

Jeannie didn't know what to say, yet his exuberance checked her. He had, after all, saved her from a great difficulty.

"Why?" she asked, backing away.

"Because I have been looking out for you."

"For me?"

"*Ah-ha.*"

It had been years since she had heard Chinook Jargon, but she remembered how Jonas had talked that way. Like the words to a nursery song sung long ago, an old memory stirred and she began to look at the young man more closely. An aristocratic face, she decided. Someone she knew. To her astonishment, she realized that he looked like Kaui Kalama.

"I know you."

"I hope so," the young man said. "I'm Kapihi Kalama, Kaui's boy grown into a man."

Jeannie gasped.

Kapihi put his finger to his lips to urge her to be quiet. His face was beaming now, so proud she remembered him.

"How on earth did you find me?" she whispered.

"I followed you. I came to help you. Those are very bad men."

"You know those men?"

"*Ah-ha.* They are smugglers. One, I think you know—Thaddeus Cooperwaite from the old English Camp. The other is Anders Gutterson, half-brother of Emmett Krill. They are very bad men."

"Dear Lord. Emmett Krill... But, how did you know they would be here?"

"I didn't, ma'am. Not until you came here."

"So you got on a boat in Seattle and followed me to Port Townsend, then here?" she whispered. "How did you know I would be on the island?"

"I followed you to Victoria."

"To Victoria?"

"*Ah-ha.*"

She pulled her shawl tight around her shoulders for the night air was beginning to bite. Out on the edge of the lagoon, the waves came in clear and cold. And for the first time since she left Seattle, she knew that she needed to be clear and cold too.

"Why?"

Kapihi shook his head. "There's no time to explain. But I know these men, Cooperwaite and Gutterson. They have done bad things for many years: smuggle whiskey, opium, cheap labor. Anything illegal, even murder. And they have done it through the firm of Campbell, Pierce and Waddell."

"My husband's firm."

"Shhh." Kapihi put his hand out again. "Please. It's not safe here. Not to talk, not to stay. Let me take you where it is safe. I will tell you everything then." He gestured out towards the beach. "I have a canoe there. We can get you to safety."

She stared across the dark beachhead. What Kapihi proposed was crazy. It must have been after midnight, possibly one in the morning. It was dark and cloudy out. Furthermore, she didn't know him. Not really. Yet she had been unnerved by the talk out there at the front of the store.

"It will take about two hours, maybe less depending on the wind and tides," Kapihi was saying. "There you will be safe. He has a very large schooner and you will be comfortable. He has men and guns."

"Who?"

"Jo-nuss. Jo-nuss Waddell. He has come to take command." He watched her face for any reaction. Her gasp was reward enough and he smiled.

"The firm's paper partner? You know him?"

"*Ah-ha.*"

408

"But how?"

"I work for him."

"Then you know you that he is really Jonas Breed, don't you?"

"For a long time now."

A noise stopped them from speaking any further. On the other side of the wall, they could hear the ropes of the bed creaking as Gilly turned over. Kapihi motioned they should go over by the door. Most of all, she should make a decision.

"I think you should wake your friend and go now," he said. "I think the men will not stay at the other house long. They mean to harm you. There will be light in three hours or so. I want to be far from here."

"I have not met Jonas Waddell," Jeannie said.

"You will find him very well." He looked at her kindly. "Be easy in your mind. I was sent to watch out for you, but I would have come anyway. In some places, it is well known that you are traveling through the islands. I wanted to come because you helped my father and you were very kind to a young boy. You have been away, but you have not been forgotten."

"Forgotten?"

"The smallpox, ma'am and what you did. And how you lost your little boy. Every mother cried for you."

"Oh," Jeannie murmured. Never once had she thought herself in that light. She had done only what was right. How long ago it seemed. She looked at Kapihi, a boy now grown into a fine young man.

"Mrs. Jeannie Naughton Pierce," Kapihi said. "I would do anything for you. I have waited a long time to give my thanks."

Jeannie sniffed at the sudden tears that came to her eyes. Powerful emotions long dormant threatened to engulf her. Not able to give him any other argument, Jeannie agreed to go with him.

It didn't take long to prepare to go. There were a few anxious moments after Jeannie first re-entered the building and discovered someone in the main store, but he eventually went out and closed the front door behind him. Tiptoeing into the room, she shook Gilly awake, then cautioned her drowsy friend to dress quickly. They were leaving for the safety of others, in particular, Mr. Waddell.

"What?" Gilly was awake now, staring at her friend in disbelief. "What on earth are you talking about?" She winced violently when Jeannie struck a lucifer and lit a candle.

"I scarce believe it myself," Jeannie said as she put what things she had brought in the buggy into her satchel. "We are in danger. Just a short while ago, I overheard Cooperwaite speak to a man named Gutterson. Both are on the shady side of the law. Smuggling to be exact and they have involved the firm. No wonder Cooperwaite was asking questions. They mean to either detain us or skirt us away before they meet with Jonas."

Gilly slipped to the edge of the bed and tried to find her shoes in the poor light. "Jeannie, dear, I can hardly keep up with you. Where are we going? We can't possibly run away from here. They have my horse and buggy. We scarcely have the means to walk out of here. And what is this about Jonas? Mr. Waddell indeed."

"We are in good hands. Would you believe that none other than Kapihi Kalama, Kaui's boy, has followed me since Seattle? Did you know that he works for Jonas?"

"No. Only that he was alive and doing well."

She gave Gilly a "you-should-have-told-me" look, then went on. "He has followed us since the farm. He says he saw everything, including the accident. He also says that Cooperwaite was spying on us."

"Oh, Cooperwaite, the rotten man. He should have been drummed out of the Royal Marines at first infraction. How will we get out of here?'

"By canoe. Kapihi says it is not far from here. Hurry!"

"Canoe? Oh, dear." Gilly had Jeannie help tighten her corset. Then after putting on her blouse and skirt, she put her belongings into her satchel. All the time, she spoke under her breath about the dangers of not knowing where they were going, the possibility of being found out, the general mood of the night. Jeannie was not moved. Ten minutes after she had returned to the room, they were out in the hall.

The building was still abandoned and closed up. For the first time since she stepped out, Jeannie realized that Cooperwaite and

Gutterson must have been very sure of themselves. She didn't believe that anyone else occupied the building. Dailey's was across the way. Not thinking the women capable of thinking of escape or even worrying about their position, they had been left alone. Which made Gilly pause one more time before they went out the door and into what might turn out to be a disaster. Out they went into the chilly dark night to where Kapihi waited in the shadows, then away from San Juan Town and into the unknown.

They went at a sluggard's pace. Moving as quickly as the women could go in the dark and the elements, Kapihi led them cautiously around the lagoon and down across the at times muddy beach strewn with driftwood and seaweed. Always on the lookout for movement at the settler's homestead above them, they avoided the occasional wash of the tide foaming in and out against their long skirts and eventually entered a strip of trees separating the first claim from a new one. On the other side was more beach and mud and a cabin built too close to the water, so Kapihi took them up behind it and continued eastward. After thirty minutes, they reached a small ridge which joined and paralleled the long, wide bay. There, they could take higher ground, but the thick stand of timber and underbrush became new obstacles for the women's long skirts. Patiently, Kapihi urged them on, pausing only once to look back at the collection of buildings lost in the dark. There was no one following them. A glance back to the lone cabin told them that no settler was awake as well. While he waited for the women to catch their breath, Gilly gave him her opinion.

"Young man, wouldn't it have been better to seek help from Mr. Higgins? He is an old soldier and a God-fearing man."

"I know him well, but he's too far from here for the help you need. Besides, Mr. Waddell can offer you better protection. The local community tolerates Cooperwaite, but they fear him as well as not knowing the true reason why they should. Higgins is not equal to his cunning. And with Gutterson present, I think it will be worse. Come, it's only a short ways." He offered Gilly his hand to help her step over some large stones in their way. To the south, the moon began to work its way through the clouds. Already, it made the waves gently moving across the bay glow with phosphorus light. Visibility along the beach was much improved. "Hurry, we must be off before we can be discovered leaving the shore. Once we are out in the channel, we'll be less suspicious."

At long last, they climbed out of the beachhead and over a small wooded point. On the other side, they came upon a group of men squatting in the sand or sitting on a single log. In the center, there was a small oil lantern, its light muted by a tin cover. Pulled up on shore next to them were two large *salt chuck* canoes. They appeared not to notice the appearance of Kapihi and the women on the ridge. As they descended to the men quietly talking there, however, four men appeared out of the trees and followed them down. They were fully armed, their rifles cocked. All told, Jeannie counted ten.

"Hey, Kapihi, you make *hyas latlah*."

"No more noise than you. I heard you far away, Andy Po."

The men laughed, then hushed when the women came down to join them. They stood up, politely taking off their hats.

Jeannie knew instantly that these were men loyal to Jonas, like the same collection of men who followed him so long ago. Yet except for Kapihi, they were strangers.

"Mrs. Pierce and Mrs. Parker," said Kapihi, "this Tenas John, Andy Po..." He quickly named off the others.

Jeannie nodded to them, then waited while Kapihi explained what had happened and why they were there.

"Sure, we can take you," Tenas John said. "I'll stay back with Mason and Tommy Pohana and continue the watch on Cooperwaite. The rest can go."

"When are you taking the schooner north?" Kapihi asked.

"This morning. Jonas wants to be ready."

"Ready for what?" Gilly spoke up.

All the men looked in her direction. Jeannie watched her friend start to say something, then stop, but Jeannie who since the afternoon felt a decidedly stronger interest in affairs around her, wouldn't let social conventions about a woman's inquiring prevail.

"If it concerns the firm, I should like to know. I have every right to know."

"Sure you are, but I think that Mr. Waddell should answer to that," answered one of the men, by his accent and the lantern's insufficient light, an Irishman. The scene was so surreal, the light from lantern climbing up their rough boots and pants like pole bean vines, leaving off somewhere below their chins.

"Does Thaddeus Cooperwaite answer to that? By his conversation, he seems quite eager to take on Mr. Waddell. Is there a confrontation brewing?"

The Irishman looked at Kapihi for clarification.

"She overheard Cooperwaite and Gutterson quite a bit."

"You're not to trouble your mind on that, Mrs. Pierce," the *shipman* said. "Mr. Waddell has things well in hand. As for yourself and Mrs. Parker, he will be most solicitous to help you."

Kapihi concurred. "We should put off now." He turned to the Irishman. "I need blankets and other gear for the women's comfort. The rest of you should make ready."

A short time later, the women were instructed to climb into the canoe and make themselves comfortable while warm blankets were set on their shoulders and around them. Canvas tenting finished off their protection from the cool, damp night air. There was a concerted effort to drag the canoe into the water, then once the bow caught the waves coming in, it lifted and lurched forward under the grunts and heaving of the landsmen while the paddlers bit into the water with their paddles. As it advanced, the remaining paddlers jumped in and they were off with a swerve. Gilly grabbed nervously onto the gunwale with her gloved hand, but Jeannie's only response was to wrap her blanket around her. She looked back where they had been moments before. The lantern was still there, its light a yellow point in the gloom, but she could see the trees and the hills behind it now and the dark shapes of the remaining men on shore. Ahead stood the edge of the bay and the cold waters of the channel. Beyond that, it was still dark, an eerie opaque nothingness receding away from them as they ventured out.

413

For one brief moment she thought of Phillip and Mina and panicked. What if the canoe were to capsize and she to drown? Would they know where she was? Worse, if they saw their mother now, what would they think? Yet as the rhythm of the paddlers became more synchronized, a sense of calm, a long forgotten contentment came over her. The bending backs before her became the men of memory when she gone down to Kanaka Town to care for Kaui Kalama. And with that memory came a renewed sense of freedom and adventure and the testing of character and fortitude that came with it; the letting go of loss into a new beginning. Above all, there was the one who drove all fear away from her.

It was odd how quickly a distant memory could come back and slam so forcefully into her, no matter how eerie the night and the circumstances from which they were fleeing. From a tiny flame taking form, it had roared into life so that it was now the only thing in front of her. Gone was her comfortable life of the past twenty years where the only struggles had been those associated with the domestic dangers of birthing and childhood disease. Just as when she set off with Andrew and all the difficulties and shame of her earlier years had become discarded, so now were the years of ease obliterated. As the canoe gained speed, the water shooting against its high bow with a sound of sizzling bacon, the unbelievable was coming closer to reality: after twenty years, the one she thought dead she would see again. With that reality, never did she feel so ill prepared.

ESCAPED

"They're what?"

"Flown, sir. The birds have flown."

"No!" His voice flying up to the darkened rafters, Gutterson's face was close to purple as he shoved Baker aside and stormed down the dark hall. The shopkeep followed meekly with a kerosene lantern held high like an umbrella. At the end of the hall, they stopped outside the women's door. Gutterson found it ajar.

"This how you found it?" he snapped.

"Yes. I'd come over, you see, to check on the stove in the store for the night and I'd..."

"Thought you'd take a little peek."

"Oh, no sir. That would be unseemly. I thought I heard a sound down the hall and sought to investigate." He pointed to the door. "It was tapping from a draft inside the room. Thought it best to shut it, then I noticed the footprints." Baker pointed to the floor. There were a set of two—one slightly muddy—at the door leading out to the outside door where at its threshold was a third larger set still damp from being on the beach. "They're those of a man. I was quite alarmed." Baker opened the outside door and shined the lantern down on the stairs. "See. They follow him out and then around to the side of the building. I took a look. They left from there and headed east along the beach."

"But to where?" Gutterson wondered when he saw for himself. "And with whom?" The beach was deserted, a pale scene now under increasingly bright moonlight

"Quite a muddle. Quite a muddle," Baker said. "It wouldn't be one of the hangers-on, would it? I'm not always assured of their reputation."

"So you think they were taken under force?" Gutterson asked as they climbed the steps back into the building. The prospect was unlikely to him, but the mere mention served a public purpose. He did not like the alternative: that they had gone willingly.

Out in the store, the front door opened and closed. A set of boots trudged across the old fir boards and stopped at the swinging saloon doors. Candlelight flickered on the hall wall.

"What the devil is going on?"

"Oh, a difficulty, Mr. Cooperwaite," Baker said.

The saloon doors swung open. "And?"

"It appears that Mrs. Pierce has left the premises." Gutterson nodded to Baker. "We'll take it from here. We'll see that a search party is put together immediately. You needn't concern yourself any further."

"But..." Baker stammered.

"Do as he says, Baker," Cooperwaite boomed from the doorway. We'll take it from here." Cooperwaite pushed the doors roughly aside so that they banged against the walls and marched down to a fuming Gutterson. Baker scurried past him, then left the store in a rush.

"What do you think he knows?" Cooperwaite asked once they were alone.

"Nothing. Thinks the women were abducted. I thought it might be a possible story for the airing."

"No. He should be silenced. No violence, of course. Just made quiet for the moment." Cooperwaite pushed in the door to the women's room. "How long ago did this happen?"

"Haven't a clue. Baker came and got me about fifteen minutes ago. He was in a flurry."

Cooperwaite raised his candle. It revealed a room that had been little disturbed. The bed was even thoughtfully made. When his candle illuminated a kerosene lantern, Cooperwaite went over and retrieved it. He struck a lucifer and replacing the chimney, motioned that they should go outside.

At the back of the building, they stared at the trio of footsteps leading off across the dark gray sand.

"Who knew they were here?" Cooperwaite asked.

"The old soldier up the hill might."

"Not possible, unless they said something before they came down. I didn't get word off to him as I promised. And they certainly didn't. But who the hell would take them away? And why? What could they possibly perceive as dangerous?"

"Maybe the widow knows more than you think."

"About Waddell? The circumstances of Pierce's death? You yourself convinced me that there was no suspicion." Cooperwaite grew silent. "And yet... it's possible," he said aloud. He *had* been pushing for information on Waddell from her. But that was not their immediate concern.

"Get some men together and send a search party out along the beach. I want to see where they went. If they cut across the claim east of here, see if they went up to the road on top. Follow them. If on the other hand if someone put in by canoe. Then it's another story all together."

~

It *was* another story all together. When the men mostly from Gutterson's outfit came back, cold and in a foul mood. Gutterson was the first to explode.

"Son of a bitch! How many?"

"Two *salt chuck* canoes," McCoy said, his red bottlenose growing brighter from his exertions outside and his fear.

"How many men?"

"A dozen or more at least from the tracks. Hard to say who. Some were barefoot, others had boots. Found this." McCoy held up a broken string of dried clams. It was a native food that only old-timers and Indians would eat.

"Think they were Indian?" Cooperwaite asked suddenly.

McCoy shrugged. "Could be."

"American or Canadian?"

"How should I know? S'Klallam maybe Saanich. The usual savages."

"Well, I don't want to hear about the usual savages," growled Cooperwaite. "Question is, why would she go with them? It doesn't make sense. Not for a lady of Jeannie Pierce's position."

"Unless," Gutterson interjected, "Waddell sent them."

"Here we go again. Now why in the hell would he do that? He's a paper partner. They're not supposed to know each other. Right? Burgess, etc.? Besides what would Waddell know about local Indians? He's not from around here."

Gutterson swallowed. "There's something missing in this picture and I don't like not knowing what it is." He suddenly shuddered. If Coward were here, he'd probably be saying that it was the ghost of Breed again. It made his skin prickle. He abruptly changed the subject and asked McCoy if he had any idea which way the canoes might have gone.

"Can't tell. Maybe east around to the new settlement. Can say this, though, the second canoe didn't put in much in before we got there. Could tell by way it slid across the beach." McCoy was proud of his deductions and wanted to tell more, but Gutterson shut him up.

"I want you to go over and see Coward. He's waiting across the Haro."

"This time of night?"

"Yeah, you take some others with you. Want him to go down to Port Townsend and keep an eye on the Pierce girl. Sort of insurance. He can say he's been asked to call on her. If need be, we can take her for insurance."

After McCoy left, Gutterson and Cooperwaite went back into the store. Reaching over the bar, Gutterson felt around for a bottle and some glasses and put them on the counter. Cooperwaite put the lantern down and watched him pour. When the glasses were filled, each man silently downed the raw whiskey. Cooperwaite held out his glass for more.

"Better load now," Cooperwaite said. "We'll split the difference and send one boat around. If it leaves now, it'll be in place like we want. Use the schooner with the steam engine. I want them pinned if there's trouble and a way out."

"Don't expect any trouble from Waddell."

"Probably not. Unless that Pierce woman shows up. Damn her! Never expected her take flight like that."

"No one expected her to go to Victoria either. When I see Burgess, I'm going to crown him good and—" Gutterson stopped in mid-sentence at the loud banging at the door. Cooperwaite drew a pistol and went to investigate. Throwing the door open, he found to his surprise a bedraggled old man in soppy wet suit and pants standing in the dark. His stiff white collar was smudged and unbuttoned, his gray mutton chop whiskers uncombed and matted.

Cooperwaite put his pistol back into his pocket and turning back to Gutterson, lifted his glass. "Do I surmise correctly that this is the very devil himself?"

"No, just his piss hole. Get in here you old fart," Gutterson yelled. "I want a word with you! Where the hell have you been?"

"You insult me, sir," the solicitor said as he came into the room. He removed his sour-looking tall hat and put in under his arm. It had once been expensive, but the beaver felt was bare in several places, like it had been scabbed over for the worse.

"Not any more than I'd berate my cur," Gutterson sneered. "May I present, Burgess, late I assume, of the firm of Pierce, Campbell and Waddell."

"I have not resigned."

"You have now," Gutterson spat. "The widow Pierce may have found you out."

419

"So it's true? She went to Victoria?"

"Worse. She just left moments ago from here," Gutterson growled. He grabbed Burgess by the lapels. "So where is the young master?"

"Drugged and on the sloop down at the old wharf."

THE TRUTH WILL OUT ONCE AGAIN

It was still early morning with just a hint of day coming when Kapihi ordered the canoe put ashore so that the women could rest. They had made it across the mouth of Griffin Bay and the headland that separated the bay from the place where the new settlement was taking form with no trouble and were now on the opposite side of the channel from San Juan Island. They had made good time and now in the ghost light of the night's last stand, they could see the black humps of the islands rising above the misty banks of unseen beaches.

"Are we there?" asked Gilly through chattering teeth.

"Not yet," Kapihi answered. "We will find a place and make a fire for you, get you something warm before we go on."

"There is no danger to being seen?"

"We have a clever little Oriental brazier. You will see. It makes no visible flame."

Following the dark shape of the shore, the men scouted for a cove they knew that was hidden behind a hill, then pulling against the tide, aimed for it. The canoe shot around the point and was brought into the ghostly presence of a narrow boulder-strewn shore. Kapihi and the Irish *shipman* were the first out, guiding the canoe upon the stony sand beach. The others jumped out and pulled it up on the beach.

"Now, ladies, you can get out." Kapihi offered his hand, helping Gilly first, then Jeannie. The two women clung to each other for support as they reclaimed their land legs and comportment. The brazier was set out and its charcoal lit. Blankets were brought over and spread upon a log in the shelter of a low white sandstone cliff. Higher up, in the dim light, they could see the dark shapes of the madrone and cedar rising above them. The men moved around quietly.

"Coffee in a short time, ladies," said the Irishman. "We have a tincture." He offered them seats, keeping them occupied while Kapihi and two others took a hooded lantern and went up the wooded hill that separated the hidden cove from the channel and disappeared into the deep black blanket of the trees. They were gone for a long while.

"Do you know Mr. Waddell?" Gilly asked their host as he poured the hot brew. She clasped the tin mug to keep her hands warm as she huddled under her blanket. She was still chilled from their ride in the open canoe. The cool air off the cove, though sweet and fresh, didn't make her any warmer.

"About twelve year. Joined up with him in the Sandwich Islands, but I've been up north around Fort Simpson in the British Columbia territories and Prince Rupert doing business for the firm for some time now, so I have been privy to all that has gone on."

"Pierce, Campbell and Waddell?" Jeannie asked. This was news to her.

"Oh no, ma'am. It be the firm of Mr. Waddell's—Pacific Northwest and Orient Shipping. He trades and ships everywhere. For nearly nineteen year now."

"Oh," said Jeannie.

"You said you were privy," remarked Gilly. "Do you know about his connection to the Queen Charlottes up there? The land of the Haida?"

"Indeed I do, ma'am. Know the whole story well."

"Has he ever remarked on it or traveled there?"

"Several times he has gone north to the Alaska territory up above the Yukon territories to do business, but he has gone in secrecy to his old haunts. I do believe that he has affection for the places. Has mentioned his time there on many occasions: the customs, the land, and its people. They have been decimated, you know. In 1862, smallpox wiped out almost eighty percent of the Haida. The villages have been greatly reduced."

"Good heavens," Gilly said in a shocked voice. "I had no idea."

Nor I, thought Jeannie. In a flash, the stories Jonas had told her on Timons came to her. They were as vivid as this moment.

"You seem to know Mr. Waddell well, Mr—" said Jeannie.

"Patterson. Indeed, I do. I'm his number one bo'sun mate."

They chatted for a bit over their tincture of coffee, as though sitting on a log in a wilderness after a wild night's escape across water was a normal as high tea in the parlor. Eventually, Gilly finished her cup and went to sit further down against the sandstone wall. Patterson puttered around the brazier and then went to smoke a pipe at the water's edge.

Jeannie, restless, walked down in her blanket and joined Patterson by the canoe. The cove was revealing itself more and more and they remarked on the prettiness of it and the beginnings of the day. The water at their feet was clear and its rhythm undisturbed as the waves drifted lazily over the pebbly edge of the beach. Her home in Seattle and children seemed far away, forgotten. She was on a different plane of life.

"Did he ever mention old acquaintances such as Mrs. Parker and myself?"

"He has spoken of Dr. and Mrs. Parker from time to time for their kindness to him. Been delighted she returned to the San Juan Islands."

"Did Mr. Waddell ever speak of me?" Jeannie held her breath.

Patterson smiled kindly at her. "No, ma'am. That is a personal matter he has not shared with me, but begging your pardon, ma'am, there's others here who place you highly in their opinion and say it is the same for Mr. Waddell. A most tender opinion."

"Oh," She felt disappointment settle hard on her shoulders. "You did not know him on San Juan Island?"

"Before my time, ma'am."

"Did he ever speak of it?"

"Aye, he did."

"Do you know of the fight?"

Jeannie had been asking so many questions that Patterson hesitated, weighing his answer, then said, "Aye, I do. It's a legend here among the islands, but for those of us who are in the knowing—meaning that the subject is alive and well—we could add a few things to it if we could. Mr. Waddell, in the local jargon, was *skookum tum tum*. His prowess is what legends are made of. He fought bravely, you know, even though he was maimed."

"Maimed?" Jeannie's voice cracked.

Embarrassed he might have let something slip, Patterson concentrated on getting his pipe lit and jammed it into his mouth. Jeannie looked for an explanation from Gilly, but she was sound asleep in her blankets, her body slumped back against the sandstone wall they were taking shelter under.

"You didn't know then?" he finally said.

"No," she murmured, "I didn't know." She was about to ask for more details, but Kapihi and his men returned and beckoned to Patterson to join them. They huddled for a moment, then Kapihi came over.

"We've got to go. The tide's changing in our favor and we wish to be with it." Are you ready, Missus Pierce?"

"Yes. I'd like to be away from here as quickly as we can, but I do wonder if you would walk with me, Kapihi. For just a moment. I would be so grateful."

Kapihi beamed. He said something to one of the Kanakas, then with a serious face, beckoned her to start walking along the beach.

The little cove was quiet. She could see the trees individually now. There was light in the sky to the east. Some birds were stirring in the trees. She wrapped her blanket tight around her as it was still quite chilly, but her thoughts were quite hot and agitated. They strolled along the beach.

"How are your mother and sister?"

"My mother is well. She took a new husband long ago and lives at Lummi near Whatcom. My sister, Noelani, is a pretty young woman, but has always been wild in her ways. She ran off at fifteen with a Scots miner. They are still together and a son."

"And you?"

"I have a wife and two sons," he said proudly. "They live in the Hawaiian Islands."

"You are away from them a lot?"

"It's the sea, ma'am. I see them about twice a year, but sometimes they come on the voyages over to here."

"Ah." Jeannie sighed, pulling her blanket even tighter in her uneasiness. The small talk was over.

"You are troubled, Missus Naughton? *Sick tum tum?*"

"Yes, I am." She cleared her voice. "You know how I regarded Jonas in times past."

"*Ah-ha.*"

"Mr. Patterson has told me a terrible thing."

"*Wah.*" Kapihi looked back to the camp.

"He told me that Jonas was maimed in the fight. No one ever told me, not even Mrs. Parker who saw him just a couple of weeks ago. Tell me, is it true?"

Kapihi drew himself up. His face was sober.

"Is it?"

"*Ah-ha.*"

"You said he was all right!"

"He is, ma'am," Kapihi said with great feeling. "*Hyas kloshe.* Jo-nuss is very fine. You'll see." He tried to soothe her worries, but she continued to fret.

"Missus. Parker told me that he could not come because he was injured. She did not tell how badly. It was badly?"

Kapihi looked down.

"Was it?"

"Missus. Pierce. Why do you want to make yourself *hyus sick tumtum?* This is an old story."

"Where you there? You left with Jonas."

Kapihi was silent.

"You were there. Oh, you must tell me. Please, Kapihi."

"Missus Pierce..."

"Please."

Kapihi shook his head miserably. "I promised Jo-nuss I would not say anything." He sighed. "But I could not deny you this." He looked back to the camp. "Come. We'll go further from here. Then I will tell you."

They walked to the end of the beach blocked by a landslide down to the water's edge. Kapihi stopped and invited her to sit down one of the many large boulders strewn there.

"It was a long time ago," he said, "but what do you want to know?"

"Everything."

Kapihi sighed, then launched into his story. For Jeannie, it would be the hardest one to bear.

Quietly, Kapihi told her of the fight and their flight from the battlefield to avoid the authorities.

Then Kapihi told her about how Jonas was maimed.

"Please, don't tell me anymore, Kapihi. I can't bear it," said Jeannie. She got up from the boulder and walked away, feeling sick to her stomach.

"I'm sorry to distress you, ma'am, but you asked."

"Yes, I asked. I just never knew. I'd always thought him killed outright. Maimed." Jeannie went over to the bank where gnarled tree roots dangled down from the trees on the ridge above. Wiping away the tears that flowed easily down her cheeks, she took a moment to compose herself. "It hurts to think of him suffering." She turned around. "I'm sorry. You were so young. Just a boy. And you remember this."

"He was my father's *kahpo*, his best friend and—a great *tyee*. Now he is mine."

Jeannie played with her gloves. "What happened after that?" she asked in an unsteady voice. "Did you stay?"

Kapihi thoughtfully bowed his head, then looked up. "Yes. Jo-nuss was very sick. When it was finally dark, there was a great discussion about what to do. Collie and Moki knew that the Bostons and the King Georges were all looking for him. He couldn't be taken to Port Townsend and he couldn't go into the British interior. Doc-tin didn't want to move him, but Collie thought he had a better chance if they could get him to my mother's people. It was a good thing we had left San Juan for the smaller islands. It gave him a start. I went to sleep. When I woke later that night, they had put Jo-nuss into a *salt chuck canim*. He was all bundled up in blankets. I went down with my candle lantern to look at him. He looked very bad. Moki said he was all mixed up and talking to the spirits."

"Did he ever speak clearly?"

"Once. He opened his eyes and looked at me. I was standing in the water looking at him. The *canim* was like a coffin on the water. He was already laid out. He knew me, though, and smiled. Told me to be good. That was all. Collie came over, but Jo-nuss was asleep again. Sometime later, they left for my mother's village."

"Did you see him after that?"

"Not for a long, long time. Maybe ten, eleven years. It was a great surprise. I heard the talk. I thought that he was dead too. I was just a boy. I didn't know that he was quietly hidden away. I just knew that he was very sick. A year after I thought he died, someone sent money so that I could go to school. Then, when I was fourteen, I began to go to sea. First, California, then finally, the Hawaiian Islands, the land of my father. There I met Jo-nuss. In Owyhee."

Jeannie bit her lip, afraid tears would overtake her again. It was still hard thinking of Jonas alive somewhere else all these years, yet he had risked his life to hear word of her getting away.

"Did he know you?"

"Oh, yes. Very well. All those years he was the one who paid for my schooling and the care of my mother and her family."

"Was—is he well?"

"Oh, yes, Missus Pierce." Kapihi smiled broadly, his black eyes shining like polished coal. "He is *hyas skookum*, very powerful. He has a hand like this"—Kapihi made a fist with his left hand and moved it like there was a hook in it— "but he is the same Jo-nuss. The hook hand makes him fierce. He is an even greater *tyee* than before. He has many ships and many *shipmen* under him. He goes everywhere: to China, the British Northwest Coast, California."

"And now he is here," said Jeannie.

"*Ah-ha.* He has come home."

Home. Jeannie looked to east where the sky had continued to lighten so that more of the mountainous islands were visible in the growing light. This had once been home. A place where she had promised that she would never leave. She turned and smiled at Kapihi. "Thank you," she said. "Even if it has been hard, I thank you." She looked down the forested beach where Gilly was standing up and straightening her skirt.

"How much further is it?" Jeannie asked.

"About forty minutes, I think. We should go. There is trouble behind us and you will be safer with Jo-nuss and our men."

"Then let's go," said Jeannie, even though she wasn't sure any more why she wanted to.

TOGETHER

"**G**ood God," said Collie under his breath. "Is it who I think it is?"

Breed made no other comment than to say that he would personally wring Kapihi's neck, but his heart wasn't in it. His shoulders stiffened as the canoe pulled alongside the schooner and bumped against its painted side. He stepped back, a dull pounding building in his chest.

"I guess, all hands." Collie called the morning watch over to help him man the boarding ladder for the passengers.

"Mind yourself there," he called down to Gilly and grunted his approval as she was assisted onto the first wooden tread by Kapihi and a companion. Behind her was Jeannie Pierce.

Breed tried to keep his emotions banked down but he was curious about what the years had done to her. He was not disappointed. Though windburned and chilled from her exposure out in the canoe and surrounded by the dark frame of her bonnet, time seemed to have been gentle to her, giving definition to her high cheeks and oval face. Her figure was still lithe and full in the places they were supposed to be, not given away to middle age dumpiness so many women seemed to achieve at her age. In short, she was beautiful. The dull pounding in Breed's chest turned into a knife.

Toketie. Putting his hands behind his back, Breed backed off and walked aft to the doghouse where he called down to Cookie in the galley.

When the women were on deck, Collie greeted them with guarded courtesy. "Ladies, this is an honor. To what do we owe this visit?" He smiled at Gilly who was in the forefront of the party, but gave Kapihi a good scowl.

Gilly brushed down her skirt. "An encounter with a perfectly dreadful man." She gave a shiver to show what she thought of him, then not waiting for Collie to respond, called down to Breed who had not come forward.

"Jonas, are you going to be standoffish?"

"No, dear lady. It was not my intention. Welcome." Breed smoothed down the little dab of goatee on his chin and came slowly forward.

"You are not happy to see us?" Gilly asked.

"In truth, this is a bad time..." he said.

"There was trouble, *kahpo*," Kapihi blurted out.

"Trouble?" Breed's voice carried across the deck like a trumpet, but the thick, new- morning air stopped it from going beyond the schooner's edge. "That true?" He looked at Gilly, avoiding Jeannie.

"Do you remember Thaddeus Cooperwaite of the old Royal Marine camp? He thought it best to confine us at San Juan Town, though at first I didn't quite understand what for. Jeannie said something about smugglers." Gilly came around Collie and swept down toward Breed. He decided to meet her half way so as not to appear rude. The women's arrival presented a number of problems, the first of which was what to do with them. He couldn't just drop them off in some cove. They would have to come along.

"Cooperwaite?"

"And a Mr. Gutterson whom I suspect has some family relation to that old scoundrel Emmett Krill. Kapihi was there and heard it all." Gilly shook out some sand from her skirt. "A wild night indeed."

Breed looked beyond to Jeannie and for the first time acknowledged her. He tipped his captain's cap to her, but kept his left arm behind his back. "Jeannie," he said quietly, almost a murmur. "You are looking well despite your ride." He wondered how she felt towards him.

"I'm fine," she said. "You are looking well, too, Jonas. How wonderful to see you again."

Breed cleared his throat a little too loudly. "You must all be chilled. I've arranged for coffee and a small breakfast. You may retire below immediately."

"A capital idea," said Gilly. "Come, Captain Henderson. And Kapihi. You must show me where to go. I'm sure Jonas wishes words with Jeannie." With that, she put her hand through Collie's arm and urged him to proceed, leaving Breed no time to protest. Suddenly, the deck was deserted.

"A bloody conspiracy," Breed grumbled, then softened. Jeannie was still waiting at the bulwark.

"I'm sorry, Jonas. Perhaps this wasn't wise, but Kapihi offered a way out."

"What were you doing in San Juan Town?"

Jeannie told him how the horse bolted and they lost their wheel; how Cooperwaite appeared and gave assistance. "Later, I became suspicious when I overheard him talking to a man named Gutterson. Who is he?"

"Emmett Krill's half-brother." He started to say something, then thought better of it. "You shouldn't have come out here. What possessed you to wander through the islands unattended?"

"Why, I came because I learned you were alive. I wanted to see for myself."

Jeannie's words hit him hard. Long suppressed feelings well up. "You came looking for *me?*"

"Yes. I thought I saw you on the docks in Seattle some months ago. After Andrew died, I decided to investigate. It was only a half wish. I didn't really expect what I saw was true. Then I received confirmation. I first went to Victoria where I learned that Gilly had returned. The rest just sort of happened."

"So you set out looking for me. Why, after all this time?"

"Because I wanted to know why you didn't come for me."

Breed stepped back, shaken. He felt his cold shell break away from him though he couldn't keep the bitterness out. "And have you discovered the answer in your travels?"

"Yes, Jonas, I have. You shouldn't have waited for me. Not when your life was in such peril."

"Ah, Kapihi. My chronologist."

"Don't be hard. He loves you like a son."

"He exaggerates."

"He told me the truth." Jeannie came forward, her sand-mottled skirt sweeping the boards of the deck. "I could not live with myself now I know you survived when you could have died as I believed. All because you waited."

"Sounds much too complicated."

"It's not. Oh, Jonas, I'm so sorry." Jeannie's eyes filled up.

Breed didn't know what to say. Jeannie still unsettled him.

"Why don't we go down? We can talk in my quarters."

Down below, at the back of the salon behind the companionway, Jeannie stepped into a comfortable room with bookcases, a desk and several gas light fixtures. One was set over a round eating table. In the middle of the room there was an opened skylight which provided generous light. Next to the built-in bookcases was a small bureau with a large oval mirror. Facing it directly it across the room was the sleeping quarters: a bunk bed built into the wall half-covered by a curtain. The wood paneled walls and brass fixtures added a richness to its simple seafaring sensibility. Yet it reminded her of the cabin on Timons Island. Jeannie sat at the table placed on a rich red Oriental rug.

Breed took her shawl and before she settled in, hot steaming coffee was brought in by a white-haired, wizened-looking man with hairy forearms. From a silver pot, the man poured coffee into a teacup that would rival Jeannie's tea set. For Breed, he filled an old ceramic mug.

"*Mah-sie*, Cookie," Breed said. He nodded that would be all they needed.

After the cook left, Breed took off his coat and hung it up on the coat tree. She chose not look at him directly, but in the mirror over the small bureau, she could see for the first time the hook protruding out of his left shirt sleeve. Its very appearance made her heart sink. It was a weathered-looking gray piece of steel, bent at the end like a question mark. Where his wrist and hand should have been, there was a leather cap that held the hook. She supposed an armlet went under his sweater sleeve. He used the hook deftly, slipping it under the neck of the coat and placing it on one of the coat tree's branches. She looked down at her coffee when he came over to the table.

"It's not to your liking?" He indicated the coffee.

"No, it's fine, Jonas." She helped herself to the little pitcher of cream.

"Good." He reached over and took his mug. With the hook, he took a cloth napkin from a little stack on the tray. She waited for him to sit, but instead he moved back over to his desk. When he dropped the napkin, Jeannie gasped, but with practiced ease he picked it up with a swipe of the hook and placed it on the desk.

"Don't concern yourself, Jeannie. It happened a long time ago."

"Does it hurt?"

"Sometimes. There's a pain where the limb is missing, but it's a pain that can be mastered. Little ghosts."

She started to say "so sorry" again, but she seemed to be repeating herself so said instead that since she left Seattle, she had become acquainted with her own little ghosts. "Time seems to have been twisted back on itself."

"Ghosts?"

"Jeremy. I have been thinking so on Jeremy."

Breed smiled softly and nodded his head. "He was a lively little lad."

"You used to say he was *hyas skookum*."

"So he was."

You once thought that of me too, Jeannie thought, but she did not voice it. She took a sip of her coffee while he settled back on the edge of his desk and nursed his mug. And since he did not speak, her eyes began to stray and fell on a picture setting next to him. Set in a brass frame, it held the image of a young woman: dark hair parted in the middle, high cheek bones and skin as light as the silvery tone of the tintype. Despite the rigid pose, there was a quiet beauty about her as she sat with her hands folded in front of her.

"That's my wife, Annie McDougall."

"She's pretty, Jonas."

"*Ah-ha*. She was. Dead these past ten years."

"Gilly says that you had children."

"A son and a daughter. I only buried Hannah the other day out in these very islands. Like her mother, she had the consumption which seems to strike at Kanaka and Salish people alike."

"I'm so sorry, Jonas. I don't know what to say, except my own understanding of the deep grief you must feel. And your son?"

"Ransom is studying medicine in Boston. London after that. It's his heart's desire. Been gone for a year now."

"Ransom. That's an unusual name."

"It's for the ransom I paid to be free." He looked pointedly at her. "It was for Annie. After the fight, I was hidden and cared for by Sally Kalama's family. The Nooksack village was deep in the wilderness. Annie's father was a trader at Fort Langley in the British Columbia Colony. Her mother was part Stó:lo, part Kanaka. She came down to see one of her aunties in this village. Found me occupying one of the benches in the long house. She stayed, then when I was stronger, went with me to Hawaiian Islands. I had, by then, learned that you had married." He scowled. "I did ill by her, at first. I reformed myself. Ransom was the debt I owed her and my own freedom. I've never regretted it."

Jeannie swallowed. He was defending himself, but the bitterness in his voice troubled her. She had never known him like that, but then there were twenty years between them and memory.

"Have you been happy, Jeannie?" It was a simple question, asked quietly.

"Yes, I have. It's been a good life. I have a son and daughter too. They are good children, grown into adults. And it has been more than a life of teas and social niceties. I have tried to make a difference in the community, especially for women and children of all backgrounds and situations. We have a women's league and a literacy society for the poor, of which I play a part."

"I'm glad for it. You deserved it. It's what I wished for you."

Jeannie took a sip, then put down her cup. "I'm sure you did, Jonas. It has been totally satisfying, yet in the last three days I have come to wonder if it was contrived. Was it real? And did I really have a say in it? Tell me, when did you decide to become Jonas Waddell?"

"I suppose Kapihi has enlightened you on that?"

"No, I found reference to your new name in papers Mr. Simpson held for me at the Victoria office. They belonged to Andrew."

"Ah, Andrew. My partner. Never were two so linked."

"He was angry with you."

"I'm sure he was. He was a rather stubborn, hard-headed man. Now he's gone. I'm sorry he's left you a widow with fatherless children. For that, I truly am."

"But he cheated you."

Breed scowled. "How would you know anything about that?"

"I didn't. Not until the last few days. He took claims from you."

"That is another matter. Not worth discussing here." He mechanically sipped from his mug.

"At least you could tell me how and when you became Waddell."

"I made the decision once in Honolulu. It was my mother's maiden name."

"And you had no commerce in the Pacific Northwest before that?"

"No, not until after Annie died. I brought her home here, you see, and when I saw the islands and great mountains again, I felt a longing to be here, but with the boundary issue still not settled, I decided I could not safely come, so I sent Collie."

"Even if you had been exonerated?"

"*Ah-ha.* But it was more than that. My children were small and they needed me. Besides, I already had commerce enough in the Hawaiian Islands and Hong Kong."

"Yet you bought out over half of the company in less than two years later."

"That's true."

"And you met with Andrew. By what he wrote, he was furious to learn you were Waddell."

"He was surprised. That's true as well."

"And you continued to meet, conspiring to keep this partnership a secret from me?"

"No. Collie did the business for me. And after that, Mr. Simpson in Victoria. He is a very able man, Mr. Simpson. Very upstanding and honest."

"My uncle chose him."

"Indeed, he did."

Jeannie fidgeted with her napkin. "Did you ever see my uncle? Did he ever know that you were alive?"

"I was tempted to tell him. Archie and I had a far deeper friendship than you may realize. He supported me when I returned to white society in the 1850s, even though there was a suspicion of me in Victoria. I have always been grateful. I know he defended me during those hard days after Kaui Kalama was murdered, but Archie was in ill health the year I took over the firm. I worried it might put further strain on him as I could only continue my exile. Instead, I let him know through my associates that as chief partner in the firm, Waddell would insure the solvency of the company and it would be ruled according to the principles he believed in."

"And you kept it secret all these years."

"I thought it best."

"For whom? Not for me, did you?"

Breed's silence was his answer.

"Did you buy the firm out for revenge, Jonas? Against Andrew?"

"No," Jonas said, raising his voice slightly, "I did it for Archibald Campbell who was my friend and who was being cheated out of his share by the mismanagement of the company."

Jeannie gasped and looked at him in disbelief. "Are you implying that Andrew was deceitful with my uncle?"

Jonas got up from the desk, his face flushed. "Do you want me to answer that? Enough, Jeannie. I think enough has been said."

"Do you?"

"You shouldn't have come. I should pack you back into the canoe and send you away, but I need my men."

"I wouldn't go. Not with words such as these hanging in the air." Jeannie's voice rose and became hard. "You don't know the price I paid."

"You don't know what you are getting into here," Breed said harshly. His eyes flashed with anger.

"I know that Gutterson intends to manipulate you and have you join his smuggling trade."

"You heard him say that?" Breed laughed. Some of the anger went out of his face.

"Why is it so humorous?" Jeannie asked.

"He doesn't know what he's bought into either." Breed picked up his mug. "We need to join the others. I have preparations to make before we set sail. The hour is coming quickly."

"What hour?"

"The hour of justice." His words flew at her.

She had no chance to tell him about Phillip gone missing.

Breed escorted Jeannie into the warmth of the schooner's galley. Both subdued and closed-mouth, they avoided Gilly's curious look. Once he let Jeannie go ahead of him, Breed stayed back near the doorway. They could have been on the opposite ends of the world.

Jeannie sat down next to Gilly on the cushioned booth seat at the galley table and without a word, scooted in. A new cup was given her, but she declined.

"Jeannie, you must take something," Gilly whispered. "At least, some marmalade and these delicious biscuits."

"No, thank you. I'm quite all right."

"You haven't had a thing, I can tell."

"I'm fine," Jeannie protested under her breath. She glanced at Breed, afraid he was watching, but he was engaged in conversation with an older man at the doorway whom she suddenly realized was Neville Hector, the one Breed's friends called Doc-tin. Breed listened intently, then nodding, stepped back into the salon. Somehow she knew he was not coming back.

"Mrs. Pierce," Doc-tin said, "May I welcome you? It has been some time since we met. I hope that you are comfortable."

Jeannie brushed aside her hurt feelings and smiled at him. "Has it been twenty years? I could scarce believe it after our canoe ride last night. How familiar it seemed."

Doc-tin came next to the table. He took the hand she offered and bowed over it. "Madame, the years have been kind to you. You are as lovely as ever."

Jeannie truly smiled now. "How kind you are, Neville."

"It's the truth, so help me. May I?" he asked, indicating an anchored captain's chair opposite the women. He eased into it cautiously. "Jonas has asked me to make sure that you are settled. We will be underway now in just a short time." He reached for the coffee urn and poured some into a ceramic mug.

"Where *are* we going?" Gilly asked. "Or should I say where are *you* going?"

"Up to the smaller islands north of here. We want to be ahead of Gutterson and his men."

"Any particular reason why?" Gilly asked. She had to speak in a loud, unladylike voice for suddenly there was a raucous rattling sound that seemed to fill the ship. "What is *that*?"

Jeannie, still stunned by her reunion with Breed, looked up through the galley skylight, but could only see the varnished wood of the mast shining in the early morning light. She drifted again, barely paying attention to the conversation next to her.

"The anchor, ma'am. The winches are being employed."

"Not by hand?" Gilly leaned in.

"Heavens, no. This schooner is a modern ship. It has a steam engine to do the duty of what would be many men in the past. It's been designed after those fishing boats in the east. Takes only a small crew to man it while the rest are out to sea in their dories. Jonas found it suitable for these waters here. Of course, in our case, the winches leave it free for our men to do their duty."

"And what is that?"

'Now, Gilly, if I may again after so many years claim that name freely, this matter is best left to us, but if you insist I will only say that as customs officer for the district, it is in the way of revenue collection for which this ship is doubly suitable."

"So this is official business?"

Doc-tin cleared his throat. "It's legitimate enough. It will all be duly reported. We should be able to find a safe haven to anchor the boat and keep you in safety."

"In safety?"

"We're meeting Gutterson on shore. He doesn't know the extent of our intentions."

"Oh," Gilly said.

"You're expecting trouble?" Jeannie asked, suddenly engaged.

"Jonas wants to be cautious. Especially where Cooperwaite is concerned."

"And why is that?" she said, her voice half lost in the increasing noise overhead as another winch began to hoist the main sail. Someone called out and feet began to scramble around the deck. Up the stairs in the chartroom, the captain's clock struck three tinny bells into the morning watch, its voice nearly lost in the commotion. She turned and looked behind her at the little brass clock screwed to the wooden shelf behind her. It said five-thirty in the morning.

"Cooperwaite is the only one who can identify him," answered Doc-tin. "Might make things a bit sticky."

"Gutterson doesn't know who Waddell is, does he?" she said.

"No, but Cooperwaite surely will recognize him. He must not see Jonas until the appropriate time."

Gilly gasped and clapped her hands together. "You intend to entrap him, don't you?"

"He's a bold smuggler. A revenue boat followed him down from New Westminster, British Columbia a couple of months ago. They knew he had the goods, yet when they boarded, they found nothing. Later one of the men observed a halyard rope dangling off the stern. Probably dragging his haul, then cut it loose when the customs men got too close. He got clean away."

"It wasn't the only way, was it? He made use of the firm," Jeannie said.

"*Ah-ha*, he did. Crafty too, though that's more of Gutterson's making. Cooperwaite's been providing the hideouts, mainly. Has the more troublesome goods buried on some of the islands north of here, we suspect. Opium, for instance."

Jeannie shook her head. She had always thought Cooperwaite a pompous, opinionated sort, but not a man of a criminal nature. He had sunk low since he left the marine camp so long ago. "What *do* you know of Mr. Cooperwaite?" she asked.

Doc-tin scowled. "Just know he joined the gold rushes up in the northern interior for a couple of years, then returned to this region at the time of the settlement of the boundary issue. Homesteaded, but that has been a rather dubious cover for his real activities. When he came into Gutterson's crowd, I don't know, but he's been an efficient rogue. His activities haven't been known by the general public."

Doc-tin put down his cup. "Now, if you will excuse me, I have to go topside. Before I do, however, I should like to offer a place for you to rest. After your journey last night, I'm sure you wish to sleep. A place is being made ready for you at this moment."

"What happens once we're at our destination?" Gilly wondered.

"You'll stay on board here. You will be quite safe."

"You seem occupied with the word, 'safe,' Hector." Jeannie stirred on her seat at the table. "This is the second time you have said it. I fear that you're not telling us everything. Was our discomfort with Mr. Cooperwaite more than our imagination was creating? Were we in real danger?"

Doc-tin flushed. "Ladies, what *is* it about you, this propensity for suspicion? My wife knows when I tell her I am going fishing exactly whether or not it's fish I'm after."

"You are evading the question."

"There's more to it than smuggling. There is reason to believe he has committed murder—perhaps more than once."

Both women gasped in unison.

Doc-tin stood up. "Now ladies, if you would be so good as to let me show you your quarters. We are underway now. You may find them a place of refuge." He motioned to a young Indian boy working at the stove in the galley. "Will you come with us, Jimmy? Find *hiyu paseesie*, pillows."

Gilly scooted out from the bench and went towards the hallway Doc-tin indicated, but Jeannie held back at the table.

"Gilly, will you go? I wish to speak to Doc-tin. If you don't mind, Hector."

Doc-tin shrugged, then gave a few instructions to the boy. Gilly gave her friend a reassuring smile, then with the boy leading the way, followed him down the narrow hall now rising and falling gently as the schooner made way across the cove. When they were gone, Jeannie clasped her hands in front of her and set them on the table.

"Troubled?" Doc-tin asked.

"He will not speak to me. He only intimates difficulties yet will not say what they are."

Doc-tin grunted softly, then sat back down in his chair. "I take it that it was not a happy reunion?"

Jeannie played with the beaded material on her reticule. "I don't know what I should have expected after all this time, except some warmth. I feel he blames me for his injury."

Doc-tin leaned over his hands and said earnestly, "Oh, no, dear, he doesn't. He feels inadequate. No, that's not the word. He's as nervous as a schoolboy on meeting you again."

"Jonas? He sounded bitter."

"He has much on his mind. Your coming surprised him."

"You speak as though he never meant to seek me out at all."

Doc-tin shook his graying head. "In time. Just too much to deal with. The firm has been in a crisis since Pierce's death. The death of Jonas's daughter only complicated matters more. Her loss has been devastating."

"Yes, of course, Hannah. Well I know what it is to lose a child." Jeannie sighed lightly. Doc-tin smiled gently at her. "Was your meeting so difficult?"

"Jonas implied Andrew cheated my uncle."

"Oh, dear."

"My solicitor, Burgess, said that all was well, but I know it is not well. Mr. Simpson, our representative in Victoria, has said that Burgess is not at all trustworthy. Now, my son Phillip is missing. He was supposed to be with—" Jeannie's voice broke, exhaustion starting to overtake her. She composed herself. "Phillip is supposed to be with him, but Burgess is also missing. Does this have anything to do with this Gutterson?"

Doc-tin worked his mouth, like he was trying to get rid of a bitter taste. "Possibly." He leaned in. "I do assure you that we are aware of your son's disappearance. Some hours ago. Jonas sent men to look for him. I guarantee that he will be found."

"How did you know?"

"One of Jonas's men found out." Doc-tin didn't elaborate. "It's one of many troubles in the firm."

He went on to tell her of the discovery of smuggled goods, the false records and hidden numbers and earlier run-ins the firm had years ago. He also spoke of some of the legal wrangling over Breed's former claims and Breed's handling of the firm once it came under his control. He even intimated at some of the personal struggles between the men from the time Pierce knew that Breed was still alive to Pierce's recent entanglement with Anders Gutterson. While the cook clattered around in the galley kitchen, they sat for nearly thirty minutes at the table. When he was finished, Jeannie looked up at him with large, sorrowful eyes.

"I can't stop thinking about his wounding. Kapihi told me he waited for me to be on my way with Andrew before he would submit to you. I hate thinking of him suffering."

"He only suffered until he knew you were safe, until the edge of the sword took the poison away, until the decision was made for him to go to Hawaii. After that, he started over."

Jeannie swallowed. Her voice became smaller. "Did he say anything when he heard I married?"

Doc-tin grimaced. "Not with words. He had been very ill for weeks, but finally improving." Doc-tin reached for the pot on the table and poured himself some more coffee. "After he learned of it, he did close himself up and waste away. Medically, I had done all I could. But his spirit was missing."

"Oh." Jeannie swallowed and turned away, afraid to look at Doc-tin. "Is that when the girl came? Annie McDougall?"

"*Ah-ha*. She would sit with him for hours as he lay on the bench in her family's longhouse. Eventually, he took interest enough and his health improved. Mind you, I didn't really know her that well. I wasn't always able to be there so I had no inkling of anything between them. But I will tell you she was a proper young lady from what I saw. Well educated and refined as best her parents could give her in that wilderness. Her marriage to him came less than a year after they arrived in the islands."

Jeannie's eyes filled up. Tears began to silently roll down her cheeks. "I never knew. I thought him dead. I thought I would never be the same. And—"Jeannie looked at Doc-tin and judged him. *Should I tell him?* She looked into the galley. The cook was gone. She took a big breath and leaning in, whispered "—and I carried Jonas's child. Could I really say no to Andrew?"

Doc-tin's head jerked up. His glasses went askew. For a moment he was speechless, but Jeannie could almost see his racing thoughts on his face as he collected them. "Bless you, dear. Now it all makes sense."

He laid his hands over hers. "I knew you were true to Jonas. I knew there was an explanation."

Jeannie sniffed. "And you do not condemn me?" Her lips trembled.

"Oh, no." Doc-tin's voice thickened. "I think I love you even more." He squeezed her hands.

Jeannie bowed her head. Relief flowed through her. Finally, she looked up. "Do you think Jonas guessed?"

Doc-tin shook his head. "He may have wondered, but I don't think he's ever seen a portrait of your— son. What do you want to do now?"

Jeannie pulled her hands away and dabbed her eyes on a handkerchief. "I seem to be adrift in some grand plan. Of course, I will do what Jonas wants me to do while you carry out your action, but I do hope Phillip can be found. Then, when everything is settled, I will tell Jonas."

Doc-tin smiled softly. "Very admirable. Whenever you choose to tell him, I will support you. If you choose not, the secret stays with me."

Doc-tin got up. "Collie says that Jonas was cheated. But maybe everyone has been cheated out of what was, what should have been. Yet, now you too must let it go. After today, everyone must let it go."

Jeannie sniffed again, seeking a handkerchief from her reticule. "You keep saying after today. I don't understand. Are you speaking of the arrest of Cooperwaite and Gutterson and how it will solve the firm's present difficulties? Or of the past?"

Doc-tin frowned, a deep sadness clouding his eyes, "It's more than about smuggling and corruption in the firm. It's about Shells Shining."

Wilson woke at the first sound. His fingers touched the pearl handle of his revolver slipped under his mildewed pillow. From outside the fly-specked window set in the rough cedar board wall like a square Cyclops eye, a winter wren began its dizzy call. Wilson stared at his pocket watch leaning against the lantern set on a barrel next to his bed. It said six o'clock, but the summer sun had already been up for hours and pecking at the ring of the giant cedar trees around the homestead. Wilson sat up and listened again. On the other side of the wall, came only the stamp of the horse that had been led in last night from the rain. Wilson got up and pulled up his suspenders, then went in his stockinged feet to the door that led into the main part of the barn. He listened for moment, the revolver cocked, then opened the door.

There was no one there. He made a quick check, then stepped back into the room and closed the door, pocketing his revolver. He put on his boots and slipped out the side door set close to the cedar trees. The air was cool and heavy with morning dew, stirring lazily around the boughs and understory of the tall giants. He took a few short steps and he was in their quiet shelter where he could observe the homestead. He held himself close to a shaggy trunk and waited.

"You pretty damn good," a voice said next to him.

Wilson jumped, then relaxed. It was Lakit, Sikhs's son-in-law.

"I heard something, but wasn't sure what it was."

"I've been here a short time. I saw you stand up through the window. There's no one else."

"It's not very secure here, then."

"No, it's pretty good. There's one *hyas* swamp behind here. You have to go around all that skunk cabbage. Come through and you sink to your thighs."

Wilson checked to see if Lakit had come through the swamp. He was dry.

Wilson looked back towards the side of the barn. Beyond it, he could see the farmhouse. The back porch door was shut, the hand washing pan still upside down. No one was visibly awake.

He looked around the forest, half hidden in mist. He knew something was coming, assuredly as the odd, half-remembered twinge beginning to tighten in his gut. It was a cool, semi-shrouded morning like this when he left his Union encampment set in a forest and never looked back.

"Jo-nuss say he see Cooperwaite?"

"No, he hadn't. You know Cooperwaite?"

"I know Cooperwaite. *Hyas mesahchie.*"

"I'd say it goes for the whole bunch. Coward, Krill, Cooperwaite."

"Someone's awake up in the house," Lakit said. He pointed at the smoke rising out of the stone chimney atop the shake roof of the building and adding depth to the mist already hanging there.

Wilson wiped his mouth and mustache on his handkerchief, then pocketed it.

"I'll go offer my help, then keep an eye on the road. I'll see about breakfast."

"Well, lookit that." Laki nodded down the dirt lane. A lone figure was walking up in the open.

"Company," Wilson said. "Time to work."

ANDREW

"**K**ah-po? We're here."

Breed looked up to the island that lay in front of them. "Good," he said to Collie.

Breed was pleased they had made good time from their last position, reaching the inlet in under two hours and ahead of Gutterson and his men. The weather had cleared. That would translate into a comfortable landing and arrangement of his men. Sikhs, Tenas John and the other Songhees and S'Klallam men were to be under cover the whole time, placing themselves throughout the island in case there was trouble. Others from the crew would reconnoiter, locate any extraordinary watercraft and destroy it. Once the exchange was made, Doc-tin could step in and arrest Gutterson and any others.

Whether Cooperwaite would be there or not was unknown. Breed hoped that he would be. He had known about Cooperwaite's collaboration with Gutterson for some time. There was some conjecture that he might have had a hand in Pierce's death, for it had been no accident. Breed was more interested in Cooperwaite for a separate matter. He felt that he had things in good order for the meeting.

The only thing troubling him now was how coldly he had treated Jeannie. Meeting her had not gone as he had imagined it. He had

intended to approach her after Gutterson and his organization had
been dealt with, but her impetuous decision to go to Victoria and
subsequently to Gilly Parker's homestead on San Juan Island had
thrown him off. Worse, her sudden appearance wrecked any notion of
a discreet meeting. Thrown together so quickly after so many years
apart was disconcerting. Everything he had practiced saying, failed.
Instead, he had become angry over her questioning his motives for
buying the firm. Once again, Andrew Pierce had come between them.

His arrangement with Pierce had worked well. At least once a year,
Collie would come to the Pacific Northwest and deal with any important matters in the firm of Campbell, Pierce and Waddell. Pierce
served on the board as its president and was effective enough, but
behind the scenes, it was Simpson who saw to the firm's overall financial soundness. The firm became solvent again and grew. Pierce was
an affable spokesman for the firm and served it well in that capacity.
Over time, he began to make much of his position's social and cere-
monial duties, touting his success as a businessman and community
leader. Pierce had become an important figure in Seattle, hobnobbing
with other businessmen and the most influential politicos in the territorial legislature.

He began to delegate some of his duties to others, taking credit for
any successes. Breed didn't care. He was busy with his own interests
in the Pacific and in British Columbia to the north to pay much more
attention to Pierce. It was only during the last year that Breed had
become impatient with Pierce. When smuggled goods were discovered in the warehouse in Port Townsend, Breed ordered an
accounting to be made discreetly. Events moved quickly after that.
First, questionable appointments were investigated, then Gutterson's
infiltration was discovered. Further digging uncovered Cooperwaite's
involvement. At that, Breed made a momentous decision—he would
return to the Pacific Northwest and meet with Pierce.

They met in December, across Elliot Bay and around a headland
from Seattle. It was a hilly, sparsely settled place, the few isolated
homesteads there surrounded by massive trees and wetlands popu-
lated with skunk cabbage and bracken fern. The only road was a trail.

It was a clear, sharp morning when Pierce came ashore in a skiff and walked up the stony beach until he saw the trail that led up onto the bench of land above. When he saw Breed, he hesitated, then continued on. Breed stood underneath a massive cedar, bundled in a sweater and an unbuttoned wool coat. Two canvas chairs were set next to a small folding table on which food and a coffeepot had been set out.

"It too cold for you?" Pierce asked as he declined the cup offered. "Your blood has grown thin, Breed."

"It has been some years since I lived here."

"You intend to stay?"

Breed's eyes flashed, but didn't answer. To him, Andrew Pierce was a study. He hadn't changed much over the years. He was slightly balding, his hair a faded blonde and cut fashionably to match his beard and sideburns. He was still tall and thin—though he had a slight paunch—and except for lines around his eyes and mouth, he was still handsome in a long, angular way. Just older. Yet, there was arrogance underneath the affability that was hard to ignore. He had come so far, had done so well. It showed in the way he held his head, the straightness of his back. Pierce hadn't had a hard day's labor in years. For Breed, it had been his way of life. He felt that he could not command without showing that he could shoulder his own weight with his men.

He invited Pierce to sit down, but Pierce remained standing, his eyes fixed on Breed's hook hand. Breed ignored Pierce's stare. "As you wish." He stepped away from the chairs, nodding to Collie Henderson behind them.

"Are *you* feeling important?" Pierce asked sarcastically as he looked sharply in Henderson's direction. "You command so many."

"Are you feeling threatened?"

"You know damn well, I am. How dare you imply that I had anything to do with this."

"That's the point. You didn't. You weren't paying attention. Something has been amiss for months. Simpson wrote a report."

Pierce snorted. "A report!"

"Yes, a report. It was given to you. Didn't you read it?"

"Not initially. There was some important legislation pending at the time. I was occupied."

"Now are *you* feeling important?"

"Maybe I am. Maybe I am in a position where I can finally get you off my back. We won't be a territory for much longer. And I have friends." Pierce had been there for only a few moments e was already boiling with resentment.

Breed smiled sardonically and shook his head. "You forget who the primary partner here is. Your political chums don't frighten me. I think you should, however, be frightened of Anders Gutterson."

"I never heard of him."

"Well, you should. He's Emmett Krill's half-brother." When Pierce shrugged in disinterest, Breed went on. "Their family history is not important. Their illegal activities, however, are another matter. It appears little brother has outdone big brother."

"How?"

"Smuggling goods and laborers, prostitution, extortion, gambling. Not to mention opium. He has apparently been doing business with our firm for some time."

Pierce blanched.

Breed sat down in one of the chairs. He pushed aside the cups with his hook, then using the tip of the steel appendage, drew a leather-bound book to the edge of the table.

"Sit down, Pierce. Please." He reached for the book with his good hand and put it in his lap. The hook flipped it open and between hand and hook, Breed got to the page he wanted.

"You should watch that new boy of yours, Frederick Howell," Breed said. "I don't trust him. Don't know exactly what he does, but I believe that he reports to Gutterson, somehow."

Pierce continued to stand. "I picked Howell," he said meekly. Breed ignored him.

"This ledger is a list of scheduled shipments between Seattle, Port Townsend and Victoria for the past year. It details the contents of the shipments. On the surface, it appears legitimate. The discovery of the smuggled goods last month, however, tends to dispute that. Yet, they have moved smoothly through the delivery system without alarm. Closer scrutiny suggests that there might be another ledger to ghost this one. That this has been going on for at least a couple of years." Breed tapped the page. "The answer is somewhere in the accounting. There were some difficulties again, weren't there?"

"With the firm?"

"Just some minor problems. That panic in the late '70's. Some mine closings, lumber mill failings. That couldn't have helped."

"Yes," Pierce mumbled.

"Could have left a door open, though. I'm not suggesting that you were tempted to act rashly again as you did ten years ago."

"But you will remind me of it." A muscle in Pierce's jaw flinched.

Breed closed the book and placed it on the table. "That is on your conscience, not mine."

"My conscience! You're a murderer and instigator!"

"Enough!" Breed shouted. He slammed his hook down on the book, gashing its rich red cover, then shot up from his seat. Pierce flinched. There was movement behind the cedar. Collie appeared with two other men.

"*Kahpo?*"

Breed waved him off. "It's all right. Just a policy discussion. Got a little heated. Would appreciate it if you would replenish the coffeepot, Collie. I should like a hot cup. I'm sure Andrew would too."

Pierce cleared his throat. "Yes, thank you. That would be would be considerate. It is rather cool out."

Breed walked to the edge of the woods. Down in front, two men waited for Pierce on the beach. Beyond their skiff, the water was as gray as a school slate. Sheep grazed in a cleared field on the heavily-forested island across the Sound. Wispy clouds scattered across a blue sky. A pleasant scene, despite the damp chill and slight breeze off the water. Though it felt cold to him, Breed had forgotten the mildness of the winters here.

"In my youth," he said, "I could be out on a day like this nearly naked and think nothing of it. A cloak made from a wool blanket and a cedar hat was sufficient. I could work for hours hollowing out a

451

cedar log, burning it, shaping it until it was put into the water as a magnificent canoe."

"I cannot imagine what it would have been like to be in such a heathen place under such circumstances."

"That is the difference between us. You could never countenance anything that you felt beneath your understanding." Breed turned around. "Such as friendship. You were my friend once and I trusted you."

"So we are partners now and you do not trust me. That is your doing."

"Should I? Stop calling me a murderer, an instigator for something that happened years ago when this was still a nervous, unsettled place. I was exonerated, pardoned for that day."

"For killing Emmett Krill and others in the fight, yes. But in many minds, not for Engstrom Pratt who lost his head so despicably."

"You still think about that? Those were unsettled times, Andrew. There was a whole people who were decimated by smallpox and trickery. The northern tribes who raided for riches and glory. Yet most of our countrymen did not bother to make the distinction between friend and foe and grouped them all as one."

"Does anyone know who killed Pratt?"

"It has taken me many years to find out, but I know it was not Comes Shouting's men, though they had every reason to do so. It was a Quileute. Pratt had cheated him a few weeks before over on the Olympic Peninsula. Pratt probably thought he could do it again."

"Can charges be made?"

"No. The Quileute is dead and it would be difficult to prosecute the rest of his men. It does absolve Comes Shouting, who still lives."

"Then what of the woman, the one who was abused and left for dead?"

Breed stiffened suddenly. His eyes grew hard. He changed the subject. "What are you the most afraid of? What do you hate?"

"That you covet my wife," Pierce blurted out.

Breed moved away from him and did a strange thing: he raised up his left arm and sighted the hook up with a thin cedar sapling fifteen feet away. "Isn't it odd that I come from so far to be here, yet you do not ask after my voyage nor my feelings at being here after so many, long years? You do not ask after *my* family." He lowered his arm. "Do you know that I have a beautiful, lively daughter and a son any man would be proud of? Do you know the state of their hearts and affairs? Have you ever asked or cared?"

"You have bound me to you. You will never let me forget!"

"That you wanted me dead as was rumored? That you could have Jeannie freely with just a little lie? That you took my lands?" Breed was angry now. "Covet her? I loved Jeannie Naughton. I would have done anything for her," he shouted. He raised his left arm and shook the hook. "I could not come because of *this* and because people feared and hated what they could not understand. So I trusted you. *You*, Pierce." Breed's voice was loud and filled with anger. Collie and the other men reappeared. They did not go away this time.

"But..." he went on, his voice beginning to soften, "once I lost her, I did not covet her. All these years, I never approached her nor made myself known to her as I have to you. You know that. You're pathetic, Pierce. I don't think you know her heart, even after all this time. She would never leave you, married as she is. She made a vow to you. Breaking it would be too hurtful."

"You don't think taking over the firm was coveting? You have access to everything I own."

"No, and you know the truth to that. Archie Campbell was my good friend."

Pierce began to shake. He recklessly blurted out, "Tell me this, then. Did you ever lay with her?"

"You bastard!" Breed shouted. "Is that what you think? My coveting? Is that what has poisoned you since you've known I was alive?" He started to bring the hook up and slash it down onto Pierce's head, but he checked himself. He punched the man in the mouth.

Pierce cried out in horror as he was thrown backwards.

From the corner of his eye, Breed could see Collie pull his sword, but his concentration was on Pierce who was fumbling to wipe blood from his mouth with a handkerchief.

"You're sick," Breed said.

Pierce choked and spit out blood. His eyes filled with tears. His hands were shaking.

Breed made eye contact with Collie. "Collie. Whiskey, please." Collie sheathed his sword and returned with a whiskey bottle. Breed took one of the cups on the table and filled it halfway. He shoved it at Pierce who first balked, then downed it in one gulp.

"We have a problem, Pierce. It is not who has what," said Breed. "It's what has been done to the firm. It needs to be corrected immediately. I fear physical harm, if it is not."

Pierce's head shot up. Breed shook his head. "Not from me. Gutterson and Cooperwaite. For the good of the firm, can we put aside personal feelings and be clear on that?"

Pierce cleared his throat and gently daubed his mouth with his fingers. "What of Cooperwaite? What can he do?"

"Copperwaite's quite dangerous. He's been smuggling for years. Gutterson may do the daily, dirty work—which was recently exposed —but Cooperwaite is a higher stakes player. He's not ashamed of murder, especially since he knows he might have been found out."

"Do you have proof? The authorities should know."

"They will know. But not right now. At first, we need to find the ledger. Bring it in as soon as you can."

"Me?"

"Yes, I'm relying on you to do it. The ledger is somewhere in the firm, perhaps in plain sight."

"And what will you do?"

"Return home. I promised my daughter Hannah a trip to San Francisco this coming year. You will be told how to reach me. When you find the evidence needed, I'll come. Remember that you can rely totally on Wilson. He will protect your family."

Pierce nodded, cowed.

"You can redeem yourself, Andrew. You can make it right."

"And how would I do that? What else must I do?" he asked bitterly, the taste of blood still in his mouth.

"Be happy with Jeannie and make her happy in genuine ways."

It was the last time Breed saw Andrew Pierce. The following April, Pierce found the secret ledger. Breed came back to Seattle to meet with him. The meeting never happened. Pierce was found drowned near the boat where they were to meet. The ledger was not with him. It was in the possession of a street urchin Pierce had instructed to give to the man with the hook. Breed found Pierce dead. The boy alive with the ledger, then disappeared.

THE PLAN

W hile the men divided themselves up for dispersal through the island, Collie and Breed stayed back for a last-minute review with Doc-tin. The women slept below, giving the three men the opportunity to talk openly. They sat on seats in the chart room and went over their strategy for the meeting with Anders Gutterson. It was to be a small group without Doc-tin's presence as he might be recognized as the customs officer in the region. Collie and Sam Hunter, a crewmember chosen for his clerk-like looks, would come out with Breed along with Kapihi. Breed was already dressed in his best suit in order to present himself as someone out of place and easily duped.

"You've put on weight, Jonas." Doc-tin said.

"A temporary situation." Breed patted his chest and belly with a wry grin. It gave off a dull sound. Underneath his shirt, a horsehair-filled pillow had been tied to the top of a lid from the galley stove to give him bulk. The primitive costume device hung from his shoulders with belt straps.

"But are you armed?"

Breed picked up a Remington double-barreled derringer. "I have this, but I should be fine as long as Gutterson doesn't become suspicious." Breed looked down into the galley where he could only see the table and floor. "The women are still asleep. Probably better that way. Patterson's staying back. It should be adequate protection, don't you think?"

"I think so," said Collie. "We were nearly an hour ahead of Gutterson's men. They made for the other side earlier on."

"The first group of men can go."

"As we speak, *kahpo*."

From the deck they could heard movement as the first group went over the side into canoes.

"Now we should go," said Breed.

They landed on a fine gray beach dotted with clumps of tall, sharp-edged grass. Ghostly shapes of trees and other natural flotsam bleached by the channel waters lay strewn about the length of the beach. At the center of the low, dog-bone-shaped island, there was a natural opening between two small forested hills. Snowberry bushes formed a scattered hedgerow on their flanks, backed by tall madrone and big-leaf maple trees. The canoes were beached further away and secured, then the men dispersed into the trees and brush. Breed took the center path going from the beach into a sheltered glade followed by Collie and Hunter. There they used a path well-known to both of them. It rose gently up from where they stood and was wide enough for two abreast to pass easily

"We're to meet on the other side and south of here," Collie explained to Hunter as they walked along. "Gutterson will be there along with some of his crowd. Not more than four as agreed, but only two to talk. You and Jonas, Gutterson and his pick of the litter."

"Where does this trail go?" Hunter asked.

"It winds through the trees there, then cuts back above the edge of the water on the other side," Collie answered. "It's all sandstone around here. There are some big boulders there, so you can't get down every easily to the beach. Have to go up into the trees again and go around. Gutterson wants us to meet there."

With that, Collie left him to join Breed who was walking ahead of them.

The trail turned as Collie described, breaking out into a narrow, pleasant bay. It was deserted except for a lone gull skimming its way across the water. Its cry echoed between the low bluffs at either end of the bay. The waters seemed expansive as there were no islands directly in front of Breed and his men, only channel water flowing out with the tide. The beach was a long, narrow strip of sand, but large boulders prevented easy descent. They were dry and smooth, providing little traction for the boots the men wore.

Breed stopped to look briefly, then continued on the trail that followed the jumble of the boulders. A hundred feet later, the trail came to an abrupt stop. The only way to continue was to go up. Breed grabbed an exposed root of one of the cedar trees and pulled himself up into a mixed glade of maple, cedar saplings and madrone trees. Collie followed, carefully placing his boots in the natural footholds like Swiss cheese holes wind-blasted in the sandstone wall. When they were on top, they picked up the trail again and followed it along under the cool shadows of the trees. It was very still and no one talked. The water seemed far away, encaged behind the rusty-red, slender trunks of the madrone trees, but occasionally, they had a glimpse of the beach would come through. It was still deserted. They made good time.

After climbing steadily, the trail narrowed and began to descend into a deep glade. Before they reached the bottom, the trail split in two. Breed pointed in the direction of the path where the sky was visible among the trees. Salmonberry bushes and stinging nettle dominated its edges. Soon they reached the edge of the bay. The beach was gray and sandy with a large collection of beached driftwood. To their left, a sandstone cliff which supported the forest they had just passed through on top, rose about thirty feet into the air. To their right, an even higher cliff rose above a stand of trees that intermingled with grasses and sedges lining the beach. The cliff's summit was hidden from view. Breed's party made their way out onto the beach and stopped.

"This should do, *kahpo*." Collie said.

"As good as any, Breed replied.

THE SUM OF ALL EVIL

For a moment Jeannie stared at the plank boards above her and wondered where she was. Then she remembered. She was on Jonas' schooner somewhere off San Juan Island. After her humiliating meeting with him and her frank talk with Neville, exhaustion claimed her. She had lain down on a bunk bed provided her in the bow of the schooner. She must have fallen asleep instantly. Now as she examined her surroundings she became aware that, save for the gentle rocking of the ship, the vessel was entirely quiet.

"Gilly?" she called out. When there was no answer, she threw aside the blanket someone had laid over her and sat up as straight as the headroom under the top bunk could allow. The room was somewhat dim and smelled of tarred rope. Across the narrow space on the other side of a ladder, she could see a bundle on the opposite bunk. A patch of sunlight splashed across the panel in front of the pillow.

"Gilly," she called softly to the thatch of strawberry blonde hair peeking over the wool blanket. There was still no answer. Her friend appeared dead to the world. Jeannie sighed and put her legs over the edge of the bed. At her feet were her boots. She put them on and picking up her shawl, went back through the passageway she remembered led to the galley.

"Where is everyone?" she asked. She found the boy Jimmy working on a pot in the sink. The galley was small but efficient-looking. There was a wood-burning stove and oven, and several working counters and cupboards for storage.

"They went ashore. Long time now."

She looked up through the opened skylight. The day appeared to be partly cloudy. "We're actually here? I thought it would take hours."

"It took maybe two hours. You like *kaupy?*" He pointed to coffee mugs hanging from hooks on the low beams.

"Yes, please." She took one down and came over to the counter where the day's meals would be laid out. He poured her a steaming cup then went back to the sink.

"Are you the only one here?" she asked.

"The *shipman* Mr. Patterson is here. Everyone else went in boats."

Jeannie smiled at him. He was a young boy, maybe ten. His arms were skinny as sticks and his body seemed lost in his gray flannel shirt, but he lifted the heavy iron pot with little trouble. He caught her smile and grinned, a dimple appearing in his brown cheek.

"You know Jo-nuss very well," he stated.

"Yes, I know Mr. Waddell."

"He's O.K. Be back bye and bye."

"Have you known him a long time?"

"Everyone knows Jo-nuss. Me, I'm his cabin boy two years."

"So young," Jeannie said.

"My *tillicum* are dead. Captain Henderson found a place for me." The boy's black eyes gleamed. "Now I go everywhere. Have you seen San Francisco?"

Jeannie said that she had and took a sip of her coffee, then paused. Above her a voice she could not identify came through the skylight. "Is that Mr. Patterson?"

"*Ah-ha.* I think so."

"I should like to go up. Thank you for the coffee." She gathered her skirts and went up the stairs into the chart room. It was a comfortable space with built-in cushioned seats and a chart table and stool. A number of maps and charts were spread out on it or pinned to the wall behind it. A single kerosene lamp made of brass hung in the corner next to a framed lithograph of pheasant hunting. On one of the cushions was a dated copy of *Frank Leslie's Illustrated Newspaper*. She looked back to the chart table. A journal was open, a gold tipped pen laid in its center. An entry for the day was half-finished. Though she realized that she hadn't seen Jonas' handwriting in years, she instinctively knew it was his. Next to the journal was the mug that she had seen earlier in his cabin. She laid her hand thoughtfully on the page, but chose not to look at what he had written as it was unseemly, even if it were as dry as a mariner's notation might get. She heard the voice again accompanied by a new one.

"I suggest you climb back down. I don't care if you are the Queen of Sheba."

Jeannie ducked her head and looked up the stairs onto the deck. The voices were coming over by the bulwarks, but all she could see was the open skylight on top of the doghouse and the mainmast beyond.

"I've come for your protection," said the new voice. "I want to be dead of them. I insist that you tell Mrs. Pierce that her solicitor is here."

"There is no Mrs. Pierce here."

"Then I shall seek your protection anyway. I've been most inconvenienced."

There was arguing, some swearing on Patterson's part and then the solicitor was on deck. Jeannie stayed where she was, curious to hear Burgess explain himself. She could certainly visualize him without daring to look. A portly middle-aged man with dainty hands and feet, his gray muttonchops and mustache tended to puff out like a frustrated hen's ruffled feathers when he enunciated his words. From his voice, he was out of sorts.

"Are you turning yourself in, Mr. Burgess?" Patterson asked pointedly. "You'll get no sympathy here."

"I know not whatever for."

"For cooking the books, I should think."

"Sir, you insult me!"

461

"Tell that to the judge." There was movement toward the deck-house, but Patterson's clear, lilting voice was still over near the bulwarks when he spoke again. "Go sit down. And you down below, put off now."

Jeannie strained to listen and for the first time, heard the chortle of a small steam engine. It couldn't have been someone from Jonas' party. Patterson sounded angry. She lifted up her skirt and climbed the short stairway to the deck, ducking her head as she came out the open hatchway. In front of her was Burgess, sitting on the doghouse. To her right was Patterson. Still speaking to someone down on the water, he held a shotgun discreetly in his right hand. Neither man saw her until Burgess suddenly turned. The man's face went white.

"She's here! Mrs. Pierce is here!" the solicitor shouted as he lumbered awkwardly to his feet.

Patterson turned to stare at the older man, then swung back, bringing the shotgun into play, but it was too late. There was an explosion of sound and the bos'un fell back, his hand digging rigidly into his neck as if he could clamp the sudden rush of blood with his bare fingers. He lay on his back on a neat stack of ropes. His feet kicked violently against the side of the ship. He began to swear, then choke, his Irish lilt rising with fear. Burgess did nothing to assist him. The chain of events was apparently not what the solicitor had counted on and he began to moan that he had only done what he was told to do and surely he was done for.

Jeannie did no better. She stood frozen. Everything had happened so fast and with no reason. Now, things moved slowly. Burgess was talking to her, pointing to the gunwales. Miraculously, hand still to neck, Patterson had rolled to his side and, in a pitiful effort, was trying to reach toward the shotgun. She thought he called her name, but it was someone climbing up the boarding ladder. Her own heart pulsed in her throat, then the trance broke. Pushing Burgess away, she went to help the dying man.

"Run... t'.. Jimmy," Patterson whispered when he recognized her. "He'll hide ye." His shoulder and shirt front were soaked with his blood. It caked his cheek like a mud splatter. He worked his mouth, then gurgled out, "Run!" That was all he could manage. He sank back to the deck.

"Too late," a cultured voice said. "You might as well stay." Topping the rail was Cooperwaite accompanied by a foul-looking man. The black-haired creature smiled at her crookedly, displaying several missing teeth. Both men were armed with rifles. Cooperwaite climbed over and slipped down onto the deck. He reached down and picked up the shotgun. He opened it up and took out the shotgun cartridge. Beneath his feet, Patterson sighed heavily, then lay still.

"You've murdered him," Jeannie cried. She had taken a kerchief out of her skirt pocket and was putting pressure on a wound that seemed to swim with blood. The kerchief was soaked.

"How touching," said Cooperwaite. "Gramble, see to the solicitor. Tie him fast. Jeannie, you will come with me."

"I'll do no such thing."

"You've no choice in the matter. Either I take you or I'll let Gramble do the honors as I have no patience for female hysterics. You," he said to Patterson, lightly tapping him with his boot. "Who else is on board?"

Patterson did not answer. His bloody hand had fallen away from his neck. He was looking up at the mainmast where the red telltale was gently turning in the breeze. The sky was a sultry blue, last night's weather a dim memory.

"Never mind," said Cooperwaite. "Get up, Jeannie."

"I can't. It's not right."

Cooperwaite's voice turned surprisingly soft. "He's nearly gone, can't you tell?"

Jeannie looked down. Patterson's brown eyes were open, but they were becoming clouded. She took away the kerchief. Patterson didn't move.

"See, the business is done." Cooperwaite reached down and pulled the man off her lap, then took her by the hand. "Get up, Jeannie." He pulled her up, then nodded for his partner to put Burgess in the boat.

Burgess started to squirm. He shouted, "You promised to let me go! How dare you!"

"Stuff it, you little shit." Cooperwaite pushed him into Gramble.

"Wait," Jeannie said to Burgess. "Where is my son? He's supposed to with you."

"He's well taken care of," Cooperwaite said. "Now, get into the boat."

Jeannie felt the blood drain from her face. *They have Phillip.* It was difficult to keep composure with shaking knees, but she suddenly felt that no matter what, she would not let Cooperwaite see her cry or show fear. Neville-tin had promised they would find Phillip. That gave her courage.

She looked down at her skirt, appalled at the large bloody stain there. Her hair was coming undone. She knew she looked terrible, but she no longer cared. From deep inside, a hard, gnawing feeling was working at her. She never thought she could hate someone so completely.

"Now you, Jeannie. Be a good girl. I regret this, I truly do."

Jeannie glared at him and let him help her to the gunwale where he lifted her up. "Where are you taking us?"

"Oh, to the island. I wouldn't miss the rendezvous. It sounds so romantic. The word, that is. It's a business meeting after all. Tell me, what is our Mr. Waddell like?"

"My husband's partner?"

"Come, come. I know that he is the owner of this ship."

"I don't know. On my life, I never met him before last night."

"Then why did you go with him?'

"I didn't *go* with *him*. We went with an acquaintance of Mrs. Parker who assured an easy trip."

"In the middle of the night?"

"You must understand our situation, Mr. Cooperwaite. You must forgive me, but the ill repute of the town. As for the acquaintance, I had no idea he was associated with Mr. Waddell."

"Do *I* know Mr. Waddell?"

Jeannie knew that she was in danger here, but so was Jonas according to Neville's warning.

"He must not see Jonas."

"No, I don't think so. Before our introduction, I couldn't have picked him out of a labor line."

Cooperwaite stared at her. "Why the sudden distrust of me?"

Jeannie answered quickly. "Not distrust, Thomas. I said, discomfort. It had been all a rather horrid day. This—gentleman—had seen the accident and came to inquire after hours. One thing led to another. We didn't wish to spend the night there. And it was too late to alert you." She looked down at poor Patterson. His jaw had become slack and he still lay in the position into which that Cooperwaite pushed him. A large pool of blood under him was spreading out across the deck of the schooner. "But now, what should I think of you?"

"Indeed. At this point, I don't think it matters. Move along."

He handed her down to Gramble who was already in the steam boat. Burgess had been put in the bow where he was ordered to sit, leaning up against the wooden side. A bundle of heavy rope had been thrown into his arms to hold him there. Avoiding him, Jeannie held unsteadily to the edge of the roof of the pilothouse and surveyed the rest of the steam boat as it rocked uncomfortably against the schooner. From what she could see of the little vessel, its only purpose was to hold the battered steam engine amidships, right in the center of the vessel. There was barely room for anything else.

"In there, Jeannie. Take a seat." The pilothouse was small and tight with only one seat, an old barrel with a mildewed cushion on it. There was one lone window, set in front of the helm. It was gloomy spot, the whitewash flaking off the fir board walls. Behind her was a bin of sorts. Several canvas bags were stacked in it. Jeannie sat down and watched as Gramble cast off. She could not see higher than the last rung of the ladder on the side of the schooner, but she could see across the deserted inlet to the forest shore of the island. Had Gilly heard the shot? Jimmy surely did. And who on shore? Jeannie peered through the dirty glass, but saw no movement on the beach nor on the bench of land above it. She desperately wished she had listened more carefully to Hector's description of the island. Perhaps she could ascertain which direction they would have gone and warn Jonas.

Cooperwaite came in and took the helm. Outside the steam engine came to life and began to move the boat away. The little steamboat was surprisingly quiet. Cooperwaite headed it towards a section of the island where a stand of madrone stood like undulating rusty sentinels. He didn't speak to her, ignoring her uncomfortable perch on the barrel, but eventually he did turn to look at her. He saw her bloody hands and gave her a cloth to wipe them clean. Jeannie took it without a word.

"You realize that you have complicated matters for me. I had thought to see you without all this commotion. Now, I'm afraid I'm going to have to take you with me. Perhaps quite a distance from here."

"I cannot think that you would harm me, Mr. Cooperwaite, despite the cold-blooded murder of Mr. Patterson, but why take me anywhere? There is nothing that I can add to whatever you are going to do."

Cooperwaite smiled at her, the scar by his eye belying the friendliness he seemed to display. "Oh, I think that you add a good deal under any circumstances. You are, after all this time, still a splendid and fine-looking woman, Jeannie Naughton Pierce. There was a time when I was quite infatuated with you. Unfortunately, you did not return the favor."

"Am I at a disadvantage now because of that?"

"No, not at all. I would say that you are most favored. Especially since you are widowed." He looked at her pointedly, his eyes straying over her face, and then slowly down her figure. Briefly, he looked out the window to check on his direction, then continued speaking in a tone that made Jeannie become increasingly uneasy. She pulled her shawl more closely around her, making Cooperwaite smile again. At that, she straightened up, keeping to her promise not to show fear.

"What happened to you, Mr. Cooperwaite? You had such promise."

"My Marine career?" He smirked. "I'm not so sure it would have advanced any further. There were so many intrusions. Difficult to watch the men desert and head for the gold mine fields in Chilliwack and further north. You've probably forgotten that, British honor and all that. I think forty-five deserted from the New Westminster post just the month of July, 1860. And several left the camp right there on the island. I would have gone with them, but there were other matters to attend to. Sweet matters, to be exact. Besides, I needed my salary. I went later and did make some sort of fortune." He paused. "But that was a long time ago."

"So long ago that you have forgotten every honorable thing as a Royal Marine?"

Cooperwaite's lips parted slightly at the question, his eyes stared vacantly at her under its sagging eyelid. "Bloody hell. Why do women always make something out of a monkey suit? Our whole existence here was to boost up some native trading forts. What's so honorable about that? I was glad to be rid of it."

"I think you did care, Mr. Cooperwaite. Once upon a time. What changed you?" Jeannie hoped that by talking she could improve her chances of escape from him.

Cooperwaite gave her a strange little smile. His eyes had dilated in the dim cabin, giving him a haunted look. "What, indeed. I'm afraid that's not open for discussion." He shifted his eyes away from her and set his mouth. He would say no more. He looked back out the window and returned to his task of piloting the boat.

They were well away from the schooner now and approaching the head of the protected inlet it had been anchored in. Jeannie wondered if the inlet was part of a large hilly island densely covered with trees. She could see sandstone cliffs under the foliage. There could be more coves on the other side, she thought. This could a popular place to rendezvous. She had heard of hidden sandstone caves on some of the islands in this area. Perfect for smugglers.

"Must we go to the meeting?" Jeannie asked.

"I'm afraid so. I have a vested interest, you see. You might be interested as well." He was silent for a moment, his eyes on his task. He seemed to be looking for a place to weigh anchor. When he made his decision, he put his head outside of the cabin. "We'll stop here, Gramble. Make ready to go ashore." He turned to Jeannie. "We'll disembark here."

Outside, she could hear the sound of the anchor splashing. The steam engine seem to slow down, then cut out altogether. The inlet became instantly quiet. The boat glided along for a ways, then stopped on its tether. It turned slightly, then began to become attuned to the rhythm of the inlet's water. Jeannie thought she could hear waves lapping on the shore.

Cooperwaite put a rope through the helm and tied it back to a hook on the wall. "Please go outside and turn to your left," he told her. "We'll take the rowboat over."

Jeannie stood up and walked outside. Gramble was at the stern, checking the oars in the rowboat. She looked to the bow where Burgess still sat with the coiled ropes in his lap. He looked miserable. His high collar had popped and was dangling around his neck like wayward wings. His cheeks looked like overripe strawberries. Not much like the fastidious solicitor he had been for the firm. Jeannie suddenly felt sorry for him, even though he was surely as guilty of smuggling as Cooperwaite and Gutterson were.

He raised his eyes to her. "Forgive me, Mrs. Pierce. I hope that you were not injured."

"Only my opinion of you, Mr. Burgess. My late husband trusted you."

"I..."

Cooperwaite cut him off. "I'm afraid we'll have to save this for another time. There's not a moment to lose. Carry on, Gramble. I'll see you on the other side." He took Jeannie by the elbow and pushed her in front of him. The space between the side of the steamer and the pilot house was as narrow as a ledge. Her skirt squeezed through the area with a bit of tugging. Cooperwaite helped her down into the rowboat while Gramble held it fast with the painter rope. As she sat down on the seat, the last thing she saw was Burgess sitting on the deck holding the ropes. He was the image of dejection, his mutton chops hanging down on the sides of his face. As they pulled away, she wondered what would become of him. Perhaps, she thought, I should worry about myself.

THE PARLEY

On the beach, Breed put down the burden he carried on his back. It was a small folding table. Hunter and Collie untied two canvas chairs from their backs. As if on cue, a sloop came around the bluff at the mouth of the bay and made its way in. There was action on board as sails were brought in and preparations made for anchoring.

"Look to your places," ordered Collie to the others. "You too, Kapihi."

Hunter laid a knapsack on the table and took out a pen and ink set. He wiggled a folder out, but left it in the knapsack. Finally, Hunter set a decanter of sherry and a couple of crystal shot glasses on a little tray in the middle of the table. When all was ready, he stepped back and unslung a rifle from his shoulder. The meeting place was ready for business.

"Give that to Collie for now, Sam," Breed said. "Secure your derringer, if you would." He checked his coat pocket to make sure his own was there. "Collie, you'll do introductions, then step back. Looks like they're ready to lower a boat." He took a telescope out of his coat pocket and squinting, brought the landing party into his glass. Gutterson was getting into the large dory along with some men Breed did not recognize. Cooperwaite was not with them. He searched the boat, but could not find him. Disappointed, he collapsed his telescope and prepared for their arrival.

It took several minutes for them to land and pull the dory up on the beach. Collie was the first to meet them, helping to bring the craft on shore. He wiped his hands on his pants and stepped back when Gutterson got out. Breed stayed where he was. It took a good deal of effort not to burst out laughing. Breed had seen actual pirates in his day, but nothing came close to Anders Gutterson in personal appearance and selection of wardrobe.

He looked vaguely like the tintype they had seen earlier, but in person his face was even more like his deceased half-brother. The comparison stopped there, however. He was not as burly as his brother. When he removed his green felt hat, the balding blonde hair underneath was matted and pressed down below his ears like a fallen halo. His nose was red from drinking and his blonde beard was stained.

His clothes were no help. He wore a dark green sack coat with a tan vest underneath, all sizes too tight while his pants seemed like they would fall off. It would have been a mistake to think him a buffoon, however. Breed thought he would fit in anywhere in the world as a wharf rat. There was no doubt that he could be dangerous. He was as shifty as he was wiry in frame.

"Captain Henderson, I presume?" Gutterson asked as he came over to Collie. He smiled at him, but already his eyes had shifted to Breed who was standing near the table with Kapihi. Breed had dressed as a gentleman, down to the diamond pin in his Ascot tie.

"I am," answered Collie. He shook his hand and turned to Breed. "May I present Mr. Jonas Waddell of Honolulu?"

"Pleasure," Gutterson said. "I'm Anders Gutterson. I was hopin' we'd meet." He waved his hand at Kapihi as he waded through the sand to Breed. "That your servant?"

Breed pretended not to hear. He stood with his left hand in his jacket pocket and waited for Gutterson to come close. When Gutterson extended his hand, Breed shook it and sniffed.

"So you are the one who has been grazing my fields." Breed spoke in a low voice so that the gentle morning breeze took away the words from his mouth, but Gutterson caught them. He flushed with anger, but it evaporated quickly when he saw Breed smiling.

When Kapihi offered him a glass of sherry, Gutterson said, "Very nice." The shot glass seemed to disappear in Guttersonn's rough, meaty hand. He turned back to his men and waved them forward. They had been waiting suspiciously near the dory. They lowered their rifles as they advanced.

"Gentlemen. I believe that you have something to discuss with me," Breed said as he took one of the glasses and raised it to Gutterson.

"Indeed." Gutterson motioned again and one of his men came forward with a large satchel. He downed his drink and was astonished when it was filled again.

Breed directed him to one of the chairs and for the next few minutes they exchanged pleasantries. He let Gutterson ask him any questions about his trip over, operations in Honolulu and the Pacific and his business in the Pacific Northwest. Breed gave him impressive details. When Gutterson became more personal, Breed reminded him that they were gentlemen and changed the subject. They could have been sitting in the men's smoking room at the most swank men's club instead of on a beach on an unoccupied island. It was pleasant with midmorning fast approaching. The waves lapped lazily. After a second round of sherry had been consumed, Kapihi offered cigars, though Breed declined. Gutterson chose one carefully, then launched into new territory.

"What did you think of your partner, the late Mr. Pierce?"

"An affable figurehead. Mind you, he was never in charge."

"You were?"

"My agents. Captain Henderson, for one. I was more than well-informed." Breed talked authoritatively, choosing his words carefully.

Gutterson's's eyes narrowed. "How long have you known? About the operations?"

"Long enough to have you arrested."

Gutterson nearly spit out his cigar in mid-draw. "You have a dangerous sense of humor."

"All the more to see what stuff you are made of. This is not a child's game we are embarking on. I need to know if you have stomach for more intriguing fare. Tell me, did you ever meet my partner face to face?"

"Pierce? No." Gutterson grinned crookedly. "He was too much concerned with civic affairs than muck his hands in some warehouse. He fooled me, though. Got a spit of conscience and did some digging on his own. One of my spies found him out. Put an end to that." Gutterson looked at Breed curiously. "You don't seem in the least appalled."

At that point, Breed took his hook hand out of his pocket and put it on the table. "That's because you and I are businessmen of the same ilk. How do you suppose I make my millions? Did you personally do the business?"

Gutterson stared wide-eyed at the hook. "I lied," he finally said. "I met him on that one occasion, so the answer is, yes."

"Come, come. This has not left you speechless, has it?" Breed was thoroughly enjoying himself as he pointed the hook at Gutterson's men, though the admission of murder disturbed him.

"Why don't you dismiss them, as agreed? My clerk will stay. The others will retire to a proper distance. I'd like to see what you have to offer."

The men on both sides moved back. When Collie passed in front of him, Breed scratched the tab on his chin. Collie betrayed nothing, only the faintest twist of his lips. Breed responded by reaching for the decanter of sherry and refilled Gutterson's glass. It was of the finest quality, with a smooth sweet taste. Gutterson sampled it greedily, dripping some of the liquid on his chin.

When the men were placed, Gutterson drew the satchel to him and opened it up. He removed a wooden box and placed it on the table. When he realized that Breed would be at a disadvantage in opening it up, he proceeded to do it himself. Inside the box were small tins marked with a commercial label reading, "quinine."

"May I?" Gutterson asked Breed. He chose one of the tins and opened it. It was filled with a white powder. Opium.

"What do you think?"

Breed leaned down to sniff at it. He took a pinch and rubbed it between his fingers. "A good quality."

"You bet. This ain't all. Folks want the queerest stuff. Australian wool, Chinese laborers."

"I don't deal in human cargo."

"Not to worry. There's a whole list out there. All easily concealed."

"You forget that it was found out."

"Not with you controlling the picture."

Breed looked at the opium. "And it comes in from China via Victoria and the Gulf Islands?"

"Right over Haro Strait or the 49th north."

"Where did you hide it before?"

"Now, I thought we was gentlemen. That's a secret for me to know. *My* hidey holes."

Breed looked around the beach. "I'm sure that you have a few right here. A perfect spot. The traffic is a bit slow."

"So's the law." Gutterson chuckled. He took a sip of sherry. Breed hoped he had lost count of how much he had consumed.

Gutterson smiled wickedly. "I've got a partner. Name of Cooperwaite. He deals with this here high-end stuff. Now if we were to be all together in this—had a perfect place so it would always be an inside job without the rest of the firm knowing the true business end of things why that would be right fine."

Breed put the lid back on the tin. "Well, you interest me. You do indeed."

"Then it's a deal?"

"It's a deal," Breed said, shaking on it. Then he proceeded to tell Gutterson his vision of things. That took another twenty minutes and more sherry. While Breed took out documents from the file in his knapsack, Hunter kept the shot glass full. Breed showed Gutterson where to sign, which Gutterson did with a flourish. Then Breed signed the papers, making sure everything was properly blotted and preserved. Finally, Breed stood up to stretch. Gutterson followed suit, then excusing himself, went off to piss into the water. Breed waited patiently, putting their signed agreements in order and the satchel in Hunter's possession. The smuggler's men watched guardedly, not trusting everyone as Gutterson had. Breed looked in Collie's direction. He looked a little wary. It had gone almost too smoothly. Breed thought about that. What could Gutterson gain at this point? It would be over in a moment, anyway. Once Collie and the others had Gutterson's gang covered, Doc-tin could make his appearance. He looked out across the bay where the sloop was anchored. No movement there. No one else had come ashore.

Hitching up his pants, Gutterson walked back to the table where the papers were stacked.

"Got one more thing now that the papers are signed." Gutterson snapped his fingers and two men standing by the dory whipped off a canvas cover over some cargo. Only it wasn't cargo, but a disheveled young man. His hair and clothes were filthy. His eyes blinking at the sunlight, his face had several days' growth of beard. As they pulled him up to a standing position. Breed could see he had been drugged.

"Thought I'd turn him over to you now we're partners. May I present, Phillip Pierce."

Breed looked at the young man. Blonde and fair.

Finding his footing on the beach, Phillip wrestled away from his handlers and brushed his clothes off. "Keep your hands off me," he said, and he stared at Breed, his face angry and scared at the same time.

Phillip Pierce.

Only Breed wasn't looking at Jeannie's son, but Breed's own father as young man, long remembered in a miniature Breed carried from his boyhood to shipwreck to Haida Gwaii and back—all his life. In an instant, Breed knew the truth behind Jeannie's decision to go with Pierce and the secret she carried alone all these years. It near broke his heart. Phillip Pierce was his son.

"I'll take him," Breed said, then all hell broke loose when high up on the ridge to the left of them, a voice screamed out his name.

"Jonas! Oh God, Jonas!"

He turned toward the scream and took a bullet on his breast as he moved. The crack of a rifle followed. The bullet smacked him viciously, digging the sharp metal edges of the stove lid into his chest and belly, then ricocheted into the stub cap on his left arm. A second shot and a female voice shrieking in a high pitch of pain followed. By then he had fallen into the sand. The pain agonizing.

All around him there was chaos as everyone yelled and swore. Gunfire followed, booming like cannon above the stream of profanity and exploding the sand into stinging fragments around Breed's face. Something heavy fell near him, but he laid still and face down, the wind nearly knocked out of him. He heard Collie's voice and Hunter's. The bullets no longer came from above, but from the trees near the bay and close to him. So he stayed still, the metal digging into him and making him bleed. He prayed that Phillip was safe.

"You son of a bitch!" Gutterson yelled. The firing continued, but it was being directed into the woods. Jonas wondered if they were losing, but if he tried to reach for his gun he would be dead. Boots crunched on the sand and someone stood above him. A rifle went off next to him, then another. The sound hammered at his ear drums. Suddenly, he was roughly grabbed by the collar and dragged.

"I got him! I got him!" Gutterson screamed. Another hand seized him and his body was lifted further away from where he had fallen. He lay as limp and heavy as he could, keeping his mouth slack and his eyes half-closed. He was carried as far as the sedges and grass and then tossed unceremoniously on his side on the other side of a large driftwood log. It took every effort not to groan as the lid cut into him in new places, adding to his agony, but he rolled away from the log and lay still. The gunfire resumed earnestly nearby, but Breed already knew that he was in unfriendly company. He had not been rescued, but captured by Gutterson.

"Shit. What the hell happened?" yelled Gutterson as he reloaded behind the safety of the old rotten log. "This your doing?" He kicked out at Breed who did not move. "Check him," the smuggler said to his companion.

Something jabbed Breed's shoulder and he was pushed onto his back. Hands rifled his coat pockets and found the derringer. Immediately it was tossed away. Then the man leaned down to examine Breed, his right eye squinting. Breed brought the hook up in a rapid, tight swing and swiped it across the man's eyes. Screaming, the man fell back, dropping his rifle as he wiped the blood out of his eyes.

Gutterson turned in surprise, but was too late to avoid the hook again as it snagged him on his coat and pulled him down against his screaming, kicking comrade. Gutterson roared and swore. By the time he had struggled into an upright position, Breed was gone. Like a ghost, he had disappeared. With the rifle.

RECKONING

This is all a dream, Jeannie thought, as they climbed steadily through the leafy woods. Once on shore, Cooperwaite moved quickly. Taking her by the hand, he had led her across the sand to a narrow gap in the bench where he made her go first and scramble up. On top, he motioned her to the right and several steps later they were on a trail that went to the woods. She looked wildly from side to side in hopes that, somehow, one of Jonas's men was nearby. She had been aware of the Songhees men onboard the schooner. She had seen one in the salon before she retired. Perhaps there were others. Collie. Someone.

"Wait," said Cooperwaite. He made her stop on the path. Jeannie welcomed the pause. She was out of breath. She pulled at her hairpins and let her hair cascade down around her shoulders. It was better than letting it struggle on her head like the tower of Pisa. She looked down at her skirt. She was sure the blood stain had soaked through her petticoat, but it was drying.

Absentmindedly, she lifted her foot and examined one of her high-top boots. It pinched horribly and the heel was nearly twisted off. Not the sort of walking shoe she'd buy in the future. She put it back on and thought, if there *is* a future. Dully, she looked at Cooperwaite who was listening to the woods around them. The path had branched. She wondered if he was lost.

"Ah," he said suddenly and turned to her. He smiled when he saw her hair down. He nodded in approval. "Let's go."

"What if I don't?"

"Now, Jeannie. Let's not play games. I never thought you the sort. In fact, I always thought you were a level-headed sort of girl, not prone to simperings and smelling salts. Quite admirable in such a beautiful lady." He took a step toward her and reached out for her hair. He took a bunch and twisted it until it pulled sharp against her scalp. Gently he pulled her hair back, forcing her to tilt her head. "I say go. You go."

"Of course. May I have some water, though?"

Cooperwaite stared at her, then released her hair. "You're in luck. I actually have a flask. He reached into his coat pocket and brought out a silver flask. He pulled out the stopper and handed it to her.

Delicately she took a sip, then sputtered. The water made her lips pucker. The flask had been used for some sort of alcohol previously.

Cooperwaite laughed. "Take it easy. There's plenty to go around."

Jeannie nodded, unable to speak. She looked at the flask. There was a monogram on it: ASP. She gasped. Andrew's initials. She looked at Cooperwaite in horror.

"It's not what you think. I came by it accidentally. After his untimely death." He grinned crookedly. "I've always wondered about that. What you saw in Pierce."

"That's none of your business."

He laughed again, then abruptly stopped. His face drew dark. "Oh, I'd say that his business *is my* business. Quite a lot of it." He looked up the trail, then took out his watch. He made great ceremony of opening the lid. Jeannie watched him warily. She jumped when he snapped it shut and smiled at her. "Just about everything."

He leaned his rifle against a small tree, then moved so quickly that she was unprepared to protect herself. Seizing her by her arms and pushing them tight against her sides, he angled her back off the trail, then in one motion forced her violently down on the ground. He

478

threw himself on top of her with all his weight and laughed when she began to struggle and tried to bring her knees up.

"Thaddeus! Don't do this!" she cried. Jeannie twisted and turned, but she was helpless against his strength.

Pulling her arms from her sides, he put them by her head. Jeannie felt like a stick puppet, her hands and body not in her control. He leaned over and breathed on her.

"Oh, you are the beauty. Simply splendid." With that, he kissed her coarsely on the mouth.

She fought him and succeeded in moving her face away from him. He let go of one of her hands and used his free hand to grab her and twist her face back at him. He plunged his mouth again on hers, ignoring her fingers trying to tear at his cheek. He kissed her throat and ear, laughing at the blows and scratches, but eventually, he grabbed her hand and forced it back down to the ground. This time he tucked it under her hip, then pressed his body into hers. They were breathing heavily from exertion now. Cooperwaite smiled again, then tore at the buttons on her neck. The fine cloth ripped.

"Thaddeus!" Jeannie was defiant, but fear was creeping into her voice. Her eyes would not leave his as they implored for some last remnant of decency. Cooperwaite sat up and straddling her hips, dug his knees into the ground, pinning her more. Jeannie swallowed and chewed her lips. She became still.

"That's better," he said. He pulled away the shirt cloth so the delicate lace camisole was exposed. He pressed on the corset, muttering, "Damn contraption," then yanked the sheer cotton cloth above it away. The tops of her breasts were exposed. Jeannie turned her head away as he leaned down and kissed her. His free hand squeezed one breast while his lips explored the deep cleavage. With her so still, though, he soon became bored and sat up half way. He stroked her hair.

"There was a time once when I would have killed for you. Oh, yes," he said when she looked surprised. "Remember Breed? That *siwash* misfit? I saw how he looked at you that day of the picnic. Convenient how he took advantage of you after my fall. He planned it all. I could have killed him, but Emmett Krill beat me to it."

"Mr. Breed never took advantage of me, as you are now. You set yourself up."

"Touché. I like a little verbal repartee before the amusement."

"You will have nothing."

Cooperwaite snorted. "Oh, I'll have it all." He seized her skirt and began to yank it up toward her hips. Jeannie twisted under him and tried to free her hand, but he was too strong.

Jeannie looked away. When he rocked on top of her, she whimpered.

"There, there. No tears. No tears at all. You're the sensible sort." Cooperwaite sat back straddling her. "What *are* we going to do? I must see Waddell. I'm curious, after all. He'll be easy to find. I know these woods like the back of my hand and more. This is my haunt, you see."

He brushed a finger on her face. "On the other hand, I simply would like to stay and continue this conversation. This sweet conversation."

He sighed dramatically. Jeannie wondered if he was going mad. They were in the woods and Jonas' people must be here. Perhaps if she screamed. Something warned her, however, that it would be useless and would only make Cooperwaite madder still.

Suddenly, he unbuttoned his pants and exposed himself. At that instant she knew she could not stop him.

"Thaddeus, please!" she cried.

Cooperwaite laughed. "Thaddeus, please. I like that. Yes, indeed," he said and brought his face down close to hers. "Oh, you'll say that. Again and again."

In her fear, Jeannie seized the open collar of his shirt at his neck, grabbing a chain hidden underneath. It came out before he knew what was happening; before he realized that she knew exactly what was hanging on it, shining like an abalone coin after all the years.

It was a labret. Shell Shining's labret. And Jeannie held onto it in fear and grief. For this was the undoing of it all and the catalyst for the tragedy of the past twenty years. Kaui Kalama came for Jonas and Jonas went seeking too late. All the players took their places over this: the rape and murder of an innocent Haida woman.

What changed you, Thomas?

What, indeed. I'm afraid that's not open for discussion.

This is what he was speaking of on the boat. She stared at him and knew he was not only mad, but very dangerous.

"Give that to me," he barked and yanked it out of her hand. He stuffed it back down inside his shirt.

"You killed her. Shells Shining."

Cooperwaite's face turned dark. Jeannie was surprised to see fear as well as rage. She cringed, but took his stinging slap on her cheek without crying out.

"Because you wouldn't have me, you bitch. Do you hear? After all the bloody teas and niceties," he snarled. "Oh, she was strong and wily, but I took her and had my amusement." He patted his throat. "Got an extra souvenir too." He sighed. "You shouldn't have seen that. I would have preferred to have it kept secret."

"They'll know."

"Who'll know? Nobody's going to know."

Jeannie started to say the Songhees, but said the Haida instead.

"Haida?"

"They were on the boat with Mr. Waddell. I believe he brought them from Fort Simpson."

Cooperwaite blanched. "Why?"

"I have no idea. We didn't speak much."

Cooperwaite sat up stiffly. The sudden change in his demeanor was unsettling. A haunted look crossed his face and he pulled back from her. His look was full of regret.

Jeannie closed her eyes. He was going to kill her. She would never see Jereminah and Phillip again. She would never see Jonas again. Never speak to him and say the words to him she really wanted to say. She opened her eyes and looked at the trees above her. She was glad they would be the last things she saw. "Get up, Jeannie. We have to go."

Jeannie had been unaware that he had climbed off her and dressed.

Self-consciously she sat up and pulled her skirt down to her ankles. She pulled the top of her shirtwaist together as best she could. She wiped at the bits of leaves in her hair and stood up.

"Give me your hands."

When she saw that he would bind them, she turned one of her hands into the palm of the other so that the kerchief he used crossed the top of one of her hands, not the wrist. She pretended that it hurt, but he never said he was sorry.

He pulled her up, then moved her out onto the trail pushing her toward the branch to the left. "We've got to move, so move."

They moved quickly, making their way through woods that now rose up first gradually, then more sharply until the trail came at last to a sandstone cliff. Cooperwaite came up by her and showed her the way. She would be able to climb with her hands bound without difficulty. He pushed her onto the rock and pressed his body into her. He breathed into her hair.

"Just this one last task, then I can get on. You'll come, of course." He pushed her up, touching the back of her skirt as he did so. Jeannie went higher to avoid him, but found he could quickly climb alongside her. When they came to the top, he was already there to help her up.

"Over there," he pointed. He directed her toward a trail going across a ledge on the rock face. The top of the ridge was sandy and slippery. Jeannie did not look down. The trail went on for some ways, turned and went up, coming out on top of an open, grassy space. It was nearly treeless and she could see out to the water.

"This way," he commanded and they moved down into the trees, but still walking on what was mostly rock and grass. The trees thinned around them. They came out onto a ledge high above the big-leaf maple trees rising up from below. Suddenly, she could see down to a beach where men were standing around. A large dory was beached on the sand. A table and canvas chairs were set out in the middle of the expansive beach. She stared down at the group. One of them she knew instantly. It was Collie. Another was Kapihi. The other had his back turned to them as he talked to a man much shorter in stature than he was. She knew that set of shoulders. Jonas.

"Open up," said Cooperwaite. "Though I know for a fact that they can't see us, with the trees there, I don't particularly want them to hear you. You're so unpredictable." He pushed a kid skin glove into her mouth. It tasted sweet and dry, making her mouth water. He checked her hands and slipping another scarf through them, tied them to her waist.

"Now behave." He moved her next to him and unslung the rifle from his back. The men below were gathering at a table. One was at the table stacking papers.

Cooperwaite squeezed Jeannie's arm. "That Waddell? You don't have to answer. I believe that is."

Jeannie nodded. She prayed that Cooperwaite wouldn't recognize him.

"Looks a lot younger than I imagined, though he has quite a paunch when he turns to the side." He released her and checked the rifle. He didn't notice that she was working with her hands, turning them so they were cupped flat in prayer. It created a gap in the first binding and she began to discreetly make her hands free.

The proceedings continued down below. Papers were organized, the satchel exchanged. Cooperwaite watched everything with a studied detachment. Jeannie watched in horror as Phillip appeared form the dory on the beach. He looked bedraggled and weak. Jeannie could barely hide her terror.

Suddenly Cooperwaite stiffened. Jeannie's heart sank. Breed was facing them fifty feet below, then looked up into the trees. For the first time, his features were very clear.

"What the devil. Waddell is Jonas Breed?" He seized Jeannie roughly by the arm again. "What sort of trickery is this?" he snarled at her. "What are you up to?"

When Jeannie shook her head that she didn't understand, he slapped her face, then pushed her away. To her horror he shouldered his rifle and sighted it at the men below. Regaining her footing, she twisted and turned her hands until one of them slipped out, then pulled the glove out of her mouth. The trigger was cocked. Cooperwaite was taking aim.

"Jonas! Oh God, Jonas!" she screamed, then rushed at Cooperwaite to put his aim off. The rifle went off like a bomb near her head. The sound ricocheted against the cliff. He put his hand on her face and pushed her back to get another shot off. She lunged at him again, but the second shot went off as quickly as the first. She grabbed the stock and tried to pull it from Cooperwaite's hands. He turned her around and as she lost her grip and fell, she could see that Jonas was on the ground. Her right hand still bound to her waist, she landed groveling at Cooperwaite's feet.

"Whore," he said as he bashed the rifle butt onto Jeannie's free forearm.

Jeannie screamed, but in one last effort grabbed him by an ankle and upset his footing. She pulled and pushed until he slipped on the sandstone and in one unceremonious motion fell over the ledge onto bushes growing below the rim.

"I'll kill you!" he roared and swore as he snagged onto some roots and branches and stopped his fall, but no one heard him. His voice was lost in the outbreak of fighting down below. He pulled himself close to the cliff and looked for his rifle. It was stuck barrel down in some brush below him. Gripping the roots with his left hand, he reached over and touched it with his fingers. By repeatedly playing the barrel, he gradually worked it into the palm of his hand and grabbed it. He wasted no time after that. He was no longer immune to the fighting below. Shots were hitting leaves in the tops of the trees and gouging out chips in the cliff. Turning, he pulled himself up over the edge of the cliff only to find that it was deserted. Although he searched for as long as he could safely manage, he never found her

PEACE

As soon as he pushed Gutterson onto his companion, Breed was up and running with the rifle. Keeping low as he could with the metal lid flopping against his chest, he leaped through the reeds and grasses until he came into the safety of woods. He continued running until he came up against the high sandstone cliff. The fighting was going fiercely behind him, but it was coming from new quarters. Once he recognized the reports of the rifles and sidearms, he was confident that Sikhs and the others had joined in. Gutterson had fooled them, landing a party before he had come himself, but it was luck that got them past Breed's men. To confirm Sikhs's presence a war cry he hadn't heard in years came rising up from the beach, sending chills up his spine. He turned once to locate Gutterson, but he was not visible. Breed continued on. He hoped that Phillip had enough sense to find cover.

Breed worked his way through the brush against the cliff and satisfied he couldn't be seen, undid his shirt, exposing the contraption he had put on in jest. It had saved his life. Over his left breast, a ragged tear in the horsehair pillow marked the path the bullet had taken. The pillow was burnt at its edges. He put a finger in it and could feel the dent in the metal. He threw off the pillow and gingerly lifted away the lid. There were cuts in his chest near his shoulders and on his hard belly where the lid had pounded into him from the first bullet's blow. An ugly gash on his right side showed the track of the second. Breed considered himself lucky.

The fighting behind him was becoming sporadic. He buttoned up his bloody shirt, tucked the tie into a coat pocket and took up his rifle. At the cliff's base, a narrow lip of sandstone rose up gently, widening as it went until it came to a wide ledge and an opening to a cave. Looking back down through the trees Breed saw with great satisfaction Gutterson coming out onto the beach with his hands raised. He was relieved to see Phillip with Sikhs. Phillip would be in good hands. Collie was limping, but he had a pistol aimed at the smuggler. Breed tried to locate Kapihi and Doc-tin, but didn't see them. Every minute counted. He had to get to the top to Jeannie.

It was dim and cool in the cave. He searched his memory of this old haunt. He grinned, went to the back wall and chose a slim chamber that went up. As it narrowed, he went on his belly with the rifle out in front. The sandstone was damp, smelling of sea water and small animals. He used his hook hand like a claw to pull himself up. The chamber came out into a wide open space about ten feet high and full of reflected sunlight. Standing up, he turned and faced a wide opening out to the bay, hidden to the outside world by tall leafy trees. At the far end, sandstone floor slowly rose, bringing him into another chamber next to the one below. It too was opened, for the sandstone face of the cliff had been sandblasted ages ago into giant Swiss cheese holes. He stood still for a moment listening, deciding which way to go. He looked up at the stony ceiling, then went to his right.

The cave narrowed there and grew dark. As he climbed up into another chamber, he ended up crawling on his hands and knees again. He moved without a sound. Carefully, he put his head through and stopped to listen. From far-off, a little animal skittered across dry leaves. The space was very dark and had a coolness speaking of age. As his eyes became accustomed to it, he was aware of a presence over in a corner. Quietly, without scraping the hook or his clothes against the rock, he lifted himself into the cave and stepped back to the wall.

The presence stayed the same: a pale, nearly invisible gray. For several minutes he stayed patiently where he was. Gradually, a soft sound came to him, like the trembling of a young fawn upon discovery. The presence drew itself in and held its breath, a movement that touched Breed deeply.

"Jeannie, is that you?" he whispered.

"Jo-Jonas?"

"*Ah-ha.*"

Something inside Breed broke. All his anger and hurt scattered. What stayed was his memory of their time on Timons, the sunshine coming through the cattail weave in their secret bower, her warm body against him, and the cardamom smell of her Brown Bess soap. *Toketie.* As she rushed into his arms in the dark, dank cave, he was afraid fear, not love, drove her until her groping hands found his face and she kissed him full on the mouth. He held her close and rocked her. "*Toketie.*"

Eventually, she said in pinched voice, "Oh, Jonas. I thought Cooperwaite shot you dead."

"No, your warning saved me."

Jeannie sniffed. Breed fumbled for his box of lucifers and struck one. Holding it above her, the harsh flame in his hand caught the features on her face. He was shocked to see a swollen mark on her cheek and her hair all tangled and wild. Her shirtwaist was torn. "Did he hurt you?" He barely controlled his anger.

Jeannie sniffed again. "He frightened me, that's all."

"No, Jeannie, he assaulted you. Are you sure you're alright?" He shook the lucifer out when the flame reached his fingers and lit another to continue talking. The flame threw a yellow light on her. Her cheeks glistened with tears. She trembled anew as she pulled her blouse to rights.

"Jeannie," he said tenderly. The lucifer went out. He pulled her against him. She rested her head upon his chest.

"Where is Phillip? Is my son safe?"

"Last I saw, he was with Sikhs."

"Thank God."

Breed drew her closer.

"How did you find me?" she whispered. "When I ran away I fell down into some opening. Once I was in, I just kept going, though I despaired I would never get out again."

Breed snorted softly. He tightened his arms around her and gently rocked her. "This is an old smuggler's cave. It has many chambers and passages that go throughout it. I would have found you. You are *kloshe tum tum* to me."

Jeannie made a little sobbing sound in her throat, and then snuggled closer, her hands in fists against her mouth. Neither said anything for some time. There was peace and safety in the dark.

Eventually, Breed kissed her on the top of her head. "I'm sorry I was so cold to you." His voice was thick. "Didn't mean to be. Just worried something like this would happen."

"I know. I understand now." She cleared her throat. "And I'm sorry I got angry. It was just the shock of seeing you, all the lies about the firm. Oh, Jonas, Cooperwaite boarded the ship and killed poor Patterson without a care."

"*Wahh.*" The news was a hammer blow. "And Jimmy? What of the boy? And Gilly?" The cuts on Breed's chest throbbed. He felt like he had aged ten years.

"I think they are safe." She straightened up. Breed let her go and struck another lucifer so he could see her.

"What will happen now?" Jeannie asked.

"Time to get you back to the ship. Then I'll go for Cooperwaite."

"Oh, Jonas, please be careful. I think he is quite mad."

"Obviously."

"No, insane. He killed Shells Shining."

"How do you know that?" Breed's voice echoed off the cave walls.

Jeannie cringed, then found her voice. "Because I have seen her labret. Cooperwaite has it on a chain around his neck."

"Christ!" Breed threw away the dying match and stood up. "The bastard." He backed away and turning, let the darkness hide his rage and grief. "*Toketie tenas wincom,*" he murmured and walked away. He stopped at the cave wall and braced his hand and hook against the cool, damp rock. For some time he did not speak.

"Jonas?"

"I'm sorry," he said thickly. He came back to her. "No wonder you were frightened. You saw the beast he is."

"Shells Shining. I'm so sorry."

"I know you are." He felt drained. All the years of wondering came to this. He cleared his throat. "I've known for several months now that Cooperwaite was on the south end of the island the day Shells Shining was abducted. I just didn't have the physical proof, except he has been suspected in a number of attacks on native women over the years. Each time, however, the implication was they were immoral women, so of no consequence. No one cared to lay official charges." He leaned over her. "Let's leave this place and go into another chamber where there is light. Can you walk?"

"I think so. I'm just stiff."

She groped for his hand and he helped her stand. Breed lit another lucifer to locate the entrance to another passage. He picked up the rifle and led her across the chamber where it narrowed again, but kept its height. He led her, feeling his way until they came out into another room. He struck a lucifer, exposing a space like a view down a man's throat.

"Is this where you came from? "he asked her.

"I'm not sure."

"There is a passage that goes up, but we're going this way."

As Breed led Jeannie into a new area of the caves, she felt her confidence coming back. She had been terrified of facing Cooperwaite alone. The space grew lighter as they went through. Suddenly they were in a chamber where they could see without a lucifer. Further down, the cliff face opened up again and they could see out into the trees. The day was bright outside. From far-off, there came the sound of sporadic gunfire. For the first time she could see his bloody shirt and coat.

"Oh, Jonas. You are hurt."

"It's not as bad as it looks, though I'm bruised, I can tell you."

He gave her a reassuring smile, then saw the cloth around her waist and the way her hands had been tied to it. He saw her left wrist. It was heavily bruised.

"Jeannie, why didn't you say something?"

"It's nothing. A little tender, perhaps." She rubbed it lightly and winced.

"Nothing? Don't you see the way you hold it?" He gently reached for her hand. Supporting her hand and forearm in his one hand, he pulled the sleeve back as delicately as he could with his hook. The wrist and forearm were badly swollen.

"Did you do this falling down your rabbit hole?"

"No. After I warned you, Cooperwaite pushed me down and smashed my forearm with his rifle butt."

Breed swore and shook his head in disgust. "Doesn't it hurt?"

"It aches something fierce, but it's tolerable. It stings only when I move it."

"Because it's broken."

He ordered her to sit down and searched the cave for a piece of wood. Finding a flat slab of driftwood in a stack against the far wall, he made a splint, carefully binding the driftwood from her forearm to her hand with his silk tie. He used a piece of petticoat for a sling. She was amazed how he used his hook hand to do it.

"There. That should do until Doc-tin can fix it." He sat down next to her.

"*Mahsie*. Now let me see your arm, Jonas," Jeannie said. "I think it's still bleeding. You should bind it."

"Not much. The stub cap was struck, that's all."

"Let me see."

Reluctantly, he took off his coat and carefully pulled the sleeve over the hook one-handed. Underneath was the leather armlet.

Using the fingers on her good hand, she wiped away the blood, then pulled back when she touched something sharp. "Is that a metal fragment?" A jagged piece of metal stuck out of the leather.

"So it is."

"Then we must get it out." She had stuffed her reticule in her pocket before she lay down to sleep on Breed's ship. An ivory case held a pair of tweezers and an ivory nail buffer. Without asking, she pinched at the scrap. It was jagged like a narrow handmade arrowhead, its point apparently piercing all the way through to the skin. He gazed intently at her hand when she began to work at the scrap, but otherwise he made no sound. A little twist, a tug, and the bloody piece was free.

"I should clean out the wound. There could be more. If I may—"

Undoing a buckle at the head of the stub cap, she helped separate it from the strap that went up his arm to his shoulder under his shirt sleeve and removed it. On his own, he removed the cap.

"You always do this yourself?" she asked.

"Yes. It's an old practice." He said no more, as if he were waiting for comment from her when the cap came off. Though it revealed only a blood-stained cotton stock covering the end of the limb, there was a noticeable change in the structure of the forearm: it simply tapered off, its end atrophied from long years of disuse. But Jeannie said nothing. Very gently she slipped the sock off, exposing the pale, dry forearm and a narrow, bloody gash.

"See, it's just a scratch, Jeannie. Nothing more. I'll wash it out later."

"I could at least wrap it," she said. She tore off a small piece of her petticoat and wiped away some of the blood that hadn't dried. She worked with her head down, but her eyes couldn't keep off the end of the limb. It came to a conclusion of flesh that looked like the puckered top of a narrow gourd with the stem off. When she dabbed near it, the bone felt close and hard, yet she discovered the muscles near the elbow were stronger than she thought as if he worked them somehow. His upper arm was strong and muscular.

Breed leaned against the rock wall and closed his eyes. Jeannie finished cleaning. She intended to wrap a new piece of cloth around

491

the arm, but discovered it would be difficult with only one hand. She wondered if she should put the bloody sock back on instead. Perhaps it was needed to keep the stub cap in place. She was about to ask when Breed spoke.

"Did you think about me Jeannie? All those years..."

Jeannie stopped dabbing and looked at him. "For a long time, I thought of nothing else.

Then after a time, I had to put it all aside. I buried the hurt deep in my new life. Worked hard to keep it down." She smiled wistfully. "But I didn't completely forget. How could I? Sometimes in the evening just when the sun was going down behind the islands and the Olympic Mountains to the west of Elliot Bay, if I should see a *salt chuck* canoe going out, I would remember the canoe ride from Timons to English Camp. I would remember the stars, the way the paddles stirred the night water and made it twinkle with the sea lights. You were always in the back, guiding me home."

"Did you feel safe with me then, Jeannie?"

"Yes, I felt safe." She patted his arm. "Should I wrap it full for the cap?"

Breed leaned over and looked at her progress.

"I was going to bind it with a piece of cloth," Jeannie declared. "Do you have a clean sock? I don't think I can do it one-handed." She flushed, suddenly realizing that he did everything one handed.

"You can put another layer on. I don't have a clean sock. Here, I'll hold the end while you wrap."

Jeannie lifted up the edge of her skirt and ripped off another piece of petticoat. As she resumed wrapping the bandage with his help, she looked out toward the opening. There were birds in the trees and she tried to identify them. If there was any fighting, she couldn't hear it.

She felt exhausted and her lower arm ached as though throbbing hot needles struck it. Jeannie put her head down, but she was suddenly aware he was looking at her. His presence was so strong. The hair at the nape of her neck began to rise, not out of fear but of feelings long dormant. Was this why she had gone looking for him? When she had enough courage to look at him, she found him smiling wistfully at her. She smiled back. He kissed her, then leaned his shoulders back against the sandy, hard surface of the cave wall.

Jeannie ducked her head down and looked at the exposed limb. The forearm was like an animated piece of wood. She thought of how ill Jonas had been. Here was the proof. She thought of him on Timons, coming out of the water with the crab baskets in *both* hands. She tried to continue wrapping the limb, then stopped, feeling sick to her stomach. Tears sprang into her eyes. She had not waited.

"Jeannie?" He reached over and touched her cheek. "If it bothers you, stop. You needn't worry about this. I can do it myself."

"I didn't know."

"*Ah-ha.*"

"I thought you were dead."

A tear dropped onto his arm. Jeannie sniffed and wiped it away, then weeping bent down and kissed the spot. It made her feel even sicker, but she felt she had to do it to get over her revulsion over the maimed limb.

"Jeannie, stop."

She looked at him again and tried to smile. "Were we so young and naive to believe that we could have withstood anything? That we could never be apart?" She looked up at him. "I did wait for you. Just not long enough."

"Jeannie," Breed said in a thick voice. She was surprised he was near to tears. "*Toketie.* God." He swallowed hard. "I know. I know why you went with Pierce. Phillip is my son, isn't he?" Jerking forward, he gently wiped away one of her tears, then kissed her on her wet cheek. "He's our son?"

"Yes, Jonas." She took his hand. "He's yours. I truly thought you dead. I couldn't shame my uncle. I had to marry."

Breed sagged against the rock wall. "Pierce. You did it all alone. All these years. Did he know?"

"I don't believe so."

"Was he a good father?"

"Yes. He loved Phillip." She finished wrapping the limb. "How did you find out? You've never seen Phillip before, have you?"

"No, but he looks exactly like my father. To see Phillip near took my breath away." He started to say something else, when he froze, his hand going for his rifle. Out near the trees, a flock of birds took flight.

"What is it?"

He put a finger to his lips and whispered. "Shhh. Not sure. Stay here."

Keeping to the wall, he moved further to their right, mindful of exposure through the holes in the sandstone rock face in front of him. At the end of the cave, he stopped and edged his way over to the opening. He lifted his rifle, laying the long barrel across the crook of his arm. Like a stick on a stick, it looked absurdly ineffective.

Jeannie picked up the stub cap with its hook, wondering if she should toss it to him, but he was absorbed in watching something below and she heeded his command to stay put.

Suddenly, he began to sight and track something, then froze. His whole body was perfectly still and she remembered the night before the fight when they had walked to the Royal Marine Camp and had encountered Collie and his men coming for Breed in the woods. He could fight. As she watched him now, she was both frightened and reassured.

Breed held his position for some time. Eventually, he crawled silently back to her. "There is someone below," he whispered. "Hard to tell if he is alone."

"Where are Collie and Neville?"

He pointed his head to the left of the opening in the cave face. "We have traveled some distance from where the beach is. These passages lead back to the other side of the hill."

"Won't they be looking for you?"

"They'll come..." He stopped in mid-speech. Below them a shotgun boomed. Jeannie gasped and clutched her arms. Breed scooted across the floor on his belly. Peering carefully below, he took one look and withdrew immediately. A second boom followed by the crack of several rifles sent him back to the wall by Jeannie. He picked up the stub cap and hurriedly put it on. The firing increased as the fight resumed.

"What's happening?"

"There are men below. Not mine. They are working their way up."
He gave her his hand. "We're going to have to move. We'll go
this way."

"Can't you stop them?" she asked.

"And give ourselves away? Not with you here, love. It's too risky,
Toketie."

Jeannie wasn't even aware he said, *Love*. It was so natural. Obedi-
ently, she rose and hugging the wall, followed him across the cave to
an opening that revealed itself only when they were directly in front
of it. He checked the straps on his stub cap one last time, then shifting
the rifle in his hand, he went first through the crack in the wall.
Instantly, they were thrown into darkness and the dank smell of wet
sand stone.

"Put your hand on my arm, Jeannie, so you won't get lost. It's a
narrow way that works its way up with some confusing turns."

"There's no light?"

"*Nawitka*. Not for a long space."

Behind them, they heard voices above the fighting. As they made
their way deeper into the passage, the noise and confusion was swallowed up by the silence of the rock.

RESOLUTION

"Jeannie."

In the thick darkness of the passage, Jonas's voice seemed to come from a long ways away, even though he was so close he could touch her.

"I'm here, Jonas. Did you see anything?"

"No. You can come now."

"And the guns?"

"They have subsided. We'll be safe here, I assure you." Jonas came closer to her, the cloth of his coat lightly rasping against the narrow sandstone walls of the passage. His boots echoed strangely behind him.

"Do you think we have been followed?"

"Into the cave where we were? Possibly. But not here. The passages are too dark and convoluted. Gutterson's men can only make a stand. Odds are, they didn't have enough time to climb up."

"What is ahead of us, then?"

"A chamber that opens up to woods. At this point, we have turned back to the west where the schooner is. What trail did Cooperwaite take you on?"

"We went to the head of the cove before he put the anchor down, then directly to the shore and through the woods there. It was quite pretty, though at the time, I did not enjoy it."

"Did he take you on the trail leading you up to the top of the cliff?"

"Yes. Is that where you think he is?"

Breed paused thoughtfully. "I'm sure he would have seen the fight's end, but I doubt he'd attempt a rescue—he has no manpower. His only hope was to turn back to the mail boat. He should have made his way back there."

"Then who was below us?"

"More of Gutterson's men, most likely." Breed shifted something in the dark and Jeannie remembered that he was still carrying the rifle. "Come, Jeannie."

Jeannie reached out and felt for his hand. Her hand came in contact with the cold metal of the hook. She was glad he couldn't see the shock on her face. Bravely, she gripped the steel and wiggled it in her hand. "Lead on," she answered and was rewarded with a chuckle.

It wasn't far to the light and an open chamber. Once in it, Breed had her sit against the wall while he checked outside. She sat down and hugged her bound arm, relieved to rest. She was becoming increasingly exhausted from the pain, but dared not burden him any further. She brushed her hair back with her good hand, then pulling her legs up under her skirt, leaned back to watch him stand at the opening in the rock.

The sun was bright out there, its light filtering through the big-leaf maple trees whose top leaves stirred gently in front of the cave. From where she sat, they looked like jagged green and translucent soup plates, reflecting patches of light on the opening and the side of Breed's face. She looked for the things she remembered about him and decided that he hadn't changed much. The old tension was still there: the way he held himself was not tamed by the excellent cut of the clothes he wore. He was watching intently down below, his rifle aimed.

Where had the years gone? Jeannie wondered. And where will they go now that he knew why she didn't wait?

Eventually, he turned back to her and smiled.

"Jeannie. I think we can go down. Sikhs is coming. I can see him."

"Oh, thank Heaven." She struggled to get up, her legs and arm aching fiercely. Breed shouldered the rifle and came to help her. When their hands touched, she felt energy between them. He must have felt it too.

Breed cleared his throat. "I'll get Doc-tin to fix you up in no time and then get you home. I promise you." He held her hand lightly as they stood close to each other, then he motioned for her to follow him. At the opening, she looked down and saw that there was a ledge just below the lip of the entrance. To the left, it angled slowly down, hugging the side of the cliff until it disappeared into the depth of the leafy woods below. To the right it went up. Breed stood on the ledge below her.

"See, it's wide enough for a goat cart. You won't lose your footing, Jeannie, even with your arm in a sling." He offered his hand and helped her down. "I'll go first. We'll be down in no time." He started to go down when a voice called out.

"Tut, tut. Always the gentleman. What a bore."

Jeannie gasped. Further up on the ledge Cooperwaite stood with a Colt .45 aimed at Breed.

"Stand down, Breed."

Breed didn't move. "What do you want?"

"What do you think? Safe passage. I shall take her with me. Come Jeannie, another adventure."

"Stay where are you, Jeannie. It's over, Cooperwaite. Listen, the fighting has stopped." Breed moved back up to cut the space between them, but Cooperwaite was quicker.

"I said, stand down, Breed, or I'll shoot her dead, I swear." Cooperwaite shifted the pistol abruptly so that it was now aimed at Jeannie. He came down in three big strides and motioned for her to come toward him with his free hand. "Come, Jeannie."

"For God's sake, Cooperwaite. Let her go. She has done nothing to you."

"She has played me the fool, though I commend her loyalty. I wonder if Pierce ever thought about it." He smiled wickedly, then suddenly grabbed her by the sleeve and pulled her up alongside him. He kept the pistol on her and started walking backwards up the path.

Breed slowly lowered his rifle, then sensing danger threw himself against the cliff as Cooperwaite suddenly fired his weapon at him. The bullet caught Breed on his left side, causing him to grunt and tumble back down the ledge. Cooperwaite tightened his grip on Jeannie's wrist and began to half-drag, half-pull her the remaining yards to the top.

"No! Jonas!" Jeannie screamed. She pulled back and tried to see where Breed had fallen, but the overhanging branches of several trees blocked her view. The trail was empty. "Jonas!" she wailed.

"Move!" Cooperwaite grabbed her broken arm through the sling. Jeannie cried out and obeyed him, stumbling over her skirt and into Cooperwaite's arms. "Later, my love. Now move!" He pulled her by the sling and she followed to avoid further punishment. They were soon on the top. To her horror, she saw that she was not far from where Cooperwaite had first brought her, though this section of rock was treeless and devoid of any brush or grass. It was a wide, flat expanse of rock, segmented like the designs on a gigantic gray tortoise's back. At its edge to the west, the tops of cedar and madrone lined up like a low sylvan picket fence. Beyond, she could see down into the cove where Jonas's schooner was anchored. Beyond rose the tip of San Juan Island. Cooperwaite pushed her toward the other side. She went as far as the edge, then stopped and turned on him.

"Why did you shoot him? He would have let me go."

"For satisfaction, I suppose. I don't like being trifled with. Business partner, indeed. Now be a lamb and move. Down there."

"No, I won't go with you. I don't care what you do."

Cooperwaite laughed. "You continue to amaze me, Jeannie Pierce. Forgive me for thinking you some pampered pet. I've been quite wrong. You're magnificent. Now move."

"No. I won't go another step. I can't. I'm exhausted."

Any patience Cooperwaite had, dropped like a stone. He reached out to slap her, but she was ahead of him and simply slumped down to the ground, safely away from the cliff's edge.

"What are you doing?" he yelled.

"Doing what I have meant to do all along—resist you."

Cooperwaite kicked her in the legs. She bit her lips, but did not cry out. "Fool!" he bellowed, then began to look around furtively.

"You should do as Jonas said. Give it up. His men are everywhere."

"Get up!" He aimed his pistol at her. "Look at me."

Jeannie looked, her heart pounding in terror. The fact, was, however, she *was* exhausted. The broken arm had sapped the rest of her strength. She could not go down over the edge because she would fall. She didn't want to fall, so she remained where she was.

Cooperwaite pulled the hammer back and she thought how odd it was that in three days' time all she had known about life and cherished had been sorted out and put in order. At this final moment, it was even clearer: she had loved her life as a mother to Philip and Jereminah and mother to Jeremy and in many ways, wife to Andrew and all that had entailed. Yet next to her children, there was a summer where someone had loved her for herself and shown her adventure and love of a simple nature.

She looked at Cooperwaite and thought, *if Jonas is dead to me again, then I shall still have that summer.* She pulled her shoulders up and watched Cooperwaite's face go from fury to surprise as he suddenly convulsed and grasped his chest. Bright blood began to flow from between his fingers. Gasping, he slumped onto the ground. A rifle report echoing around the rocky top sounded. Instinctively, Jeannie scrambled away.

"Jeannie!"

To her great joy, Jonas Breed came bounding across the summit. When he came alongside Cooperwaite, he kicked the pistol out of the dying man's twitching hand, then squatted down by him.

"Jonas." She couldn't say anything else. She looked at his side where there was a small amount of blood on his coat. He did not seem badly injured.

"Are you all right?" he asked. He squeezed her shoulder, his face barely concealing his deepest fear that he had come too late.

"I'm all right, Jonas. And you?"

"I'm fine," he said, then smiled grimly. "I'm sorry. I had to use what Cooperwaite gave me—a good whack on the ribs—to get away. My rifle had only one shot left and I couldn't chance wasting it." He laid the weapon down on the ground and reached over to Cooperwaite. The man was on his back with his legs drawn up in agony. His arms were flung out where he fell. He had no nerves to move them. He worked his mouth like a fish out of water. He turned his head when Breed touched his neck and began to open his shirt.

"Are you a tamanass?" Cooperwaite asked vacantly.

"I'm no spirit, Cooperwaite, but I will be the last thing you see before you go to hell."

"I've seen you before. Out there on the water."

"In your nightmares. I've been looking for so long." He pulled out the chain with Shells Shining's labret. He bit his lip and swallowed as he held it reverently in his hand, then yanked it from Cooperwaite's neck.

"Water," said Cooperwaite.

"I have none."

"My pocket. A flask."

Breed sighed. "Tell me about Kaui Kalama. Who told him I was in San Juan Town?"

Cooperwaite grinned, his lips exposing blood-etched teeth. "Who do you think? I wasn't about to give myself away." He coughed and asked for the water again. Breed searched and came up with the flask. He poured some water into his hand and gave it to Cooperwaite. The man sipped, then choked. Bright blood sputtered out of his mouth and down his chin, mixing with water in little streamlets.

"You tell Emmrtt Krill?"

"Maybe... I think... he had... his own little score to settle." Cooperwaite breathed with great effort. "Didn't... like the Kanaka ...snooping around nor your ....interference, for that matter, into... his trade. The alarm was just going out about that..." Cooperwaite didn't finish the word. He gave Breed a sneer. "I took her to spite you."

Breed grabbed Cooperwaite by the shirt front, his face enraged and bitter. For a brief moment he held him off the ground, then threw him back. Cooperwaite cried out in agony.

"Jonas, have pity," said Jeannie.

"Pity? There's none for him. What he did was unforgivable. He'll have to suffer for it."

Jeannie gently touched Breed's arm. "Not here. He can't hurt anyone any more here."

Cooperwaite tracked his eyes dreamily to her voice. "I thank you, madam. I will dream of you when I sleep—" He stopped in mid-sentence; his head sank back. He blinked his eyes like they were growing heavier. He finally closed them, then opened them suddenly.

"Oh, no. Keep them away." Cooperwaite sought to touch her, but he couldn't raise his hand any higher than his side. "Keep them away." His head lolled to the side, his eyes wide with terror.

"Who?" Jonas looked behind him but neither he nor Jeannie saw anyone.

"Those bloody *siwashes*. Haida. No," moaned Cooperwaite and struggled to push himself away. He kept looking in that direction.

"No one's there," said Jeannie.

"Oh, they are here all right," Breed said bitterly. "All those good people you abused. The Haida, Songhees, Kanakas."

"Keep them away." Cooperwaite continued to thrash his head and shoulders from side to side until, to Jeannie's horror, he succeeded in rolling himself over. The momentum sent him rolling again beyond Jeannie's reach until he went over the side of the cliff, his body crashing through the tops of the trees and bouncing and spinning down through the branches to the ground far below. His voice screamed like a banshee until it was cut short.

Jeannie sat back on her heels and put her good hand over her mouth. Her stomach surged, and her mouth went sour. Breed put his hand on her shoulder, squeezed it and then got up.

"What did he see?" she whispered when she was collected enough to speak.

"Justice." Breed raised his hand in greeting to Sikhs who was standing nearby. "Maybe something else. *Klahowyah*, Sikhs."

"*Klahowyah*, Jo-nuss. You look pretty damn beat up." He came over and inspected Jeannie with a kind eye. "You okay, Mrs. King George?"

When Jonas made a face, Sikhs burst out laughing and said he was making *hee-hee* just to see Breed's reaction. "We get help for you. I am so happy to see you, Mrs. King George. Everyone is so glad that you have come again."

Jeannie lifted her strained and tired face up to the old man and thought that she had never been so grateful to have someone say what he had just said.

"And I am happy to be here too." She started to get up to greet him, then collapsed in a dead faint. *How typical, how expected*, she thought as she passed out. *Never again.*

Jeannie woke to the sound of a seagull calling from outside. She opened her eyes and discovered that she was in a simple whitewashed room. There were lace curtains in the single window and bright ladyfinger flowers on a maple highboy across the room. A slight breeze stirred in the room, disturbing the motes descending through the center of the sunlit room. She wondered if it was early afternoon. She pushed back the covers and found that she was dressed in some-one's simple cotton skirt and blouse, not mourning clothes. Her broken arm was encased in a plaster of paris cast and placed in a clean piece of muslin cloth for a sling. Outside the window, she heard voices. She sat up, tested the strength of her legs on the floor and then put on her boots as best as she could manage with one hand.

Out in the main room, she found a comfortable space with settee and chairs and an old-fashioned open fireplace. A fire made of drift-wood was crackling there. Rag rugs covered the fir plank floor. A corner was devoted to books. There was a table with lamp on it and pictures on the wall.She wandered over to the pictures. One showed Neville with his Indian wife and two young boys. There were other photos of the family taken in various studios over time, all set in simple frames. She was about to leave them when she found to her surprise, a photograph of Jonas Breed with his wife Annie. Jeannie recognized her immediately. With them, was a young man with dark hair and eyes, yet he looked so much like Jonas that she gasped. *Ransom.* She knew Ransom was younger than Phillip, but standing tall behind his mother he showed the same confidence his father had. The girl next to him had to be Hannah. A lovely young lady with light hair and complexion. So this was Jonas's family. Jeannie sighed. *These are our histories we must adjust to.*

Jeannie went over to the screen door. Before her, beyond the porch and beach below, was a magnificent view of open water with one of the large islands on the other side. The day was warm and inviting. She opened the door, causing its hinges to screech. To her right, someone stood up quickly and closed the book he was reading. It was Jonas Breed.

"Good afternoon," he said.

"Is it already?"

Breed laughed. "For the second time in two days."

"Days? I've been here days? Dear heavens. Where are Jereminah and Phillip?"

"Mina's fine. Wilson has been with her all the time. I sent Phillip down with Collie to bring her here. I expect them here this afternoon."

Jeannie stepped onto the porch. "Is he alright?"

"Yes. Gutterson drugged him. Collie sobered him up. He was talking non-stop to Collie when I left."

"Did you speak to him?"

"Briefly. He's grateful for his rescue, but I think has a low opinion of me."

"All this will take time, Jonas."

"I know. He doesn't need to know about me. He is grieving for his father. I certainly grieved for mine." Breed cleared his throat. "Come, Jeannie. Sit. Please. Doc-tin says you need rest."

"Alright." Jeannie sat down on the padded bench he offered her. He went and sat on a chair next to the porch railing. It was made of twisted driftwood with a tick pillow for a seat.

"Where are we?"

"This is Tenas Point. Doc-tin lives here with his wife Mary and their boys. We thought it best to have you mend here. The schooner was a bit cramped."

"You said Wilson was with Mina. Was there trouble?"

"Wilson had it well in hand—long before it went anywhere. I'll tell you about it later."

"Where's Gilly?"

"She's here. Out with Mary somewhere. She'll be glad to see you upright. She was quite distraught when we found her on my schooner, but has recovered."

"Thank goodness." Jeannie sighed and studied the wonderful view in front of her. "Such a lovely place."

"*Ah-ha*. Doc-tin's been here since before the boundary claim was settled. Said it would take dynamite to get him out of here."

"What happens now?"

"Doc-tin has had his hands full with all the papers to file. A lot of comings and goings. Both the American and Canadian authorities were interested in Gutterson and his gang. And there was considerable talk about Cooperwaite. They found his wife, buried out in the back of his place. She may have found out about his smuggling activities. May have planned to report him to the authorities. Apparently, even Gutterson didn't know she was dead. Cooperwaite won't be missed."

Jeannie shuddered. "I owe you everything. For saving my life, for bringing me here." She looked around and decided that it offered a comfort of home long forgotten. "What happened to Mr. Burgess?"

"Alive and talking his head off. As you suspected, they tried to get rid of him. Knocked him on the head and threw him off the boat. Thought if all else failed, the cold water would do him in, but they didn't count on Jimmy. Jimmy was able to pull Burgess out along with Gilly's help."

Jeannie shook her head and sighed.

"What?"

"What shall I tell my children?"

"Tell them you had an adventure."

"Oh, Jonas, it has been more harrowing than that. My whole life in question. I don't think I'll ever be the same."

"What are you going to do, give up the mansion on the hill?"

Jeannie snorted. "I don't know. But I can change. I can come out here more often. I am too restless now. And then there is what to tell Phillip and Mina about their father and the firm."

"Tell them nothing. They don't need to know as yet. It will be kept quiet. Doc-tin and others will see to that. It's a private company matter. The public will be too busy with tales of smugglers. Besides, I owe it to Andrew."

"Andrew?"

Breed looked down, then away out to the channel. He studied the island opposite them it for a while, then looked at her. "I think you should know about Andrew's death. I feel I'm to blame for it."

"Blame? How?"

"The first and only time we ever met was last December."

"December? He was moody that season. I've often wondered why."

"We did not always see eye to eye. He resented me great deal."

"As a partner, or truthfully, was it over me?"

Breed paused thoughtfully. "I think it has always been over you. Last winter, he was particularly difficult. Jealous."

"Were you?"

"Ah, Jeannie. It would be wrong for me to answer that. Only that I told him that I would never upset your life. He didn't believe it. We had words. I didn't come to fight him. I came only because I wished to bring Gutterson and his crowd to ground. Told him that I would return to the islands."

"But you came back."

Breed got up and went to stand at the top of the porch steps. He put his right hand in his pants pocket. The hook hand rested on his hip. He looked back at Jeannie.

"Andrew found a ledger that I hoped existed," Breed answered. "He sent word that he had it. I think at that point, it became very dangerous for him. Frederick Howell, that solicitous solicitor-clerk in the Seattle office, is one of Gutterson's men. He and Burgess had been working the books for months. He must have warned Gutterson. I was to meet Andrew when I arrived in Seattle. At the last minute, I suggested that he have someone else carry the ledger for him. As it was, that was a fatal mistake. When it was not on his person, he was murdered. Or murdered for it, when discovered that he didn't have it. We'll never know."

"Murdered." Jeannie put a hand to throat in shock.

"I'm so sorry."

"Why wasn't I told?"

"In part to protect you, but also to throw off Gutterson and Cooperwaite. Customs wanted to make them feel infallible."

"Do you know who did it?"

"Gutterson. He confessed to me on the beach as we were negotiating before the fight broke out. He'll hang for it, small comfort as that is."

"Oh." Jeannie swallowed. Tears formed. She wiped them away.

Breed turned and smiled wistfully at her. "It wasn't the outcome I had planned on."

"No, I'm sure it was not." She sniffed and looked away. A pair of sea gulls shot by, then stretched out their wings and rode across the channel on the rising air. She watched them without a word, then remembered that Jonas might be waiting for her to say something. "It wasn't your fault. He knew what he was doing and what he wanted for doing it."

Breed smiled wryly. "I still regret it."

Jeannie stood up and came over to him. "Poor Andrew."

"Poor, Andrew, indeed." Breed cleared his throat. "If it's any reassurance, he died instantly."

Jeannie put her hands over her mouth. She took a moment to compose herself. "Thank you for saying that. It does help. For all his faults, I believe that he cared for me and especially for the children." Jeannie sniffed. "Do I have anything to fear?"

"No, the danger is past. All the parties have been apprehended.

Anders Gutterson was quite cooperative on that account. Besides, you have always been protected and it will continue."

Jeannie puzzled at that, then suddenly understood. "Wilson. It's Wilson, isn't it?"

"*Ah-ha.*"

"Oh, Jonas," Jeannie said in exasperation under her breath. She shook her head and walked to the other side of the landing. She ran her fingers over the smooth, peeled log pillar next to the steps, then stopped at a knot and gently made little circles around it. Across the water she could see the outline of a sail coming up the channel.

"We'll see you back to Seattle with your children," Breed said. "I've thought of giving Simpson a raise and assigning him to the Seattle office there. The railroad is coming. It will bring prosperity. Simpson can help you with any remaining affairs. He will be an excellent manager for the firm. May even make him a partner. Do you intend to continue to go to the board meetings?"

"Yes."

"Good. That's good." He took a step down.

"What about you, Jonas?"

"I'll have to be in Seattle for about a fortnight—I've been ordered to speak at the inquest into Cooperwaite's operations and his demise."

"You haven't been arrested, have you?"

"It's only a formality. I should be free to leave."

"Leave?"

"Yes. I have things to sort out."

"Oh. Then you *are* returning to Hawaii."

"At some point. Collie will manage what needs to be managed. Andy Po is taking over a position there as well."

"What will you do in the meantime?" Jeannie asked with a sinking heart, for she was beginning to realize that he was leaving much unsaid.

Breed indicated that he wanted to go down to the beach. "That sail might be the *Toketie,*" he said. He didn't speak until they were at the water's edge. The sun was warm on the gray sand, drying it into tiny mounds. Little insects scurried over the bits of driftwood and dried out green-glass seaweed. The water was so clear and cold that the pebbles lying beneath it appeared to be under glass. He picked one up and fingered the wet, smooth pebble in his hand.

"I have always wanted to go north, to see the old places of my youth. Now that I am back here in the open, I have the freedom to do so. I'll be going by schooner with Sikhs and Kapihi. We may make part of the voyage by canoe. I'll be gone for six months at least."

"Six months? So long? I won't be seeing you again?"

Breed turned and looked down at her. "*Toketie,*" he said gently. "I'm only going away for a short time." He took a cloth out of his pocket and opened it. Inside was Shells Shining's labret. "I want to return this to her brother. I plan to stay there for a while and become reacquainted with old friends. I'll take things as they come."

"And then?"

Smiling softly, he put away the labret. "I don't know. It depends on you. I'd like to come back when your period of mourning is over. I'd like to call on you."

"Call on me?"

"*Ah-ha.*" He gazed straight at her, his face hopeful, then, his face reddened. "Forgive me," he said.

"For what?"

Breed swore under his breath. "I don't know." He rolled the pebble around in his fingers. "I have *no* idea what I am asking. Haven't a clue. I certainly don't expect things to be the same, Jeannie. What's done is done and we are no longer young people with years ahead of us. And I'm no opportunist, though Lord knows, you've always been wearing black all the times I've known you."

Jeannie laughed at that. "And you have not taken advantage before even when I was not in mourning? To hire someone to watch over me? What were you thinking?"

"I was thinking that I was free to do so with Annie's passing, though I have felt a certain betrayal to her memory on my part for it."

"I should like to know more about her."

"Thank you. She was a good woman and companion. A good mother. I loved her dearly, though God knows... well, that is done these long years. I am not asking for any promises. There are no debts to collect. I just want to see you from time to time. I would enjoy that."

"So you want to be proper and call on me."

"*Ah-ha*. Minimize any prospective tongue wagging…"

"Oh, Jonas." Jeannie put her good hand over her mouth as tears stung her eyes. "You don't have to ask." She came over to him and took his hand—his hook hand—and laying it on her breast, embraced its hard, smooth metal.

"You are *hyas skookum* to come so far," she said.

Breed smiled softly at her turn of words. "I suppose I am."

"And what was between us is not utterly dead."

Breed made a soft noise in his throat and bowed his head. Jeannie put her free arm around his shoulder and hugged him.

"You told me once," she said against his neck, her warm breath caressing the skin next to his collar, "that sometimes things happen that we have no control over, yet we manage somehow. Sometimes we are better for it. Sometimes we are all *mistchimas*."

"Yes" Breed said.

Jeannie continued, "Let us at last release our bonds, Jonas. Let us move on."

"Only if we go together."

The schooner tacked to the left and then again before it was in front of them. Gilly came down to the beach to hail it in along with Jeannie and Breed. There was a new easiness in the air as they stood side by side, Jeannie's arm slipped through Breed's.

Sikhs saw it all from up on the forested hill and was glad. The spirits had told him it would be so. Tomorrow he would give his adopted son a new name. Then his son would be truly free.

GLOSSARY

Chinook Jargon was a trade language developed around 1800. Prior to European contact the Chinook people controlled the trade on the Columbia River for centuries. Trade came as far away as Vancouver Island and present day Montana. When English and American fur trade companies showed up in the early 1800s, the trade tradition continued. Chinook Jargon is mostly Chinookan with words from both the French and English languages.

ah-ha---yes
Boston---American
camin---canoe
chak-chak---eagle
elan---help
hyas---big
ipsoot---hide
kahpo---brother
Kanaka---human being; name for Hawaiian in 19th c.
King George---British person
kiawali--to love
klahowya---Greeting
kloshe tum tum---sweetheart

ilihee---earth
mahsie---thank you
mistchimas---slave, captive
ow---younger brother
sikhs---friend
skookum---strong
skookun tum tum---brave heart
sikhs---friend
tenas---small
tenas wa wa---all talk
tot---uncle
tyee---chief
toketie---pretty
wake---no

Author Notes

One of the curious bits of Washington State history is the infamous Pig War. On July 15, 1859, an American settler on San Juan Island shot a Hudson Bay Company pig. The incident nearly brought the United States and the United Kingdom into war.

Since 1846, when the Treaty of Oregon set the international boundary between the United States and present-day Canada, the water boundary had been in dispute. Listed only as "the channel" in the treaty, there were in fact two channels, Rosario and Haro Strait. As early as 1845, the Hudson's Bay Company, operating at Fort Victoria, claimed San Juan Island. When the Americans counter-claimed the island in 1853, HBC established Belle Vue Farm and ran huge numbers of sheep. The unfortunate pig was the only victim of the escalating tension, but its demise was on course to an international crisis.

Names such as Captain George E. Pickett, later of Gettysburg fame and 2nd. Lt. Henry M. Robert, of *Robert's Rules of Order*, were some of the Americans in Company D who responded to the American settlers' plea for protection. The standoff was peacefully settled in late November, 1859. The island would be jointly occupied by each country's military force until an international committee would determine where the international water boundary would lie. For the next 12 years, officers at both camps got along quite well, dealing with such issues as smuggling, settler disputes and claim jumping. All of the San Juan Islands were awarded to the United States in 1872.

For the sake of storytelling, I have moved up certain dates pertaining to English Camp. The Royal Marines landed on March 23, 1860. Though the commissary was built early on, the Royal Marines including officers spent the summer in tents. The housing on Officer's Row also commenced later that summer. It was just more fun to have the house for the assistant surgeon built so Gilly Parker and Jeannie would have a place to stay.

Horse races did happen at American Camp. I moved Pickett's race up a year for storytelling. His horse did bolt from the race. To learn more, go to the San Juan Island National Park website: https://www.nps.gov/sajh/learn/historyculture/the-pig-war.htm

Mike Vouri, retired ranger at the national park wrote about the Pig War and the Royal Marines. Check out his excellent books, *The Pig War* and *Outpost of Empire*.

The presence of Hawaiians in the Pacific Northwest for over two hundred years is another intriguing historical bit. Hawaiians, or Kanakas as they were called in the 19th century, were an important part of the Hudson Bay Company's labor force. The first Hawaiians to see the Pacific Northwest came with Captain George Vancouver in 1793. When HBC established Fort Vancouver on the Columbia River in 1824, Kanakas were there. They could also be found at the sister HBC fort, Fort Langley (1827) in present-day Canada and at Fort Nisqually in Washington (1855). Kanaka Town was an actual place on San Juan Island. It was located not far from HBC's Belle Vue Farm on San Juan Island where Hawaiians worked as shepherds.

Friday Harbor, today a popular resort town on the opposite side of the island from Bellevue Farm Island, received its name from Peter Poalima Friday, a Hawaiian shepherd for HBC. The smoke drifting above his wooden shack above the harbor was a guide for seafarers for many years. The harbor became known as Friday's Harbor. Sadly, when the San Juan Islands were awarded to the United States by the international boundary panel, the Hawaiians had to leave as they were considered British citizens. Many left for Victoria or for Salt Spring Island and other islands in British Columbia. Peter Friday's son was born an American citizen, so Peter Friday stayed on for several more years.

The people of the Salish Sea (Vancouver Island, Olympic Peninsula, San Juan Islands and upper Western Washington) are Coast Salish. Starting in the early 1850s, "northern Indians" (Haida, Tlingit and Tsimshian) began to make the long journey down from lower

Alaska and British Columbia to raid Coast Salish communities or to trade at Fort Victoria. As Americans began to homestead on Bellingham Bay and on Whidbey Island, northern Indians became a threat to both settlers and Coast Salish peoples. Several blockhouses were built on Whidbey Island. Fort Bellingham, commanded by Captain George E. Pickett, was built to protect the settlers there. Today, Haida, Tsimshian and Tlingit communities can be found in Seattle. Known for their art, they are part of the great renaissance in the Pacific Northwest.

ABOUT THE AUTHOR

Award winning author, J. L. Oakley, writes historical fiction that spans the mid-19th century to WW II. Her characters, who come from all walks of life, stand up for something. She is the recipient of the 2015 Bellingham Mayor's Arts Award for writing and history, 2015 WILLA Award finalist for historical fiction and the Chanticleer Book Reviews Goethe Grand Prize winner 2016 for post 1750 historical fiction. A University of Hawaii Manoa graduate, she has been curious about Hawaiians in the Pacific Northwest ever since she arrived in the Northwest. It is a story few people know.

Oakley loves writing in noisy cafes and exploring local history, but when not writing she enjoys teaching history hands-on to school-age kids and for historical organizations.

To learn more about her novels and novellas, go to http://amzn.to/2uewppR. If you enjoyed this novel, please consider writing a review.

J. L. Oakley can be found on:

Twitter at @jloakley

Facebook https://www.facebook.com/JLOakleyauthor/

Website: https://historyweaver.wordpress.com/

Made in the USA
Coppell, TX
13 June 2020

28043431R10292